BY RU P

Surfers

October Song

THE SEED

City of Dreams and Dust

A Haven in the Stars

FATE AND THE WHEEL SERIES

A Time of Ashes

Hunting Gods

The Ice Queen's Song (coming soon)

Connect online:
https://twitter.com/RuPringle
https://rupringle.com/fiction
https://www.facebook.com/authorrupringle
mailto:ru@rupringle.com

A HAVEN IN THE STARS
The Seed Volume 2

FRACTAL SYMMETRY

First published in the UK in 2020 by Fractal Symmetry
Version: July 2020
(http://fractalsymmetry.com)

ISBN: 9798664219289

Proofread by Sophie Houston mailto:sophie@rjfhouston.com

A list of **Principal Characters** is provided at the end of the book.

—:—

For Will

PROLOGUE

DRIP, DRIP, DRIP.

Plip-plink, plip-plink.

After a spell of absence, the cavern's dim micro-galaxies once more cast their blue-white illumination. Each day now they crept a little higher up its walls. The rise of their ephemeral civilisation could be seen as a freeze-frame animation of remembered stills, oozing up the walls like moonlight.

With the galaxies rose Tom's spirits. It was as though the two things were connected: some forgotten genetic part of him, which delighted in natural cycles, calling to him like a voice from the bottom of a deep well. Winged forms, felt and heard more than seen, flapped through the sluggish airs of interconnecting passageways, their bodies twisting, uttering squeaks and clicks at the limits of hearing, warm in the darkness.

Once they entered the chamber, however, they fell silent, passing in haste, eager to be elsewhere.

Snuffles echoed in the gloom. Water dripped into pools as it had always done. Had Tom's mind required mathematics in order to understand, it could have devised any number of complex equations to describe the chaos of watery noises.

The little white-haired man had come to see him again today. The organiser. It had been a while since his last visit, and the human had sat dutifully before the most fertile source of his nightmares, battling to maintain an open mind despite reflexes which screamed for him to slam it shut.

Tom might have liked the man, he decided, if he were a man himself.

It struck Tom, perhaps for the first time, that he might like many of his unsuspecting charges. Even those who openly detested him, for he fully understood their loathing. More than that, he *cared* for them.

Why? They would never thank him. He was too alien. Too uncomfortable.

Like most questions, this one was rhetorical. He cared because, despite their frailties, they too had been willing to die for others who could never understand what had been done for them (and were unlikely to offer thanks if they did). The real question, though lay in the answer – which created more questions, which generated answers and questions of their own. All of them branches of an infinitely complex tree.

Questions, answers … he'd stepped into the trap again. Human linearity was infectious. Sentience was rooted not in reasoning, as his enslavers had believed, but in *feeling*. Especially for others. The most pea-brained creature capable of self-sacrifice for another was more truly aware than the most dispassionate genius. *Compassion!* How ironic that a world with a wistful reverence for finer feelings had been so obsessed with the quest for cold intelligence.

Compassion alone extended consciousness into the worlds of others. Only a society combining the awareness of every self in a living, evolving web, was the multiple, rather than the sum, of its parts. It was this feeling, which he'd once thought he'd nowhere but within himself, that bridged the gap between *them* and *him*. The knowledge that he now assisted those who had, however unknowingly, lent purpose to his existence suffused him like a drug.

He would die for them.

And when he did, the world would see precisely what he was capable of. It would be something no human would ever forget.

The snuffling became a gurgling. Then all was still.

PART ONE

1

FULL ACCESS

HAZEL PEERED BLEARILY around the circle of faces. Though most of the forty-three present knew each other well, some hadn't seen each other for months, in some cases years, and they chatted enthusiastically.

She closed her eyes and her mind and tried to drown out the babble.

It had been an exhausting journey from Haven's Gate, and the burns on her arm felt like they were still on fire. She turned, gazing up through the viewing wall at the gleaming blue semicircle hanging over everyone's heads, wishing she were on it.

The pink-skinned, white-bearded man at the head of the oval table slapped his hands on its polished wooden surface, and conversation quickly died.

'Right, thank you.' He cleared his throat. 'You all know me, Zhelkar Porro, but just in case there are any of you who've been asleep the last forty years, I and my partner Dorrin,' he motioned to the plump, walnut-skinned woman with equally lively dark eyes sitting beside him, who smiled briefly, 'are overseers of defence according to State of Emergency law, as well as other things of less immediate relevance. One or two of you who are new to duty on the *Comhairle* may not have met before, but the sooner we start this meeting the better, and I'm not going to fart about with introductions. We have more urgent matters to discuss –'

'Shouldn't Tom be here?' The voice belonged to a bony-faced, brown-haired woman Hazel knew she should recognise. Faces around the circle glazed or looked awkward.

'You mean, Cedra, shouldn't this meeting be in Tom's cave?' Hazel had her now: Cedra Hornbeam, from Hollytree. A pain in the arse. Even her mannerisms were maddening. 'I thought everyone knew by now, but I'll take this opportunity to make it clear. Again. Tom can no longer be moved. He never liked being moved in the first place.'

'But we need him up here. Are his whims so important that we should put them before our safety? What's he doing in that hole of his anyway that's so vital?'

Zhelkar's eyes hardened. He was as Hazel had always imagined Tolkien's Gandalf – in looks, if not height. *Wizards are subtle, and quick to anger.* The real wizard, however, looked nothing like a wizard at all. More the way she imagined Aragorn. She wondered for a moment where he was. The thought brought with it a twinge of concern.

'Enough!' Zhelkar snapped. 'Cedra, shame on you. This is neither the place nor the time.' Cedra adopted a glowering silence, content to have made her point. 'I agree it's not ideal, meaning we cannot rely on Tom's guidance to the extent we've become accustomed to. However, this should bring home just how reliant on him we've become. Perhaps *over*-reliant. Should we all run around waving our hands because he will not mollycoddle us?

'Besides,' Zhelkar added scanning the circle of faces in irritation, 'Tom is fully aware of the situation, and said his presence was not necessary. I hope that will put an end to this futile side-track.'

Probably knows the outcome already, thought Hazel. *And with the waves of loathing emanating from this room of supposedly enlightened people, I wouldn't blame him for not wanting to be involved.* Zhelkar peered probingly around the table.

'So,' he continued, when no further challenge was forthcoming, 'this meeting is a product of our investigation of the anomalous supernova of the star known in our charts as A …' he peered critically at the screen before him, 'Five … Three-Six-Eight-Five-Four-One-Zero. What a mouthful. You have the details as they were available in front of you. I assume you've all taken them on board?'

There was vague nodding from around the table. He clasped his hands together, and his expression became sombre.

'Most of you, I think, knew Sarana Pohae, who was in the org that was killed during the incident. She will be sorely missed. Her partner and close friends are planting a tree for her some time in the next week. I believe they've chosen an aspen.

Anyone who wants to come will of course be welcome. Some of you will also have travelled with Willowseed, who was tragically just a youngster, but already an org of great bravery and character. Its closest kindred and friends are holding a deep-space ceremony in two days. They say any of us who wish to pay our respects are encouraged to do so.'

The wizened little seventy-year old seemed suddenly very old, but he continued.

'We have here with us Hazel, who most of you will know through her dedication to intelligence, deep-space scouting and Lancer liaison work.'

I doubt that's the main reason, thought Hazel, darkly. Zhelkar was just being kind.

'Hazel was in one of the two orgs which survived the extraordinary events referred to in your briefs. I gather more information has come to light since we received the first transmission from Haven's Gate.'

He looked up from his handwritten notes.

'I know you must be very tired, Hazel my love, but please tell us what you know. You know you don't have to stand.' He flashed a small smile of reassurance. Hazel felt the warmth behind it and returned the feeling.

'Feel free to ask any questions after I've finished,' Hazel began, trying to sound less awkward and weary than she felt. She took a steadying breath. 'His name, he has told us, is Wood McCorkindale. He says he's from a planet called Sandsea, which is about halfway from IPEC's geographical centre to its perimeter, on the side nearest us.'

Diagrams and images flashed and rotated on holoscreens above the table's dark central well, keeping pace with her commentary.

'Apparently, he was confronted with corruption high up in his father's company, for whom he was halfway through a degree in astroengineering, begun when he was only fifteen. It seems he took it upon himself to investigate. When his prying was discovered, he turned to his father, who disowned him and kicked him out of the family home.'

There was a murmur from around the table. Frowning and head-shaking.

'He was quickly tracked down by the company, and vividly described and visualised being thrown out of an airlock and forced, in fear of his life, to mine the asteroid belt of the star which caught our attention three weeks ago, using the specialised mining vessel you see on the screen.'

Above the centre of the table twirled a model of the ship she now knew as *Oscar*. Layers were steadily stripped away to reveal internal structure.

'Our records show it's a design dating from almost two hundred standard years ago. The vessel has no interstellar capability, which effectively imprisoned him within this deserted star system for more than six years.'

'That's slavery,' observed Zhelkar, causing wide-eyed nods from some of the others.

'Indeed. However, he was not alone on this vessel. I sensed another mind on the ship …'

'Sensed? Are you the telepath?' The speaker was a young, dark-haired man Hazel did not recognise.

'Yes, I'm the fucking telepath, alright? Can't you tell, arsehole?' She leaned towards him, on her feet now, jabbing a finger at one of her eyes, both of which she knew would now be burning brightly red. 'Or are you colour-blind as well as stupid?'

The man flinched as waves of fury permeated his brain.

'Like to stick me on a stage and see what little tricks I can do wouldn't you?' Hazel narrowed her eyes. 'Yes, I can tell. I can show you if you like?'

'Please, please,' broke in Zhelkar Porro, with considerable urgency, standing and raising his palms.

'A practical, *personal* demonstration. Would you really like to see what I can do? Would you?'

'Hazel! Shane Summersea! Please!' Zhelkar slowly lowered his hands. 'I'm sure nothing … *derisory* was meant by the question. Was there Shane?'

'Oh, no,' stammered the sweating young man. He seemed to be shrinking into his seat. 'There wasn't, please believe me. No, I, ah … Please accept my apologies if my question sounded, eh … *wrong*. I really am most terribly sorry.'

He tried to meet Hazel's stare but made it only as far as her chest. Realising what he was staring at, he paled even more, eyes snapping downwards. Zhelkar glared at Hazel with the full force of half a century's accumulated respect.

'Well,' sniffed Hazel, seating herself. 'Apology accepted.' None of the room's other occupants seemed to know where to put their eyes. 'As I was saying,' she continued, looking pointedly away from Summersea, who was now peeping between his fingers almost from beneath the table, 'it appears this machine has an exceptionally powerful thinker on board. We didn't get much out of McCorkindale regarding its origins, but – although this may sound unlikely – I believe it to be a true artificial intelligence. A *mind*.'

There were sceptical noises from around the circle.

'It seems self-aware and concerned for the consequences of its actions. It has access to a sizeable database, and it can definitely learn. It has agreed to cooperate with us, so long as it can communicate directly with McCorkindale, with whom it has developed what I can only describe as a friendship.'

There were raised eyebrows at this.

'I think some of you need to open your minds a little. I can't pick up the machine's thoughts yet as I'm not … ah, *tuned* for something so different. Perhaps the best analogy I can give is one of you trying to eavesdrop on a language of odours.'

This caused a murmur of nervous amusement.

'As Tom has shown us, emotion lies the root of sentience – and I have experienced emotions from this machine. Strong ones. Is this so impossible? The machine describes its own brain as parallel in principle to an organic one. I can find no way to explain what I've felt and observed other than concluding that it has a mind of its own. And a smart one at that.'

She continued without waiting for a response.

'The next thing is the vessel itself. We don't understand how, and both McCorkindale and the AI – which, by the way, calls itself "Tink" …' there were a few smirks at this, 'no Peter Pan quips, please – were very tight-lipped on the subject, but the ship has onboard a power source which is frankly baffling. *It* was the source of the SOS messages.'

Had she been less tired, Hazel might have found the expressions of disbelief greeting her from around the table hilarious.

'I know,' she commiserated. 'Those pulses approached the output of a star. I'd have found it incredible myself, had I not seen what you are about to. We have facts, and though we can't explain them yet, we'd be foolish to disregard them.'

The lights dimmed and a reconstruction of the brief battle played out in 3D in the air above the table-top, drawing gasps from its audience.

'That was a fully-armed federation cruiser,' continued Hazel as light returned. 'Using full-blown Puke military shield technology. Ton for ton, perhaps the most potent warship they have. I don't know what the outcome would have been had the cruiser used fusion warheads, but when you consider how many scouts we've lost to fast cruisers such as these … And I'm betting we've seen only a fraction of this monstrosity's potential.'

She paused, allowing the implications to sink in.

'I think it's important to bear in mind at all times what we owe to McCorkindale. And to this artificial intelligence. It was only through their actions that I'm here to talk to you today. Before I make my final proposition, are there questions anyone would like to ask? Points anyone would like to make?'

The others looked questioningly around at each other, some shrugging in ways that made Hazel itch to slap them. Zhelkar and Dorrin sat back in their neighbouring chairs with apparent unconcern. Hazel knew otherwise.

'This sounds pretty weird if you ask me Hazel. I really don't see how we can afford to take chances.'

The speaker was Sander Leafdance, who peered at her intently from ice-blue eyes which seemed full of mischief despite the seriousness of the issue.

'Shouldn't we – well, I suppose I really mean *you* –' he grinned in a way that was totally disarming, 'just give 'em the old memory brush-and-scrub and boot 'em back to the federation? Forget the whole thing. Even bringing them to Gamma …' He wrinkled his prominent nose. 'I know that's already done, and I *think* I understand why you did it and everything, but it still seems a mite risky to me.'

'We had no choice Sandy,' she said, 'and that brings me nicely to my proposition, so please forgive me for going straight on to that.'

Hazel drew herself up, and slowly and deliberately scanned the room, causing many of those present to look away.

'Quite apart from the practical difficulties of trying to give amnesia to a very alien mind which has the apparent power of a *sun* at its command if it decides it doesn't like us any more –

11

what I'm basically saying is that it can't be done, at least, not safely, and not by me – we can't afford not to take risks.'

She took a deep breath, not enjoying the prospect of what was coming next. Zhelkar had begun to look agitated.

'Most of us have assumed that we can stay hidden for ever. This is extremely naive. I believe, although I will probably be lynched for saying this –' she glanced nervously at Zhelkar, who was now visibly alarmed, and then at Dorrin, with whom, as always, it was difficult to tell, '– I believe that we have only a few years, five at most, before the Pukes find us.'

There was a crescendo of startled and angry cries. Some around the table glared at her accusingly. Sander Leafdance stared wide-eyed at the table, hands splayed on it as if for support. Others fixed their gaze expectantly on Zhelkar and Dorrin, who sat in stony silence.

'Deny it, then' called Hazel over the din.

The noise died. All attention was suddenly on the Porros. Zhelkar regarded Hazel squarely. Eyes which normally twinkled now smouldered, all humour gone.

'Hazel is right,' he admitted. 'I hope you will all understand why we didn't make this common knowledge.'

'Then what are you saying?' The voice was that of Tooni Snow. 'That it's all been a waste?' The big, dark, thickly bearded man waved an excited hand at the planet filling the room's viewing port. 'All this has been a *waste?*'

There was stunned silence.

'I think we should all listen to what Hazel has to say,' ventured Dorrin, calmly. As far as most around the circle could tell, her expression had survived the whole meeting without a flicker of change. She gave Hazel a half-nod no-one else caught. Hazel coughed.

'We, ah …' She coughed again. Mother, this was harder than she'd imagined. 'We should seize every potential opportunity with both hands. I believe we may now have the weapon we need.'

'What – this mining thing?' The speaker was Cedra Hornbeam. 'It's an antique pile of junk! And how by the Great Mother do you suggest we get hold of it? This character and his silicon collaborator aren't going to just hand over their ship to us.'

Hazel glared for a precisely calculated moment.

'We don't need to get hold of it.'

'Then how –'

'We persuade McCorkindale to join us.'

The room was silent. All eyes were on her.

'It should be possible,' she went on. 'He's an outcast, just like us. I'm willing to bet that if he wanted to join us, the AI would follow suit.'

'And how do you suggest we go about this? I'm sure I'm not the only one here who would never trust a mercenary. Mercenaries have a habit of selling out to the highest bidder.'

She allowed a smile to leak through. 'That's not what I have in mind. We *show* him. Show him what we have here. Something no one else can offer.'

'Don't give us that!' Cedra scoffed. 'The only thing Pukes understand is that money of theirs. You can't expect to interest one of *them* in anything that doesn't involve adding points in their credit system.'

This created a murmur of agreement. Hazel looked daggers at her.

'You genuinely think that would work?' asked Zhelkar. He seemed surprised.

'I think it has a chance.'

Zhelkar nodded thoughtfully to himself.

'Well Hazel,' he said, 'I suppose you're in a better position to make that judgement than anyone else.' He pulled at his beard. 'So, tell us. What's he like? What kind of character is he?'

Agitated, Hazel tilted her head, taking a few moments to consider.

'He's ... unusual. He must have been a survivor to keep himself alive at all, let alone stay sane doing what he's been forced to do, in hopeless isolation, for so long. I can't say I've ever experienced anything like him. He's ...' she sucked her lower lip, struggling to turn images and feelings into words. 'Very inwardly focussed.'

'You mean introverted?'

'Not really. Well, yes – a bit. She prodded her chin with a forefinger. 'More *imaginative*. His mind is a fully functioning world, as though he's compensated for the inadequacies of the world outside by exploring and expanding the one within. It just doesn't seem as rigidly connected to external reality as, well, most people's minds.'

13

'Is he on the spectrum?' Tooni Snow. 'You know, like Asperger's?'

'No!' She frowned. 'At least, I don't think so, although he's clearly intelligent. Don't misunderstand,' she went on, seeing the way expressions were changing, 'I'm not saying he's a nutter either. Although he is a little odd. I haven't –' she searched for an adjective for what she knew would be a hard concept to understand, '– fully *calibrated* him yet.'

Fidgeting, she glanced at Zhelkar. She'd backed herself into a position where she needed to explain far more than she wanted to.

'Every individual's perception of the world is different,' she pushed on. 'To see the world through another's eyes, so to speak, I have to go through a sort of cross-referencing process which takes time – but my first impressions of his mind are … it's very vivid. Like walking through a forest and *feeling* it, when what you're used to is two-D images. You might call him a daydreamer, but it's more than that.'

'But do you really think you can trust him?'

Hazel realised that she'd wandered off the point somewhere. 'I think there's a good chance, but I should point out that I can only "read" thoughts that are crystallised. Conscious or semiconscious ones, if you like. I can't just "delve in" and extract someone's innermost secrets – they must first form a thought, which makes it quite possible to keep things from me. I can trick someone into revealing thoughts unintentionally. Or encourage thoughts or memories that will … ah, twist a person's perception in order to get at information a person's mind is protecting. But that's a last resort. It's not pleasant. It leads to damage.' Hazel scowled, obliged to offer the clarification, but very ill at ease.

'So, I can't automatically tell if someone is hiding something,' she went on. 'But, from my initial impressions of McCorkindale, I don't think there's a deception in his head. He's like a kid, really. Innately trusting, even naive, but with a childlike cynicism. His childhood was truncated when he was exiled, and it shows. If he's lying in any way, I haven't spotted it – although, probably because of his inwardly-focussed nature, I did find him hard to read sometimes. He didn't let much slip, other than what he wanted us to know.

'The impression I got was that he helped us out of a sheer pent-up sense of injustice. His anger was ... ferocious, but afterwards he felt acute remorse for those he killed. At the moment, he's just confused and mixed up. I think he long ago abandoned any sense of control of his life.'

Eyes defocussed, she nodded to herself.

'I think I can persuade him.'

Leaning forward, Zhelkar regarded her sternly. 'Hazel,' he said, 'this is a serious matter. No outsider has been allowed any kind of access for decades – and, even then, under circumstances far less serious and delicate than these. There is also the issue of quarantine and the treatment he will need to undergo. Is he strong enough?'

'We don't know yet,' admitted Hazel, using a thumbnail to pick at a callous on her palm. 'I left before physiological or immunological tests had been made, although I would guess that he is.' Zhelkar stroked his beard thoughtfully.

'I confess that I have grave misgivings. However,' he sighed, 'in the circumstances I believe you may be right.'

He looked at his partner, who nodded. He swept his eyes around the circle of faces.

'If anyone has any objections in principle to the stranger having *full access* ...' he paused to let the words sink in '... you had better speak now – or, as they say, in future stick a sock in it.'

When no-one spoke, he focussed his attention squarely on Hazel.

'How long will you need?'

Hazel inflated her cheeks. 'Several months. At least six, I think.'

There was the briefest pause. 'We probably have that long to play with.' Zhelkar glanced again at Dorrin, who dispensed another nod. 'Though I'd far rather it was less. Is six months enough?'

Hazel set her jaw. 'It'll have to be.'

'Very well. You're in charge of him during that time. Hazel, with things as they are, I think even six months is pushing things, so the sooner the better, eh?'

She shrugged.

'Do what you have to do,' he went on, 'but if your suspicions are aroused ... *Please*, for all our sakes, do not take

15

unnecessary risks. I imagine I don't have to stress that too much?'

She swallowed. 'I'll do my best.'

'Of that I have no doubt.' Zhelkar smiled kindly. 'Sorry love, but I want you back at Gamma Station as soon as possible. From now on, he's all yours.'

He turned his eyes to the table and seemed to shrink. His voice became quieter, almost a mumble.

'I'll tell Tom, of course. I'm sure he'll agree.'

2

SNAKE

>HI TINK! *Seven days already. How are you doing without me for the first time in your life?*

>*I hope you're not lonely.*

>*Myself, I think I feel more alone right now than at any time in the past few years, which says a lot about what a good friend you've been. I'm basically a prisoner here. Again. What's keeping me going is the thought of being able to see you soon, and also the prospect (distant, at the moment) of discovering what's behind all this. It would be OK if I could talk to you, or even better have one of* Oscar*'s drones here for us to talk through, instead of having to use this thing, but they won't even let us use tight-beam signals.*

>*I don't think it's because they don't trust us. At least, not entirely. Our new friends must be very anxious to keep themselves a secret – from what I've gathered, they hardly ever beam or broadcast transmissions themselves. I think they use communications missiles even for short-range stuff, which is impressively paranoid! I presume that's what they'll do with this message, provided they send it like they promised. The only way I can see them getting it to you is putting it into an airlock for one of your drones to pick up. If you reply to this, tell me if that's what they do. It might be useful info.*

>*I'm sure it's the confederation they're afraid of, or some part of it. That seems to make most sense, although I'm still finding it hard thinking in terms of 'outside' IPEC, which I grew up thinking of as the whole world. My best guess so far is that we've stumbled across a Freelancer society, or empire, which is keeping quiet either because they're smugglers, or (somehow, I have a hunch this is maybe closer to the truth) they've separated themselves entirely from IPEC.*

>*Either way, the future doesn't look promising if what I've heard about Freelancers is true. I thought at first we'd found the mythical aliens! I've had glimpses of some properly weird stuff, and, despite having spoken to what are either real people or masterly fakes, I still can't convince myself*

that's not part of what's going on here. I'm itching to get a look inside one of those wild little green spacecraft.

>*I'm fairly sure I'm inside that rotating green sphere. I've experimented with flicking things across the room, and they loop slightly in one direction. 'Gravity' here must be caused by rotation and centripetal force, which is my main reason for thinking I'm in the sphere, although such a setup seems primitive. Why don't they just use AG?*

>*Our new friends don't seem to go for complexity in a big way in general. Or comfort, come to that. Things I took for granted at home just aren't here. Six years trapped inside* Oscar *should have prepared me for this, but it hasn't. It's not that it's actually *uncomfortable*. They've obviously gone to a lot of trouble to try and make me feel at home.*

>*Maybe that's it! They really are trying to make me feel at home, and to give me things they imagine I would like. I get the impression they're finding it difficult not because they haven't the resources or the technology, but because they really don't know how. It's not second nature to them, and they're trying hard to put themselves into my psychology. I'm probably not explaining myself very well, and this probably all seems prosaic to you anyway, but the impression I get is strong, and I'm finding it a little unnerving. I feel naked, almost. Alien. Perhaps they are aliens after all, but just look like humans. Perhaps they're in disguise!*

>*Perhaps I'm letting my imagination run away with me.*

>*But don't worry about me yet. They're treating me well. I have new clothes, which are seriously wacky, but they fit, and now a four-room apartment all to myself! Luxury compared to life on board* Oscar. *And food! A modern dispensary which gives me food which doesn't taste like a chemistry experiment!*

>*There's HV, but, amazingly, just twenty-one films are available, and they're all crap and very old. There aren't any programme channels I'm allowed access to. I've not been allowed out of my cage even once and I have to tell you I'm getting really restless. Everyone I've seen has been very polite to me, and I must admit that, whatever the reason for this, I'm enjoying not being treated like scum for a change. To my face, at least.*

>*Their reactions to me are confusing. They seem grateful, even reverential (an odd feeling!), but also awkward, as though they don't know what to make of me, or what to do with me. It's almost as though they're embarrassed about keeping me in here, if you can believe that. In particular, the tall, dark-haired man who watches over me half the time gets really flustered when I hassle him about letting me out. He keeps me guessing of course, though very politely. 'Don't know when, you'll have to wait, not our fault, blah blah blah.' Yech! But at the same time, I'm only writing this*

because I'm almost certain they'll transmit it, even though it's encrypted. I have no idea why they're like this, or what they're hiding from us, or why, and it's probably futile to speculate. Time will tell, I suppose, but one thing's for certain: I can't take being caged like this for much longer!

>*You said in your last message that you've told them everything they wanted to know, except about* Oscar. *Although (strangely, perhaps) I still don't have a bad feeling about this bunch, who- or whatever they are, remember what we agreed. You can't be too careful. I have a lot more experience of people than you do, and it's taught me that you can never, ever trust anyone.*

>*Hope you're OK. I'll write again as soon as I can. See you soon (hopefully).*

>*Your favourite organocarbon snob.*

>*END MESSAGE*

Wood chewed for a while on his lip. Then he painstakingly picked out letters on the unfamiliar keyboard to type SEND. He hit the return key and sighed, rubbing his newly depilated chin, hoping his transmission wasn't already being decrypted and picked apart for evidence of rebellion.

Having assured him that the message had been sent (honestly, absolutely no doubt about it), the screen's wafer-thin rectangle faded to darkness and another image began to fade in. Silky green tongues undulated from its base as though in a current of water. Colourful shapes began appearing from off screen.

At first, he took them to be fanciful spacecraft. Then he saw that they had the ambience of life. They waved and wriggled translucent fins, propelling themselves across a background of deep blue splashed with swirling stars. At the front of their flattened bodies were distorted, scaly parodies of human faces, in which bulging silvery eyes twitched, and grotesquely protruding lips rhythmically opened and closed …

Wood rose from his chair and ripped the terminal's wired connection from its socket in the wall. Blank, the screen folded silently back into its tiny box. For a moment he tried to recall the images, wondering what deranged imagination could be responsible for such creations. As they reformed in his mind, he pushed them away in disgust.

Anger flared. He paced to the far wall of the living room and faced it, arms folded.

'I've had enough!' he cried. 'I've put up with your shit until now, but if you think you're going to keep me here *any longer* without telling me who, or what you are, and why I'm still inside this bubble, you're in for a shock.'

There was only silence. He pounded his fists on the unyielding surface.

'*Do you hear me?*'

The wall's pale green began to darken. He seated himself on the sofa facing it, glowering at where he knew the white-coated man or woman would appear. As green faded to transparency, he found himself staring into the dark eyes of a tall man with coppery skin, strikingly uncluttered features, and fine, jet-black hair which hung around his shoulders and mirrored his eyes.

'I see your arm is better.'

'Yes,' the man replied, in thickly accented Standard, flexing his arm to prove it. He never smiled much. Wood found himself glad for this lack of pretence. 'Thanks to you, just burns and bruises.'

'I want out of here,' declared Wood. 'Immediately.'

The man, who'd said his name was Berry, rose from his seat – a sofa much like the one Wood was sitting in – and went through the familiar routine. 'We'd like that too, believe us. But there are good reasons you can't, yet. It's for your own safety. Truly sorry.'

Berry looked pained. It could almost have been genuine.

'If it wasn't for you, I'd he dead,' he said, as though this explained everything.

'So, let me go.'

'Could enlarge your quarters for you. That help?'

Wood didn't reply. He inspected the lampshade, a latticework of rough fibres, brownish in colour. He'd never seen anything quite like it. 'What's that?' He demanded.

'Sorry?'

'The cover for the ceiling light. What's it made from?'

The man seemed momentarily speechless. 'Sorry,' he mumbled, looking away, 'don't know.' He was obviously lying, although Wood couldn't imagine why. 'Wasn't responsible for the decor. Could get it changed if you don't like it?'

'You *won't* keep me in here much longer. And you won't be told when your time is up.'

'Oh?' was all the other man managed. He seemed surprised and angry – and possibly, thought Wood, just possibly rattled as well. Maybe, at long last, he was getting through the facade.

Wood stared at the floor and said nothing.

Presently the man turned his head at something. Something he'd seen? A sound? His eyes focussed on the transparent barrier, as though an image was projected there. His expression softened. He seemed excited. He forced a smile Wood's way.

'Looks like your wish might soon be granted. Hold on for another hour. Things might begin to explain themselves then.'

Wood grunted. 'Oh, I do hope so.'

THE HOUR'S SLEEP Hazel had snatched returning to Gamma Station hadn't been remotely enough, but the pill she'd taken was doing its job. She stomped along the main trail through the inner sphere, gazing in undiminished wonder at the patchwork of cereals, root-crops, orchards and thick hedgerows which curved above her head, all illuminated by sunlight shining through the skin of the ecosphere. As a born Havenner, the spartan claustrophobia of the ecospheres was something she could enjoy for brief periods, but not for any length of time.

Ah Haven. She hadn't been there nearly enough of late.

She pushed aside the wooden door and announced her presence to the greying, heavy-jowled man at the desk.

'A weird business this, Hazel,' he declared, shaking his head. 'Quite what this character's supposed to do for us, I can't fathom. We should be sending him back where he belongs. Isn't a Puke alive can understand anything but their own sweet self, if you ask me.'

'Thanks for your advice, Yarrek.' He nodded. 'But I didn't ask you.'

The corridor was a short one, though its upward curve was still visible. Hazel didn't enjoy the Coriolis effect, even on a habitat the size of an ecosphere. It felt like your feet were being faintly but insistently pushed out from under you. Worse, its direction depended on your orientation relative to the spin.

She found the room she was looking for. As anonymous as the rest, but for the number inexpertly painted on the bare metal door. 'Berry?' she whispered, knocking gently.

After a few seconds the door opened, revealing a face smiling with relief.

'Hazel! Hiya. Flight okay? Ah, see you've lost your sling too. Just as well. We were starting to look like twins.'

'Berry, *dearest*, the only way you and I could look like twins is bandaged head to toe, and then only to the blindest of bats. Did you get the report from the meeting?'

'Yup.'

'What d'you think?'

'That you're mad. Zhelkar and Dorrin are mad if they gave the go ahead. We all know about Tom's sanity. Did he give the go ahead?'

'Berry,' she growled, vision clouding, 'you know nothing about Tom. *Nothing!*' He held her gaze for a second, but knew it was a lost argument. 'Anyway, Tom had nothing to do with it. He will approve it though. Count on it.'

Berry seemed to deflate. Then he shook his head. 'Damned if I know how it came to this,' he muttered. 'History of the world, I suppose. Sorry. You'd better get on with it.' He jabbed a thumb over his shoulder. 'Still can't help feeling this is a massive mistake.'

'How is he?' asked Hazel, changing the subject. Berry drew himself up.

'Making threats. Think he and that monstrous machine out there had a pre-arranged agreement that if he wasn't back by a certain time, the monster would come looking.'

'Seems sensible.'

'Knew all the time, didn't you? And you still went ahead with this.'

'We don't really have much to lose, do we?'

He sighed. 'Perhaps. But be careful. There's more to Mister McCorkindale than meets the eye.'

'Oh, I know that.'

'Snake made me feel *I* was being interrogated. And that lampshade – who put a thundering hemp lampshade in there? Everything was meant to be synthetic! Straight out the blue he asks what it's made of, leaving me gaping like a landed trout. Knows I was bullshitting, and he'll wonder why. Makes me wonder what other oversights we've made. Tell the truth, to start with I thought he wasn't all there. Sat staring at nothing or flicking toothbrushes or castor wheels across whatever room he was in. But he doesn't miss a trick. I hope to fate the thinker's been properly purged, and he won't start seeing flocks of birds or shoals of fish next. That'd *really* set him off.'

Hazel pursed her lips. 'With luck, it won't matter soon.' She peered up at him, knowingly. 'You really don't like him, do you?'

'Well ...' Berry smoothed a hand over his slender neck. 'He saved my life and everything. Yours too, and I'm grateful. But ...' He exhaled, heavily. 'No. Don't like him. Gives me the creeps.'

'You shouldn't let him get to you.'

'I'm not.'

Liar.

'Look, you going in, or what? Had as much of your friend as I can take for one day and could do with hitting the sack for a few hours.'

Hazel blinked, wondering why Berry was being so hostile. 'I have to see the Doc first and get her report. No use bringing him out if he'll just die, is there?'

Berry was clearly in two minds about whether or not this was the case.

ELDER OF HEALING Indora Hibiscus ran through the data with a sense of methodical calm, slowly sweeping the columns with her placid brown eyes, lips pursed yet still curled at the corners in her perpetual lazy smile. Hazel tracked her progress to the bottom of the page, awaiting a conclusion. To her, the data was meaningless.

Eventually, Indora nodded.

'Yes,' she concluded, with great solemnity, touching a gnarled hand to the red dot painted on her wrinkled, olive forehead: a mannerism Hazel found drove her to distraction. 'Yes, I believe we can be certain enough now to proceed. Though his body shows evidence of severe trauma around a year ago, he has recovered. Physically, he is surprisingly fit in view of his confinement and the stresses he must have been living – or perhaps I should say *surviving* – under. Although the boy still needs a good feed.'

There was one of Indora's characteristic pauses. Hazel fidgeted, itching to reach down and wind up the woman's spring.

'He has a healthily high erythrocyte count, and a promising, but of course redundant, lymphocyte count. His immune system is not too degenerative, although it will, of course, need to be carefully primed. We will have to proceed with caution.

'Physically, he has a vigorous and robust metabolism. Indeed, he has an exceptionally low basal pulse rate of just thirty-five beats per minute, and all response times are excellent, although his blood pressures are lower than ideal. He has large lungs for his small size, and good bone structure.'

She paused again, and it was only her infectious placidity which held Hazel in check.

'His digestive system is less fragile than we have had reason to fear, although it is of course unable at present to digest our normal diet. It would take him several weeks at minimum to become accustomed to eating what we do, and it is fair to say he would experience much discomfort. The inoculations will also give him symptoms much more acute than would be expected in our own.'

She lost momentum again and sat there, sagely nodding to herself. Hazel's impatience finally bubbled over.

'So, all this means we can go ahead? It's not going to kill him?'

Indora turned her smile up a notch. 'No, no. That is unlikely. Although there is, of course, that possibility. He may experience some terrible reaction to something or other. But he is young, and, in Orphaned terms, strong. I think he will be able to take it, yes, without too much trouble. That is not to say he will *enjoy* it, you understand. He will think his world has ended!'

Hazel slumped with relief. 'Thanks Doc.' She patted the older woman on the shoulder and rose from her seat, turning in the doorway as she made to leave. 'You do realise the importance of this?'

Indora smiled. 'Do not worry, my flower. I shall take good care of him physically. The other, more difficult, part is up to you.'

A ROBUST-LOOKING young woman strode into the room, her loosely-curled reddish hair bouncing with the energy of her stride. Wood greeted her with a level stare. She flung herself into the soft chair on the far side of the screen and pushed the dark glasses she wore up a nose which looked as though it had been broken at some point.

'Hello there,' she said, smiling, and the smile seemed to radiate genuine warmth. Cocking an ankle on one knee, she draped an arm over the back of the chair. 'My name's Hazel. We haven't met personally before, but you saved my life.'

'I've heard this before. Are you going to let me out of here voluntarily, or not?'

The woman seemed unperturbed. 'I must apologise for our treating you this way after what you've done for us already, but I hope before long you'll appreciate our position.

'We want to repay you,' she told him. 'You're a fugitive. We can offer you somewhere to stay, if that is what you want. A *home*, Wood McCorkindale. The alternative is that we can take you back to the edge of confederation space.'

'You're finally letting me out of here?' Wood couldn't conceal the hope in his voice.

'We are. However, if you decide to stay with us, I must warn you that it won't be easy for you. There'll be much discomfort involved. If you choose to leave, you'll have to do so now, and we'll escort you out the same way you came in.'

His eyes narrowed. 'What kind of discomfort. Why?'

'I can't tell you, yet. You might not believe me if I did. I'm sorry. You'll have to trust us for the moment.'

Wood blinked, amazed at the request. 'I'm not trusting anyone *one nanometre* until you at least tell me who, or what, you are, and why all this shit about secrecy.' He tilted himself forwards. 'What are you hiding? How the hell do you expect me to trust you? You've told me nothing!'

The woman unfolded her leg. She matched his movement, fixing him with a gaze that was somehow intense even beneath her dark glasses. 'I believe you have an enquiring mind, Mister McCorkindale. There are things I could show you which I'm sure would reward the risk.' Lifting a corner of her mouth, she gestured above her head. 'Haven't you seen enough to whet your appetite? We mean you no harm. If we had, harm would already have come to you.

'Trust us.'

HAZEL STUDIED HIM for a few seconds. She didn't have to read his mind to tell that she had him hooked.

3

WHY WON'T IT STOP?

THE WASHROOM was a cubicle two metres wide. It was sulphur-yellow save for one wall, which was a physical mirror, and a floor of dark tiles which were hard on the knees. On the wall was a shower hose. Made of fibrous composite, the toilet was a brown trumpet which vanished into the floor.

Wiping away strings of mucous, Wood raised his head from the toilet opening. His reflection was a shade of green he'd never imagined in human skin. Neither had he imagined it was possible to feel so dire. Further stomach spasms were on the way.

'What's happening to me?' Panic rose along with more bile. His stomach strained against long-empty confines. He plunged his head back into the bowl and a dribble of clear, yellow liquid poured between his lips. Acid liquid scalded his anus, gushing down his legs inside the fabric of his trousers. *Disgusting!* He coughed uncontrollably. 'Oh God. Why won't it stop?'

He retched yet again, barely registering the hand Hazel was holding against his back.

Hazel was fairly certain she'd never seen anyone so ill either. Watching was enough to make her nauseated, without the stench of him and his ejecta. At the same time, he was so heartrendingly forlorn that she found herself bedevilled by some deep-seated urge to cuddle him.

'I've never smelled anything so bad,' he wailed. 'Foul air keeps pouring out of my bottom.'

'Take the injections,' she implored. 'It'll get worse. Imagine what this will be like after a few days?' *If you survive that long.* She stroked his sweat-drenched back. Wood retched yet again, and sneezed, so that more bile dribbled out of his nose. He barely had the strength to support himself on the toilet rim.

'I want to die.'

'The injections will make it stop.' *Eventually.*

'Why is this happening?'

'It's what tried to tell you. The microorganisms. Tiny lifeforms which are now inside your body.'

'Uunh. Like … a horror 'vid.'

'It's natural.'

'Then why aren't you all like this?'

'We get that way sometimes. Living with them has meant our bodies have mechanisms to protect us, so even if we do get sick, we usually recover. You won't. The injections and pills I offered will prime your body so it can use its own defence mechanisms.'

Wood sneezed again, several times, leaving him more exhausted than ever. A titanic burst of wet flatulence echoed around the tiny room. Hazel took an involuntary breath, causing her to gag. 'I don't understand any of what you're saying,' he wailed. 'I've never heard of any of this.'

'I'll explain later, but please: in the meantime, take the injections. If you don't, *you will die.* Understand?'

Wood stared at her with an expression of sheer terror, then buried his head in the toilet bowl once more. 'Oh God,' he croaked, straightening, wiping his chin with a shaking hand.

Hazel moved back to the doorway. She put her hands on her hips and waited. Eventually his head turned half towards her.

'Damn you, do anything you want. I couldn't care if you killed me at the moment.'

SIXTEEN HELL'S TEETH-class courier ships tore through the strange substrate of hyperspace at velocities few other manned spacecraft could have hoped to match. Little more than a shield-protected cylindrical frame to which an outsize thruster, a sac of hydrogen, twenty nuclear missiles, a tiny living module and a Thomson field generator were attached, each half-kilometre long vessel was invisible to the rest but for sluggish radio pulses transmitted for positioning and communication.

Hyperspace was neither a comfortable nor a natural place for humans to be. The appearance of emptiness was false. Objects became practically invisible at distances of more than a few kilometres, yet exploratory probes had taken recordings and measurements hinting at a form of structure. With humans and their machines ill-equipped to view that structure, however, whatever it constituted remained mysterious.

As far as Aral Nikumi was concerned, the courier's lack of provision for passengers to view their surroundings was a blessing. Hyperspace was something not even seasoned sailors relished: the sense of inchoate hostility to human life was too strong. It was well documented that even if a starship's passengers had no knowledge that they were in hyperspace, stress and unease increased, and conversation faltered. A mythology had developed around it.

He glanced at Kettering, who was snoring in the seat beside him – intense, somehow, even when unconscious, his severely cropped blonde hair now dirtied with grey. Nikumi envied this ability: sleep was something he managed only in a bed, and then fitfully. His implant could intervene, but that kind of sleep was not the same.

One of two rooms in the entire vessel, one stacked on the other, the cabin was a beige-walled box fitted with rows of skinny seats and little else. The smaller upper cabin housed the three-strong crew. Facing Nikumi in the opposite row sat Lieutenant Commander Eagleberger – long since fit for duty after two years rehabilitation with her cloned arm – and Tactical Officer Arjum Jeetwa, who was now a fully-fledged, and respected, Special Branch technician. In his own row, freshly promoted Lieutenant Commander Ishti Waranika was industriously chatting up one of her colleagues: a soft-eyed, hugely muscled man Nikumi knew as Special Branch Officer Calter, although he he'd lately been assigned the naval rank of Sub-Lieutenant. The man seemed to swell under the praise gushing upon him. There was a hot twinge in Nikumi's chest as he thought of his ex-wife, Sonma.

The rest of his loyal subordinates from *Violator* were split between five of the other couriers. Lounging in the remaining seats were a dozen of Nikumi's new command, hand-picked from the ranks of Special Branch. Their crash-course in Divide and Rule-class operation had been efficient and effective, but Nikumi found himself wishing for a more seasoned crew. If only to make integration with navy personnel easier.

Perhaps he'd simply been exposed to too much navy thinking. His previous command, it seemed, had left an indelible mark.

Even with the staggering manpower, firepower and organisational power at his disposal, Nikumi's mission was daunting. There was no case that he was aware of in all of history where so much hinged on one man. He could neither crumble nor make a poor decision. The plan now in operation was a cunning one, and the odds should be heavily stacked against the enemy. However …

Try as he might, he still could not put himself in his enemy's shoes. Their motivation remained one that he couldn't fathom. Arguably the most vital step towards overcoming an opponent was to understand them, and the simple truth was that he didn't. The Lancers, by contrast, were transparent. He could picture himself in their position quite easily – even sympathised with it. This had made him highly effective when planning and executing Lancer-related operations for the Joint State Security Service.

This mission was different – something which created a knot of unease in the back of his mind. Despite his encyclopaedic knowledge of the matter, there remained too many unknowns for him to feel fully confident. The portrayal of the 'Freaks' (as Josey Fox's mysterious group was now officially known) as doomsday cultists worked only to a point, beyond which it hindered true insight. He had a strong feeling that things were far more complicated than apparent.

Not that this lessened the threat.

The sense of purpose permeating the canned atmosphere of Hell's Teeth class Confederate Vessel *Mind Bender* was formidable. Not even the Lancer problem had, to Nikumi's knowledge, generated such unity. This was despite fifteen days already in cramped tedium. Usually on such journeys, tranquillisers were necessary to stem the flaring of tempers.

Not on this flight.

The thought was uplifting, and he clung to it.

'LISTEN UP, LADIES AND GENTS, this is your friendly tour-guide speaking. Hope you enjoyed the ride and the views – we'll be dipping into real-space for another high-speed refuelling in just over a minute, so I'd appreciate it if you stow anything spillable.'

Good. A break from routine, however small. No chance to stretch legs though. A subtle vibration went through the vessel as the main thruster fired to slow the backwards-hurtling vessel's speed towards something a normal spacecraft could match.

Nikumi thanked God that Satan was not on board. He and two drugged-looking female 'companions' had been given a specialised courier of their own, manned by a small army of thinkers slaved to two other couriers in the fleet. The thought made Nikumi's lips curl. By laws applied to anyone else, the creature should not have been allowed to live, let alone under the protection of the Service. It burned, but there was nothing Nikumi could do. For the plan to work, Satan was perhaps their key asset.

'Here we go folks, hang on to your hats.'

A tremor went through the cabin. Waranika ceased her seduction and tensed back in her seat. A holoscreen sprang to life behind the wall opposite the cabin airlock. It showed the fast-approaching hydrogen sacs in a line against the stars of truespace, each attended by a bowl-shaped utility tug. There was a subtle feeling of movement as the sixteen delicate-looking couriers pirouetted to face the fast-approaching fuel sacs, which themselves were travelling at enormous speeds relative to surrounding space. A thud reverberated through the cabin's thin fabric as the spent sac was jettisoned astern. The broad shields forming the bows of the spacecraft parted, clearing the way for the new sacs. The view shifted slightly as *Mind Bender* adjusted its trajectory using its near-vestigial attitude thrusters.

Then the fleet were upon the fresh sacs, gulping them into their skeletal innards using invisible manipulator fields. There was a jolting second thud, and mechanical sounds filtered through the cabin's structure as clamps locked on and fuel-feeds connected. The thrusters fired again.

Within another minute, a different kind of jolt signified the return to hyperspace, and the screen disappeared.

Nikumi thought back to his meeting with his mentor for the past three years, the JSSS's Supreme Chief Jesus Hussain, and the legendary James Marcell. An unholy alliance, it had struck him, even at the time. Since then, he'd often pondered the relationship between the overlord of Unicorp (and, some said, the most powerful man alive) and the Interplanetary Economic Confederation's supposedly impartial Joint State Security Service. He hadn't known what to expect of Marcell. The man certainly had presence, in abundance, and was obviously not a man to cross.

Nikumi had never met anyone he trusted less.

He recalled Hussain's words in the final minutes of his incarceration – his reward from the JSSS's covert Green Section for discovering the LGO, or 'Little Green Object', beyond IPEC space, all those years ago. *Your life will be beholden to people whose identities may surprise you, and whose aims you may neither like nor understand.*

Arching in his seat, he stretched to ease cramping muscles. His mind itched to wander, and for a moment he allowed it to. He'd never been told the identity of his ex-wife's lover. This, he'd been told, was necessary to protect both himself and the man involved. He would never meet either again.

He hoped their assignments had been dangerous ones.

LEANING BACK ON pearlescent sand, his head against an ornate Moroccan pillow, James Marcell studied the report on his implant's display, which seemed to hover in the sky beyond his antique Armani sunglasses. He waved away the brunette who was massaging his testicles with enthusiasm but less skill than he would have liked. She sloped off along the beach to join a game of volleyball with the other girls.

Matters appeared to be progressing well. Hussain seemed pleased. Courier missiles were spreading between every one of IPEC's hundreds of thousands of communications nodes, the message they bore fanning out towards the most distant reaches of the confederation at speeds unattainable by manned craft, multiplying unstoppably until it numbered in the millions. Each carried a single message: catch Josey Fox. Soon there would be not a single planet, colony or complex which didn't know what to look for.

An expensive exercise, he reflected, but necessary.

He rose stealthily to his feet, waded into the warm water, and swam towards the false horizon.

4

INFLIGHT ENTERTAINMENT

WOOD McCORKINDALE STEPPED stiffly through the door of the single-storey prefab building which had recently been his home. Surprised by the intense aromas the breeze brought to his nostrils, he lingered on the scuffed aluminium step, gazing in wonder at the patchwork of browns and greens, spattered with brighter colours, which arced in a concave band above his head.

He felt better now. *Much* better – although, backtracking, he realised that he still felt unwell by most of his standards prior to his exposure to the biological world those twenty-five endless days ago (at his own insistence: idiot!). Despite his unfamiliar clothing and fading rashes of angry pustules, with his hair trimmed and tied back and his beard shaven, he looked almost respectable. He still wore a nappy. The team in charge of his 'adaptation' had explained that his diarrhoea would continue for at least another week, which apparently meant seven days, as his guts adapted to the civilisations of microorganisms flourishing in them. The cocktail of stenches which were constant companions now – of his bowels, his sweat, even his breath – were something he couldn't imagine ever getting used to.

He was finding what he saw around him similarly difficult to assimilate. The entire sphere was made of living tissue. Many such structures existed, Hazel had told him. They were self-regenerating and repairing, capturing energy from sunlight in an improbably subtle process called photosynthesis.

Beginning their lives as seeds in the soils of planets with suitable carbon dioxide-rich atmospheres, they grew by fixing gases into molecular building blocks. After several years, having grown into discs hundreds of metres across, they were raised into orbit. There, by liberating dissolved oxygen and nitrogen, they inflated to form hollow spheres which were topped up via specialised tanker vessels until the ecosphere had grown sufficiently large and strong to inhabit. Planetary soil was spread around the interior, and plants – which Hazel had explained were the group of organisms from which the ecospheres had been derived – grew either in this thin mineral layer or supplied with nutrients from the ecosphere itself. These plants provided the basis of the occupants' diets.

The organisms now swarming in unimaginable numbers in his gut were the reason he could now digest plants. 'It's a mutually beneficial arrangement,' Hazel had explained. 'They get a meal out of it, and so do you. It's called symbiosis.' The plants and the ecospheres themselves continually recycled atmospheric oxygen as it was turned to carbon dioxide by its human inhabitants. They also recycled other waste. Once established, the whole system was self-sustaining. All powered by sunlight.

It was all weirder than his most fevered dreams.

'Are those ships – the organics …'

'Orgs,' interjected Hazel, hands jammed in the pockets of her favourite pair of brightly patterned trousers as she waited beside him at the door. 'We call manufactured ships nonorgs. Which sounds kind of banal, now I tell it to someone else.' She set off along a foot-polished path through wind-rippled fields of what McCorkindale now knew to be cereals. 'Watch your feet,' she called back to him.

He stepped over a ripple in the sphere's wood-like inner skin. It might have tripped him had he still been looking up. 'So are orgs the same as this?' he asked, as he waddled to catch up. Overhead, small buildings clung to the colourful stripe looped around the ecosphere's equator. Multilegged little vehicles crept over it, harvesting or planting fruits and other crops.

'They're similar in that they're derived mainly from plants. But they're much more complex and have a mammalian nervous system.' Anticipating his query, she said 'Mammalian. That describes mammals, which are the group of organisms to which you and I belong. Look – I know you must have a million questions, but I'm not a database, and I won't be able to answer most of them properly without going into fundamentals. You'd be better going through a library, but I'm afraid we don't have one here. For security reasons. All I can usefully tell you now is that the orgs are sentient, reproduce by fission, and propel themselves by manipulating spacetime. We avoid thinking about that last part too deeply by calling its visible effects an "aura."'

They were approaching the terminus of a monorail, where an archaic-looking, brightly hand-painted car waited. 'Amazing,' he mumbled. 'Can they use this manipulation for defence as well?'

Keeping anything from Wood McCorkindale, reflected Hazel ruefully, was going to be a struggle. 'They can deform space around themselves so that electromagnetic beams or projectiles can get no closer than a few centimetres.' Feeling his next question form, she added 'Which is what you saw when the orgs were fired upon before you destroyed the IPEC warship.'

McCorkindale was impressed.

'Unfortunately, though, IPEC's latest weapons can fry our orgs without a direct hit.'

'You could probably boost this field somehow. I presume it's gravitational? How do they generate it?'

'Please get in.' Hazel gestured inside the car. Within was functional seating for thirty, all facing uphill. Hazel waited for McCorkindale to choose a seat, then sat one seat away from him. The car accelerated smoothly up one of the five rails which curved like spokes uphill to the spinning ball's axis.

She'd yet to answer his question. McCorkindale, however, was a persistent bugger. 'I was asking, how do the ships – the orgs – distort space? What's the process involved?'

'Be patient. I'm sure you'll find more than enough to occupy your curiosity later.' She peered at him through the dark glasses she'd worn since their first meeting. Her eyes had been injured during the attack, she'd told him, sensitising her to light, but the glasses, along with her evasiveness, had expanded a bubble of unease at the back of McCorkindale's mind. She watched him ponder that, given everything he'd seen so far, and the fact that both he and his motives were unknown, it was perhaps unsurprising that these people were obviously hiding something. Hadn't they been more forthright than he could have expected? Maybe she was just trying to lead him in gently?

Maybe.

'Are you sure your friend will be alright about you not being around for a while?' she asked, keeping her tone light. 'I hope there aren't going to be problems.'

McCorkindale didn't like the sound of that. The car was now tilted a good forty degrees to the ecosphere's axis. Apparent gravity had already halved. 'He won't enjoy it much, but he's said he'll go along with it.' He turned suddenly penetrating eyes on Hazel. Berry was right: he was highly deceptive. Even his thoughts were unpredictable. 'I still don't see why we can't go wherever we're going in *Oscar*. The same way as we came here.'

She didn't reply for several seconds.

'There are rules,' she said, holding his gaze, steeling herself for the draining process which would erase his recollection of the previous weeks. 'As I told you.' He turned away. 'I didn't make them, and they can't be broken. Even for you. No non-organic ships are allowed.'

'Then this place, or thing: whatever you're taking me to see; you must be pretty desperate to make sure IPEC can't find it.' Focussed on her again, his eyes narrowed. 'What are you people doing out here?'

Hazel looked away, out of the window. They were climbing almost vertically now. Around them the walls of the sphere shone a warm green-orange, shot through with darker veins and pipes like blood vessels. She could feel her hair lifting as apparent gravity became negligible.

You should start wiping him now.

Then again, these were reasonable questions, under the circumstances.

'We aren't without our insurance policy in this,' she said at length, facing him through a fan of floating hair which she brushed aside with a hand. 'You're now a carrier of plague. If you leave us without being decontaminated, you'll bring disease and death potentially to billions of people who have no immunity. You'll be the cause of at least one catastrophic epidemic. I hope you can appreciate you wouldn't be popular.'

McCorkindale's gaze hardened, though it became less formidable as his eyes lost their probing quality. 'I see. Now that's out in the open, don't get any ideas about jacking around with Tink or the ship. If he doesn't hear from me when he thinks he should, or if any of you try any funny business, he will make the loudest noise this part of the galaxy's ever seen.'

'I'm glad we understand each other.'

They disembarked from the monorail. Pulling herself along by a tangle of woody railings, Hazel led the way along a throat-

36

like tunnel lit by patches of green chemiluminescence in the walls. Soon the passageway merged with five others to form a single irregular tunnel around six metres across. Monorail tracks from the gullets of the three largest tributaries ran equidistantly along the walls of the combined tunnel. The handrails petered out, replaced by metal rungs driven into the tunnel's brown skin.

McCorkindale allowed himself a flush of pride as Hazel glanced back and was surprised to find him following with ease at her heels. A tubby monorail tractor slid by in silence, towing machinery. The driver, a middle-aged man called Evening Sky, cheerfully returned Hazel's wave.

'This way.'

She beckoned McCorkindale down a side passage with 'Dock 46' painted on the living passage wall. After twenty or so further metres the passage ended in a structure like two tightly clenched lips. Gliding past her, McCorkindale pulled his face towards one of the lips, sniffed it, and tapped it with a knuckle. The surface was hard, but pliable, as if pressurised. He pushed himself out of the way as Hazel moved forward, unable to hide his curiosity as she rubbed a polished patch to one side with her fingers.

With a rustling sound, the lips parted.

'Come on,' Hazel pulled herself, legs-first, between them. Then she saw his face. 'It's an airlock, that's all.'

Apprehension in every movement, McCorkindale put a hand on each lip and pulled himself after her. Though short, the tunnel beyond was disturbingly like some giant body-part for someone unfamiliar with such things. It ended in a metal chamber, on the far side of which was a conventional airlock door. Hazel palmed the control pad. The door slid open and he followed her through.

'Watch the change to gravity,' she warned, catching herself on bent legs as her weight became apparent. Grunting with surprise, McCorkindale planted himself face-first into the floor. 'Sorry, I should have said that sooner.'

She stared down at him, hands over her mouth.

'Um, you okay?'

He propped himself on his elbows and nodded balefully, probing a grazed chin. His pale face was flushed pink. As he picked himself up, Hazel had to turn away to hide the fact that she was trying not to wet herself.

The small cabin of the spaceship was spartan metal and siliplastic with panes of nearly indestructible transparent diamondglass forming the front and much of the sides of the hull. McCorkindale, who'd expected an org, looked like a child confronted with a disappointing gift. The docking area was an irregular cavern on the ecosphere's axis of rotation. Fanning over its luminescent walls were networks of irregular pipes, on some of whose largest swellings, lips, like those via which they'd entered the airlock, were visible. From others, Orgs sprouted like vine fruit, no two the same. Many of the swellings sported metallic boxes – nonorg airlocks like the one they'd just negotiated. They could have been nailed on by a drunken god.

Hazel strapped herself into the pilot's seat, gesturing for McCorkindale to do likewise in the co-pilot's. Having charged the reactor, studied the little onboard thinker's summary of pre-flight checks and confirmed that McCorkindale's harness was secure, she thumbed the docking clamp release, grabbed the joystick and dabbed the pedals. Manoeuvring thrusters thumped, the view spun around, and a circle of stars grew ahead. Hazel picked her way between other small spacecraft and playful flocks of bright green objects the size and shape of rugby balls.

'Org crèche,' she explained, following McCorkindale's gaze. 'Normally, orgs don't grow much until they're nine or ten years old.' She felt his excitement as the dock's entrance passed and the spinning ecosphere began shrinking behind them. Ahead, bright against the stars in all its gothic glory was *Oscar*, the filthy old mining vessel he'd come to call home.

She pointed at the stern section of the IPEC cruiser *Born to Destroy*, looming a few kilometres further away in a halo of its own debris.

'Why did you make us bring that?'

His attention was still locked on *Oscar*. For a moment, she thought he hadn't heard.

'Be patient,' he replied, mockingly. 'You might find out later.'

She smiled, without humour. The truth was that she already knew what he wanted it for.

That was why she'd risked the lives of so many to bring it here in the first place.

5

LANGUAGE OF THE MIND

SPROUTING FROM THE WALL was a semicircular excrescence like a bench, furnished with a maroon and green check-patterned rug and scattered with brightly patterned cushions.

McCorkindale sat on it as though afraid it might bite him.

He looked about him with childlike awe; at the chemiluminescent patches illuminating the org's interior, at the bumps, veins and smooth patches in the curving walls. Here and there were areas through which he could see stars.

'Is it what you expected?'

His nose wrinkled. 'Not sure.' Hazel nodded encouragingly. 'It's very, um … I mean, there isn't anything *in* here.' He thoughtfully gnawed his lips. It was a relief to see them without scabs. 'How do you control it?' As he finished speaking, he released a barrage of obscene, wet noises, finding, to his dismay, that his nappy still required. Hazel coughed as he turned crimson. *Aww, Great Mother!*

'Nothing to be ashamed of,' she told him.

'I'm really, really sorry.'

Trying not to breathe, she bum-shuffled away from him. 'Mmmm. Not ideal, is it?' He seemed to be trying to shrink into the seat.

'Will it always be like this?'

'You should settle down within a month.' *I hope.* 'Four weeks, or three tendays.'

'Three *tendays?*'

'You'll get more used to it as well.'

He went into a coughing fit, pulling a disgruntled face as he recovered. 'You were telling me about the orgs.'

No, you were asking. Which is different, sunshine. Hazel inspected a palm. 'You're asking the wrong questions. *We* have no control.

We're passengers. Most orgs would go to extraordinary lengths to be of service – it's in their nature – but they spook easily, and they get tired. We're decent to them, and they trust us. We respect their wishes and concerns.'

'But how do you navigate? How do you even communicate with them?' Hazel thought that he looked a little green. He was peering at the stars with a hint of desperation.

'That's what I keep trying to tell you: *we* don't navigate. Their brains are complex navigational organs. They can navigate more precisely than the most advanced navcomp systems. Although, as with hyperspacial travel, things are less predictable over longer distances.'

'Hold on a minute … You're telling me … that you don't use hyperspace?'

Hazel raised her hands in amused frustration. 'Well, I was *trying* to save the best bit. Our nonorg vessels do. But no, orgs don't. Hadn't you noticed?'

'Then, what …?'

'They travel directly, point to point.'

McCorkindale's mouth was hanging open. 'But … then … why are astroengineers still … pissing about in hyperspace if you can go direct?'

'Because they *can't make it work*. People have tried since the early days of interstellar travel, but inorganic technology just isn't sophisticated enough yet to overcome the practical problems involved. Finding hyperspace was an extraordinary fluke, well ahead of its time. Technology hasn't yet fully come to terms with that, let alone something as complex as direct travel. Panspacial put it in their "future ideas" file long ago.'

'Then how …'

'The orgs use wormholes.'

McCorkindale looked at her as though she were mad. 'This isn't some holovid. How can you squeeze this –' he gestured wildly around the cabin, whose appearance was still freaking him out, '– through a hole smaller than an atom!'

'I never said we just 'pop through' them. That would be impossible.' In McCorkindale's eyes was the panic of someone whose world was unravelling. She could sympathise. It probably felt as though much of his academic life was redundant. 'Please – I'm neither a physicist nor a biologist, so I can't go into this in depth. You'll have a chance later to meet people I'm sure would love to elaborate. As I understand it though, our model of how orgs work is based on something called Wheelerian topography.'

'… The membrane of spacetime is a froth of quantum-scale holes, tunnels and bumps and so-on.'

Hazel was surprised. Could he know of org history? It seemed unlikely. And besides, saying anything on *that* topic might invite questions she did not want to have to answer.

'That's the idea,' she said, carefully. 'The model's an old one – more than five hundred years, in fact – but it's the best we have. I've heard the orgs described as using this surface the way we use our feet and hands, though I'm sure that's a gross simplification. There are even smoother regions they avoid, a bit like ice.'

Though McCorkindale gazed around the org's interior as though he wasn't listening, Hazel knew that he was hanging on every word.

'That's how they travel sub-light. You were asking how they travel interstellar distances. Orgs can also use the pits and wormholes as progenitors for forming links between widely separated points in spacetime. At a quantum level, we think orgs have cracked the code by which mass tells spacetime about itself. They tell it fibs: such intricate and convincing lies, they can bend and mould it like four-dimensional putty; even tie it in knots. We think the energy required to power all this is 'borrowed' from one or more mirror universes in a tricksy quantum accounting operation I don't pretend to understand. But the upshot is that orgs can create a small volume of spacetime connecting points separated by hundreds of light years, while maintaining a gravitational gradient in it gentle enough that they aren't torn apart as they pass through.'

McCorkindale digested this. It had occurred to him that something didn't add up. If, as Hazel had hinted, the fundamental principles were poorly understood, yet at the same time this was a process too complex and subtle to have been just stumbled across, how had these bizarre creatures taken to space travel in the first place?

'Not convinced?' Hazel laughed, more nervously than intended. *Damn*, he was sharp. 'Don't blame you.'

He was truculent now. 'There's something you're not telling me.'

She dodged the remark. 'At least you've not pronounced it "impossible". They say the proof of the pudding's in the eating, and you'll be eating pudding any minute.' His look suggested that she might be dangerous. Her giggle surprised him. 'Sorry. A local expression.'

'You,' observed McCorkindale, 'are baiting me.'

Hazel kept her expression neutral. Then a smile pushed through. She turned her eyes to the floor. There was silence for a few seconds.

'The orgs. You asked how we communicate with them. Ask it.'

'Ask it?'

'Yes, just ask it anything. Oh – and, being sexless, they aren't offended being referred to as "it".'

'Um, hello?' he began, eyes raised, feeling foolish. Then he placed fingers against the sides of his head and grinned.

It was as though a clear bubble of thought had materialised precisely between his ears.

-Don't be bashful- -:I: am not that different from the :intelligence: :you: call :Tink:- -:Worry: unnecessary- -Capable :hands: will take you safely-

There were no words he could identify. The message was a flow of forms, tones and depths, more immediate and intimate than words could ever be.

-Although no :name: is necessary in :mindspeak:- -call :me: :Tumbleweed:- -:Org: :names: are intrinsic in :shapes of the mind:- -If :you: refer to :me: in :non-mindspeak: please use this :name:-

'Tumbleweed?' *Okay, concentrate. -So this is :your: :voice:?-* Once again, he was surprised that both speech and understanding came more or less naturally.

-Inasmuch as :I: have one-

-:Telepathy:-

-Your :power to observe: = :uncanny:- Sarcasm! He grinned wider.

-You always :speak: to :each other: like this?-

-Always-

-Limited to :short-range:?-

-:Distance non-dependent: but only theoretically- -:Distance: :muddles:- -:Interference: from others- -:Org: :intellects: distinct :beacon: empty :space:- -:Conversation: across :light years:-

This was a little unclear, but he thought he understood the creature's gist. *-Then … :communication: must be :instant:?-*

-Between :orgs:, correct-

-But … how?- Ah! *-:Quantum entanglement:?-*

-Every :telepathic being: contains :entangled material:-

'Bloody hell,' he squawked, aloud. *-:Mechanism:?-* *-How are :you: :telepathic:?-*

-:Symbiosis: Same as :human:- …

There was the feeling of intrusion on the conversation, like shouting above which words could not be heard. *-What's wrong?-* he asked, but there was only a feeling of static, like an empty screen. Hazel innocently examined a broken fingernail as Tumbleweed bubbled into McCorkindale's consciousness again.

-We are soon to make the first :connection:- *-:You: will experience small :discomfort: most likely-* *-Like wearing :internal organs: on :outside:-* (sensations of mirth).

Oh God. *-And that's :funny:?-* Connection. Suddenly he could visualise clearly the process involved.

-For us, it is quite :hilarious:- *-Every :time:-*

The experience was as disorientating as on that first occasion, during *Oscar's* unlikely rescue tendays ago. Again, McCorkindale's reaction was of claustrophobia and alarm. The sense of compaction reversed, becoming an outward pressure, as though he was extruding in a horrifying way from inside himself. He was glad he couldn't see what was happening outside.

He felt dizzy. Bilious. 'Oooh ...'

Then his head was between his knees, aching muscles protesting as his stomach turned itself inside out.

'Uuunh. God.' He wiped his mouth. 'You get used to *that?*' Ashen, he watched as his discarded breakfast was sucked into the spongy brown floor.

'Oh yes,' said Hazel, prising a pack of water for him out of one of the storage organs behind the seat. 'The novelty soon wears off.'

-That nice?- he asked Tumbleweed.

-Your :poison:- *-my :breakfast:-*

-Yuck-

Part of the wall had cleared to reveal a segment of some softly luminous brownish-red globe with a brighter speck visible against it. Rising, McCorkindale reached out to touch it. It was a flat screen, seamless with the rest of the wall of the org's internal spacer, though the image it portrayed had a slippery 3D quality.

The speck in the view could have been any colour in the eerie light.

'It's a sheet of cells containing electrosensitive pigments,' Hazel explained. The boy was like a sponge: she could feel him soak up everything she said, and his insatiable thirst for more. 'Dyes which change colour under electrical stimulation. There's a dense array of neurons serving the pigmented cells of the screen. The picture's a combination of pigments changing colour, and the cells – which are called chromatophores – shrinking and expanding. Orgs have a lot of control over their own morphology, and they know humans like to see what's going on.'

Where are we? he asked Tumbleweed. He was finding the communication already more fluid, like someone losing a stilted foreign accent.

Approaching :Beta Station:, orbiting the brown dwarf called :Walnut: How would you like to see your surroundings properly instead of using that pokey little screen?

He pondered this. *Okay.*

'Whooaaaaaargh!'

The immensity outside the ship poured into his protesting brain. McCorkindale was still aware of the cabin, could still see Hazel watching in thinly-veiled amusement, and still feel the coarse material covering the faintly throbbing bench he was now clutching for support. Simultaneously, he was floating, bodiless, in space, able to see in all directions at once.

Except that it was not quite *seeing*. It was perceiving in a way which was new. Yet it felt oddly familiar, overwhelmingly *sensual*, and – even once he was over the initial shock – quite breathtaking.

Glowing softly from its internal fusion source, the tiny ecosphere of Beta Station cowered beneath Walnut's thunderous magenta globe. The failed star loomed so overwhelmingly that it seemed to be in the process of toppling on to the fragile bubble. As McCorkindale watched, pair of brilliant stars – one intensely green, the other neon red – were slowly eclipsed by the edge of the brown dwarf's atmosphere. *Limetree and Firebrand* commentated Tumbleweed. In the opposite direction was a fat orange star, more a circle than a point. *Cyclops*: a huge red giant. The galaxy was a silvery band, half obscured by an arch of nebulous blue light laced with filaments of purple and black shadow. *Trene's veil.*

A much larger, almost spherical org was approaching through the weird purple dusk. It slowed itself with uncanny precision, and Beta Station began to recede. The two strange spacecraft remained barely metres apart, as though locked together by an invisible forcefield. Tumbleweed had obviously sensed McCorkindale's forming question.

By sharing auras, we travel more efficiently. It's less of a strain on my battery-organ and makes it much easier to gossip. (Auras? Ah, yes – that purplish pallor. A drizzle of photons at the violet end of the visible spectrum, a by-product of the complex bookkeeping required for the orgs to borrow from one universe what was fleetingly used in another.) *Would you like to meet my friend?*

McCorkindale's mouth opened. Hazel felt his hesitation; his spike of self-doubt and fear. *Yes, I'd like to.*

A very different presence swam into his head, like consciousness into a dream. It was beginning to feel a little crowded. *I am pleased to :join: you. I :experienced: what you did for us. I have :intimacy: with :Albatross2: and :Birdwing:, who owe all to you. I am Starquest.*

Starquest seemed an altogether more sober org than Tumbleweed. McCorkindale could sense, powerfully, the reverence behind the images and feelings. Overwhelmed, he tried to focus on a response, but couldn't pin down or organise his conflicting jumble of thoughts.

We are honoured by your :opening-of-mind: to us. We shall keep your :language-of-mind:, and treasure it. Should you ever desire it, we will bear you to the farthest star.

Hazel smiled at his scarlet face.

'You opened yourself right up to them,' she explained. 'You were obviously confused and affected, and you let them see that. It's a gesture they revere very highly – to them it's a sign of great trust and intimacy. They've been very complimentary about you. I think you just made a couple of good friends.'

'Oh.'

A two hundred percent increase, reflected McCorkindale. *I'll have to keep this up.*

AS HAZEL HAD EXPECTED, the next 'connection' felt less uncomfortable than the previous one, and McCorkindale managed to keep down what remained of his morning meal. He found himself once more plunged into Tumbleweed's sensory world.

Ahead, a bright sliver marked the edge of a planet: an utterly dark circle against sparsely scattered stars. Mesmerised, he watched the sliver fatten as a bright sun rose over the horizon, casting golden light on stacks and swirls of cloud as the terminator retreated and the orgs bled momentum to their invisible interface. As night was peeled away, a close-orbiting red moon cast a shadow which skimmed towards the orgs above dazzling clouds and gleaming blue oceans, revealing itself as slightly oval as it advanced towards the edge of the darkness.

From space, at least, it was the most beautiful planet McCorkindale had ever seen.

Hazel was equally engrossed in what Tumbleweed was showing her. After what could have been minutes or hours, McCorkindale was disappointed to find himself back in the cabin.

Hazel smiled at him.

'I should have something momentous to say,' she said, rubbing a thumb over one of the pads of hard skin on her palms. 'You're the first outsider to come here … for nearly forty years, I believe.' She swallowed. 'Well, this is it. This is home.'

She swept aside a strand of hair which had dangled unconcerned over one eye throughout the voyage – an unconscious gesture which wasn't lost on McCorkindale – then took one of his hands in both of hers. Her smile was solemn now.

'On behalf of everyone, Wood McCorkindale, welcome to Haven.'

6

JUST PEOPLE

ALONE AGAIN, Tumbleweed dropped silently towards the clouds, wrapped in a slippery cocoon of tortured space.

As it plummeted, the living starship began to replenish drained reserves in ways that Wood did not understand. He felt its unmistakable pleasure, like a swimmer surfacing for breath after a spell underwater. Planes of high cloud zipped past. The table-top of a huge thundercloud approached, blinding white. In the darkness beneath its overhanging rim, columns of rising vapour flashed eerily as lightning writhed over them. The org plunged into the inky confusion of cloud below. Blinded, Wood wondered what other, alien senses the org used for navigation.

What a violent place.

Abruptly, they emerged over an ocean that mirrored the glowering ceiling above. Travelling at an unlikely speed just above groping waves, the org caused barely a ripple. A rocky island grew ahead. Wood could see other small shapes speeding away from it. They were soon lost in the grey line where the sky met the lashing sea.

The org slowed, and a rough shoreline passed below. As Tumbleweed rose above the twisted lavas of a steep hillside, Wood could make out a pair of dark openings in the mountain high above. He knew instinctively that this was their destination.

It soon became clear that the openings were very large indeed,

They passed into an underground space through a mouth which must have been a couple of kilometres wide and almost as high. 'Is this, ah … non-human?' Wood asked quietly.

'These caves were formed when a magma chamber near the surface emptied, although I'm sure it's unusual to find volcanic caverns anywhere on this scale. You're familiar with vulcanism and plate tectonics?'

'Um. Sort of.'

'This is a volcanically active world, still undergoing a lot of crustal movement. This place is long since inactive though.'

That's Reassuring.

The openings were soon bright patches shrinking in the darkness behind. Light strips overhead revealed that Tumbleweed was descending a broad tunnel. Presently, the org turned a lazy corner and a vast underground cavern hove into view.

Wood was transfixed. He'd been in spaces as large, possibly – but none had filled him with such awe. This chamber was the result not of human labour, but of pure chance.

The uneven floor had been smoothed into flat terraces, connected by ramps. Many were occupied by orgs of greatly varying shapes, sizes and shades and patterns of green and yellow. The largest, Wood estimated, were almost a hundred metres long. While no two were identical, there were themes: big and almost spherical, medium-sized and shaped like stubby hotdogs, and relatively tiny, rounded ones which huddled together or floated around the cavern like gangs of unruly children. Many platforms were sprinkled with finned or winged shapes which he guessed were atmospheric vessels. Mostly brightly coloured, there didn't seem to be one decorated the same as another.

Below the cavern wall, on the two largest, highest platforms, lay three spacecraft which could have contained several *Oscar*s each. *Cargo haulers*, he thought. They looked unimaginably old. Where any modern spaceship would have had one, each sported no less than five rings of curiously angular Thomson Field Generators. Dust-dulled, and projecting an air of dereliction, they seemed almost part of the background. As the org descended, Wood saw that one of them had visibly sagged in the middle.

Towering over everything, lodged like an improbable crystal in the rust-coloured wall of one corner of the chamber, was a gigantic, dust-dimmed prism. From its uppermost facet a network of immense tubes fanned into the rock of the chamber's ceiling.

'That looks like an oxygenating plant.'

'It is.'

'It looks kind of derelict.'

'It hasn't been used in two centuries.'

He squinted. 'How come you didn't need it any more?'

'We ... developed other sources.'

Tumbleweed was now settling towards a big terrace neighbouring the cavern wall and a row of low utilitarian buildings. The org was already below the roofs of some of the larger hangars. 'Wait a minute – *centuries?* How old is this place?'

Hazel's lips pursed thoughtfully. 'Well, the oxy-plant over there was installed almost four centuries ago.'

Wood could tell that his expression wasn't edifying. 'But ... even if I accept what you told me about the age of the human race, surely that's back near the beginning of space-flight?'

'Those three ships on the upper terraces were among the first ever true interstellar craft.'

Wood said nothing further, giving up, at least for the moment. His ignorance seemed fractal. Each revelation spawned too many new questions for Hazel's explanations to keep pace.

Tumbleweed touched down on the dusty platform without so much as a vibration. Rising as the weird organic airlock rustled open, Hazel gestured for Wood to follow. Tumbleweed's presence between his ears felt disarmingly eager. *I hope you enjoyed your flight with Tumbleweed Starways.*

Thank you. It was educational.

I hope the privilege of transporting you is mine again. :Bag-for-rejected-stomach-contents: unnecessary next time.

Looking forward to it.

THE STEP DOWN OUT OF Tumbleweed's faintly obscene-looking airlock-lips to the dust of the cavern floor was quite a long one. There was no ramp, and no reception committee. In fact, not a single person was in sight. The nearest building was two hundred metres away, and they were obviously expected to walk.

Wood wasn't sure what he had expected, but he felt curiously let down.

'We don't stand much on ceremony, I'm afraid,' confessed Hazel, shouldering her small travel bag. 'I can see the lack of formality might seem rude if you're not used to it, but Havenners are fine once you get to know them. Usually. This way.'

She ushered him towards the closest building, which had a blue-painted rolling door in the side, and rows of dark windows. Wood rubbed his arms against an unanticipated chill. The damp air bore a curious thick smell he'd never experienced before. 'You might want to get cleaned up in the toilets here,' she told him. 'I've got some fresh nappies for you. You know – diapers?'

A figure was running towards them waving an arm wildly over his head. He slowed to a walk as he approached, a smile cleaving his long, angular face. He wore filthy green trousers with inexpertly patched knees, and a mud-coloured pullover which sagged unflatteringly about his waist. The creases of his smile made his chin, covered in fair stubble, look even longer.

Stopping a couple of meters away, he propped his hands on his hips and regarded them both with active, intelligent eyes.

'Hazel, Hazel! How are you? I never got a chance to say hello at that last meeting. I'm so glad to see you.' He hesitated, as though he might normally have embraced her, and surveyed Wood methodically from the feet up. 'Is this 'im?'

Hazel scowled. 'Sander, you disgrace. Couldn't you have put on something clean?' She studied him with distaste. 'Can't you be more *polite* to our guest?'

His face fell. 'Oh, sorry,' he said, 'We don't stand much on ceremony here.' He wiped a wiry, black-stained hand on a trouser leg and held it out. It was unclear whether the net transfer of dirt had been from hand to clothing or the reverse. 'Sander. Sander Leafdance. Call me Sandy.'

Wood took the hand with intense suspicion. Its grip could have crushed rocks. 'Wood McCorkindale.'

'Oh, everyone knows who *you* are! Very pleased to make your acquaintance.' The man said this with disarming sincerity, but then ruined the effect by turning offhandedly to Hazel again. 'I'm due a spell at Juniper, so I've been asked to fly you two over.'

'*You?*' Hazel exploded. 'You were the best they could do?'

Wood had backed away a couple of steps and was eyeing Sander with a mixture of foreboding and disbelief. Opening her mouth as though to apologise, Hazel caught Wood's gaze. She rolled her eyes. Wood felt a helpless smirk spread across his face.

Seeing Wood's mirth reflected in Hazel's expression, Sander turned towards Wood. Wood felt his grin vanish. Sander put hands on his hips and peered between the two of them.

'Shall we go?' suggested Hazel with a grin.

THE SURFACE EFFECT VEHICLE skimmed low over lashing waves, clearing spray from the windscreen by rhythmic horizontal slashes of its wiper blades. The cabin was tiny, but what the small aircraft lacked in interactive furniture it made up in clever use of space, slotting four reasonable bunks, a toilet-cum-shower room and the cockpit into an area just three metres by three. Like everything McCorkindale had seen so far, the cabin was rather Spartanly functional.

At the cavern, which Hazel had referred to as 'Hades', he'd quickly cleaned himself up and put on fresh clothes provided for him. The clothes were well-worn but comfortable. Once underway, Hazel had suggested that Sander use the on-board shower, and when he refused, had wrestled him bodily into the cubicle. Sander had seemed to enjoy this. He'd emerged five minutes later, pulling on his own fresh clothes even as he dried himself with a small, blue towel. Every bit as threadbare as the ones he'd removed, the clothes were at least clean. The process had left him looking little less dishevelled.

He and Hazel talked as though they'd known each other most of their lives, gossiping and joking. Wood soon lost track. After half an hour of watching the waves which scurried by, feeling lonely and lost, he rose from his seat and went for a shower himself.

Hazel watched him go.

I don't think we're being very professional about this.

Sander shrugged. *There is no easy way, Haze. Can't stick him on a pedestal. That's sure to come back in your face. He's going to feel alienated enough before very long. He's got to feel we're just people.*

You're right, of course. Even so, don't you think you overdid it ever so slightly?

Sander grimaced as he was subjected to a cartoon image of his neck being throttled to terrible thinness until his eyes and his tongue bulged from his head. *Who says I was overdoing anything? I was just being me!*

That is precisely what I meant.

WHEN McCORKINDALE OPENED the narrow door of the shower room some time later, sunlight was glittering off the waves ahead, lighting them from behind like tumbling green solar-sails. In the distance a jagged, glittering band of pearlescent white seemed to hover above their crests. McCorkindale squinted, leaning forward.

'Is that … ice?'

'Sure is,' declared Sander proudly. 'Well, strictly speaking it's snow.'

'Like … you mean, water ice? Not carbon dioxide?'

'Er … Yes.'

For a moment both he and Hazel thought that McCorkindale might start bounding around the cabin.

'From what I've seen, this is one funky planet you have here.'

Sander darted a look at Hazel, then beamed his easy-going grin at the younger man. 'You think so?'

The mountains grew rapidly. Studying the small screen before which Sander had draped himself, McCorkindale saw that they were heading due west relative to Haven's spin, at one and a half thousand kilometres per hour. He returned to his seat and watched the approaching coastline.

As it drew closer, he saw to his astonishment that, beyond a narrow shore of dark rocks and golden-red sand, it wasn't any colour or texture he could have expected.

It was brilliant, wind-blown, emerald green.

7

ELEMENTS OF RISK

SPACE TRAVEL WAS, all considered, as dull as tapwater.

Olea Hudril's fantasy had been of thrusting starships, ripping through mysterious fabrics into exotic micro-universes. Voyaging to outlandish destinations with a sense of motion and occasion.

After the initial excitement leaving Renascido, Jo Fox's fancy starship might have been an office pod for all the sense of voyaging involved.

A couple of hours in hyperspace had been sufficient to sate her curiosity. At her request, the windows were now opaque, confining her view entirely to the rather cramped cabin. Not that they hadn't found entertaining diversions. Her suspicions about Jo as a lover had been accurate. Once she'd pushed beyond a charming, totally unexpected, layer of bashfulness, he was empathetic, playful, eager to please, and more than adequately equipped in all the ways which mattered.

After the first couple of tendays, however, what Jo called 'cabin fever' had set in. Matters were not helped by the atmosphere of tension which persisted despite Jo's veneer of calm.

Lounging naked on the king-sized bed – now in couch mode – Olea refilled her glass with champagne. 'This is a very long leg outside real space, isn't it?'

As for much of the last two day-cycles, Jo was seated, equally naked, at the folding desk behind the pilot's seat, tapping industriously at a keyboard. It was a nice view, as it showed off his inexplicably toned muscles, but she had no idea what he was doing, and he was – at least by his standards since revealing to her that he was the universe's most wanted man – unusually taciturn on the subject. It seemed to be some form of message.

Olea studied the cabin. The ceiling had a soft, silvery finish in a pattern subtly like skin. Morphtec was heavy, apparently, and all the fittings were made of a featherweight silicon polymer, with subatomic enhancements to reduce its mass. According to Jo, she could have lifted the cabin interior and all its furnishings with one hand.

The tapping ceased. Olea found Jo facing her, hands propped on his knees. He was wearing his serious expression, in which, perversely, his features were at their least striking.

'I'm trying to put as much distance as possible between us and the message following us,' he told her. 'Build up speed while we're in hyperspace, rather than shed it by dropping into truespace to orientate ourselves.'

'But if we stay in hyperspace too long,' she protested, 'don't we risk re-emerging inside a planet, or another spaceship or something? Or getting lost, and coming back round where we started? Especially seeing as we left truespace from inside Renascido's exclusion zone. I thought hyperspace was intensely curled or something, which makes the margin for error increase with distance travelled outside real space? Exponentially,' she added, to emphasise her point.

Jo cocked his head. 'None of that's wrong. The recommended maximum interval is generally twenty-five light years in truespace. We've gone at least two hundred and twenty, which is, of course, highly illegal. We'll need to drop out within the next day to triangulate our position, so we don't end up in the wrong side of space entirely, and after that I plan to make numerous drop-ins and outs. But I need to press our advantage.'

'Is that not risky?'

'There's always a risk. Which is why the rules were devised. They're based on what was felt to be "acceptable risk" for civilian traffic. If everyone did what we're doing, the percentage of traffic lost would cause uproar. For a single individual journey, though, especially as we're aiming to drop out in interstellar space, the risk is actually reasonable.'

He regarded her for a second, with a hint of frustration.

'Olea … I still worry that you haven't quite realised what we've started. At this moment, the fastest possible courier missiles will be fanning out behind us. There will be *millions* of them. They will be spreading news of our departure to every single inhabited rock or tin can in Interplanetary Economic

Confederation space. Every military unit, police force and bounty-hunter in existence will likely be looking for us, and they'll bring their fastest, most heavily armed, most capable spacecraft with them. Soon, word will overtake us. There will be nowhere we can go, nothing we can do, without being captured or killed.'

Olea swallowed. 'Do we have enough fuel?'

'This ship is somewhat customised. You'll have noticed that the cabin is rather small. That's because the main drive and the hydrogen reserves are abnormally large for a ship this size. The TFG's more powerful too, so we can exit at higher velocities. But even so, we can drop in and out only five or six times before we must refuel. That's better than courier missiles, which can manage only one exit – two in an emergency – but it's not a reassuring safety margin.'

'Isn't that kind of a problem?'

Jo stretched his arms towards the ceiling, arching his back, making his abs stand out. 'It's our first four refuelling stops that I'm most concerned about.' He rubbed his eyes and placed his hands behind his head. 'For those, we'll need to use commercial orbiting and deep-space complexes. The first couriers will be very close behind. They're much faster in a straight line than we are, and priority information takes only seconds to turn around at a communications and refuelling terminal.

'We have the advantage that the message will have to relay itself through whatever terminals are nearest – meaning the alert will have to travel further than we do, and it'll also be delayed by the time each missile has to spend decelerating for each exit. Added to that, we had a small head start, and an element of confusion might help, too. It's going to be tight, but if we can get past that first refuelling stop, we should be in the clear. I've left fuel dumps and other provisions in deserted planetary systems along our escape route. No one should bother us there.'

He pursed his lips.

'Unless we're very unlucky.'

8

SYMBIOSIS

HAZEL HUGGED DORRIN, and then Zhelkar, warmly on the veranda, and seated herself in the cool shade on the wooden swing-chair suspended from the crossbeam.

The chair was deep and quite high off the floorboards. Hazel wasn't tall, and her legs dangled as it swung. *Like when she was a girl*, thought Dorrin. For a moment, she found herself looking at the fiercely independent little five-year-old who'd obstinately made the veranda her home twenty years ago. Refusing to sleep inside, staring each sunset over the ever-changing waters of the lake until the autumn's chill made her too ill to protest any more. Her eyes were still the same. She wondered how something could burn so fiercely, and not diminish.

Neither Dorrin nor Zhelkar spoke, content to listen to the echoing calls of waterbirds somewhere out in the lake. Gazing out at the sun rippled water, Hazel seemed slowly to absorb its qualities until her eyes grew tranquil too, like forest pools.

She turned to face them, and a smile split her broad, high-cheekboned face, dimpling her cheeks. Recognising the signal, Zhelkar said 'so how's our friend?'

Hazel looked at the lake once more.

'Okay. I think. He's using the library. I mentioned the word "library", and nothing I could do could persuade him to stay away. He was dithering around outside the archive building – he was so confused! Half of him wanted to go in and try to devour all the information we've got right away, and the other half wanted to go around ... fondling and smelling all the different bushes, trees, insects and everything.' She snorted. 'It was hilarious!'

Dorrin shot Zhelkar a look, which he greeted with a raised eyebrow.

'I got him a remote terminal,' Hazel went on, 'and when I left him, he was sitting under a tree by the lakeshore, giving his terminal the third degree – all the time staring about as if he couldn't cram in enough information at once.

'So how would you say he's … acclimatising.' As always, Zhelkar was choosing his words with meticulous care. Hazel scrutinised her calluses.

'Fine, I think.'

'Has his reaction been what you expected?'

She cocked her head, looking up at the sky. 'Well … no. Not really. To be honest, I'm not sure *what* I expected. Seeing this place crawling with all these different living things came as a big shock to him to start with. Perhaps not surprising, given that until a few days ago he had no concept at all of anything apart from humans and machines.'

She did her characteristic to-fro, contemplative head bob.

'He's getting over that now. He still finds the concept of having organisms inside him quite horrible though. He has nightmares about it. And small, crawly things give him a real fright. It's really funny!' She put a fist to her mouth in a vain attempt to stifle a very girlish giggle.

'But his interest is … captured, shall we say?'

'You could say that. He might be horrified –' another giggle, 'but he's also fascinated.'

'Darling,' said Dorrin, 'it sounds like you're doing a good job. It even sounds like you're enjoying yourself.'

'I am,' she answered, with a look of perplexity that could have been trapped wind. She'd made it plain that she hadn't expected to enjoy babysitting the strange young Puke man in the slightest.

'What's he eating?'

Hazel laughed out loud. 'Same old momma Dorrin! Always have your priorities straight.' She smiled at the woman who half-filled the old wicker sofa, head cradled under her partner's skinny, wrinkled arm.

Dorrin arched a mildly indignant eyebrow.

MCCORKINDALE WAS EXACTLY where Hazel had left him.

Wearing a long-sleeved T-shirt and shorts, he was crouching below a pine tree in the leaf-litter by the water's edge, squinting into the low sunlight at a coot leading a flotilla of comically frantic chicks amongst the waterweeds. His expression was hard to read. He found them endearing but was unsure why. He wanted to wade into the water and … well, *touch* one of them, but was afraid of wriggling things in the mud. He was overwhelmed by a barrage of strong and unfamiliar smells, from pine sap, sun-warmed soil and the grass and flowers lining the lakeshore to rotting vegetation and bird shit.

Sensing Hazel's presence, he shot her a glance, then gazed again after the hyperanimated blobs of feathers, who scampered after their mother out of sight behind a clump of rushes. Hazel pushed her sunglasses up the bridge of her nose and strolled towards him.

Might as well take that ridiculous thing off, you know. Couldn't you have worn contact lenses or something a bit less obvious?

She stopped dead.

'How … how …' Realising she was stammering, she clamped her jaw shut. There had been no warning – nothing! Straightening in that oddly slow-motion way of his, McCorkindale turned to face her, evening sunlight illuminating his unruly straw-coloured hair, which fidgeted in the breeze.

'I suspected when I met you,' he said, squinting into the sun again. 'It fitted, somehow. There was a voice in my head on my ship, before I …' his eyes dipped, 'did what I did.' He looked up again. Picked out by the sunlight, his large irises were the purest blue Hazel had seen, bluer even than Sander's – the colour of forget-me-nots. He rubbed his endearingly small nose, sneezed violently into a palm, looked in alarm at the results, and wiped them on his shorts. Hazel was still too stunned to respond. 'It wasn't an org. It felt different, though I can't describe how. Things which happened when we came here in that org got me thinking. I keep feeling things too – like soft brushes in my head. One of the first things I looked up in the library was "telepath".'

Oh, thunder and shit.

'At first, there was nothing there. As if almost every reference had been erased.'

Hazel felt her cheeks burn.

'I couldn't find any explanation of how it works,' he continued, avoiding her eyes, 'but one of the files you neglected to wipe cleanly mentioned that the, um, irises of telepaths change colour depending on brain activity. And you just happen to have worn dark glasses since I met you.' He crossed his arms, eyes finally meeting hers, daring her to explain.

'I would have told you.'

The eyes flinched away. 'You said I could trust you.'

'I'm sorry.' She knew her that body language suggested otherwise.

'Come on, then.'

She took an involuntary step back. 'What do you mean, "come on then"?'

'Let's have a look.' He shrugged, sheepishly – a movement so awkward that it could have been coordinated by a committee – and motioned the glasses off with a hand.

Hazel wanted to run.

After some thought, she removed them, dropped them in a pocket of her cargo trousers, and stood, blinking, with her arms clasped around her. She felt utterly naked. McCorkindale shuffled towards her into the shadow of the trees, squinting slightly upwards into her face.

With effort, she raised her eyes defiantly to his.

'Oh wow,' he said. 'That's *amazing*.' He took in every detail of her eyes, noting their almond-shape and the faint epicanthic folds which spoke of Asian in her thoroughly mongrel ancestry, and, she was told, made her seem younger than she was. 'Um, what does deep red mean?'

Through his eyes, she saw hers blaze. 'Irritation. Anger. Or frustration. Depends on the shade.'

It was McCorkindale's turn to redden. 'I'm sorry. I didn't realise you felt … *bad* about it.'

For a moment Hazel was incandescently furious. 'The price for my "gift".' She spat the word. 'I can tell what everyone is thinking. Perhaps it's only fair that everyone should know what I'm feeling. The difference is, I can choose to mind my own business.'

McCorkindale looked away.

'How did you hide what you were thinking from me?'

'Why should I tell you?'

Because if you don't, you idiot, I'll have to wipe your memory, and you'll be sent back to the Pukes. She didn't externalise the thought. 'You were saying something about trust. Works both ways.'

59

Studying his borrowed sandals, he fiddled in his pockets, obviously considering whether to answer her or not. He squinted into the tree branches. 'I suppose … if I don't want you to know something, I try not to materialise the thought.'

Hazel was intensely sceptical.

'You gave me clues on the org. I just relax and …' he pushed his lips out, throwing up his hands, 'I don't know – sort of empty the thought away, before it's had a chance to form properly. If I didn't focus on it, I figured you might not either.'

She just looked at him. His downy, almost white eyebrows were pushed together.

'Is that so strange?'

'I've never met anyone before who could do that.'

'Oh.'

They watched each other, McCorkindale over folded arms, Hazel now with hands on her hips. Unexpectedly, she found that she'd made a decision. A smile curling a corner of her mouth, she turned towards the lake.

'So, what *else* did you learn from the library today?'

At the edge of her vision, his boyish face lit up. In some ways, he was still a more open book than anyone she'd ever met. 'A lot that I don't understand at the moment. I must be like someone trained in infographics or something trying to learn astrophysics from first principles. Most of the references lost me completely.' He toed the dirt, and said with unexpected gaucheness, 'Hazel … um, d'you think you could help me? You're the only person here I really know, and I'm kind of … All this biological stuff is … weird.'

'I can show you around for a few days as well, if you'd like.'

McCorkindale returned her smile with a sudden, dazzling grin. 'That would be great! I'm feeling … a bit lost here.' His face fell. Hazel winced: he was pulling his sleeves down, rubbing at the horrifying self-inflicted scars on his forearms. Especially when unsure of himself, he had a habit of making sure they were covered up. 'I miss Tink.'

'Then I've just the remedy. I know how awkward it is when you don't know anyone. We're invited over to Zhelkar and Dorrin Porro's place for dinner.' She tilted her head, hoping her gaze seemed welcoming. 'Would that be a start?'

His eyes had become like a hunted animal's. She'd forgotten how unused he was to company. What he felt was much stronger than mere awkwardness. He fingered his lips. 'I *think* so.'

'Don't worry.' She forced a smile, 'it's nothing remotely formal. Just be yourself and relax. Though I think it might be fair to warn you about Dorrin. All I can say is, I hope you have a healthy appetite.'

'Oh. Well, yes.' His eyes were wandering away again. 'It's slowly coming back.'

He was obviously preoccupied by something.

'By the way,' he ventured, after a lengthy pause. 'Something some of the kids were saying. Um, what's a "Puke"?'

THE LARGEST OF THE CABIN'S three rooms was walled in unfinished pine logs. Laundry dried on spider's-webbed racks suspended from the rafters. Framed leaves, feathers and photographs and paintings of people, sailing ships and forest landscapes decorated the walls. On a waxed cabinet in the corner, crammed with well-thumbed books of yellowed paper, beeswax candles supplemented the flickering light of a log fire. Beside the cabinet a reflector telescope stood on three sturdy legs. A soot-blackened bellows and a rough painting of Juniper Lake took pride of place above a mantelpiece jammed with seed cones, seashells, wooden and stone carvings of animals, and a stack of defunct solar cells. Ornate rugs cushioned the foot-polished wooden floor.

'This is one of the largest towns on the planet?' Wood exclaimed over a forkful of fruit pie, eyes still roaming in wonder at his surroundings. 'How many people?'

Seven of the current population, including three young girls that Hazel had last seen almost a year ago, sat in a rough crescent round the fire. Zhelkar lounged in an old wooden chair with curved runners which allowed him to rock back and forth, making the floorboards creak. McCorkindale and Hazel sat at opposite ends of a surprisingly comfortable threadbare sofa, hemmed in by cushions of clashing colours, while Dorrin occupied a heap of similar cushions in a chair opposite Zhelkar. She made it seem like a throne. Cross-legged on yet more cushions on the floor, the children talked quietly, paying occasional attention to the conversation of the grown-ups.

Cushions, Hazel had explained, were a hobby of Dorrin's. Dirtied plates and empty glasses lay on the rug before the fire.

'Around two thousand,' mused Dorrin, scooping up another mouthful with unhurried efficiency. 'At any one time.' There was something about the quiet woman which McCorkindale, like Hazel, found calming. 'There are six hundred and fifty-two towns and settlements around the planet, and many temporary encampments.'

'Why so few people? Um, incidentally, this –?'

'Blaeberry and Apple. Pie.'

'Hmmm. It's … scrumpshush. Mmmm, sqwumpshush.' Still chewing, he wiped away purple juice which had oozed from his mouth using a sleeve of the handknitted jumper Hazel had lent him after the sun went down.

'I don't think my baking has ever had such praise,' said Dorrin, inscrutably. She raised an eyebrow. 'Verbal or tangible.' Hazel averted her gaze, trembling with the effort of keeping her face straight.

'Indeed,' breathed Zhelkar, eyeing Wood with an expression somewhere between fascination, humour and scorn. Dorrin interlocked plump fingers.

'Why so few people? That's a deceptively complicated question you've asked there – Wood? Is that what you prefer to be called?'

He hesitated, then nodded.

'A good name. You could be one of us.' She gave him a searching look, then a little sigh. 'The answer goes back an awful long time. It's a history in itself, and I doubt you'd want to hear it all.'

Wood noticed that the three young girls had stopped talking and were looking expectantly around the adults. Throughout the evening the eldest, a brown-skinned, black-haired girl of around six, had been watching him with round, disquietingly direct dark eyes. Apparently speaking for the other two as well, she'd asked 'Are you really an Orphaned? Are you a Puke?' Sparing her a nervous glance, Wood popped the last morsel of pie in his mouth and patted a stomach which was visibly bulging. He placed his empty bowl on the floor beside the sofa.

'I've nothing pressing to do.'

Dorrin's eyes conferred briefly with her partner's. Zhelkar gave the slightest nod.

'Well,' she began. 'It's a long story, beginning nearly half a millennium ago, and it has to do with everything you will have seen today.'

She broke off, apologetically. 'I'm sorry my dear, you'll have to forgive me if this is starting to sound like a bedtime story. In fact, that's exactly how I used to tell it to a certain little girl sitting not very far from here.' She looked warmly on Hazel, who turned away, embarrassed, glad that her eyes were unreadable in the dim light. 'It was the only way we could get her to sleep, for a while.'

McCorkindale (no – *Wood*, Hazel admonished herself) stared between the three of them. He hadn't realised. Yet, now that he saw it – saw their closeness – he felt no surprise. He was drowsy in the reflected warmth of the fire, whose burning gases were so unaccountably hypnotic. Revelations and concerns seemed to lose their potency before it. Even the unfamiliar aromas of woodsmoke and hot resin seemed unaccountably soothing. For a few seconds the only sounds were the crackling of logs, and the peeping of waterfowl across the lake.

'A bedtime story,' he murmured. 'Yes. Maybe I could use a bedtime story.'

She felt the ache of the stolen years of his life; the need to catch up. Here, amongst strangers, in what he saw as a primitive shack, somehow that was what he felt he was doing. In flashes, he relived the flight to Juniper across forested coastal mountains; his shock at seeing birds: human-like, yet at the same time utterly inhuman. The glittering seas of the huge Hughes Gulf, and the Crystal River Canyon: a twisting, granite-walled trench into which cascades thundered from glacial side valleys. She felt his heart race: he'd never seen anything like this. Where the valley seemed to end, the aircraft had banked beneath a towering rock pillar through the rainbows of a two thousand metre waterfall above which lay hidden meadows cleaved by a foaming river. Finally, there had come the exhilarating swoop over moorlands, and then forests once more, inexorably down to the liquid-gold expanse of Juniper Lake, on which wooded islands were scattered like tears. The town of Juniper itself had been invisible from above the trees but for a handful of roofs rising into the canopy, every square centimetre dark with solar panels.

Dorrin's look seemed to ask if he was serious. He nodded drowsily, and the large woman beamed at the smaller figures on the floor. 'Dorrin is a *seannachie*,' Hazel murmured into Wood's ear, leaning across the sofa. 'A storyteller. She's famous for it.'

Dorrin leaned down towards the children. 'What about you sprogs? Would you like a bedtime story?'

'Is it bedtime already, auntie Dot?' demanded the second eldest, aghast.

'What if we make this a most unusual bedtime story? One you don't have to be in bed for. Unless you want to sleep here afterwards, which you're welcome to do. It's a special story. Your mas and pa won't mind.'

The sprogs conferred briefly and nodded, except the youngest, who just blinked.

'It's little bit long, I'm afraid, and parts of it are sad.'

'That's okay auntie Dot,' chirped the eldest, whose name was Pine. 'We're old now.'

Dorrin settled back into her seat. 'Very well then.' As she began, her voice seemed to become the quiet focus of the flame-lit room, and the world outside bled into memory. Closing his eyes, Wood felt the fire's flickering warmth begin to penetrate parts which had been cold for longer than he could clearly remember.

'Long ago, there was a planet. It was quite an ordinary little planet as planets go. It had rocks, and mountains, and volcanoes, and its own moon – which, admittedly, was a large and handsome moon – but all in all, it was much the same as so many other cooling balls of molten rock dotted here and there around the galaxy.'

The children were silent now, devouring her words with the same rapt faces Wood remembered from his brother and sister as they watched HV.

'Even so, there were things about this planet which might have been considered a little unusual. It had wide, restless, rolling oceans, and it had a thick, muggy, atmosphere.

'Now, it has to be said that the atmosphere was not something you would really want to breathe. There was almost no oxygen in it at all, and it was full of horrible poisonous gases like methane and ammonia. And the oceans were not really somewhere you would ever want to swim. They were very hot, and full of acids and other nasty things, and would have dissolved and boiled your flesh from your bones.' The children leant back in mock-horror as Dorrin leant towards them, hands clawed, eyes round. 'In fact, it was such a hostile place that any little girl or boy foolish enough to have walked on to its surface would have been very dead indeed, within seconds.' Dorrin looked sternly at her youthful audience, who giggled.

What's all this about?

Hazel cast Wood an admonishing glance.

'For thousands of millions of years,' Dorrin went on, 'the planet orbited slowly, round and round its small, yellow sun, in all its barren hostility.

'Then, one day, something extraordinary happened. Quite by chance, groups of complex molecules became stuck together in a way which allowed them to *copy* themselves. Life had begun, in the stormy oceans of the planet.

'Slowly at first, and then faster and faster, these groups of molecules copied and copied themselves, and began to grow in number. But as anyone who has heard the spread of news from mouth to mouth will know, copies are never entirely accurate. In this way, as these groups of molecules – organisms, you might call them – copied themselves, so they slowly changed. And as they changed, they became more and more complicated, and bigger and bigger, joining together to form different structures, and finally different groups of structures. As time went on, over millions of years, they changed themselves into more and more varied and complex forms.

'Life had begun the process we call evolution.

'Now, the earliest of these living organisms all lived without oxygen. And they did so quite happily for a billion years – until, one day, there evolved a new kind of organism which would change the planet for ever. These new organisms did something none of the earlier organisms could do. A molecule called carbon dioxide was to be found everywhere – it formed most of the thick, muggy atmosphere, and was dissolved in the deep, grey oceans – and they found a way to use sunlight to break it apart, using the carbon part to build their bodies, releasing the oxygen part as waste.

Before very long, they had grown in the oceans to such numbers that as they died, and drifted to the sea bed, they began sucking the carbon away from the oceans and the atmosphere, storing it as they became squashed, and squeezed, over thousands of millions of years under the weight of countless gazillions of their kind which drifted down in layers on top of them. The pressure from all the countless dead organisms raining down on them from above, burying them and squeezing them, eventually turned them into rocks. And so, very gradually, these tiniest of living things changed the atmosphere into one which a whole profusion of new lifeforms could breathe. An atmosphere containing oxygen.'

'For billions more years, the lifeforms – the *organisms* – continued to evolve. Many came out of the oceans and spread over the land, and then even into the air, gliding on the ever-changing currents of air which swept over their endlessly evolving planet. And still they grew in number and complexity until they included almost every size, shape and colour, and every part of the planet you could think of. Many died out, often in great waves of death, for in many ways the planet was still a harsh and dangerous place. Great rocks fell unpredictably from the sky, killing all organisms which could not either hide, riding out such catastrophes, or copy themselves quickly enough to adapt. The atmosphere itself was still changing. Temperatures rose and fell, hot for millions of years, then becoming so cold that much of the planet was buried beneath solid ice. All the different types of organism, which were known as *species*, had to find ways of adapting to such changes, or die.

'And so, the cycle continued, unsteady, yet unbroken, evolving ever more variety, covering the planet with a rich, living skin called the biosphere. And in that skin came to live the organisms we call animals, and fish, trees, grasses, flowers and other plants, insects, arachnids, crustaceans, and fungi – and all the tiny invisible microorganisms upon which the countless other lifeforms depended to give them life. And the planet shone with the blue of the oceans, and the rich green of the land, and the pure white of the clouds swirling in the light of its small, yellow sun, like the jewel it was.

'Then, one day, evolution brought forward a second lifeform which was to change the planet for ever.

'Now, this lifeform was no more different from other lifeforms than they were from each other. But it had the unusual combination of a large brain, clever hands with which to shape the world to its desires, and, most importantly, it was aggressive and ambitious.

'This lifeform called itself "mankind". And it called the planet on which it found itself the Earth, after the rich soil which this abundance of life had created. Within the blink of an eye, it had claimed the planet as its own.

'In an even shorter eyeblink, it cut down and burned the great forests which once covered much of the land, replacing them with organisms created solely to supply its endless appetite. By the billions, it hunted the animals which inhabited the land, and sucked life from the seas using great machines it built for the purpose, taking only a tiny portion of the creatures it caught and throwing the rest away, dead. Slowly at first, but then faster and faster, other lifeforms began to disappear – a few at a time, then hundreds, then thousands, then tens of thousands every year.

'Strangely, it seems mankind had expected to continue in this way for ever. The reason may never be known. Perhaps mankind simply forgot that it was part of a community of different lifeforms, and set about destroying this community, bit by bit, like a person without sense sawing off the branch on which they are sitting. Perhaps the individuals making up mankind could not understand the instincts which led them to breed, and multiply, and breed, and multiply, until their numbers were so enormous that there was nowhere mankind was not, and the world could not contain them.

'Yet still their numbers grew. And the poisons from their homes and their machines soured the rivers, and the oceans, and even the air that they themselves breathed; sucking the life from the other living things which still managed to survive. Their cities and their enslaved plants and animals devoured the land like something cancerous, and wherever they went, the planet died. Some of the poisons they produced meant that even the sun's rays, which until now had sustained life, began to kill the surviving plants, even those which mankind had altered in order to feed itself.

'Within a heartbeat of the planet's long life, it had become so sick that it began to die.

'And mankind, seeing the ruin it had made of its home, found ways to escape to the stars, and made homes on other planets, tunnelling into their dead surfaces for the metals and rocks and other things which the Earth used to provide. It found giant gas planets with thick atmospheres made of molecules from which it could make food, so that everyone could now be fed without the need for plants or animals. And it built great machines which produced oxygen from carbon dioxide so that everyone could breathe without the need for plants. Eventually, it came to believe that all the other life of the Earth, upon which it had once depended for food, and air, and life – everything – was of little importance.

'But mankind found that it had taken its problems to the stars. Its home planet was sick, and it had brought the sickness wherever it went, in the form of plagues of other organisms which had adapted to survive alongside mankind. For, by its actions, mankind had unwittingly chosen for survival, from the once uncountable different species of the Earth, only those organisms best able to compete: organisms able to infect its bodies with diseases, or to stow away on its starships, or in its homes, eating or contaminating its food. Those organisms most immune to all the medicines, and the poisons, and the other weapons it used, ever more desperately, to try and control them.

'And so it was that, as mankind became ever more at war with what remained of the life of the Earth, as it forgot all the good things that this great well of diversity once had been, it grew to hate all life that was not its own.

'On the overcrowded Earth, terrible diseases spread, like a fire through a gum forest, killing billions, spreading even between the stars by the spacecraft upon which mankind now depended to feed itself. Slowly but surely, mankind's past was catching up with it.'

Dorrin paused. For a moment, she might have been carved from wood. The fire made snapping noises.

'One day, a decision was made. No one knows who made it. Perhaps it began as an idea, and gradually more and more of the individual people who made up mankind heard about it, until, finally, enough of them agreed for it to happen. Perhaps one of these people, or a small group of them, decided the way things should be, and made it so.

'However it happened, one day mankind decided to end the problem once and for all.

'People from every place mankind had spread to among the stars were herded into the mightiest city mankind had yet built on the Earth. This city was called Rio de Janeiro. For those of you who don't know, a city is a little like the towns we have here on Haven – but larger and more crammed with people, and buildings, and machines, than you or I could imagine. Once the city called Rio de Janeiro was crammed almost to bursting, it was sealed inside a giant bubble to protect those inside from what was to come.

But getting into the city wasn't simple. There were too many people to fit, and entry came at a cost. Only those who either had power over other people or who agreed to think the way those who controlled the city did – something mankind called *religion* – would be protected from what was to follow. There were other reasons people were left outside. Some didn't want to go into the bubble. Some arrived too late to get in. Some couldn't be contacted or didn't want to be.

'And then the world was sterilised.

'Every last organism, even the ones within mankind's bodies, was killed, using lifeforms which mankind had designed for this one purpose: a powerful brew of viruses and poisons which attacked every living thing except mankind itself.

'They poured toxic powder on to the Earth and bombarded it with neutron bombs and deadly high-energy particles. They set fire to the remaining forests, and the grasslands, and the crops, and released the virus there as they had inside their protective bubble, and did the same in their spaceships, and the cities and environment domes which, until now, had been spreading on other planets. They scoured space for survivors fleeing in spacecraft and destroyed these too, with the fire of nuclear weapons, to make sure that not one single non-human organism could survive. The process lasted for a generation. And they called this, the greatest mass-murder of living things in all of time, *the Purges*.'

Flames flickered. The children were silent, their eyes round. When Dorrin began again her voice was quieter.

'When at last it was safe for the survivors to return outside, they began the task of collecting the dead remains of trees, which were now very valuable. All over the planet, which they renamed 'Born Again', in what would become the language we know as Standard – people sought out what the fires and the bombs had spared and took away what they could. Those who were quickest, or were in groups powerful enough to take what other groups had already found, became very rich. When I say rich, I mean they had a lot of money, which was a kind of points system these people used to try and measure happiness.

'When the wood was gone, they tore away the dead bushes, and scraped away the dead grass. They burned it in fires to warm themselves and to cook the insects and animals which now lay scattered everywhere – never decaying, as there were no longer any microorganisms to return their goodness to the soil. The times after the Purges were hard, and once the wood, and the grass, and the dead animals were all gone, there was even less to go around than there had been before.

In just a few years, mankind had removed almost all traces of the life which once covered the planet which had birthed him. The winds and rains caused by the changes he had made washed and blew the once-fertile soils into the sea, carving valleys and canyons where once there had been forests, and savannahs, and cities. The Earth was barren for the first time in over three and a half billion years.'

Wood found his mind alive with startling images, as though from his own memory. Huge tracked vehicles tore desiccated tree stumps from the ground with cavernous, toothed jaws. Tiny figures scurried in their wake collecting branches and logs to stash in overladen little four-wheeled vehicles. Some of the vehicles were crude, wheeled platforms pulled by filthy and ragged men and women.

Hazel? Are you doing this?

'Now,' said Dorrin, 'you could be forgiven for thinking that this was the end of the Earth, but that was not the way of it. A century and a half before the Purges began, one of the billions of individuals making up mankind had a vision. Realising what was happening to the Earth, this man began to gather around him, in secret, a group of followers.

'This was the man we call "the Professor".

'At first, it was the Professor's hope that he and his followers might help some of the other lifeforms to endure long enough that, one day, they would be free to roam and evolve on the planet called Earth once more. Before long, however, the Professor realised the terrible truth. It was too late for the Earth. There would always be too many people, and their hunger too great, for there to be room for animals and plants except those which where to be used or eaten by mankind. And so, as the first spaceships began crossing the huge, empty distances between stars, the Professor went searching.

For many long years he searched, for somewhere just right. Somewhere the rest of mankind would never find, no matter how hard they looked.

'Then, one day, the Professor knew that he had, at last, found what he'd been seeking all this time.

'It was a planet with wide, rolling oceans, and high, snow-covered mountains. It had deep lakes and clear, tumbling streams. It had great, wide, lazy rivers. All that it lacked was an atmosphere you could breathe. And, as the Earth would become, it was barren. Completely, utterly lifeless, desolate and dead.

'He called the planet *Haven*, in the hope that it would someday be a safe home for animals and birds, and insects, and fish, and fungi, and plants – and all the organisms which are too small to see without using a microscope. And he brought with him, in his three great starships, the *Daker*, the *Nyirenda* and the *Pemba*, the sad, tiny fraction which was all he could save of the endless variety of life which had flourished on the now ruined Earth. And so, he set about bringing life to the barren planet of Haven.

'He had brought with him tiny organisms which could change the atmosphere and turn it into something which animals could breathe – but on their own these would have taken many thousands of years. Time was short, so he helped them by building great oxygenating machines powered by nuclear fusion, and in less than a century the seas were teeming with plankton and other small organisms, and the first trees and grasses were growing in the barren soil. Soon there was enough plant life to begin recycling the oxygen by itself, and so he turned the machines off, and they stand to this day, as silent monuments to this time.

'Now that there was somewhere for them to live, the Professor began releasing the animals which had been kept in cryogenic compartments, in enclosures of their native habitats, or merely as genetic codes stored in data drives. Little by little, life began to flourish on the awakening planet of Haven. The forests spread and grew into what we see around us today.

'But the Professor was never alone in all this. He had help. He took with him five thousand chosen others: men, women and children who had all sworn to protect what the rest of mankind was determined to destroy.

71

'These five thousand are our ancestors, and all of them made a promise. They promised that they would never, ever allow what had been done to the Earth Mother to happen again. And so, to ensure that it does not – to ensure that the Earth did not die in vain – we keep our numbers small. We tread lightly on the thin soil of our planet, and we leave each other, human and non-human, the room we all need, hoping that one day we may redeem ourselves for the terrible crime committed by our kind.'

The fire sparked and crackled, burning low. In the distance, an owl hooted.

9

VERY DEAD

EVEN WITH ITS CHAMELEON field inactive (a feature which used as much power as a large city), Paradise, also known – primarily amongst bureaucrats – as Area X, was visible in the depths of interstellar space only by the occlusion of distant stars.

In the enhanced, networked image provided by the approaching Hell's Teeth squadron, the base was unprepossessing: two squat, dark cylinders orbiting lazily about one another, their surfaces marked only by proximity-visible navigation cardinals sprinkled around unseen gates to the ports inside. It was only as the spacecraft drew near that the size of the structures became apparent.

At a little under two thousand kilometres from end to end and six hundred wide, the two cylinders – which some forgotten wit had dubbed Adam and Eve – were the reconstituted fragments of a minor rocky planet which had been demolished and transported piecemeal to its present location. At the time of its construction eighty-nine years ago, Paradise had been a pinnacle of deep-space technical achievement. Every few years another hundred or so kilometres were added to each cylinder to keep pace with the growing confederal fleet.

Despite their dimensions, the gravitational pull of the two honeycombed tubular structures was weak, so they'd been spun to provide a force equivalent to a comfortable 0.9G at their circumferences. This was largely a safety feature: changes in spin were likely to be less problematic during an attack than gravity generators failing. The spaceports spanning the axis of each cylinder, however, were non-rotating, and employed gravity fields where needed.

As the hard-decelerating squadron approached Eve, the featureless cylinder just wouldn't stop growing. There was a thump as *Mind Bender*'s main drive cut out, followed by smaller thumps as manoeuvring thrusters fired, and a detached sense of motion from the holoprojected outside views as the ship pirouetted to face its destination. Visible in the holoprojection's extremities, the other couriers kept a tight formation as the immense armoured door of the naval base yawned to receive them.

'Ladies, gentlemen,' said the pilot's voice over the intercom, 'we're now on docking attractors. Please remain in your seats 'til we get the green light. Thank you for flying Paradise VIP Class. We trust you enjoyed the ride, and do hope you choose to fly with us again.'

The gaping maw swallowed them.

Within, a vast, bright cavern receded into a distance fogged by clouds of service drones and small spacecraft. Fortresses and other large starships hung at conflicting angles, like abstract decorations. Several Divide and Rule-class fortresses were clearly under construction, their matt grey pinched cubes lacking corners, or sections through their middles. On all sides as the fleet of fast couriers advanced, battlecruisers, cruisers and destroyers slipped past, all kilometres or tens of kilometres in length, stacked in skeletal maintenance gantries or in ranks of launch silos like toys in a shopping mall display. The uninitiated Special Branch volunteers in Aral Nikumi's team stared at the projections, open-mouthed.

'Busy,' observed Kettering, eyes shining. 'Haven't heard of this much activity since the war.' He rubbed the stubble on his spade-like chin. 'Looks like they're preparing an invasion.'

'That,' said Nikumi, 'is precisely what they are doing.'

'They've been briefed?'

'Word reached them here a month ago, I imagine.'

'Nice of Green Section to tell us.'

'Need to know.'

Kettering looked pointedly away. Though the commander was dedicated to his new responsibilities, Nikumi knew that he resented every minute of his five years' captivity. He wasn't alone.

'There she is!' The voice belonged to Ishti Waranika, who had an arm draped possessively around Sub-Lieutenant Gul Calter's pyramidal neck. 'Good old *Violator*.'

Behind an older, slightly smaller fortress loomed a familiar shadow with the outline of a squashed square, identifiable by its pattern of lights. In such surroundings it could have been a scale model. She craned her head back towards Nikumi, and Calter peered round at him as well.

'Reckon we'll get her back?'

'Don't raise your hopes too much.' Nikumi said this with a dark grin, which Waranika returned.

'This time we'll make her true to her name, eh?'

The dock's gravity grapples took over and the small fleet arced towards one of a cluster of feathery cones sprouting from Eve's complex inner surface. As they approached, the cone resolved into an array of landing platforms fanning from a central spindle.

With a carefully orchestrated thumping of thrusters, *Mind Bender* drew up beside one of the larger petals as the rest of the fleet were sent to platforms of their own. A window of the cabin screen showed docking clamps pulling the vessel the last few metres. A hovering utility drone sped towards the vessel from the direction of the spindle. It dragged a ramp up to the airlock hatchway before *Mind Bender* had even stopped moving.

The door to the pilot's cabin opened.

'We're down,' said the pilot: a small, intense man with a goatee. 'Safety and radiation checks will take a minute, so please stay seated. When we've got the go-ahead, make your way down the ramp and take the open gravtrain quickly to the spindle. At the top of the spindle there's a conference room where Admiral Abdul Grisham will meet you for your briefing.'

DESPITE THE SAFETY FIELD, the view of four hundred kilometres of nothing in a direction which, in the local gravity field, at least *felt* like down was deeply unsettling – particularly with dozens of moon-sized spacecraft moving around. Emerging from *Mind Bender*'s airlock, Special Branch's Paradise virgins peered over the edge of the ramp in alarm. Two stumbled, one of them covering his eyes and then vomiting on himself.

Waiting for Nikumi at the end of the platform was an immaculately presented man with dark eyes, a shaven head, and a maroon uniform jumpsuit. His black beret bore a triangular red badge. Military intelligence. He extended a hand.

'Lieutenant Kalim Greene, sir. Security.'

The hand felt like a glove full of rocks. 'Commodore Aral Nikumi.'

'Sir. I'm to escort you to the briefing room. With your permission.' Standing aside, he gestured towards the marked strip demarcating the gravtrain.

'Lead on, lieutenant.'

The others followed in more-or-less disciplined single file. Above the level's other platforms loomed further Hell's Teeth, seeming dangerously close to the larger rosettes of the upper landing platforms. One by one, the gravtrain surged the procession of officers, and the air surrounding it, forward. It was like being suspended in a series of invisible bubbles travelling at a relative eighty kilometres an hour.

'You boys and girls have been busy since I was last here.'

Greene nodded. 'I'm limited in what I can tell you,' he said, expertly using the momentum of his arms to face Nikumi, 'but yes. The entire base was put in the picture thirteen standard days ago, and we're expecting a full-scale offensive any time after the next tenday. I've never seen everyone so energised. Everyone here just wants a go at these Freaks, or whatever we're supposed to call them. We won't be short on motivation. They're out for blood. The rate of work here's been fifty percent over projected estimates. Personnel are skiving sleep hours so they can put more into prepping the strike force. The fleet is over-subscribed: too many volunteers. Lancers never generated this amount of fire.'

'The Lancers were never this much of a threat.'

Greene gave Nikumi an odd, searching look. 'Commodore? Where did all this come from? How has this all suddenly blown up? No,' his eyes lost their focus, 'on second thoughts, don't answer that. I've a feeling I neither need, nor want, to know.'

Nikumi returned his look with sympathy. The spindle was approaching. The gravtrain slowed as it entered the broad doorway serving the docking area. '*Violator*,' he said. 'Do you know – is it *Violator* we will be getting?'

A curt nod. 'Sir. She's been extensively refitted with all the latest toys. We think you'll like the improvements.'

'That will please the boys and girls.'

Greene's eyes narrowed slightly. 'Sir, if you'll forgive me – do you know anything of this Troubleshooter project? This new weapon we've been promised?'

Nikumi was already shaking his head. 'No need for me to be tight-lipped about that. I know no more than you, possibly less.' He pursed his lips, gazing back along the line of officers. Similar lines had formed along the neighbouring platforms, radiating from the spindle like spokes. 'Lieutenant,' he murmured in a confidential voice. 'What arrangements have been made for Satan?'

A subtle pause that wasn't lost on Nikumi. 'He's being escorted to a safe holding by armed drones under pre-programmed thinker control. No people in the chain. When he reaches the end of the ramp, they're going to zap him with tranquillisers. He'll stay tranquillised until you leave.'

'He won't like that.'

'Paradise's view is that he's not our problem.'

Nikumi grunted. 'Understandable. But thanks a lot. And …' he hesitated. Found that his mouth was dry. 'The two women he was with?'

Greene stiffened. For a moment, there was something in his eyes that looked like rage.

'You don't know? They're dead, sir. Very, very dead.'

10

CORRIDORS

OFFICIALLY, this was the largest meeting of governments in the history of mankind.

Unofficially, it almost certainly was as well.

It was certainly the only occasion of which James Marcell was aware when most of the presidents, prime-ministers, kings, church officials, and other assorted heads of the nations and colonies of IPEC had physically assembled under one roof. Not to mention legions of admirals, generals, and heads of commerce and industry. Previous occasions which had approached such a scale, most of them during the Lancer Wars, had largely comprised VIPs with the prefixes 'lieutenant-' or 'vice'. Which gave some idea of how seriously the current threat was being taken.

All because of one godforsaken planet and its tribe of loonies. Marcell ground his teeth.

Renascido's Central Governance Chambers had made a war effort of its own during the past tenday to cater for the vast contingent now descendent upon it. The building's Morphtec had hollowed out a half-kilometre wide conical amphitheatre, terraced with conference tables around an array of giant holoprojectors. The tang of ozone created by discharge from the electrical systems was noticeable from Marcell's seat in the third terrace from the top. Most of the three thousand or so VIPs already seated below were talking animatedly. Latecomers filed inside in steady droves from concealed doors. Amplified by the cleverly-shaped chamber, the rumble of human voices and footsteps was oppressive.

Another first, Marcell noted, was that, despite the staggering number of politicians and representatives from outwardly competing corporations present, the meeting almost certainly remained secret. The news would leak, of course, and soon, but when that happened, it would do so in a controlled way. The public would be exposed to a flurry of wild-sounding, easily deniable rumours. After a healthy interval, these would be substantiated by well-known figures whose reputations would be loudly and publicly destroyed for supporting such crackpottery.

Only once such exposure had embedded the idea of mankind's hidden past in the public consciousness would it be allowed to morph from the ramblings of a foil-hat-wearing fringe to something acknowledged by governments and science, and, finally, enshrined in official policy.

If there's time.

Like all large, hastily organised meetings, this one was thinly-orchestrated chaos. At least linguistic barriers were in the past, where they belonged: Portuguese wasn't a template Marcell would have chosen for a universal language, but it did the job. The speaker of the chambers, Bernadette Quiong, if anything more famous – and certainly better loved – than the presidents who'd come and gone during her sixteen-year tenure, stood to address the house, her imposing mini-skirted figure towering a hundred metres into the chamber, rotating so that all could benefit from her steely, black-eyed gaze.

Her blood-red lips parted.

'Ladies and gentlemen. Now that we have all had time to arrive, access the vids, and take on board what they mean, it is time for me to open the house for this urgent debate. I bring to your attention the grave import of the topics to be discussed. By consensus, this debate will continue until all avenues of importance have been resolved, and courses of action decided.

'Never has humanity so needed clear guidance. Though they may not know it yet, the people of our hard-won confederation are entrusting their futures to you. First, a point of order. While it is customary in the chambers to stand while speaking, and to sit when yielding the floor, for practical reasons, and in acknowledgement of the numerous traditions represented here today, this requirement is temporarily waived. That said, if anyone feels more comfortable standing, knock yourself out. To open the debate, I call upon Mr Carlito Andritsos, Supreme President of the Republic of Renascido.'

Standing as the speaker seated herself, the dapper, white-haired president treated the video drone hovering before him to a suitably weighty glare.

'Ladies, gentlemen, your majesties,' he began. 'Your honours, your graces and eminences. Thank you all for coming. We have all seen the recordings. We have all listened, I assume, to the detailed histories provided to us. To some of you, much of this will be new. To most of you, I suspect all of it will be new. The rights and wrongs of this withholding of information are for another debate. I'm pleased to say that every nation represented within this house today has declared solidarity by placing its military at our collective disposal. What we are here to decide is how best to proceed with its deployment, and what steps can and should be taken to avert catastrophe.'

Andritsos hooked his thumbs behind his lapels.

'It is my proposal that, short-term at least, we accept the plan presented by the multinational thinktank which has devoted itself to studying this developing situation for the past standard decade. They are in a unique position to advise us on the nature of the problem and its solution.'

'Proxima Centauri,' prompted the Speaker, with a toss of glossy hair. A towering image of Ned Hachilika, Supreme Head of Proxima Centauri, faded into existence opposite that of Andritsos as the president sat down.

'You say,' began Hachilika, his domed forehead furrowing as he leant back in its seat, 'that the rights and wrongs of the situation are for future debate. I refute that. It was criminally negligent, and an unforgiveable abuse of trust, for those who knew of this to keep it from *any* of the governments directly concerned. We have all been put unduly at risk.'

His leathery, bronze face was composed, but his eyes smouldered. He waved an arm. 'By harbouring this "thinktank", whatever such a term proves to mean, your government, Mr Andritsos, was complicit. And now you seek our unconditional support?' His image leant forwards so that it seemed to come within striking distance of Andritsos's. 'What else have we not been told? Proxima has been prepared to grant materiel under the request made to us under emergency conditions. However, before we go *any* further, I move that a principle be established whereby a guarantee of freedom of information forms the basis for further agreement.'

Andritsos's eyes bulged. 'Freedom of information, are you *insane?*'

'I mean, within the corridors of power.'

'I see.'

There was a pause. Marcell thought that the president might have glanced up at him, just for a second.

'Regarding the allegations my respected friend has made,' said Andritsos, addressing the speaker with the heavy-lidded air of a college lecturer humouring a slow student, 'can he not see that it would have been suicidal for our knowledge of this threat to have spread earlier? This Josey Matlow Fox is the worst combination of dangerous maniac and genius. If the extent of our intelligence had become known to him before our current trap had been set, who is to say what he might have done? He could have planted capsules of these … ah, *organisms* at strategic points all around the confederation.'

'And who is to say he has not done so?'

The president raised his hands in exasperation. 'Quite! Which is precisely why this meeting, and a carefully coordinated course of action stemming from it, are vital. However, our profiling and behavioural models suggest that he will not have taken such action – *yet* – although the possibility must be considered very real, and containment measures are high on the agenda for discussion later. It is more likely that he has other mischief planned, though we can only guess what form that may take. We must all stay vigilant and expect the worst. However, with regards to your point about secrecy – this will be a long debate, and, if only to circumvent all the usual jockeying so we can crack on with the important stuff, I agree. May I have the floor?'

Hachilika nodded. Andritsos' expression grew solicitous as he stood again and scanned the chamber, making the tufted ends of his white eyebrows protrude eccentrically.

'Can we quickly table the motion? Calling for unrestricted access to all available facts pertaining to the current threat by all those with clearance?'

'Unless there are objections …?' elicited the Speaker, allowing a suitable pause. When none were raised, she intoned 'Cast your votes now. The motion is that all available facts pertaining to the threat posed by the terrorist Josey Matlow Fox, his acolytes, and non-human lifeforms be made available to parties with clearance. Cast your votes, please.'

Revolving numerical figures scrolled on the holoscreen as votes were logged. Eighty-four-point-two percent in favour. Abstentions at five percent.

'The motion is passed.'

Apparently mollified, Hachilika nodded. *Can he really be so naive?* Despite its geographical centrality, reflected Marcell, Proxima Centauri was a backwater.

'Good,' harrumphed Andritsos. 'Now, the most pressing concern is our short-term strategy. Our plan must succeed. And let's think for a moment now what that means: to succeed.'

Putting his hands on his hips, he thrust his chest out above his modest paunch and rotated slowly, sweeping his eyes methodically over of the ranks of surrounding seats, missing no one.

'To succeed means the total and complete annihilation of every single organism that is not human. *Not one* microscopically small organism can be allowed to survive. Think what that means. It means one hundred percent-effective containment. It means absolute superiority in every aspect of operations. It means overwhelming force. Each and every vessel of theirs must face a hundred of ours. Each missile of theirs must face *a thousand* of ours. There must be nowhere for any of the people harbouring – *breeding* – these organisms to run to. Nowhere for them to hide, and no time allowed for them to get there if they could.

'As a backup, and to ensure the eventual extermination of the threat, I have been advised that the genetic codes for the original Purge range of viruses and the formulae for the poisons, along with stocks of the more durable ones, have been in safe storage at a facility whose existence, until today, was a closely-guarded secret. A program for their mass-production is underway we speak.

'While safeguards must be observed – many of the toxins are every bit as lethal to humans as these other lifeforms – within a few tendays we should be in a position to begin spreading them tactically around the confederation to ensure that any outbreaks are contained before they can become a plague. Once the planet believed to be the primary infective reservoir is found, we will be able to deliver both the viruses and the poisons in the form of bombs. Combined with more conventional neutron bombs, these should kill every living thing within tendays. However, our think-tanks caution that the uncertainties inherent in this approach should only ever make it a failsafe, complementing, rather than superseding, our military operations.'

'New Monaco,' broke in the Speaker. Andritsos rolled his eyes and sought out the delegation, whose location was highlighted by a subtly flashing halo.

'Your Majesty.'

He sat, arms folded. New Monaco's long-faced, grey-haired Queen Isabella Grimaldi the second swept steady brown eyes around the chamber.

'Mr President. I appreciate the urgency of the situation and applaud your dedication to its swift resolution. However, I would caution all here not to, so to speak, throw the plate out with the food. Forgive me, but it seems clear to me that the possible link between this planet and the apparent vitality of its inhabitants is being underplayed. This is of particular concern given the alarming health trends reported not just in New Monaco, but, I am given to understand, similarly around the I. P. E. C. Compared to the immediate threat posed by this Josey Fox, and what he and his people have apparently been up to, this problem is harder to conceptualise. Therefore, perhaps, it has less power to frighten and alarm.'

The queen propped her fists on the annular conference desk and thrust her prominent jaw towards the chamber.

'But it frightens *me*, ladies, gentlemen – and I put it to you that this development is, in the longer term, equally grave. If my sources are correct, our confederation's best-funded thinktanks and research institutes have little to offer regarding potential solutions. The only concrete suggestions I have heard involve cybernetic modification – a practice currently banned, or at least straightjacketed, by conventions laid down by the church.

'I suggest that these two problems may be connected, in ways not currently clear, and that in the resolution of one should be sought a solution for the other. I urge us to look upon the immediate situation not simply as a threat, but also as a potential resource. While the costs and complications of containing these nonhuman lifeforms may be greater than those of simply annihilating them, so, too, are the potential benefits.'

'Your majesty,' began Andritsos levelly, rising once more. 'Once again I must thank you for a most challenging and erudite argument.' Marcell chuckled: Andritsos's use of euphemism was famous. 'However, the fact is that our resources will be sorely taxed simply eliminating the problem. The planet we seek is almost certainly much further from IPEC space than the most distant Lancer worlds. Deploying a fleet there that is sufficient to get the job done safely will consume a major portion of our military and other resources. Projections are that we may face a confederation-wide recession of at least four standard years as a consequence of funding this operation.' Supporting his argument, charts and diagrams flashed up in the air beside the president's projected image. 'Neither should it be overlooked that this will leave our society vulnerable to Lancer incursions. Which is another reason that secrecy is paramount.'

'Nonetheless, Mr president,' responded the queen, 'if there is any truth in the rumour that these "Freaks" possess the key to a cure for our ailing collective health, might not the risk be worth taking? However different from us, these are, fundamentally, people we are dealing with. Might it not be possible for us to reason with them? They are, after all, if intelligence on the subject is to be believed, centred on a single planet. We are an entire interstellar civilisation, with resources to match. Faced with our combined military might, surely they will realise what they stand to lose?'

Andritsos's exasperation was clear. 'In my view,' he said, not bothering to stand, 'no, your majesty. And that view is backed up by our think-tanks and thinker ranks. These people will not respond to such reasoning. Have you made your proposal, your Majesty?'

The Queen drew herself up. 'I suppose I have.'

'The Vatican,' said the speaker. Andritsos nodded, clearly anticipating support.

'The position of the Church,' declared Pope Ali Horst III, his hologram towering sternly above the chamber as he rose to his feet, 'is that this planet and these lifeforms are an abomination, and should be eliminated.'

Andritsos blinked. 'That's it?'

'The church has spoken. They are unholy, and must be destroyed.'

'Thank you, Your Holiness, for putting the church's position so succinctly.' Still seated, the president turned to the Speaker's platform. 'May we take the vote, madam speaker?'

'What, exactly, is your motion, your majesty?' asked Quiong, her brow knotted as she looked towards Queen Isabella.

'That the confederation exercises restraint, aiming for pacification and quarantine, rather than annihilation, with a view to urgent scientific study.'

'Please cast your votes for the motion proposed by New Monaco.'

Thirty-two percent in favour. Marcell sat back. Considerably more than he'd expected. 'As always, your majesty,' said Andritsos, on his feet again, 'the house is grateful for your stimulating contribution. Our conscience, if you like.' His face darkened. 'I only wish that a conscience was something we could better afford.

'Now, to the meat of the discussion – and forgive my haste, but we find ourselves at a juncture where every minute may count. We have two issues to decide. Firstly, the theatre of operations will be very remote. This means that weighty decisions will have to be made within the taskforce without access to democratic process. Does the taskforce enjoy the express permission of the heads of state here assembled to oversee the deployment of materiel and personnel, in whatever manner the command structure sees fit, for the elimination of this threat, on behalf of all nations here represented?'

'Please cast your votes.'

Eighty-eight percent in favour. Marcell wondered if the voters fully realised what this signified. Amongst the dissenters were the queen of New Monaco, who was sulking, and a couple of dozen colonies from parts of IPEC which were furthest from the menace. Even so, a spectacular figure.

'Secondly,' Andritsos went on, 'we come to the Troubleshooter development, or project, of which most of those here are – until now, often unwittingly, it must be said – joint consortium members. Owing to its nature, a protocol has been developed to weight commercial and political contributions in this vote. On your screens are the details of two motions, which I urge you to analyse carefully. The first is a technicality, but concerns validating your support for this protocol.'

'Please cast your votes.'

After a noticeably protracted pause, the figures for the vote appeared. Seventy-one percent in favour.

'Good,' said the president. 'Now to the second, crucial, motion: your support for accelerating the Troubleshooter project to its conclusion.'

'Please cast your votes.'

Seventy-nine percent. *Good enough.*

'Thank you. Finally, for clarity, I move that the project be put at the disposal of the naval task force, under the direct control of Fleet Admiral Abdul Grisham, for use however he sees fit. This deployment may be looked on as Troubleshooter's trial-run. Risks are involved, but my feeling, shared by our thinktanks, is that it's an asset we can ill afford not to use. It will involve the staffing of no less than one-point-five million specially trained servicepeople, who are receiving a crash course as I speak. Do you have my support?'

'Please cast your votes.'

Ninety-seven percent. Never, in his five centuries of commercial dealings and politicking, had James Marcell seen such a figure in a critical state-level vote (an unrigged one, anyway). Troubleshooter did that to people. It brought them together. It made them feel good.

Carlito Andritsos had visibly relaxed. 'Very well,' he said, with a tiny bow. 'My thanks, ladies and gentlemen, Holiness, Your Graces, highnesses.' His eyes dipped to his personal screen. 'The courier is being uploaded with the results of the votes … it is now underway. I commend you all on your strength of purpose and your unity. With such resolve, I have little doubt that mankind will triumph once again. Your countrymen and women will be proud of what all of you have achieved here today.'

Looking drained now, the president blew a lungful of air out through puffed cheeks and collapsed back into his seat.

'Now, about those containment plans. Then we can move on to specific details and the costings.'

11

EMERALD LAKE

'THIS IS MY FAVOURITE PLACE.'

Hazel's eyes mirrored the aquamarine of the lake, which in turn mirrored high spires and spikes of pink rock. Seamed and flecked with patches of snow, the peaks trailed banners of cloud against an early evening sky. Although the sun was still high, its light was rich and mellow. It made the granite glow.

'The sun's a shade orange compared to the original apparently,' she went on, unconcerned by the discontinuity of her monologue. 'Earth's, I mean. So they called it Amber. Amber's the resiny stuff you've seen oozing out of pine trees. Has that lovely smell.'

Raising her head, she inhaled the aroma of the pines which jostled round the little sandy bay and spread to the precipices beyond the lake.

'Moon's a lot smaller too.' Hazel gazed at the squashed, pink sliver drifting over a prominent triangular mountain she'd earlier called 'Bighorn'. 'Earth was almost a binary system before they got rid of the moon. Ours is a runt by comparison. There's a whole community of plants creatures that depend on the movement of the seas caused by the moon's gravity. Tidemaker, we call it. Our moon. A lot smaller, but much closer, so the effect is similar – although it orbits a lot faster, so the tides are a bit manic, though not nearly so impressive. In places on Earth, the ocean used to go up and down twelve metres every day.'

Feet in the air, chin rested on forearms half-buried in warm grains of silicon dioxide, gypsum and mica, Wood was enjoying a pleasant weariness and the play of sunlight on his face and the backs of his legs, content just to listen. He was still adjusting to the variety and sheer intensity of smells and other sensations permeating the air of this bizarre world. Until two tendays ago he'd never experienced wind on his skin. Not all such sensations were pleasant. At nights especially, the wind was sometimes so chilling that he feared for his safety. Invisible particles in the air, some apparently produced by the trees and other plants or bizarre lifeforms called fungi, made him perpetually want to sneeze. A thousand things seemed to make his skin itch.

Powered surface vehicles were forbidden beyond the vicinity of Juniper, and Hazel had suggested that they travel as far as the lake using the precarious two-wheeled vehicles he'd seen townspeople riding around, using their own legs for propulsion. Once Wood had demonstrated – to Hazel's disproportionate amusement – that he was utterly incapable of riding one, she'd suggested walking. 'It's only eighteen K.'

'Eighteen *kilometres?*' He'd gaped at her, like one of her planet's fish. 'Can't we take an SEV or something?'

'I am *not* taking an SEV to Emerald Lake. Even for you. You can walk.'

And so, they had. The narrow path had weaved between great tree trunks where birds called woodpeckers prowled, drumming their beaks noisily against bark, through thickets of scratching shrubs, and grassy, strongly-scented clearings where enigmatic boulders stood amongst tall yellow, pink and blue flowers, looping butterflies, and chirping crickets. As they gained height, pines had begun displacing the airier, mouldier-smelling spaces of the broadleaf forest. Raptors wheeled above the treetops.

The journey had taken all morning. At every corner of the path, Hazel would stand waiting for Wood, hands propped on the hip-belt of her backpack.

It was Wood's second day without his nappy, and the first he could remember feeling truly healthy. Even so he was, he had no trouble admitting, very tired. Hazel seemed as overflowing with energy as ever. Despite his own backpack having been virtually empty, however, he felt a sense of achievement. No one he'd ever heard of before coming to Haven had walked so far in one go.

They'd spent much of the time talking, Hazel describing the life of the town, or other parts of Haven. He'd often found himself watching her. Silent now as she stared over the crystalline waters of the lake, she seemed somehow a focus for all that he could see, hear and feel around him.

Amber dipped steadily towards the turreted skyline.

'We should think about something to eat,' said Hazel, abruptly. 'We can catch some fish if you want.'

The look Wood gave her was blank.

'You know? To eat?' She held up a fist and mimed mastication. Wood felt his lips curl in horror.

'But they're alive!'

She shot him a wicked grin. 'Not when you eat them, they're not.'

His mouth hung open.

'Don't worry, it's perfectly natural to eat other creatures.'

'Um, how … do you, um, kill them?'

She made a puffing sound as she bobbed her head. 'Fish, mostly bashing them on the skull. Deer and other running animals are usually shot through the chest with crossbows.' Seeing his expression, she said. 'We don't want to go hungry, do we?'

'But … can't you tell what they're feeling? Don't they feel pain?'

'Great Mother, yes! They're as terrified and agonised as you or I would be. I can't tell exactly what they're *thinking*, because different animals have such different perceptual frames, but they don't enjoy being killed one bit.'

There was an uncomfortable silence.

'I brought some veggie sausages. Unarguably the single most worthwhile product of human technology.'

Wood squinted at her.

'Veggie is short for vegetarian. That means people who don't eat animals. You know? People like me.'

There was a long hiatus while Wood digested this.

'You were winding me up!'

Hazel dissolved into laughter. He rose to grab her, but she was faster.

'*Son of a mother!*' She sprinted off across the sand, taunting him. Wood slumped down in the sand again. He conceded a huffy grin. 'You just volunteered to cook the food.'

'You don't think I'd let a *Puke* loose with it?' She flung herself down beside him, elbows behind her, head back, thrusting her pointed chin and full chest contentedly at the deepening sky as the breeze toyed with her hair, which hung like lava against the setting sun.

Wood found himself staring.

Soon Amber had set. Bighorn was purple in the afterglow. Hazel had gone to find firewood, leaving Wood alone with his thoughts.

Even *being* here, on Haven, was confusing. Everything he did seemed to have some unforeseen consequence – or, more likely, a sequence of them. These were usually things he'd have been far happier not having to think about. Something as simple as turning on a tap or eating the simplest item of food seemed to create, and be borne of, a nightmarish web of cascading events and processes which he felt under subtle, yet firm pressure to be conscious of at all times, if not fully to understand. There were times when the entire labyrinthine edifice seemed to bear down on him like a crushing weight.

He found himself yearning for something as mundane as exchanging a few credits for a burger or hotdog from some mechanised hatch – which, like the food itself, would have been somehow comforting in its anonymity and conformity. That, or simply being able to bury his head under a pillow and hide from it all. He studied the tops of the pines, which fidgeted in silhouette against the steadily deepening sky. For all its faults, the – albeit deceptive – simplicity of his previous life seemed suddenly very appealing.

'I don't really understand,' he ventured, eyeing Hazel with a frown as she returned with an armful of sticks. 'Where these plants fit in. I mean, you use and talk about them like they're a kind of raw material. Like, I don't know … rocks, or something. But …' He scratched himself industriously. 'Aren't they conscious then? I mean, I'd always sort of thought – *assumed* – well, that life and consciousness went together.'

Hazel's sticks clattered to the sand. 'Mister McCorkindale, you don't realise what a good question that is!' She brushed hands on her trousers. 'They certainly communicate – to a level of sophistication we're only beginning to appreciate – but I don't think human values of consciousness, pain and loss can have simple equivalents for plants when being eaten by other organisms is part of their survival strategy. Though it's a contentious issue, and that's just a personal view.'

Distracted by an itchy lump on his elbow, Wood saw that Hazel's hands were on her hips. She was regarding him expectantly. He looked up at her.

'Um, sorry …?'

Her shoulders slumped fractionally before she drew herself back up. 'Well, take these pines for example.' She gestured into the trees. 'Some can only make fertile seeds when they've been burned by forest fires. A lot of plant seeds can only grow once they've been through the guts of some bird or other animal, and having their tops eaten makes some plants send out new shoots or reproduce by splitting. See my point? If you'd evolved so you couldn't make babies without bits of you being eaten, you might not be so upset if a grizzly ran off with your leg.'

'Sorry – what?'

'A grizzly. Bear.' She glanced into the darkness between the tree-trunks. 'I'm surprised we haven't seen one yet. One of our minor triumphs: just six were left alive when the Professor brought them here, and one of those died on the journey. Some are over three metres tall when they stand up. Thing to remember is not to run.' Wood breathlessly scanned the forest edge. 'Four times out of five, just staying calm and raising your hand does the trick.'

'That's not exactly reassuring.' Huge, clawed things were lurking in the shadows of his mind. He gave a start as he saw, on his arm in the half-light, a small but unpleasant-looking insect.

'Drinking your blood,' Hazel explained. 'A mosquito. They're harmless, although diseases are carried by them in some warmer parts of the planet. You'll itch a bit, that's all.'

'Is there anything on this planet which won't eat you?' he grumbled, watching with horrified interest. 'I'd been wondering where all these little bumps were coming from. Hold on – it's got a *tube* in there! A dirty great tube! Yeech, get it off me!' He scrabbled backwards.

'Squash it. If you're feeling mean, you can pinch your skin around the bite so blood pours in until the mosquito bursts.'

He studied her, perplexed by her sudden, contradictory cruelty.

'I don't think you can worry too much about that sort of thing. You've crushed thousands of little crawly things today just by walking here, and bloodsucking insects can get so bad you'd go gaga if you let all of them bite you.'

Her gaze cooled.

'Wood, listen to me. I know there's probably not much of all of this which makes sense right now, but if you take on board nothing else, please understand clearly that this isn't some theme park. This place is cruel. As cruel as your world, in its own way. A selection process governs everything here. Parasitism and death are fundamental to it.

'We believe that accepting our part in that process is necessary to give future generations the same chance we've had. That's a stark and difficult choice – particularly if it's one of your loved ones who gets killed by some bacterial infection or rogue animal. Some here resent it. But it's a universal truth that nothing comes free. The only uncertainty is who pays. That's why your society can only ever be a time bomb. By serving individual aspirations above all else, all you've done is defer payment to future generations, who are going to end up paying in one terrible lump sum. And if you don't believe me, remember what happened to you all once already, three hundred years ago, and what you did because of it.'

To Wood's relief the insect had gone. All his uncertainty and anger poured into the look he directed at Hazel. She returned it sympathetically.

'Come on.' She sprang to her feet. 'Enough heavy talk. I'm starving. Let's get some more firewood and I'll show you how to make a fire.'

SAUSAGES SIZZLED on sticks, their smell mingling with resinous smoke under a star-specked sky. There weren't many stars apart from the Milky Way, which curled from the horizon like spattered paint. What stars there were, however, were prominent.

'See that bright green one above Bighorn? That's Limetree. It's our pole-star: everything rotates around that one. The intense red one is Firebrand. The big red one way over left, that's not quite so bright, is Goliath. Which is an absolutely massive star. You'd never believe it was five hundred times further away than Tangerine over there – that orange one – which is the second closest star to us.'

'How far?'

'Nine LYs. We're pretty isolated out here. You should be able to see Walnut, the one Beta station orbits – where we paused on the way here? – but it's way too dim. It shows up on fractal telescopes, though. It's a shame it's not summer yet, we'd have a great view of Trene's Veil. You can just see Hotshot on the horizon. That's the brightest star in Trene's Veil.'

She pointed.

'No, above that pointed tree.' She visualised it for him.

'Oh. Got it.'

'It doesn't look like a star; more like a smudge, because it's surrounded by a lot of nebulous material. It's a very young, blue star. Trene's Veil is lit up by more than twenty like it.'

For a few minutes they scanned the sky in silence, listening to the call of owls and the chirruping of frogs and cicadas.

'It's funny, you know. This place could have been made for us.' Hazel made a gesture at the sky. 'Trene's Veil keeps us hidden from every one else ...'

She fell silent, shifting the battered metal billy-can to the edge of the fire so that the vegetables boiled less frantically. Wood watched her broad-shouldered back as she adjusted the sausages again. He didn't mind admitting that he was afraid of her: she looked strong enough to tear him apart with her thick, work-roughened hands if she had a mind to, and he had the impression that boiling beneath the surface of what she allowed him to see was a temper kept barely in check.

He opened his mouth to speak, but thought better of the question. He didn't think Hazel was eavesdropping.

He decided to ask anyway.

'Hazel, why are you so afraid of the confederation? I could maybe understand why in view of the history of this place ... but that doesn't explain why the IPEC ship attacked you.'

She turned sharply to face him. He couldn't tell the colour of her eyes in the firelight, but they seemed to iridesce. The flattened crescent of Tidemaker was edging once again above the tree-spiked horizon.

'They know about us. They don't know where we are yet, but they know we exist.'

He peered into the fire. 'But why should that mean they mean you harm? Wouldn't it be a good chance to start over again?'

Hazel stared at him as though he'd said something extraordinary. 'Oh Wood, my poor, naive young man, if only there were more like you!' She laughed bitterly. 'You've already experienced why they want rid of us.'

She flung out her arms.

93

'We carry disease! None of this can exist without microorganisms, and where there are microorganisms, there will always be disease. If we wanted to do so – if we really put our minds to it – we could probably wipe out the Interplanetary Economic Confederation and kill almost every person in it.'

He chewed on that. 'But – you don't want to. Do you?'

'You kidding? All we've ever wanted is to be left alone.' She shook her head. 'We have effective vaccines for all known human diseases, which could easily be distributed throughout all the occupied worlds, just in case the screening we use whenever any of us have to visit Orphaned societies – something which, incidentally, we'd rather not be doing in the first place – fails. But that would be … economically stifling. Too *inconvenient*. In future they might want to exploit somewhere we've been first. Yes, getting rid of us would definitely be the easier, most cost-effective option.

'Besides, even then – what makes you think we would ever be left alone? This place would have to have to be evaluated, carved up. Mined for the unbelievable fortune we have in wood, should the Pukes – or the Lancers for that matter – ever get hold of it. Trampled over by millions of tourists. Owned. We have something here that can't be valued without destroying it. No one here can turn to anyone else and say, "this is mine", or "I've got more than you", because nobody owns anything. The existence of this place is an end in itself, which does not have to be justified in terms of value. It just is.

'As far as the Federation is concerned, Haven has no economic relevance, and is a potential threat. Therefore, its existence cannot be justified.'

The fire crackled. One of the sausages was burning. Hazel blew out the flames and prodded it on to a battered metal plate. The others were only slightly overdone. She drained the vegetables, then poked four blackened potatoes out of the embers, slitting them and adding butter to their fluffy, purple centres from a silicone tub. Passing Wood a fork, she pushed the plate between them.

'Help yourself.'

Wood blew on a sausage to cool it. It tasted surprisingly good. He tucked in with the hunger of a hard day's work. Moonlight played on ripples slopping on the sand a few metres away.

'You know,' he began, as the fire cooled and his belly digested. 'I used to take a car – an old burn-out I bought as soon as I got my teen license, I can't even remember the make now – and I used to override the limiters, because I was good at that kind of thing, and get it to drive me into empty places way outside the town's environment dome.'

As he scanned the dark shapes of the horizon, Hazel saw a different view: acres of red dust, crumbling rocky outcrops. A plastic bed beside a small, red and white, wheel-less vehicle.

'I used to take a duvet – you know, a thermostatic bed cover I think the packaging called it? Ran off batteries – and ... I used to stay out overnight. I used to just lie there on my back and watch the stars through the visor of my rebreather. Stars were hard to see with so many other lights whizzing about overhead. There were solar reflectors too – they only shone directly on the cities, but scattered light meant it was always light pretty much everywhere.

'I never really knew why I did it at the time. It was something I couldn't properly explain. It sort of felt ... like I was after something. I don't know. Maybe I thought that, somehow, going out there might be how I could find it.

Or maybe it was just somewhere my family wasn't. He unthinkingly fingered the pucker on his forehead where, years ago, a marriage ring had scarred him, lost for a moment in the fire's twisting pockets of glowing gases, which seemed to have such a mesmerising hold on the senses.

'I don't know if I ever found it or not,' he went on. 'I must have found *something*, because I used to go out into the desert again and again. I used to come home covered in crud, shivering because the car's aircon and the cheap stupid duvet weren't working properly. And my ... um, my father used to tell me what a fool I was being, and look at the mess, and why did I do it and all that. Everyone thought I was crazy, I guess.'

He could hear Hazel's steady breathing, and the flutter of wings as what he now knew to be a bat looped nearby over the lake. Echoing far away, some water bird made a sound like a bell. He scooped a forkful of buttery potato from a skin. Chewing, he closed his eyes, nostrils full of its thick smell and a thousand others, relishing its texture, its taste. The contrast of its heat with the cool breeze on his face and neck.

'You know, I think I understand now.'

12

THE COMPANY OF FISH

THE VIEW FROM THE SHARP TIP of Bighorn was spectacular beyond any planetary landscape Wood had ever seen. Hazel gave him a framework for it, naming prominent mountains and other topographical features, and even describing how they influenced the climate.

'Those big graceful ones in front of us to the east – they're the Snowfire Range. They go up to seven thousand metres above the level of the sea on Table Top, that big spire with the sawn off top over there. The round white one trailing the cloud is Ice Dome, which is almost as high. There are some amazing valleys among that lot, with forests of cedar, and some impressive glaciers. We could go there sometime if you want.'

Right now, Wood was too content being where he was to worry what they might do tomorrow or the day after that. 'If you like.'

'Over there –' Hazel pointed in the opposite direction, towards the west, where distant shapes thrust through several layers of cloud like spearheads of ice. 'Those are the Celestial Spears, and they're a bit higher. Fishtail, that twin-topped one, is over eight thousand metres, and Celestial Spear, just behind it, is eight and a half.' Wood wondered absently why such figures were important to her. 'We could go there too if you like, take an SEV. There are mountains in New Antarctica – the most southerly continent, which is one-third buried under a huge icecap – which go up to fifteen thousand metres, right through the troposphere, so they don't even get snow on their summits! But I don't think they're half as beautiful as the Celestial Spears.

'The Snowfires and the Spears are why the climate's so pleasant around Juniper,' she went on. 'Rain-bearing winds we get are from the west and southwest, and occasionally the east from the Hughes Gulf, and by the time these reach us, they've dumped most of it over the two ranges. There can be storm-clouds over the mountains, and we can be basking in sunshine. That line of white you can just make out in the distance in the north is one of the largest ice caps on this continent.'

Wood squinted, but Hazel's eyesight was clearly sharper than his.

'In winter, Juniper can get really cold, with heavy snowfalls. The north winds howl straight off the ice cap. There are huge, ice-carved valleys up there, much bigger than the Crystal River Canyon, which go right from the great plateaux into the sea. There's a great corrie – a bowl carved by ice – which has a back wall three thousand metres high. I hope I get time to show you!'

Wood smiled. He wasn't listening closely; just letting the torrent of information wash over him. He was sure Hazel knew this, but her enthusiasm remained undimmed, as though she might explode if she didn't find a vent for the energy trapped inside her. He gazed thirty kilometres southwest across smaller snow-splashed peaks, past the silvery rock triangle of Pearl Pyramid to the waterways and islands of Juniper Lake. He tried mentally coating it all with snow and ice. They'd crossed slippery, sugary fields of the stuff below the summit of Bighorn. Somehow it wasn't something he could imagine falling from the sky.

'I'd like to see that,' he said. 'Snow coming down.'

They'd slept in snug sleeping bags by the fire, which Hazel kept tended – to ward off bears, she said. Citing the same reason, she'd used a cord to haul their eating and cooking utensils and their remaining food into a tree behind the camp. Wood had slept soundly, reliving his desert nights of years ago in dreams full of unfamiliar sensations and sounds. To his relief, his innards had behaved, and he awoke feeling reasonably healthy.

The morning's scramble up the mountainside had proved surprisingly straightforward, though he was glad of the skinny umbilical Hazel had stretched between them as she clambered ahead over aprons of rock resembling Straubri Ripple ice cream. It had taken a morning's stiff exercise, and, though proud of himself, Wood wasn't looking forward to the descent.

By the time they reached the pines fringing Emerald Lake once more, it was late evening.

Bone-weary though Wood was, some of Hazel's energy seemed to have rubbed off on him. Without quite knowing why, he gave a sudden loud whoop, kicking his feet over his head in an aerial backflip. Hazel, who'd been walking ahead, turned. He found her staring at him as his feet hit the ground again with a thump.

'An old … er, party trick …' He reddened. Partly from his landing, which had been more painful than he cared to admit.

Hazel stared at him. A peculiar smile crept across her face.

'I don't know about you,' she declared abruptly, 'but I'm pretty sweaty after all that. I'm going for a swim.'

She ran like a sturdy gazelle over to the beach, bent to open the clasps on her boots, and kicked them off. In moments the sand was littered with clothes. Wood caught a glimpse of her pale backside before she vanished with a splash.

She surfaced with a squeal of shock.

'Well? Come on, then! It's lovely and warm.'

Her large, purple nipples, standing proudly just above the surface, told a different story. Wood hopped from foot to foot. There was a growing and very physical reason he didn't want to take his clothes off. What was happening here? Damn the woman, she was toying with him. Keeping one hand in his pocket to cover the source of his embarrassment, he went to the water's edge and dunked in the other.

He stared at her. 'It's … *freezing!*'

'Wimp.'

'You need your head examined! You're completely warped!'

'You're still a wimp.'

'Hazel … the only way you'll get me in there is unconscious or dead.'

She began splashing purposefully towards the shore. 'Deal. I'm coming to beat you unconscious.'

Holy crap. He could hardly breathe. Trying to avert his eyes, only partly wanting to, he backed away, giving no sign of capitulation.

'Have it your way,' she declared, turning her back and wading deeper again. 'I prefer the company of fish anyway.'

13

FUEL

AGAINST A STAR-SPRINKLED BACKCLOTH, the stage – wafers tens of kilometres across, stacked and interlocked like crystals – was brightly floodlit by encircling fusion-powered lamps. On and around it, a cast of thousands performed a choreographed dance of immense complexity.

Cargo trains snaked amongst skyscraper-sized marshalling towers where payloads were replenished, reorganised, or stored for collection either by tugs or interstellar haulage tractors – a waltz of segment-swapping centipedes. Deep-space ferries and superliners came and went like monstrous geometric abstractions. Smaller craft were firefly lights swarming against the frozen river of the Milky Way.

Gazing through the cabin window, Olea's eyes were round.

'All this … light years from *anywhere*.' She chewed the skin around her cuticles. 'You know, it would be wonderful to look around some of the shopping centres and leisure parks. Just for a glimpse.' Her brow creased as her focus returned to the list of attractions the Complex was advertising. 'Maybe even to, you know – buy something. Have some fun. I mean … it does seem rather a shame for *all* of that money of yours to go to waste.'

'There won't be time for that.'

This was their fourth and – however things worked out – final public fuel stop. On each previous occasion Jo had felt his anxiety grow as time was frittered away in queues like this one. Olea *seemed* largely oblivious to his fears, either too absorbed in things which were new and exciting, or still failing to grasp properly the magnitude of the forces he'd got her caught up in. He suspected the latter. The thought made his heart sink.

'We'll refuel, and then we will go,' he said. 'The best scenario puts us barely ahead of the alert they'll have sent out after us.'

'I know, I know.' Standing before the infotainment screen, she pored over an advert for one of the complex's hundred and twenty-six zero-G swimming pools. Longing was in her eyes. That she'd escaped with only a single outfit troubled her, in Jo's view, beyond reason. She was vocal about missing her sleep toner, and spoke often about her father and her friend Natalia. Jo studied her lacy black bra and rounded chin, wondering, once more, whether he'd done the right thing.

Taking a quiet deep breath, he rose from the pilot's seat, went over and took her hands in each of his. She looked uncertainly down at him. 'Listen, Olea ...'

He looked at her fingers. They were long and clever-looking – she could have been a cellist, he thought – but she'd bitten them so severely since their desperate flight from Renascido that every one was bleeding. He sighed, kissing the wounds she'd inflicted on herself, and closed his eyes for a moment. Then he raised them back up to hers.

'This is your last chance to change your mind about coming with me. Life will very different where I'm going. Sometimes it will be hard. Things you take for granted simply won't exist. There'll be nothing like ... this.'

He waved a hand at the screen, where figures splashed and cavorted in field-controlled columns of wobbling water.

'I could leave you here. Set up a bank account and a new identity for you. You'd be wealthy and invisible. You'd be free to go almost anywhere you wished.'

For a while, she gazed wistfully at the screen.

'No. I still want to go with you.'

There was considerably less conviction in her voice than he would have liked.

The comms screen flashed. 'Attention XTC2134DOB Mr Leni Tora Balinas. You have docking pad clearance: please follow the beam on "auto" to your refuelling gate. The band and docking protocol have been flashed to your thinker. If you wish to visit the main complex, please continue, *after refuelling*, to one of the private docking areas. We regret that it is an offence to use our refuelling bays for any purpose other than refuelling. On behalf of Shell Hydrogen and the historical Epsilon Nine Deep-Space Complex, thank you for your custom. We wish you a pleasant visit.'

I doubt very much that it will be.

On autopilot, Jo's ship swooped low over the surface of the filling station: one of a forest of gleaming fins and other structures sprouting from the outermost wafer of one of Epsilon Nine's crystal-shaped sub-units. Light burst from below as the refuelling bays came into view. The ship rolled to merge with a looping stream of similarly compact starships.

One of the brilliant fly-thru bays grew to meet them. Spacecraft seethed inside.

'Busy place.'

'One of the busiest,' he said. 'Population of over three billion in that thing.'

'I can think of planets with a hundredth of that.'

Equipment-tangled walls were suddenly skimming past: a claustrophobic speed-rush after tendays of hyperspace. Space became a shrinking, dark slot in the rear screen. Jo didn't speak as the ship came to a smooth stop between the delicate fingers of the docking arm. He hoped his tension wasn't showing.

'They won't really be able to catch us now, will they?'

He gave Olea a long look. 'Those who sent the message won't catch us, no – but they'll almost certainly authorise local armed forces to do so. There's a large police-force here, and a significant peacekeeping presence including naval units and infantry. While we sit around in fuel-station queues, the message which'll turn all of them against us is catching us, rapidly.'

He didn't tell her that by the ship's calculations it was already here.

A distant thump made him jump. A voice which wasn't the ship's said 'Sir, the refuelling arm has connected. How much fuel would you like?'

'Fill her as full as you can.'

Numerals in tons and credits extended busily from decimal points as liquid hydrogen was force-fed into the ship's almost empty belly.

'We might,' Jo continued, 'have the advantage that there are a finite number of available couriers. The news will reach just about everywhere, but few connections will be by the shortest possible route. It all depends on the number and range of couriers available at any given station. But it'll still be a very close-run thing.'

There was a buzz from the console. 'Sir, that's ninety point-five-eight tons at twelve thousand, seven hundred and twenty-four credits and sixty-two units. Please provide authorisation for the debit.'

Jo pressed a finger to the console touchpad. 'Go ahead.'

'Confirmed. Thank you for your custom Mr Balinas, we hope you will call again. Have a pleasant journey or a pleasant stay, the choice is yours. Remember, Shell Hydrogen: simply the best.'

There was a muffled clunk followed by a series of light taps. The view from the window began to shift. A squat blue vessel filled the view ahead as it nestled against the neighbouring docking arm. The refuelling boom concertinaing towards its hull was soon lost to sight as Jo's starship nudged back into the traffic lane.

'There's also the possibility of mites.' Seeing Olea's blank look, Jo said: 'Miniature robotic spacecraft or other drones. They burrow into objects such as vehicles, and either return to sender with intel about the host's movements and location – fortunately their size severely limits their range – or put out a beacon. I have a device which checks for them, but some of them are clever. They'll be difficult to spot.'

Brow lowered slightly, Olea nodded. 'Is it likely?'

'That I've missed some?' Jo shook his head. 'I'm fairly certain there are none on the ship. Yet.' Her expression made him wince. She understood technically what he was saying – at some level, at least, even accepted its implications – but he could see no sign that the reality of what they were doing had fully sunk in.

It struck him, like a physical blow, that he'd made an unforgiveable mistake.

The dark slot ahead grew with increasing speed. The assortment of vessels gorging themselves on their frigid nectar became blurs of colour. Then there was blackness. Stars beckoned. Jo heaved a shuddering sigh.

'Well. I'm glad *that's* over!'

Despite his qualms, he felt a surge of something like elation. Not only was the final and riskiest commercial refuelling of the journey now behind them, it had been the last such action of his life. Seeing the relief behind his grin, Olea grinned back. To his surprise, they burst into simultaneous laughter.

'Fuck,' he spluttered, adopting Olea's favoured expression. 'I'll be a gibbering wreck by the time we make it home!'

An area of screen flashed urgently on the console. His smile vanished.

'What is it?' Olea.

He hushed her with a curt wave.

'Vessel XTC2134DOB: Josey Matlow Fox.' The voice wasn't the ship's. 'You cannot escape. Make this easier on yourself: give yourself up. If you do so willingly, this will be taken into account at you trial. Nuclear missile launchers and particle beam batteries are tracking you. Fully armed naval fast attack craft are closing on intercept.'

For an endless moment, he froze completely.

Then his eyes shifted. He placed a finger on the flashing light.

'By whose authority are you speaking?'

'We are authorised by IPEC Joint Services Command to detain you. I repeat, your prospects of escape are vanishingly small. Give yourself up.'

'Ship: block all incoming transmissions.' He grabbed the joywheel. 'Aft protection on max. Any approaching craft?'

An inertial suppressor-diluted tug of sudden acceleration pressed them into their seats.

'Thirty fast interceptor craft are converging from parts of the complex,' the ship reported in its calm voice. 'We cannot out-accelerate them.' Jo began moving the joywheel from side to side, up and down. Manoeuvring thrusters thumped a staccato rhythm. Random movements, combined with distance and the speed of light, would introduce a growing element of chance for anyone targeting them with beam weapons. That didn't work for guided missiles, though. 'Ten nuclear weapons are also converging. ETA at max acceleration, one minute.'

Suddenly space on every side came alive with brilliant slashes.

'Have you made the calculations for the jump to hyperspace?' He was sweating.

'I have. There will be a small error if we do not enter at the predesignated point.'

'This is an emergency,' stated Jo. 'Start the translation.' One of these days he was going to enjoy the luxury of a hyperspace entry under safe conditions.

'This will be close,' he said, addressing Olea, still jinking. 'I thought for a horrible moment that Federal Security had arrived and set a trap for us, but I think the message must have arrived while we were hooked up. This is just the local police trying to bluff us when they realised we were slipping through the net.'

Olea's eyes glittered, saucer-like, in the light of the bombardment outside. From the look of her, reality was finally sinking home.

The starship trembled.

'Near miss,' warned the ship. 'I predict a hit soon.' Jo swallowed. The thinkers which had him in their sights were effectively range finding, casting their shots wide with the aim of corralling his ship into a narrowing cone of fire from which escape would be impossible. His eyes were fixed on the ship's countdown.

'*Here we go –*'

Rarely had a jump into hyperspace been such a welcome experience.

14

ELIMINATING EVIDENCE

TIDEMAKER HAD RISEN once more. Wood sucked the sticky crust from another of the foamy, sugary puffs Hazel had supplied, and rotated the remainder above the fire's glowing brands. There were more clouds than on the previous evening, but Hazel had assured him it wouldn't rain.

'It's usually dry from late *Giblean* to early *an-Òg.*'

He must have looked puzzled, because Hazel said: 'We divide the year into twelve months.' She began ticking them off on her fingers. '*Ceud-na-Bliadhna, Ceud-an-Earraich, Màrsail, Giblean, a-Mhàigh, an-Òg, an-Seachd, Ceud-an-Fhoghair, Meadhonach-an-Fhoghair, Deireannach-an-Fhoghair,*' running out of fingers, she returned to the first two she'd used, '*Ceud-a'-Gheamhraidh* and *Meadhonach-a'-Gheamhraidh*, based on the system used on Earth.'

The sounds she'd made were quite alien.

'It takes Haven three hundred and one-point-two day-night cycles to orbit Amber, so each month has twenty-five days, except *Ceud-an-Earraich* which has twenty six, although every five years it has an extra day to make up the extra point two. We're now in *early a-Mhàigh.*

'We also subdivide years into four seasons – *Earrach, Sàmhadh, Foghar* and *Geamhradh* – although in the tropics, they divide the year differently. Seasons reflect cycles of plant growth, which are most obvious in the mid latitudes, where there's a big difference between *Sàmhadh*, when it's usually warmest, and *Geamhradh*, when it's coldest. We get seasons because of Haven's axial tilt, although our orbit is also slightly elliptical. Juniper experiences some of Haven's most pronounced seasonal swings.'

'We talked about summer and winter on Sandsea,' Wood cut in, seizing a chance to get a word in, 'but only because of our orbit. Our axis was almost perpendicular, and of course there weren't plants or anything. There wasn't very much difference between the two seasons. We never got anything like snow.'

Her nose wrinkled. 'You're so fascinated by snow.'

'Well, it's a remarkable thing. Water as a gas, a liquid and solid, on the same planet, all at once, in the same place.' He shrugged. 'Just seems an unlikely equilibrium to be so common here.'

Hazel's eyes lost their focus as she used her stick to skewer another of the little gooey sweets she'd produced from her backpack. She held it over the fire. 'I never thought of it that way before.'

Wood sucked his own sweet off his stick. It was offputtingly charred, but tasted better than it looked.

'Anyway,' she continued. '*Earrach* is when everything starts growing after the cold months. It's my favourite season, because you can feel everything bursting into life. We're in *Earrach* now. *Màrsail, Giblean, a Mhàigh*; they're the months of *Earrach* in the northern hemisphere.

'Then there's *Sàmhadh*, when it's hottest, and all the trees and other plants lose their fresh look. Most of the growth has stopped by then. Then *Foghar*, when plants start to die back. Deciduous trees lose their leaves, and the animals which sleep through *Geamhradh* find somewhere to shelter. Including us.' She gave a little chuckle. 'It's a sad time. Well, melancholy at least. There's a great feeling of something passing away.

'Then there's *Geamhradh*, when it's dark for most of the day this far north. Some people don't enjoy *Geamhradh*, and many animals die then – a few people too – but it can be the most beautiful time of year. What am I saying?' She threw up her hands. 'They're all good, and they're good because they're different from each other.'

As she spoke, Wood's mind was filled with images – some like vague memories; others as clear as freeze-frame holos, all shot through with snatched smells – of damp, dead vegetation on foggy days in *Foghar*, or the crisp air of a frozen *Ceud-an-Earraich* morning as ducks skated comically on a frozen Juniper Lake. He pulled another sweet from its stick with his teeth, peering in surprise at the moonlight. Some of the images had felt so real, he'd been disorientated.

'Hazel?'

'Mmm?'

'Why … what I mean is … *how* are you telepathic?'

She said nothing for several moments.

'Does it matter?'

He hadn't expected such a defensive response. He thought about it, and said gingerly, and much less tactfully than he would have liked: 'You've, um, got a thing about it, haven't you?' He winced as he felt her chill almost physically beside him.

'I just don't think its any big deal.'

Rubbing his forearms, he dug his toes further into the sand. 'I only wondered how it worked, why your eyes …'

'Look, I was born like that. Alright? Why can't you just leave it alone?'

She'd turned away. He sat contemplating the fire for a while, wondering what faux pas he'd committed, why she was being so defensive. He decided, apprehensively, to persist.

'But … I didn't mean anything by it. I think it's amazing – I mean, the way you give me images like that, you hardly have to explain, because I can *see*. I love it when you do that!' He was waving his hands. 'Why is it a problem?'

She didn't reply.

'Do people resent that you're able to get inside their heads? Is that it?'

She had her back towards him now. She distractedly poked the sand with her stick, stabbing until the stick broke near the middle. She flung it into the darkness above the lake. Seconds later, there was an unseen splash. 'You don't know anything.' The words were almost snarled. 'Anything at all.'

He squinted at the apparent illogic of this, poking a finger in the sand. 'So, tell me then. If I don't know anything. Maybe … you'll feel better. If you talk about it.'

She laughed at this. 'Don't you *dare* patronise me! You of all people – stuck in that machine of yours with only a lump of silicon to talk to. What makes you think you're some psychologist all of a sudden?' She sprang into a crouch, facing him. 'You fucking Puke jerk.'

Wood rocked back, the words like a physical punch.

'Your tribe of psychos got up to entire worlds of stuff you know nothing about. Don't you dare reduce this to some self-help group issue!' She was leaning towards him now on her arms, almost screaming. 'You know nothing!' She swatted a wedge of sand directly into his face. 'Condescending prick – who the *fuck* do you think you are??'

Writhing away from her in confusion, spitting sand, trying to wipe it from his eyes, Wood was working towards apologising, explaining that he'd made a terrible mistake – and please would she try and forget he'd ever mentioned anything even tangentially connected with unusual forms of perception? – when she screwed up her eyes, and what looked like her whole body, then straightened explosively and gave the sand a wild kick, fortunately, this time, away from him.

'Fuck! *Fuck!*' Sand rained on to the lake. She was pacing about, as though caged. 'You've done it now. I can't believe this.'

She examined her fists, as though considering using them. Wood suddenly realised he was far from confident that, if things got physical, he'd even be able to run away fast enough.

'Alright.' The word was flung at him like a weapon. 'Since you asked, here it is. But I'll have to go right back to the beginning. Fuck!'

Complicated, then. How could I have guessed? Wood remained bewildered as to what he'd done. He hoped she wasn't listening in. Not in her present mood. Presently, however, she dumped herself with a growl back on to the sand.

'Okay,' she spat. 'Back in the twentieth century, starting almost two centuries before Haven had been discovered even, there were biological experiments. A very *prolonged* series of experiments. Bioengineering: that's what they called it. Ways to alter living things by manipulating genes. Early attempts were …' she exhaled forcefully, 'crude. They produced *things* … like goats with the heads of sheep, or mice which spontaneously developed cancers, for use in research. Things like that.' She hurled more sand at the lake. 'Fuck! This sounds like a bloody history lesson.'

She scowled as if resenting every second of this and debating furiously whether to go on. Rubbing leftover sand from his face, Wood avoided another eyeful of the stuff, but his conjunctivas were already scratched and sore. He began wondering whether to risk prompting her, but eventually, this time with a resigned sigh, she continued.

'Well, as you can imagine with a booming industry, as the people who did this became more adept, things got increasingly competitive.' She paused again. 'They concocted such marvels as ... legless, room-filling cows, for more efficient meat production. Pigs bred for transplants, containing human-compatible livers or lungs, and covered in ... human ears and eyeballs.' The image appearing in Wood's mind him grunt. 'The military potential of all this was realised, as you'd expect. Early developments were ... things like rats which would scurry into so-called terrorist states to release lethal viruses. Mobile virus-bombs.

'They never entirely got the hang of controlling the genetic code. It was always a case of knocking chunks out of this gene, flinging them at this gene, hoping some stuck in the right place. Even so, it was soon possible to build a group of viruses which would attack any lifeform lacking a specific DNA identifier. A finite lifespan could even be inbuilt to lower the risk of them mutating into something ... "nasty". And that, as they say, was that. The Purges.

'Anyway,' she sighed, 'not long before the Purges, there was a huge programme of tests. Some legal, some not. "Blue sky research" was what they called it. Essentially, this meant doing anything and everything their sick little minds could think of – just in case a possible application showed itself. You can't imagine some of the things they did, some of the ... creatures that were produced then.

'We have some of them here. You've travelled in one.'

Wood felt his mouth open. 'The orgs?'

'Clever boy. There were big problems with the orgs, which we now suspect was something like a campaign of disobedience. The orgs were always an enigma. They should never have worked. Some of their development team felt their components just slotted into place way too easily – like pieces of some predetermined biological jigsaw puzzle left around for them to find. Really freaked them out. Anyway, as they couldn't get them to behave, or mature quickly enough to be commercially viable – besides which they probably realised they were ultimately just too weird to sell to any potential market – the project was scrapped. No one seems to know how the orgs came to be here on Haven, although rumour has it the Professor brought them.

'The orgs were among the more successful creations. There were plenty that didn't work nearly so well. Plenty didn't work at all. You'll meet one of the sort-of-worked ones later. His name is Tom. He's asked to see you.'

Again, Wood found himself struggling for words. 'He's human, then?'

'Almost.'

'But the orgs … they're not human?'

'Part of their genome is.'

There was a brooding, uncomfortable silence. Wood sensed that Hazel was finally getting around to the point she was trying to make.

'Anyway … some experiments they undertook involved the integration, down to a genetic level, with the cells of a group of deceptively simple bacteria. Their origin is uncertain, although some believe they were engineered for military applications. That's not what I think. But, whatever, they can manipulate spacetime.'

Wood screwed up his face. 'What?'

'Much of the interior structure of each org is occupied by these bacteria, which live symbiotically with the rest of the organism. Think of them as something between a battery and a multidimensional field-generator. It's reckoned they have extensions in at least four higher dimensions – they may *be* primarily higher-dimensional lifeforms, or lifeform-like structures, the tiniest parts of which we can perceive in our four dimensions. Even our best mathematicians and physicists aren't sure about the mechanics involved, but you've already experienced one of the things they can do.'

'Bacteria?' Wood was finding all this hard to associate with the microscopic organisms he'd seen in the town library's books, recordings and documentaries.

'There were other experiments,' Hazel went on, seeming not to hear. 'Similar bacteria within this group had related effects which were also potentially useful. The experiments were successful, you could say.'

She raised her head towards the moon.

'I am the result of one of them.'

Wood's mouth opened again slightly, but he held his silence. Hazel's pleasantly robust profile was picked out as a flickering orange line in the firelight. Her visible eye glinted.

'I am a symbiotic organism. Every cell of my nervous system is fused down to a genetic level with bacteria with the ability to receive or transmit neural signals through non-geometric pathways. The ability is similar to that exploited by the orgs for propulsion, and the bacteria are physically indistinguishable from those in the orgs.

'It isn't just neural cells which incorporate the bacteria. What you see in my eyes is a by-product of the interaction of cells there with my neural activity. They absorb, and to some extent, transmit on wavelengths which reflect the signals they receive.'

Realisation dawned. *It was* Hazel *who erased those library files. And not just because of me – she didn't want* anyone *to know exactly what she was. And that time on the org,* Tumbleweed ... The puzzling feeling of interference when the org had mentioned 'symbiosis' ...

'We were another dead-end,' she was saying. 'Due for "disposal". But a few of my kind managed to escape. We were steadily hunted down. All evidence eliminated. The few who hid well enough survived in your society for nearly two-and-a-half centuries, but still they were pursued by the company who ...' She swallowed, loudly. Tears, Wood was shocked to see, were streaming down her cheeks. 'As far as I know, only one of us survived.'

There was another pause, like a held breath. Slowly Hazel raised her head.

'My mother came to Haven as a child. The Professor tracked her down and brought her here. He showed her kindness. But even here, she was ...' Her eyes lowered. She didn't finish the sentence.

'One day, she found she was pregnant.' Hazel allowed herself a tiny smile. 'Me. She spoke with me, and sang to me, every moment I was inside her – and I listened, and I learned. I absorbed the memories of my forebearers as clearly as if they were my own.

'You think you know what this means, but you don't. I've lived, cumulatively, through a thousand years of persecution. I've died fifty-five times, including being stabbed, shot, kicked and tortured to death. I've been raped and given birth in filthy back alleys. Twice, I was the one who did the raping. I've lived for years as a severed head in a tank as my mind was probed and dissected.' Teeth gleaming, she rubbed her midriff as though in pain. 'Once, I was tied to a wall, slowly opened up with a knife from my groin to my chin – and, as every thing like this was done to me, as a fucked-up little bonus I've had the pleasure of simultaneously living the whole thing from the point of view of the perpetrators. Before I was born, I knew my father's name … and that the prospect of having a … *freak* for a daughter had driven him away. We never saw him again. He could be anywhere. Although I don't think he'll be in Juniper, do you?'

'I looked for him once,' she said, more quietly, looking now at her inward-pointed toes, 'but I couldn't find him. It's as if he vanished. Perhaps his … *shame* drove him out to one of the outlying Lancer planets. Or Ceres 2, maybe – I've never been there. It's not genetic, you see. The ability. It's passed on, like an infection, from mother to child. I was *colonised*.'

Hazel closed her eyes.

'Anyway, I was born, and I could already talk to people … their minds of course – and I already knew as much as some of the adults did, and they resented or hated me for it. And the other kids thought I was strange, and frightening, and most of them wouldn't come near me. But I could still talk to my mum. Being with her was … being whole. I couldn't function without her. Half of me felt like it was ripped out of my insides and my head whenever she went away. On her missions, to the Freelancer outposts we still infiltrate. The confederation was attacking them, even then. Ever since the Purges they've had a secret organisation set up to look for evidence of life they'd missed, and it was probing, looking for us. I felt just dead. Utterly dead and alone. Like a ghost among the living.'

Wood held his breath as he realised. *Stupid!* 'Dorrin … Zhelkar, they're not …'

'My mother, Jill, was killed in an IPEC attack on the Lancer colony of Asunción when I was five.'

They both stared silently into the fire. Thoughts of what he could say, or try to say, filed through Wood's mind, only to be discarded. It was, he reasoned, perhaps unnecessary to speak anyway. Hazel would know what he was thinking.

At least, he hoped so. That way she would see that none of what she'd said made one iota of difference to the way he felt about her.

Hazel, however, wasn't listening. She was remembering the rapture of conversing in her own language and sharing in ways which no one else alive would ever understand.

15

LICENCE FOR VIOLENCE

TOWERING OVER THE docking bay like a cubic planet, *Violator* was the focus of frenetic activity. A string of huge battlecruisers and much smaller cruisers and frigates slipped, nose-to-tail, through the cavernous main portal of its brightly lit hangar bay. Maintenance craft wreathed it like a boiling mist.

On the polished marshalling yard spreading into the distance below the observation room, a portion of the hundred and ninety thousand-strong crew and infantry of *Violator* and its auxiliary vessels were arranged in neat grids, standing at ease or to attention, ready to begin the considerable logistical exercise of embarkation. Boxy personnel shuttles dropped periodically towards the yard, and when they lifted off again, the areas where they touched down would be bare. Gravity-train borne columns of fresh recruits would then snake from tunnels hidden beneath the yard, spreading like a fluid to fill the vacated rectangles.

Fleet Admiral Abdul Grisham studied the assembled might with black eyes glinting beneath distinguished bushy brows. Nikumi stood by his shoulder at a self-assured ease. He was, after all, still JSSS more than Navy.

'You have everything you need?'

Nikumi cleared his throat. 'I believe so, sir.'

'Are you quite sure? The last chance shuttle is about to depart.'

'Some of the finest minds in Special Branch have been involved in setting this up over several years. Thinker ranks overseeing the project are confident that all foreseeable scenarios are covered, with contingencies in place to cover the worst outcomes. Casualties are likely should any of these organisms get out, but our models predict that outbreaks can be contained. Even the unthinkable scenarios we ultimately win.'

'I am abreast of the situation, Agent Nikumi,' Grisham rumbled. Nikumi smiled faintly at the use of the pop-culture term: no one in the Joint State Security Service called officers 'agents'. 'I was asking about *you*.'

'I … have been more than adequately catered for. Thank you, sir.'

The fleet admiral turned a critical eye on him. 'You come highly recommended. Both Special Branch and the navy's Special Ops expressed their faith in you. I took the liberty of examining your Special Branch files – which, as Special Branch were unforthcoming, my Special Ops team was good enough to provide.'

Nikumi conceded this small defeat with a wry curl of the lips.

'Confidence-inspiring. As I'd expect of someone to whom so much has been entrusted.' The man's gaze was intimidating. 'Don't assume your name was the only one in the hat. It's a considerable step granting absolute command of so many naval resources, no matter how temporarily, to someone who is, effectively, a civilian.' He tilted towards Nikumi. 'In fact, it is unprecedented.'

What the fleet admiral was saying was that this confidence had better not be misplaced. What a pity it had been insufficient for them to have made him an admiral, instead reviving the anachronistic rank of commodore to keep him firmly conscious of his place.

'I'm aware of my responsibilities, sir,' he said, levelly. The prospect of discharging them was thrilling, galvanising and terrifying in ways he'd never previously felt. At last, a mission with an urgent, clearly defined purpose.

Nothing less than averting Armageddon.

The only crack in the memory crystal was 'Satan'. It burned in Nikumi's blood that his hands were tied in that regard. Well, he thought grimly, if it cost him his career, so be it.

For the past few months he'd studied the monstrous creature as assiduously as any aspect of this operation. Though Satan's abilities were fearsome, there were clear limits to them which the prepared might exploit. If Satan was suspected of causing so much as a headache for any of his crew, one of a range of 'accidents', mostly involving decompression, lay in wait. He'd ensured that the pre-programmed armed mechanoids necessary for them to occur were in place before Satan had boarded the ship.

If Satan knew about them, so much the better.

He watched the Fleet Admiral's eyes turned once again towards the marshalling yard. 'I note that half your staff are officers from your old crew,' the older man chuckled. 'We may make a navy boy of you yet, Agent Nikumi.'

'That you may, sir. That you may'

TEN HOURS LATER, *Violator* pulled free of its shackles and drifted majestically through Eve's cavernous docking bay, imperiously parting swarms of smaller craft. Just beyond the exit portal, it turned and fired its twenty-two gigantic main thrusters on full burn. With the twin cylinders of Paradise receding in the command decks' projected view of local space, most of the crew were singing lusty battle songs from the Lancer wars, modified for present circumstances, choreographed over the intercom.

Within another half hour, the enormous warship was lost in the shadowy depths of hyperspace, ready to wait out the long tendays at its prearranged rendezvous.

16

INTELLIGENCE

IN THE INCREASINGLY BALMY days since their return from Emerald Lake, Hazel had visited Wood regularly as he divided his time between the library and strolls through the woods around Juniper.

A lakeshore cabin had been provided for him. While he'd found it small and bare and didn't appreciate either its outdoor toilet or population of venomous spiders, furniture and decorative wall-hangings lent by the Porros and some of his new neighbours soon made it more homely, and the steps of its shady veranda became his favourite spot for study. On starry nights (as most were), he used the little solar-heated hot-tub at its rear.

His contentedness was blighted both by the absence of Tink and the distance of Hazel. Since their conversation by the lake, he had the impression that the volatile Havenner bore his company mainly out of duty.

Much of the historical footage in the library comprised audio-visuals recorded using extremely primitive equipment. Curiously, Wood found that this grittiness helped him visualise the world they portrayed. As a learning tool, the library was superb, guiding him around Earth's biomes – from taiga forests to deserts, tundra to mangroves, coral reefs to tropical cloud forest – on what felt like a voyage of discovery. There were creatures stranger, lovelier and more hideous than he could have conceived in his wildest dreams or nightmares.

Most seemed to spend much of their time eating each other. He'd begun to feel intimidated. He needed a reference point. He needed to acclimatise to the forests around Juniper with their – to him – teeming life before he could hope to understand what the Earth had been and what Haven really was.

He turned his gaze from the terminal's sail-like screen to the lake. This morning, a flock of birds of another kind he couldn't recall seeing before – big, graceful, long-necked white ones – had landed there like clumsy water-skiers. It was difficult to believe what the library had told him. Of the estimated ten to twenty million species coexisting in the geological eye-blink before the holocaust, perhaps fifty thousand – less than five percent – had made it to Haven. At least a further quarter of these were expected to perish as Haven's embryonic biosphere found its own precarious balance – and that wasn't accounting for the inevitable, yet individually unpredictable, natural disasters which had made species confined to reserves so terminally vulnerable on Earth.

Half the surviving tropical species were still to be seeded, released from captivity, grown from frozen gametes, or coded into the zygotes of other animals from gene-maps: tasks made hideously complicated by the complex symbioses without which few could survive. It was what Dorrin had described as a 'nearly-insoluble chicken and egg' problem. Without already having in place the host of symbiotic bacteria, fungi and other less closely associated insects, mites, worms and other organisms which allowed them to pollinate themselves, fix nitrogen, repel or contain infections and herbivorous attacks, and disperse and germinate their offspring, most of the trees rescued from the Earth could never hope to grow. Yet without an already established diverse forest, none of these co-dependent organisms, which had evolved in unison with the trees over millions of years, could hope to survive in the first place.

He found himself wondering what in the cosmos such diversity must have been like. The sensations generated by his discoveries – his anger over something which had happened centuries ago – still puzzled him. The closest explanation he could devise was a feeling of disinheritance. What was on Haven, though often grotesque, made a crazy kind of sense. It filled a gap, somehow.

And now, just as life was regaining a toehold, his people were apparently planning to finish the job they'd begun centuries ago.

Watching two otters forage on the shore of the nearest island, he wondered again whether he'd been given the whole story. He had, after all, only the Havenners' word that they were peaceful innocents.

Whenever such doubts surfaced, he found his thoughts turning to Hazel. Her passionate love for this place. No – love was too shallow a word.

She *needed* it. Like he needed oxygen.

That was real enough. The deep, urgent need of these people for their planet and its strange inhabitants.

He stowed the screen and left the little terminal hesitantly on the mossy grass by the steps, unused to the idea of leaving valuable items lying around and expecting them to be there when he got back. Hands in the pockets of his shorts, he ambled between disparate cabins and sheds, flowering bushes, tree-trunks, and the little boggy reedbeds the town used to neutralise wastewater and sewage. At an old wooden bridge, a stream called the Summer Burn tumbled noisily between mossy boulders into a deep pool, the energy of each falling droplet harnessed by kinetic fields from a neighbouring turf-roofed hut.

He leaned on the bridge's algae-greened rail. Shafts of sunlight made the stony streambed glow, picking out brown fish shaped like a child's drawing of a starship. He wished he was less self-conscious; that he'd joined the naked children splashing here on half the occasions he'd passed this way. He considered stripping and plunging in, but no; first there was something he had to do.

He continued along the light-dappled lakeshore. Some of the fringing deciduous trees supported structures ranging from precarious platforms of sticks to grand miniature houses with solar-panels and small rotors for generating electricity from the wind. In a clearing he passed a small boy and a girl, swinging upside down from the same rope ladder, which served a particularly shambolic assemblage of arboreal planks. The boy waved, demonstrating his lack of a need for hands. *Yes, kid, very clever.* His companion was less of a show-off.

'Rowan … I want to go down! My blood's all in my head! *Rowan!*'

Rowan ceased his vigorous swinging. 'Sara is a wus!'

Sara responded to this affront by pulling the smaller Rowan to the leaf-litter and torturing him.

As the cackling and gibbering faded behind him into the background of birdsong and rustling young leaves, the path skirted Juniper's main food storage: a long building which seemed to have been decorated by children, built beyond the reach of floods into a gravelly hillock. The town was entirely haphazard, its buildings strewn among the trees as though fallen out of the sky.

There was no shopping centre, or even dedicated shops. He'd been amazed to discover that Havenners didn't even use money, as he understood it. Anyone in Juniper for more than a month was assigned a balance sheet by Strangefruit – the town's communications grid, which ran off a group of potent little quasi-organic thinkers quite unlike anything he'd ever seen. To trade, points called 'groats' (a name with some humorous connotation lost on Wood) could be transferred from a customer's balance to the supplier's. The lack of specified prices was one of many things which had puzzled him.

'It's essentially a bartering system,' Hazel had explained as she sat on Wood's porch eating baked potatoes one evening. 'Physical things can't be owned here: materials we use are considered borrowed collectively, from Haven. Our only "commodity", if you can call it that, is man-hours. Although account's taken if danger's involved, we generally value time equally for all kinds of work. That might seem strange, but you'll find Havenners incredulous that your society rewards interesting and rewarding skilled jobs more than boring, unpleasant, menial ones which no-one wants to do.

'Word quickly gets around if someone's working inefficiently or overstating the time involved, and everyone has the right to mediation by the town council. Mediation's seldom needed, but it's useful for establishing how much work's involved in new innovations. Everyone's balance is public, which makes any skulduggery obvious. Also, that way if someone's heavily in deficit, people can offer to help by trading for non-essentials.'

'But why would they want to do that? Wouldn't they want to save?'

Hazel waved her fork. 'But that's the *point*, isn't it? We use this system to avoid economic pressures. To grow, an economy must convert resources into commodities, ever faster. That's something no finite system can sustain, regardless of how much recycling goes on, because no recycling system is anything like perfectly efficient, and the original materials still need to come from somewhere anyway.

'Our ancestors had this weird notion that, on a planet populated by billions of people, the aspirations of present generations could be met without compromising those of future ones. We used to think this was just a cynical political tool, like promising an afterlife of eternal bliss if you live according to some doctrine, which ordinary people believed because they didn't know any better – but we've since unearthed records that show many politicians and scientists, even those studying the problem of overpopulation, genuinely believed it. Apparently without irony, they called it "sustainability". Anyway, going back to groats, all a positive balance means is that you've worked more than your fair share – which is useful if you plan some relaxing time off, but that's about it. A big deficit means you're not pulling your weight, for which the council can eventually annexe you from the system.'

Wood had nodded, thoughtfully.

'People providing vital services like healing or teaching, or maintaining Strangefruit, get their "income" split between the whole town,' Hazel went on. 'A bit like a tax, I suppose – and sick people are supported the same way. But generally, how much work you do determines what non-essentials you can afford. It's quite possible to live a simple existence with almost no trade, which is what some choose. There are obligations though. Children must study full-time, after which most of us study at least a few hours a week, right up until we drop off the twig. The informality of our teaching would probably shock you, but failure to educate is considered a serious crime. Theoretically not far off murder, although we haven't had one of those yet.'

'I don't see how that would work.'

'Like all socio-economic systems, it only works because people want it to.' Seeing his expression, Hazel contemplatively picked potato skin from her teeth. 'Well, it's certainly no paradise. There can be frustrating delays waiting for work to be done, and shortfalls of certain things – and besides, people largely ignore the system and just swap favours. But most people seem happy. We've found the arrangement encourages creativity, and diverse interests. Most Havenners are jacks of many trades. We've scientists who are also artists, carpenters, musicians, mechanics, dentists, tailors, pilots, embroiderers, council members … Our mathematicians and cognitive scientists probably rival IPEC's best. Few people get bored. And they look after each other. I'll be the first to admit that such closeness has a downside, but there's a sense of collective responsibility here which sometimes I still find surprising.

Another mouthful. 'There are …' *smack*, 'similar trading systems for all Haven's communities. If you move around, you just start again at zero. Like both our society and environment, trade here is somewhat … embryonic. But the basic system's been operating for more than three centuries.'

Toying with his own, cooling, potato, Wood had protested 'But you must need real money when it comes to building spaceships and things like that? And what about the space-stations, and all the off-planet people?'

'In many ways, our stations and outpost planets are collectively like a large town. They've such a constant population turnover that they all use the same points system, called "doughnuts" for some obscure historical reason. Designing the more resource-hungry machinery we use, maintaining the automated factories and manning stations and outposts – everything not directly concerned with life here on Haven is seen as a kind of national service. We call it *tabhartas*. Our production plant on Haven is at Hades – the island with the caverns?'

Wood nodded.

'There are several more orbiting other stars and planets. All small scale compared to what you're probably used to. Large-scale tech research, manning and maintaining the ecospheres, stations and factories, and biological research and the species reintroduction programmes, are all *tabhartas*. Our duty if you like, although most people volunteer more than they have to – particularly those who like playing with technology. Since the Purges, *tabhartas* has been compulsory for everyone.'

She'd looked at him rather directly as she said this, popping another hunk of crumbly potato in her mouth. It was obvious what the look meant.

'There's a lot of flexibility,' she went on. 'You can generally find something you enjoy. I try to spend my *tabhartas* on the Carolsland reintroduction programme, which is responsible for breeding and rehabilitating species for introduction to the wild.' Carolsland, he recalled, was the smaller of Haven's two major continents, of which Juniper was the largest town. 'However, every able person is expected to do their share on the space stations and outpost planets. Some do the bare minimum, but a significant number always choose space service, either because they like challenges, or just like being in space.' Her look darkened. 'Or, like me, because that's how it somehow always seems to work out.'

She paused, as though considering what she'd just said. 'It might seem a little dictatorial,' she admitted. 'There's been occasional resentment in the past – mostly amongst Havenners who want just to sit in the woods on their own all their lives – but, surprisingly perhaps, most people just accept it. I think we're all acutely aware of what we could lose if we don't.'

Mulling over the curious mixture of anarchy and dictatorship which glued his hosts' society together, Wood approached another cabin. On its ivy-framed veranda, a woman with a long ponytail of greying hair added blue fabric to a pile by a neighbouring machine, which hummed and rattled quietly in its brainless task of cutting and stitching. Sitting herself cross-legged on a wicker chair with a small paper book, the woman saw him and waved.

'Hullo!' she called out. 'How're you settling in?'

Wood glanced shiftily about, resisting a strong urge to bolt back to his cabin. He found his legs bearing him up a bark-chipping path through long grasses and tall spears of pink flowers towards the house. He could already feel his face burning.

'Word of you's round the whole planet,' she told him, rising to meet him. Slender but big-busted, and beginning to spread around the midriff, she wore faded jeans and a black top hand-embroidered with gold and red floral designs. As she beckoned him up the steps, he saw that her cheeks and aquiline nose were ruddy, her direct eyes a warm reddish-brown. 'Hazel should have introduced you formally by now, but that's us I'm afraid. Rude!'

'Er, well, no,' he stammered. 'Not at all.'

'Well, it's nice of you to say so.' Her brow crinkled. 'You look lost, love.'

'Um, no. There's just a lot of new stuff.'

'I'd be the same.' Scowling, she shook her head. 'Can't begin to imagine living somewhere lifeless. What we have here might not be perfect by a long shot, but I'd have thought that lot,' she jabbed a thumb skywards, 'might have sated their genocidal urges the first time around.'

Though relieved to be excluded from "that lot", Wood found himself bristling.

'Sorry dear, that wasn't very tactful of me. And here am I sounding off, not even offering you a drink.' She turned her head. 'Randal!'

'No, honestly,' protested Wood, searching for an acceptable avenue of escape. There were footsteps above the muted clatter of the clothes machine, and an intense, but twinkle-eyed face appeared at the door. It was fringed with thinning grey hair and a bushy white and brown beard.

'Yes, my love-pudding? Did I hear your dulcet …'

His eyes lit upon Wood, who was trying to work out where to put his hands.

'Oh.' Wild eyebrows went up. He smiled reflexively, wiping sticky uncooked food from his hands on to the stained apron he wore. 'Ah. Hello. I'm sorry, I've only seen you at a distance until now. Probably should've had … some kind of formal introduction.' He sucked his gums and presented a hand, which Wood shook. 'Hmm, maybe I can see why not. You know, you're the first new face there's *been*. For a very long time.'

'What I was just saying. Drinks, Randal!'

'Of course. What's your tipple, son? My partner Willow here,' he draped an arm carelessly over her shoulder, 'makes lemonade, which we drink a lot round this time of year. Great if you don't need any teeth.'

'Highly refreshing,' explained Willow. 'Especially on a warm day like this.' She put out a hand as though feeling the sunshine on it.

'Thank you.'

Randal disappeared, leaving Willow smiling at Wood, rather too maternally for comfort. He studied the veranda's wall hanging: stylised herds of browsing creatures in maroon, gold and black on a green background. Presently Randal reappeared with a condensation-beaded jug filled with opaque pink liquid, and three handmade-looking pottery tankards.

'It's coloured with a wee bit of blaeberry,' he explained, filling a tankard and handing it to Wood. Wood took a sip, his cheek and eye muscles instantly spasming.

Jesus. 'I see what you mean about the teeth!'

Sat in the veranda's shade, he found himself chatting to Randal and Willow Brightstone about little of consequence. Migrations of geese, the pack of wolves which had been through the village last week, eating chickens and ducks; the black bear which had broken into the pantry of someone called Eora Aspenleaf and obliterated his stock of fudge, and how his customers took pity by taking his sweets at twice the going rate. Tracy Hornbeam, Juniper's best-known artist, who'd died a month ago of pneumonia at a tragically young fifty-two. How this *Earrach* had been unusually settled, even for Juniper, and the freakishly big trout Randal had caught in the lake. They'd answered his questions, suggesting – and sometimes arguing between each other about – the best places to see frogs, eagles, the stars, and the aurora borealis, and who was the best musician in Juniper.

'It's certainly not *you*,' Willow huffed. Randal had taken this on the chin.

'Even prodigies must start somewhere.'

'But the *fiddle*, Ran. Could you not learn something socially responsible, like the didgeridoo. Mother, it's like having a demented cat wailing at me at all hours of the day.'

Wood had laughed, and it was obviously all a bit of play-acting for his benefit, but that didn't matter. He'd quite forgotten that he'd known these people for only an hour.

He had also quite forgotten what he'd set out to do.

'Um, do either of you know where I might be able to find Sander … ah, Leafdance, I think he's called.'

'Ah. The notorious Sander Leafdace.'

'Notorious?'

Willow grinned. 'Just joking, love. Expect he'll be down at the veggies. I saw him sloping off there earlier with his toolkit, so I imagine he'll be tearing open one of the gardeners. A machine,' she added, seeing Wood's alarm. 'To get there, head on straight down by the lakeshore, then take the big path on the …'

She eyed her hands suspiciously.

'Right!' barked Randal. 'Doesn't know left from right, up from down, in from out. Wonder she can find her way about!'

Willow gave him a resounding slap on the arm.

'Ow!' He exclaimed, cringing.

'As I was saying, take the first right after the small red house. Can't miss it.

'You'd have had the poor lad walking into Juniper Lake. We'd have drowned him already.' She gave him another, harder slap.

'Ow! Look, woman, I'll have you before the council on a partner-beating charge. I've a witness!' He seized Wood's shoulder in a grip like a steel clamp. 'You'll back me up, won't you son?'

'Oh, shut it, you whining old goat.' Willow shot her partner a quick, but unmistakably warm glance, and eyed Wood's shorts.

'Do you have trousers? Are you on the barter system yet?'

He'd been arranging his arms into a knot. 'Um, well, I've some clothes Hazel gave me. No-one's mentioned me being on the system.' Willow looked him up and down.

'What do you reckon, Ran, about eighty?'

Randal shrugged carelessly, but she wasn't really looking for an answer. She went to the pile of finished jeans beside the now silent sewing machine and held a pair up by the waist.

'Don't want them too tight when it's hot.'

'I don't know if I can pay for them.'

'What? Don't you worry about that! Just take them. If you're really worried about it, we're here much of the time. Come to think of it ... we might even have some of Dew's clothes. Wait a moment.' She vanished inside the house in a flurry of feet.

'Our son,' explained Randal, smiling, though his eyes were suddenly elsewhere. 'Dew was on an intelligence mission to one of the Freelancer colonies. We're not the only bereaved ones, of course. A quarter of us here have lost someone from the missions. Cherryl was ... quite a bad one though. We lost eight. Three from Juniper.'

'Um, I'm sorry,' said Wood, not sure what else he could say.

'It was seven years ago now. Willow's right. We still have his clothes.'

Wood wasn't sure that he wanted to wear the clothes of a dead person. 'I'm sorry, but I don't understand, exactly. If they haven't found you yet, and they don't know where you are ... um, why are there casualties?'

'Hasn't Hazel explained all this? Ah.' Randal settled back into his chair and seemed to form a decision. 'No, they've not

125

found us yet,' he said, 'but they're looking. Hard. Have been for a while. They have these huge mobile fortress-things which can travel huge distances without support. Basically a self-contained fleet. We've people all the time on the Freelancer colonies nearest us. You heard of the Freelancer wars?'

He nodded.

'Yes, well, I don't know exactly the IPEC propaganda machine's slant is, or was, on this, but they never really ended. Once all free operators were driven out of the so-called Federation of Free-Trading Planets, as it was then, I imagine a great victory was claimed. But most survivors just carried on trading with confederation fringe colonies – illegally, but there was still a market because they could undercut almost anything Unicorp or its tribe of incestuous offspring did.

'Of course, IPEC wanted, and still wants, to stop this. So their fortresses maraud beyond IPEC's ever expanding boundaries, looking for Freelancer colonies to make examples of. This makes life dangerous for Freelancers, but they see the rewards as worth the risk, and have become semi-nomadic as a survival strategy. Unfortunately, there's little warning when one of these fortresses comes in. Sometimes they kill millions.

'Our relationship with the Freelancers has been pretty good. We occasionally exchange minerals from our outermost solar systems with a few of their remoter colonies for spacecraft and other items – though of course we're paranoically careful to keep our identity and location secret. They have a high degree of co-operation, and a highly efficient communications network, which we use to track confederation movements. They've also evolved an effective intelligence web within the confederation, which we plug into.'

He picked up his empty tankard, and rolled it between his hands. 'In the last decade, the Pukes have greatly intensified their offensives against the Freelancers. Maybe 'cause of us, we don't know for sure. But we do know more of us are on intelligence missions as a result. At any given time, we've over a thousand people undercover on Freelancer colonies. People like Dew. And our nemesis is getting closer. It's as if they've picked up our scent. We were all assured, mainly by Dorrin and Zhelkar Porro, who are responsible for coordinating Haven's defence –'

Wood could hardly believe his ears. 'Zhelkar and Dorrin …?' Randal raised questioning eyebrows. 'Sorry, go on.'

'Yes … the Porros always maintained that we were so well hidden, no one would ever find us. People believed them. We didn't, Willow and me. Never have. Particularly in view of the *comhairle*'s mania for intelligence missions, which make no kind of sense unless we've known IPEC'll find us all along. I think the reason we were fed this bullshit was to forestall panic. Now there's a rumour the Porros have admitted for the first time that we will be found – and soon. If that's true, then I truly can't see what options are open to us. Concealment is our only defence. Without it, we'll be just another insect squashed on IPEC's windscreen.'

Wood became aware of Willow standing in the doorway. He'd no idea how long she'd been there. A while, judging by the set of her face.

'Anyway,' sighed Randal, 'our Dew was a good lad, and we loved him very much. We'd be glad for you to have his clothes: no sense them being wasted, and we can't … wouldn't feel right just giving them to just anyone. We'd like for you to have them.'

'You can just leave them here if you like,' offered Willow, 'and pick them up whenever you want. Drop by any time.'

HE FOUND SANDER knee-deep in shrubbery: one of several permaculture patches which spread over a few dozen wooded acres and supplied the town's seasonal vegetables, nuts, fruit and other crops. The man was bending over a dirty, green-painted trapezoid box whose lid was off, exposing a tangle of clear fibres and mechanical parts. While the permaculture patch was largely self-seeding and self maintaining, it was not self-harvesting, and a wooden cart was perched immobile behind the gardener robot on eight spidery limbs. The immobile gardener had raised its four dextrous arms as though to conduct the little orchestra of carrots, cabbages and rhubarb neatly stacked in the back of the cart.

Becoming aware of his presence, Sander flashed his startlingly pale blue eyes in Wood's direction and grinned his characteristic grin.

'Hullo there!' he called, picking his way over the vegetation. 'Nice day. Mind you, it usually is at this time of year.'

Wood thought it best to just ignore this puzzlingly cryptic and apparently pointless statement. He returned the smile, warily surveying the jumble of greenery. It seemed ridiculous that food for a town could be derived from such chaos. Sander hopped on to the path beside him.

'So how are you and the fire-breathing dragon getting on?' Wood found his hand clamped between two muscular, soil-blackened paws. 'Oops, don't tell her I said that, whatever you do – she'll have me for dinner!' He mimed chewing and lip-smacking.

Wood rubbed his forearms. 'Well, um, its actually her I came to see you about, as I'm told you've known her for a long time.'

Sander's brow creased. 'Problems?'

Wood was momentarily unsure what to say.

'Oh shite – not *the* problem. Look, mate, there's certain things you shouldn't even think about. She told me you knew …'

Wood nodded.

'Well,' he continued, squinting into the sun, scratching at a cluster of insect bites on his arm, 'she's got a thing about her ability I'm afraid, and there's been nothing anyone can do about it. Must be hard for her I suppose, and some people haven't been kind to her because of what she can do. I think she's got it out of proportion, but some of us have tried to reach her for years.' He sucked his gums. 'Trust me, it's not worth it. You've just got to leave well alone.'

Wood frowned at the ground. 'But I haven't mentioned the subject for ages. She hasn't really talked to me – well, not properly – since she explained it all over two weeks ago.'

Sander stepped involuntarily backwards, almost losing his footing against a cabbage. 'She told you about … her ability? She *explained* it?'

Wood nodded. Sander gaped at the shrubbery.

'That's the most she's said on that subject *ever*. I don't think she's even discussed it openly with Zhelkar and Dorrin. Most of what anyone knows about her was through her mother!'

He gave Wood an appraising, lidded look.

'I grew up with her, you know. Hazel, me and Berry Riverdream, who you've also met. We were the terrible triplets in Juniper at one point. I've known her nearly all my life.'

While Sander didn't seem the resentful type, Wood was receiving a strong message that it was best to tread gently. 'That's why I wanted to ask you.'

Sander contemplatively picked something from his teeth. Then he delved in the bushes and produced a small strawberry, which he proffered to Wood. He stared into the trees, as though he'd seen something there. Wood shifted uneasily, holding his strawberry.

'Greater spotted woodpecker – look.'

Wood looked. It was a colourful black, white and red bird, just visible amongst the dappled shadows.

'Give her time,' concluded Sander abruptly. 'If you just show her that as far as you're concerned, she's just another person, I'm sure she'll come round. Be careful though. You won't change her. Get too close, and you'll get burned.

'Take it from someone who still has the scars.'

17

GAMES

'WE'RE BEING WATCHED.'

'Oh.'

'This isn't good.'

In the distance, the planet was a fawn crescent, completely without features as far as Olea could tell. According to Jo, it was a gas giant which had been mined for hydrogen and hydrocarbons, leaving a husk mainly composed of helium over a core of ice and rock.

She'd seen such operations on HV documentaries. The mining robots were little more than propulsion units fitted with enormous capture fields. They would condense and refine great gulps of gases as they grazed in herds, millions-strong, deep within the atmosphere, bobbing back into orbit on antigrav and mating with moon-sized purification and processing plants only to return for the next load.

The demand for hydrogen was such that large planets had been sucked virtually dry over less than a century. This particular planetary system had, Jo said, been abandoned shortly after the Lancer Wars, during which the incipient IPEC had used the atmosphere of the medium-sized gas planet she was observing to fuel its war armada.

A dark spot crept across the ghostly world's equator as one of the planet's four surviving moons blocked the rays of the distant yellow sun. 'I thought this system was deserted?'

'So did I.'

The starship had begun to feel like a prison cell. While coexistence with Jo had proved easier than she'd dared hope, Olea's cabin fever was now advanced. She found herself snapping at innocuous comments, lying in bed for much of the time and doing little but brood. At least she'd stopped chewing her hands. They were too sore. She found herself almost welcoming the prospect of a bit of excitement. 'Who do you think they are?'

Jo was studying the holoscreen intently. For once, he was fully clothed. 'All I know is that we've been scanned by radar and a few other things. Just a light kiss, as though they don't want to give too much away.' He smoothed the short hairs on his chin. 'Whoever they are, they're in orbit around what's left of the gas giant.'

'Trouble?'

Jo turned his head towards her. 'I hope we don't have to find out. But they've seen us now, and I'd have wanted to avoid that.'

What if they've found the fuel cache? She didn't say it. Jo turned his attention back to the screen.

'Ship, make us stealthy. Assuming the source of the scan is another vessel, is there a course we can follow that will let us access the fuel dump, refuel and make our next jump without contact with them?'

'The source is orbiting every six hours,' said the ship's voice, 'well inside the orbit of the fuel cache, and much faster. If we retro-brake at fifteen percent for nineteen minutes to make the course correction shown,' a new trajectory appeared on the screen, 'we should finish refuelling fractionally before the source catches us up, provided they take no action.'

Jo peered at the suggested vector. 'That's awfully close.' He ran a finger over his lips. 'Okay, make the correction. Quickly.'

'Initiating.'

The retro thrusters hissed on their stealth setting, slowing the ship with – according to the very helpful quiet commentary the ship was providing in accompaniment to an equally helpful diagram – super-accelerated spurts of cool gases. The longer their escape went on, the more Olea had felt out of her depth, and the happier she'd found herself just to let Jo get on with whatever he needed to. Her assertion that she would not be some piece of baggage was, so far, dismally ill-founded.

As the planet drew gradually closer its terminator receded, revealing a surface as uniform and smooth as a billiard ball. 'Warning.' The ship's voice. 'I have confirmed the source of the scanning. It is a solitary artefact.'

A magnification appeared. It showed a small, elongated moon, studded with regular structures.

'Its dimensions are twenty kilometres by ten by nine. It is hollow. Powered vehicles are leaving it, closing on intercept courses. We are being scanned. I do not believe that their scanning systems will currently detect us.'

Jo exhaled. 'Damn it. Hypothesis as to their identity?'

'My records show incidents of pirate activity within an approximate sphere of practicable hyperspace travel centred on this solar system. My most confident guess is that the structure we are looking at is a base for pirate activities.'

'Pirates?' blurted Olea, alarmed.

'I'm afraid we may be in for a choppy ride,' Jo told her. 'Ship, unstealth us.'

'Please be advised that if I unstealth, they will certainly see us.'

'Noted. Comply.'

Jo pulled the joywheel to the side. As the stars in the window slewed, he made a spectacular-sounding burn with the main thruster.

'That should grab their attention. Ship, how closely can you simulate a hyperspace jump, without actually entering hyperspace?'

Olea clamped her teeth together and raised her eyes to the window in the ceiling. She didn't dare ask.

'The simulation will not be entirely accurate. The pattern of particle decay will differ by a small but detectable amount.'

'Begin your simulation on my mark. Afterwards, stealth yourself immediately. Stand by. Ready … mark.'

A burst of light outside made Olea briefly close her eyes. It dissipated into the distance like a ghostly visitation. Jo pulled the joywheel gently around, then opened up the main thruster on its stealth setting.

'Warning: we are rapidly venting cold fuel reserves. If we maintain this thrust on stealth mode, our safety margin will be negligible.'

'Noted.'

'The unidentified spacecraft are maintaining their trajectory.'

The planet's wraith-like ring was now visible to Olea's unaided eye: a spectral hula-hoop. A magnification showed a blurred image of the approaching craft. Utilitarian cylinders, they lacked the distinctive hoops of Thomson Field Generators, but she'd seen enough holovid thrillers to know that what ringed each ship in their place was a detachable rack of nuclear missiles. Each vessel's nose bristled with what could only have been particle weapons. 'Can they see us?' She asked.

'They're fairly cheap Lancer tubs. I doubt they've the technology to penetrate our military-spec chameleon field. They might deduce what I've done, but I'm hoping they'll be satisfied we got cold feet and ducked back into hyperspace.' Jo pursed his lips. 'Like all spacecraft though, we can only maintain stealth by restricting our activities. As soon as we need to make any fast manoeuvres, we may as well hold out a flashing sign.'

As he spoke, the vessels began to rotate, brilliant cones spearing from their fringes. Very gradually they began to recede towards the far limb of the planet.

'Unfortunately,' Jo went on, 'our approach angle as they came out to intercept us means they'll have to wait for their base to complete its orbit and rendezvous with it as it comes up behind them. We'll be close to them all the way in, and by the time we've finished, their base will have sandwiched us between itself and them.' Seeing a message on the screen, his features relaxed. 'Ah – we've picked up the tag on the fuel dump. That's a relief: I thought perhaps they'd found it. Cards?'

She swallowed against the constriction in her throat. 'You want to play games? At a time like this?'

A shrug. 'We need something to distract us. There's going to be a lot of waiting.'

'As usual.'

'Such is the lot of man. And woman. Gin rummy?'

THE PIRATE VESSELS swung past below them and grew steadily more distant as, with agonising slowness, the planet grew, its ring now an arc of silver. Zipping past forty thousand kilometres below, a mote of dust just visible against the planet's dark side, the pirate base was wreathed in busy bright flecks.

'Looks like our friends are still in a whirl.'

To Jo's annoyance, Olea had produced another straight run. Despite being a novice at cards before their journey together, she was drawing steadily ahead. The ring passed beneath them until it curled into the distance ahead like a diaphanous motorway. Having clawed himself level again, Jo studied the ship's images and readouts. The pirate base had long ago advanced behind the planet's limb, but the preceding spacecraft were still worryingly close. 'We'll need to be careful of perturbing the ring,' he muttered. 'They'll pick that up for sure.'

'Can we avoid that?'

'Not entirely, no.'

The ring receded into the blackness of space, growing thinner and brighter until, seen side-on, it was invisible to the naked eye. There was the now-familiar hiss as the starship fired its stealthed retro-thrusters. Jo folded the cards into the box and, without exchanging a word, they both took their positions in the forward seats. A warning light began to flash. 'I know,' Jo breathed. 'I know.'

Almost imperceptibly, the ring grew again. Three hours after they'd overflown it the first time, individual particles had become visible. By a distance of a few kilometres it had resolved into a plane of evenly-spaced balls of very dirty ice, suspended in eerie stillness against the blackness of space.

According to the screen the largest balls were around thirty metres in diameter; the smallest less than two. The ring was perhaps fifty metres deep.

As the starship slipped past, its window metres from the outermost balls, the particles began to stir, as if in a faint breeze. Jo winced as he watched the disturbance. Eventually, a ball appeared which looked a little different from the rest. One of the larger specimens, its surface seemed unnaturally regular.

He examined the ship's readouts. The tanks were almost precisely empty. Although the other two ships were pulling steadily away, they were still close enough to cause trouble.

'Okay,' he said, 'this is where I go outside.'

'What?'

'I couldn't risk putting mechanical parts in this dump in case it was deep-scanned. I have to connect to it manually. Ship, how long' til the base can see us?'

'It will pass the planet's limb in approximately five minutes and forty seconds.'

Shit. 'Will they be able to see me while I'm outside?'

'I have insufficient data regarding their technology to answer that question accurately. The ring itself will camouflage you to some extent, However, there is a good chance that they will be able to see you.'

'Have you detected any satellites they could use to relay signals from this side of the planet?'

'I cannot deploy sensors on stealth setting. Would you like me to?'

Jo frowned. 'No.'

'The two spacecraft preceding us will still be hidden from the base when we become visible to it. However, two of the planet's moons are well positioned for bouncing signals between the spacecraft and the base.'

A MINUTE LATER the outer door of the starship's cramped airlock opened, and, for the first time in fifty-two years (if memory served correctly), Jo Fox stepped into space.

His throat tightened as his feet swung out of the airlock over nothingness. Above, seen through his crystalline helmet bowl, the ring was a surreal ceiling through which peeped the occasional bright star. His heart sounded like the bass drum from some of the dance music of his youth. To one side the gas giant was, even after the loss of much of its original atmosphere, oppressive. Its waxing face filled his vision, its blankness defeating attempts at judging scale. The shadows of two close-orbiting moons crept across it. Behind him, the white starship looked frail and small, something made from origami, its refuelling hose curling like an umbilical cord from the airlock towards its clasp on his skin-thin suit's propulsion pack.

These pirates are a damn nuisance.

He squeezed against the pressure of his glove. Gentle squirts of cold gas set him drifting towards the hidden balloon of hydrogen. Soon the reservoir loomed over him like an enormous dirty marshmallow. He was glad, now, that he'd camouflaged it so meticulously. The occasions when it paid to be paranoid paid for all those when it didn't.

He touched a palm to its surface and allowed the strong little field generator on his wrist to anchor him in place. With the other hand, he unclipped the bulky muzzle of the hose from behind his back and stabbed it into the friable ice, releasing a fan of sparkling fragments. Morphtec flowed into the hole, forming a seal, then a small bond disrupter ate into the pliable material beneath. He felt the tube stiffen as liquid hydrogen gushed through, jolting the reservoir's dusting of rock and ice particles into a ghostly, expanding halo.

A movement made him glance up.

The other snowballs were shifting. The stiffening of the hose was pushing the vessel and the cache apart. *Damn*. 'Warning,' said the Ship's voice. 'The pirate base is now visible around the limb of the planet.'

'How long till you're full,' he requested on tight-beam.

'I estimate five minutes.'

There was a sharp jolt as the hose went taught. Jo found himself punched face-first against the surface of the cache. A pattern of white cracks appeared in the ice around the muzzle of the hose.

'Jo? Is everything Okay?' Olea's voice.

'Fine,' he panted, tersely. 'Got a little drift on, that's all.' The cracks were growing. Barely visible jets of gas were escaping around the muzzle of the hose.

'Attention.' The ship's voice. 'I have intercepted a communication. The receding ships have reported a disturbance in the rings to their base. They have been ordered to expend all remaining fuel to investigate. They are altering course.' A pause. 'Their arc will take them one thousand, four hundred kilometres inside the ring to converge with our current position.'

Jo swore under his breath. He was beaded with sweat. 'ETA?'

'Thirty minutes. Possibly sooner. These craft will be efficient in truespace, as they have no TFG.'

'ETA if they fire missiles?'

'Minimum thirty minutes.'

'I want a list of evasive tactics.'

Jo jetted hurriedly back towards the airlock. Their cover was blown anyway: it made zero difference now that the spent hydrogen sac would jet off like a giant balloon because he hadn't resealed it. He pulled himself feet-first into the airlock. Then things happened very fast.

The refuelling hose began zipping back into its hatch in the airlock. Through the outer door Jo could see the depleted balloon accelerating through the ring, beginning to spin, propelled by a powerful jet of vaporising liquid hydrogen. As he watched, it hit another snowball, and the two flew away from each other at tangents, slowly, but with great momentum, hitting others, beginning a chain reaction.

The outer airlock door closed. 'Missiles fired,' said the ship.

'Full burn evasive!' Jo flung his helmet aside as the inner door opened and sprinted up the cabin. He'd just made the pilot's chair when the thruster came on full burn with a loud 'whap', and the hull began to rumble. Outside, the whole ring seemed to be rippling. In the co-pilot's chair, Olea had a hand over her mouth.

'How many missiles?' He was struggling to strap himself in.

'Twenty.'

'Doesn't anybody like us?' Olea.

'Ship, how soon will they converge given our current strategy?'

'Twenty-nine minutes.'

'Can we make hyperspace by then?'

'Not survivably.'

Jo bit his thumb. 'Alternatives?'

'An atmosphere-grazing slingshot at full burn will allow us to reach a point where we can make hyperspace with a seventy percent chance or better of surviving the transition before the missiles can reach us. It is possible that the following craft will not risk such a low pass.'

'Those odds are not very good!' Olea protested. 'Can't we fire on them?'

'We're unarmed.' From her expression, Olea found this unbelievable. 'Now pipe down! Do it now,' he told the ship. The spacecraft swiftly pointed its wedge-nose directly at the planet.

'Our entry speed to hyperspace will be undesirably high. Our exit will be very random.'

This, reflected Jo, was tough.

The planet grew until the starship seemed to be falling into it. Olea sat clutching her armrests, regularly glancing at Jo as if for reassurance. Only when their doom seemed inevitable did the planet begin to slip away to one side. For several minutes the universe consisted of two halves: one of darkness bisected by a sliver of silver, and one of a featureless, fawn and utterly level plane.

Then, abruptly, they were in darkness. Above, some of the stars were moving, as if under power.

'Fifty-eight nuclear weapons have been launched from the pirate base,' said the ship.

'Will they converge earlier?'

'Yes. Their trajectory is optimal for our interception. We must now enter hyperspace five minutes earlier, at a sixty-one percent probability of survival.'

Jo felt his breaths grow shallow. This was emphatically not the kind of game he liked to play. Beside him, Olea appeared to be practicing yogic breathing exercises.

The planet's nightside zipped by, visible only by its lack of stars. Ionisation of the planet's thin upper atmosphere by the hurtling starship's protective fields caused a faint glow. Imperceptibly at first, the planet's upper layers began falling away. As the starship gained more speed in its slingshot, they receded faster and faster. The horizon developed a ghostly corona, then the distant sun burst like a flare from behind it, throwing slanting light through diffuse clouds.

The ring approached once more. It zipped past in less than a minute. A rust-red moon approached, then was gone.

'ETA of first missiles twenty seconds,' warned the ship.

'Enter hyperspace at the last possible moment,' Jo told it, voice strained.

Olea stared. He shrugged.

'Could make all the difference.'

The seconds ticked by remorselessly. Closing at immense speed in a hugely magnified view from the forward sensors, the missiles from the base were clearly visible now. At this velocity, nuclear explosives were ludicrous overkill: a simple ball-bearing would have been enough to tax the ship's defences. The missiles looked like a diffuse patch of rapidly enlarging dots.

'Closing,' said the ship. Seven, six …'

'If this goes sideways,' said Jo, facing Olea, 'I think you're wonderful, and I'm really, really sorry.'

Whatever her response was, he didn't hear it. The dots drew inexorably closer, the stars behind them streaming towards a central point as the view's frantically decreasing magnification kept pace with their approach, accentuating the impression of speed. He could see a message sloppily hand-painted on to one of their circular snouts.

HAVE A NICE DAY

Hilarious.

'Three, two …'
Jo clamped his teeth together.
Space became very, very bright.

18

DREAMTIME

THE SUMMIT OF PEARL PYRAMID was a rock platform comfortably large enough for two sleeping bags, sheltered by a gnarled schistose boulder, from which slabby slopes dropped steeply on all sides. Though straightforward, the scramble up to it had been remorseless for seven hundred metres. After a couple of months exploring in the woods and meadows around Juniper Wood had breasted the final few metres feeling short of breath, rather than on the verge of death.

Hazel, of course, had arrived first. She'd watched him trudge up to the summit without the wistful smile he found himself missing – her eyes an ambiguous blue-green, as distant as the Celestial Spears huddling in shadows at the horizon. He sat heavily beside her and watched in silence as the Firedomes deepened to crimson in the sunset. In the opposite direction, the Snowfires were waves frozen against a sky which hit the horizon in explosions of turquoise, yellows, neon pinks, scarlets and oranges.

As Amber set the air grew chill, as if the door to a freezer was opened somewhere. Wood crawled into the warmth of his sleeping bag to watch the afterglow.

Seemingly impervious to the cold in just a shirt and woollen jumper, Hazel remained sitting. He studied her broad, angular shoulders and neat waist, her tousled walnut hair breeze-ruffled against the early stars. He had much that he wanted to say to her. Words he'd rehearsed in his mind many times. Edited, and re-edited.

His heart was pounding.

'Hazel,' he blurted, holding his forearms.

Wrong!

He coughed, and when he spoke her name again, it was with more conviction. She turned to him, an eyebrow slightly raised. Daylight's last gasp glinted off an expressionless eye.

'You don't …' he searched vainly for the words. His script was already in the recycle bin, '… You're never, um, in my mind any more. Are you?' He didn't think that he could really tell, not reliably, but it seemed like a good guess. She looked blankly back at him.

'No,' she said eventually, and looked away.

He waited, but she ventured nothing more. He delved in the bin and flicked back through all that he'd planned to say; the apologies, explanations …

Suddenly he saw clearly that Sander had been right. It would make no difference.

He scowled.

'Get into your sleeping bag,' he said, firmly.

She made no move. Didn't answer. Nothing.

'Humour me. You must be freezing. Get into your sleeping bag. Please?'

She frowned at this, but rose, and hauled the crumpled red cocoon from its tiny stuff sack. She shook it and it quickly took on bulk. She unclipped her boots, lay down on her intellifoam mattress, and pulled the bag over her legs, arching to wriggle it up over her body. She propped herself on one elbow and faced him with a look of annoyance. He took a deep breath and crawled into his own bag.

'I want you inside my mind,' he said, facing her as he wriggled to get comfortable on his side. 'I want you to know that, whatever I am thinking, I don't mind if you're there. I'm sorry I made you feel unwelcome. I don't think I realised how much it could hurt you.'

She remained silent, but her expression had softened a little. Perhaps.

'I want you to be in here.' he tapped his skull with a finger. 'Now. No arguments.'

'Wood, just what are you doing?'

'I want to take you somewhere.' She looked puzzled.

'Where?'

He grinned. 'To be honest … I don't know if this will work. I don't know what will happen. But you've got to trust me.'

There was silence for a moment, but for the murmur of the rising wind. Then she answered, not in his ears, but somewhere between them.

Okay. Trust. Perplexity.

Apprehension?

'Lie back,' he said. 'Make sure you're warm enough. If I'm right about this, we could be a while, I think.'

Wood, I don't …

Shush. For once in your life. Wait and see.

He felt the presence of her tentatively grow, sliding up to him, *into* him. It was a breathtaking kind of intimacy. Closeness in a way he'd not felt before.

Closer. I can feel you holding back. I'm giving you permission to go wherever you like.

I'm very afraid. He was surprised by this. *I shouldn't be doing this. I've never …*

Who is vulnerable here?

We both are. Be gentle. There must be the greatest kind of trust.

I don't understand.

I know.

There was a moment's pause, as though she were summoning up courage. Then he felt her pouring in like hot wax, mixing and immersing. There were queries there; hesitation, the need for reassurance. Gently, he encouraged and caressed her in ways he did not himself entirely understand. She filled places which had no shape, expanding and dissipating like a gas, exerting gentle pressures which told him where she was, where she ended and he began. And everywhere, she was tentatively probing, feeling with soft hands; fearful of treading too heavily.

So colourful, she said, surprised, and he felt some of her own colours, shapes, tastes and sounds. They were different from his in ways indescribable in any language but that in which they now conversed. He felt the lack of reference suddenly disturbing. *Hazel! Your perception is so different; it's like drowning – I need a reference point!*

I understand.

Subtly, skilfully, she began cross-referencing her perceptual framework with his. Its scope was fundamentally recognisable, as the regions of the brain governing the interpretation of the different senses are similar, but the form of her sensations and memories, and the textures, shapes and sensations they recorded, were something Wood had never experienced, and they built a universe which was a very different place from his own. Gradually, the process became automatic, their worlds merging in a dizzying spiral of synchronised perception, until, finally, they saw with eyes that were neither Wood's, nor Hazel's, but both.

What they beheld was breathtaking. It was perceived through a range of sensations which was more than the sum of both their lives' experience. *Wood, it's beautiful. Your world is so bright / clear / dazzling in complexity and scale / I have never seen colours / textures like these! I have never been here even in my dreams.*

Wood was too agog at what was so unexpectedly happening to respond in any coherent way, but his confused, awed thoughts ran over and through her like waves in an ocean, and she understood. *Is this what sharing really is, Hazel? Everything?*

I don't know. It's never been this way before. I've never done this. Not since … Since …

Hazel, it's all right …

Sharing before was both less, and more. I can't explain. It was different, I think.

I think I understand.

Hazel felt that she was rising – or falling, or perhaps expanding or contracting – in directions she'd never felt. There was no concept she'd possessed until now to express the parameters she felt herself exploring. *Is all this in your mind?*

I don't know exactly what it is. It seems as real to me as the other place. I came here a lot, once. I haven't been back for a while.

Her consciousness flooded with images: of a stark, metal-walled room with an old mattress on the floor, echoing cold corridors, a big, blue-white star seen through a sloping transparent wall. A haggard face in a filthy mirror; a straggly blonde beard. *Despair!* Storms of intolerable loneliness, frustration, self-hate. Brief, warm rays of desperate masturbatory relief and, occasionally, pleasure.

So that's what it's like for heterogamates! Her laughter rippled against the rocks of his mind. She felt his embarrassment like a hot coal.

You never looked before?

It seemed … impolite.

Surprise. *And you?*

She let him search, and he found that it was different, yet totally equivalent. And …

Oh Hazel. Such pain. I never realised.

No! I don't want to …

It's okay.

As the feelings were exchanged, the two of them grew closer; no longer a passive relaxation of defences, but an ever-fiercer joining until nothing was truly separate.

Are you ready? asked the part of them that was Wood McCorkindale. She formed herself around him like skin, so that he should be unrestricted.

I think so.

I haven't done this before, he told her. *Not like this. I've always been alone.*

I'll be fine.

Trust suffused him like adrenaline.

The space they were in took shape. A vast deepness dotted with a myriad bright lights: galaxies drifting and colliding across unimaginable timescales, dragged like suffocating fish on nets of dark matter as the universe unwound in cooling chaos.

What is this? Is this real?

I don't know. It sounds strange, but I don't think this is just in my head. Does it matter? The world is what you make it. Every quantum physicist knows that.

Australian aborigines, a people on Earth – they had something called dreamtime. They used to talk about dream wanderers. Or something.

You think this is dreamtime?

Their beliefs never made a lot of sense to me. Our records are incomplete. It was an oral tradition, and most of it was lost.

Dream wandering sounds like a good description.

For a daydreamer.

A chuckle. *So, are you ready?*

Yes. Take me dream wandering.

And he did.

AS AMBER'S FIRST RAYS hit the summit of Pearl Pyramid two days later, Hazel unzipped her frosted sleeping bag from Wood's, raised her sticky body away from his, and stood, naked and glorious as the dawn, arms upstretched to the unfolding sky.

Her hair unfurled in a breeze which tingled like electricity on her skin.

The world had a new vividness and depth this morning, as though she felt and saw it with a fresh, expanded range of senses. She knew, in every cell of her body, that she was a very different person from the one who had so gingerly surrendered her mind two days ago.

Wood was also acutely aware of how he was changed. Time, he supposed, did that to you – and, on some subjective level at least, a lifetime had passed since he'd so uncharacteristically ordered Hazel into her sleeping bag. There was a part of him which he suspected was now, very permanently, gone.

He doubted he'd miss it.

Hazel. The answer's still yes, of course. How could it be otherwise?

She blinked at him, inside. *Which answer?*

(Ripples of laughter) *Yes to that too. If I can remember who asked the question. Oh, it's so confusing!*

Do you forgive me?

Yes. I'm grateful.

I had to do it. You know that.

I know.

19

SMITTEN

'HAZEL!' BELLOWED SANDER from the wooden steps at the front of the town hall. 'Look who's here!'

Hazel glanced up from her apparent trance as she paced along the lakeshore path. Seeing Berry and Sander standing together, she abruptly changed direction, bounding towards them over the vicuña-cropped grass. It became clear that an almost unprecedented expression had taken over her face.

Berry stared. 'Great Mother's tits, what's up with her?'

Hazel leapt up the stairs, slammed into Berry, and lifted him clean off his feet in a hug worthy of a grizzly bear. It was easy to forget how strong she was.

'Whoa,' he grunted, 'steady! Good to see you too.'

She grinned at both of them in turn. She seemed so full of restless energy, he imagined her shooting off like a rocket into orbit at any moment.

'Berry!' she exploded. 'My sweet man!' She delivered a warm kiss to his cheek, to which he raised a dazed hand. 'When d'you get back?' She was hopping from foot to foot now, hands rammed into the pockets of her sawn-off jeans. Sander's eyebrows were raised at peculiar angles.

'Yesterday,' said Berry, still rubbing his cheek. 'Went looking for you, but no one knew where you were. Said the last anyone saw of you, you were … off some place with that Wood Mc-whatsisname.' Berry knew the name full well. This was just a micro-aggression he used to make his feelings known.

'Oh,' she replied, absently.

'We were a little worried,' Sander chided. 'All of us.'

'Well you shouldn't be.' She'd begun breezily tossing her head from side to side. 'I'm taking him to see Tom tomorrow. I can't put it off any longer. I've got some news to give Zhelkar and Dorrin. Good news.'

Berry and Sander glanced at other. 'News?' inquired Sander.

'It's confidential.' She smugly stuck out her tongue, then put a foot up on the wooden railing, and rotated it from side to side only to take it down again and rock back and forth on her feet. 'You'll hear soon enough.'

The two men stared at each other, this time in consternation. Sander's eyes narrowed.

'Haze, hon: have you been smoking some of Jake Woodvine's funny herbs? Last time I saw you, you were moping around like a puma with toothache.' She smiled, her eyes positively glowing brilliant emerald green.

'Look, I've got to go now; Bez, Sandy: love you lots. Heaps, in fact. You're the best. See you later.' With that she leaped down the steps, and scampered off in the direction of the Porros' house.

Berry could feel that his face was all twisted up. 'She's been with McCorkindale? What in the name of Amber has he been *doing* to her?'

Then he noticed that his friend was standing like a puppet supported on invisible wires. Sander's mouth was open, his eyes were glazed. His pale but normally sun-beaten complexion was as white as a newborn seal.

Berry's immediate thought was that his friend was having a heart attack.

'Sandy?' He seized the other man by the shoulders. 'Sandy! What's wrong?'

For a moment, Sander could offer only splutters. When he found his voice, it was as if an elastic band had suddenly been released.

'What's he been doing to her?! It … I … They … He's only *marrying* her? She just told me they're getting married! *Married*, Berry! Married!'

'Hazel … You mean … To … to the Puke?' Berry tottered backwards, voice rising to a shriek as he almost fell down the steps. 'To *McCorkindale?*

Moving his mouth like a fish, Sander nodded.

'To that … shrimpish weirdo from those deviants out there?'

'Come on,' admonished Sander, who'd recovered a little, 'Hazel herself isn't exactly normal. And I really think you're wrong about McCorkindale. He's the only reason you're still

147

walking around. I don't think you should forget that.' His tone reverted to disbelief. 'But I just … I mean … It makes no sense. We all *know* what she's like, and last time I spoke to Wood, he'd just come to me saying he was worried she'd never speak to him again because he'd been giving her the third degree on … you know. That Which Must Never Be Discussed.'

'Shit.'

'Precisely!'

Berry hugged himself. 'So, looks like he talked her round. Well,' he growled, 'perhaps not *talked*.' Sander made a noise with his lips.

'It can't have been that.'

'No? We don't know anything about him! He could be a real little spacefaring Don Juan.'

'Berry, the boy's being *playing with himself* for six years. Besides, we both know Hazel wasn't exactly impressed with that avenue.'

'Almost anything with a Y-chromosome living around here at one point would disagree. And some without.'

'You vindictive twat.'

'It's a fact, Sandy.'

'And way below the belt.'

He snorted. 'Psychology is overrated.'

'She's seen no one for five sodding years. Doesn't that tell you something?'

'And you think she's suddenly found what she was looking for in a *Puke?* None of us were good enough for her, so she nails the first Puke to come along?'

'Amber's light, how should I know!' Sander pulled a face. 'She obviously thinks she has. And I hope so, Berry, I really do. It's about time she had some happiness.'

They stood in brooding silence.

'Well,' murmured Berry eventually, holding his elbow, 'perhaps he's got something we don't. *Didn't.*'

Sander grinned. 'Or just larger.'

'Shut up.'

'After what you've said!' His expression sobered. 'He must have something, though. I mean, she's only known him a few weeks.'

'First laid eyes on him three months ago.'

Hands stuffed in his pockets, Berry kicked a twig off the platform. He gazed down the path in the direction Hazel had gone.

'Ah shit, Sandy.' He felt a hand on his shoulder.

'I'm so sorry, Bez. What can I say?'

'All right for you,' he muttered, more to himself than to Sander as he stared towards the lake. There was a stiff breeze today. Choppy waves jostled beyond the trees. 'I mean … she's a friend. Always will be. But …'

Sander looked at the ground.

'Funny,' Berry grunted. 'When I first saw him. It was like I knew, even then.' He waved an arm at the lake. 'Before they'd even met.'

Sander's hand squeezed. 'Bez… this might sound trite, but –' He cleared his throat. 'No, on second thoughts, it just sounds trite.'

'What?' Berry snapped.

'Well, I was about to compare Hazel's worth as a friend to most people's as anything more. But I stopped, because it sounded appallingly trite, even to me.'

'Trite isn't the word, you idiot!' Berry delivered a restrained punch to Sander's midriff, making him grunt. He became thoughtful. 'More than Steph?'

Sander rubbed his abs. 'Now who's the idiot? I'm happier with Steph than I could ever have been with Hazel. Hazel's messed up! Be realistic – you'd be miserable, both of you. Neither of us have what it'd take. What she needs is …' he scratched his long, stubbly chin, 'well, someone very weird.'

Berry clamped his hands on top of his forehead.

'Come now, stop being such a misery-guts! She looks *happy*. Can you even remember the last time you saw that? And how many close friends has she got? Be thankful one of them is still you, instead of … gurning because of what you can't have. Besides, the pool has plenty more trout in it – to use a well-worn, but nonetheless apt, proverb.'

He flapped his hands enthusiastically.

'I mean, that Aspen Sunrise working over at Hades right now … She's a little older, but I don't think she's attached to anyone, and she's *gorgeous*. And there's Moonbeam what's-her-name, from Hollytree. Okay, her teeth stick out a bit, but she's a lovely person, smart, has funbags to totally die for – I mean, those things must be full of helium – and I know for a fact she fancies the pants off you. And her legs ...'

'Yeah Sandy,' Berry broke in, almost shouting, 'but they're just fish. Believe it or not, I do not need your services as a dating agency. Sometimes Haven just seems so damn small!'

'Berry –'

'Screw it, I'm so jealous right now, I could punch my own face. And besides,' he cried, throwing a hand up towards the trees, 'you saw how Hazel looked. She was smitten! How much of her d'you think either of us'll be seeing now?'

20

BURDEN

'JO. JO? WHERE ARE WE?'

Olea had stumbled out of the sleeping area again, eyes bleary. It had seemed to her lately that all she'd done in the months since leaving Renascido was sleep, eat, and make love.

While these things were, in themselves, rarely less than pleasurable, she'd begun severely to miss – well, a life. She missed work, she missed Natalia. There were no facilities in the starship's cabin for her to make art, and while she'd experimented with a graphics package the ship's control system had cobbled together, and with daubing coloured substances extruded by the miniature dispensary on to scrolls of equally edible paper, it wasn't the same as having proper facilities. Almost more than anything, she missed being able to go somewhere *interesting* – anywhere would have done, as long as it was of her own choosing – and spend some of the money she'd earned.

Cabin fever.

She'd been woken by the jump out of hyperspace. Since their desperate flight from the pirates near the depleted gas giant, it had taken Jo and the ship's thinker several jumps for them to figure out where they were. The gas giant's gravity well had hurled them fifty light years in the wrong direction, almost into the corona of an obscure red giant star.

What followed had been a delicate dance of weighing the accuracy of their final hyperspacial exit against the need to conserve their hydrogen supply.

It had been a close-run thing.

Ahead now was another planet, almost eclipsing its sun. On the planet's night side, a crazy-paving pattern of hairlines shone redly, picking out the edges of thin crustal plates. 'We're in a solar system nobody ever visits.' Jo was saying. 'It's quite an interesting place. That planet down there is near the theoretical maximum limit for rocky planets. Around six times the diameter of the Earth.'

She was chewing her fingers again. It had dawned on her that the reason she'd lost this childhood habit might have been that her fingers were usually covered with mildly toxic paints and nanomaterials. 'Any nasty surprises waiting for us like the last one?'

'Hope not.' He drew air through his teeth. 'To be level with you, we'll be almost helpless if there are. We damaged our sensor arrays making that emergency jump and lost half our remotes as well, so we might not see a stealthed ship coming. But I'd be very surprised if anyone's been near this system in centuries. There's nothing of commercial value. That planet would be almost impossible to mine, it'd cost a fortune boosting materials out of its gravity well, and it doesn't have promising telltales anyway. There are two other planets, but they're both rocky, hot and pretty vile. We're too remote from any starlanes to be of interest to pirates.'

Olea treated Jo to her most sceptical look. He raised his palms defensively.

'I know it's not ideal, but there's nothing I can do. Good news is, after this system we really should be in the clear.'

She chewed at the inside of her cheek. 'Good.'

A diagram flicked up on to the main screen. 'Ah. Ship's found the cache.' Though he was trying to hide it, his relief was obvious. Olea scrutinised the diagram.

'It looks bigger than usual.'

'It is. I have a small errand to perform.'

She gently pushed him on the subject, but he would say nothing further.

As the sullen world drew closer it became evident that it also had a ring, though it was a shadow even of the previous planet's. Retro thrusters boomed through the hull. The ring steadily grew until its spectral grey band filled half the sky.

After a while, Olea saw that the starship was approaching an irregular little moon, which loomed over the ring's sharp inside edge like a giant Chikkin Nugget, shepherding the countless small fragments of rock which orbited the planet into a tidy hoop. As it loomed closer, she noticed that attached to it, dwarfed by the moon's heavily cratered hills, was what looked, incongruously, like a drab grey storage shed.

Unaccountably, she shivered.

ONCE MORE Jo floated through the airlock door into space, towing a refuelling hose.

Landing – or, more accurately, docking – was pointless: the moon's gravitational pull was barely enough to prevent unattached objects at its equator being hurled away into space. With such a scenario in mind, he'd built the hangar on its axis of rotation.

He drifted gently down towards the revolving nugget of rock.

At his back, perched on a weak cushion of antigravity, the ship turned against the stars, attitude thrusters spearing brightly as it matched the moon's rotation. To either side, diminutive mountains were highlighted by the intense light of the distant sun. Beyond his booted toes, charcoal-dark plains turned beyond the moon's irregular black horizon, squashed smooth by a gravity twenty times that of the planet he'd been born on, a mosaic of blood-edged continental plates spattered with glowing lakes of lava.

His hand opened against the suit's glove, firing his backpack's manoeuvring jets to slow his approach. A dab of thrusters brought his feet around as the surface came up to meet him. Another dab was required to prevent him rebounding.

Ten metres from target. Not bad.

Rather than attempt to walk, he flexed his knees and sprang in an almost straight line towards the looming hangar. Grabbing the utility bar around the door's perimeter, he pulled himself head-first towards the ground and entered the code in the control pad. The door rolled slowly into its ceiling recess, in silence but for the regular rush of his breathing, raising a thin blizzard of coal-grey dust.

With another gentle squirt from his backpack as the lights flickered on, he went inside and jammed the hose gratefully into the nozzle of the nearest of a row of twelve enormous hydrogen tanks.

The action engendered in him an unexpected nostalgia. It was eight years since he'd performed the same action in this very same place.

Feeling the hose stiffen, he pushed gently off across the interior of the shed towards a small room built against one of the hangar walls beneath towering ranks of missiles. Fifty metres long, each missile was encircled by an armoured Thomson Field generator.

The room was little bigger than the airlock to which it was attached. Inside, a keyboard and a screen were fixed to a metal shelf. With the airlock door sealed behind him, the heater switched on, and an atmosphere check complete, he peeled off the top half of his suit and hooked his legs under the metal bar which was the closest thing the room offered to a seat.

Breath smoking in the cold air, he began to type.

WITH LITTLE ELSE TO DO, Olea had watched the building through the starship's surviving sensors with growing anxiety. It was larger than she'd originally thought – *considerably* larger, as revealed when Jo's tiny figure had disappeared inside.

Since then, she'd heard nothing. His comms feed had been replaced by a curt message on the ship's screen, which the ship informed her said 'no signal'.

When his suited figure did finally appear again, she found herself sighing with relief, though the relief was tinged with unease. She greeted him at the transparent airlock door, studying his face through the sleek bubble of the suit's helmet as he waited for the chamber to pressurise.

When he finally came into the cabin, a burden seemed to have lifted from him. Sparing her a quick embrace and a kiss, first on the lips and then her scabbed fingers, he sat briskly in the pilot's seat.

The slender starship rose on spears of light away from the moon and the ring, beginning its unhurried acceleration away from the plane of the ecliptic and out towards open space.

BEHIND THE SHIP, unseen by Olea, and missing from all the vessel's information screens, TFG-equipped missiles began pouring, in wave after wave, from the open mouth of the hangar, accelerating after the retreating spaceship.

Having put sufficient distance between themselves and nearby sources of gravity, they began fanning out in all directions, soon vanishing in their own flashes of annihilating particles.

21

TOM

NEARLY THERE. How do you feel?

Wood shifted his gaze from the forest passing beneath the SEV and looked uneasily at Hazel.

'How should I feel?'

Since their return from Pearl Pyramid, he'd sensed their communication finding an equilibrium: a chaotic, yet oddly comfortable, blend of verbal and mental. While focusing his thoughts in a certain way provided something like a signal for Hazel to home in on, it was still her who had to do the searching, and no amount of mental yelling on Wood's part made any difference if she wasn't paying attention.

Already, however, the transfer felt more natural and equitable, as though they were parts of the same machine. Her withdrawal from his thoughts on their return to Juniper was, he knew, merely a taste of what she must have experienced losing the only other telepath she'd directly known. The emptiness was unsettling and profound. He couldn't begin to imagine being severed from a mind co-dependently wired into his own from birth.

Yet he knew that what he felt in her absence wasn't all to do with telepathy. 'Some people say they feel something approaching terror when they get this close,' Hazel was saying, verbally now.

'He's a telepath too?'

Not in any strict sense. 'His mind is just powerful enough to make its presence felt.'

Incomprehension.

'I think you'll see what I mean when we're there.' *Warning: he isn't pretty. And I don't just mean physically.* 'He understands the reactions people have to him, but open disgust causes him pain you can't imagine. I have to keep myself ...' Failing to think of the right word, she pictured her meaning instead. *Closed / inwards facing / guarded.* 'It was difficult when I was younger. I let down my guard for just a few moments …'

Her eyes were circular; almost black.

'I almost died. Twice. The first time … I was in a coma for eight weeks.' She shivered. 'Just a glimpse. That was enough.'

He probed gently for an insight.

No. she said. *Never.* 'Believe me, you don't ever want to know.'

Hazel guided the SEV through a maze of crumbling rust-coloured sandstone towers rising from a sloping carpet of dense young deciduous forest. Flocks of red and emerald birds exploded from the treetops at their passage. *Macaws,* said Hazel. The vehicle climbed briskly, labouring slightly as they crested a small precipice.

Here we are. She gestured to a dark opening in the sandstone wall ahead. Tilting back on its belly-fan, the craft slowed as it dropped towards a small, yellow-painted landing pad on a plinth of rock directly below the cave entrance. Wood moaned.

'I feel it. Almost … like something bad's happening in the air.'

Concentrating on the approaching pad, Hazel nodded. Her expression was grim.

'Why's he stuck all the way out here anyway?'

'He needs to be away from other concentrations of mental activity. Background noise.' *At least, that's what he tells us.* 'We could easily connect this place to Juniper by cable, but he's firmly against that idea too.' *He must know what he's doing.* 'He's our equivalent of IPEC's thinker-tanks, and a lot more besides.'

She frowned, easing back on the throttle.

'To be honest, no-one seems to know very much about him, or what he does out here.'

The vehicle free-fell the last metre to the surface of the pad, bouncing heavily on its skids.

Oops.

Hazel grinned sheepishly. Images of clumsy, lumbering animals popped up inside Wood's head. He laughed, but the noise seemed to twist in the air into something nasty. Hazel popped the door open. Big brown fruit bats flapped and screeched nervously in surrounding trees. She raised her eyebrows and drew a deep breath.

'Well, here goes.'

THE CAVE'S BELL-SHAPED outer chamber narrowed into a rough tunnel. Wood had expected plasma lighting, but it was soon clear that there would be no illumination at all. The air felt damp and unnaturally cold. It smelled of what he now recognised as fungi. As daylight faded to a bright patch behind them, Hazel passed him one of two tiny chemiluminescent torches from a pocket and adhered the other to her forehead. Like a luminous third eye, it cast a cold hemisphere of light. As Wood applied his own torch, his breath formed steaming clouds in its beam.

Certainly has a flair for the melodramatic, this friend of yours.

Hazel gave no reply.

The passage began to curve upwards, angling leftwards and narrowing again. Blocking the light of Wood's torch, Hazel's body cast skittering shadows into the uneven tunnel ahead, which disconcertingly resembled the inside of a throat. After several minutes of loud breathing and stumbling footsteps, Wood noticed that the walls had become smooth, and lighter in colour, like pale skin. Shallow steps appeared. Carved into the rock of the floor, they echoed to the irregular tap of silicon-soled shoes. The sense of dread which had begun outside the cave seemed to grow with each step until it felt like a physical force, sapping Wood's strength and will, making his feet leaden.

Hazel took his hand with a reassuring squeeze and led him on, hiding her face. The passage turned sharply right and grew steeper.

Lights off. Just press the lamp firmly with your fingers.

Lights off? He didn't want to speak aloud.

You'll be fine. Trust me. Breathe deeply.

Darkness descended. After a further two minutes blundering along the corridor with senses straining and fingers groping cool, smooth walls, a faint glow became apparent ahead.

They emerged into a large underground chamber. Even clammier than in the tunnel, the air rang with sounds of dripping water. The caves, Hazel had told him, were ancient hydrothermal veins choked with a mineral called calcite, which had been dissolved over millennia by subterranean water. On Earth, swathes of entire continents had been formed from the

158

compacted, soluble remains of ancient living creatures, creating cave systems a thousand times more extensive than anything on Haven. As Wood's eyes continued their adjustment to the gloom, he saw that central to the chamber was a cylindrical enclosure of something transparent, merging with the ceiling and floor.

Isolation chamber, prompted Hazel.

Around the enclosure, spattered across rocks which gave the impression of having run and set like wax, were the cave's sole source of dim illumination: closely packed pinpoints of silvery light, like galaxies painted on the rocks. *Glow-worms. Luminescent moth larvae.* A short distance from the isolation chamber, lounging chairs and a wooden coffee table were arranged around a patterned rug on a level part of the cavern floor. On the table was a tray of mismatched drinking cups and a what appeared to be a small dispensary.

At the centre of the transparent tank, perched on a dark plinth, was *something*. Something alive. Strain as he might, Wood couldn't see it properly. The light was too dim, and something seemed to be fogging his brain, as though his thoughts were undergoing some unknowable, and subtly terrifying, filtering process. He rubbed his forearms, unsure what was meant to happen next. His flesh was screaming for him to leave as quickly as possible.

Control it. Nothing's going to happen.

Easy for you to say!

'M Hazel and Mister Wood Javier McCorkindale,' said a thin, bubbling, nasal voice. There was a horrific frothing sound, like air being sucked into severed, bleeding windpipes. 'It is good, so good to see you. Hazel – it seems … an eternity since your angelic presence graced my empty little universe.'

The words seemed to infect the air, worming into his protesting ears and brain like the parasitic worms he'd watched in documentaries in Juniper's library. His vision spun. Hazel hooked a supportive arm around his. 'As you know,' she said, doggedly, 'I've been busy.'

Much frothing and grating. 'Hmm. Heh. And your labours have clearly borne fruit.'

Wood could tell that Hazel was suddenly irritated. 'None of the credit is due to me. I didn't have to ask or persuade. He volunteered.'

Squirming silence. Wood swayed, fighting an overpowering wave of claustrophobia, as though the chamber was saturated with too many thoughts. He took a breath to steady himself, but the air itself felt unclean and thick, almost oily. Black patches began to crawl across his vision.

'I will look at you, Wood McCorkindale. Come close against the glass where I can see you properly. My eyes are not very effective.'

Wood looked at Hazel with a jolt of alarm. Only her reassuring mental presence kept him from total panic. Numb-faced, he shuffled forwards, fixing his eyes firmly on a rock visible through the other side of the chamber. Feeling something smooth and cold against his outstretched fingers, he almost jumped. He froze, steadied by his hands against the glass, unable to keep from his face the horror and revulsion he felt.

'Look at me,' demanded the frothing voice. 'Look at my eyes.'

He ground his teeth. He was going to faint. Or vomit. Or both. *No.*

'Look at me. What you fear most is in your imagination. When fears are given shape, they lose their potency, like dreams in the light of the day. Look at me!'

He struggled, but the words had somehow cancelled control of his own body. Like a terrified schoolboy, he found his head turned, as if by a great hand, his eyes brought to bear on those of the creature in the tank.

Watery, pale, and faintly opaque, their pupils were rounded star shapes, over which fluids seeped from functionless, transparent eyelids. They were soft, ruined eyes – yet, as they stared back at him, he saw in them something unimaginably, appallingly vast. For one petrifying instant he felt that he was staring at the abyss of creation itself and not just seeing, but *understanding*, what true insignificance meant.

The part of him that he'd trained to function regardless of fear took in the rest of the picture. The eyes bulged from a mask of thinly fleshed bone above a gaping triangular nostril divided by a pale, roughly central hairline. Where a mouth should have been there was only a flap: dull, tendril-fringed tissue, which writhed constantly, dripping mucous.

Where a skull should have been, a vastly distended brain extended several metres behind the face-mask like a dark maggot. Webbed by blood vessels as thick as a finger, and sprinkled with nodules and seeping lesions, it was supported in a cradle of dark plastic. The creature possessed no chin, that he could see. The neck was a collection of tubes and rings of bright cartilage, clearly visible through the thin membrane which covered them. Processes and spikes of bone emerged through the skin around the creature's spine, which was twisted sideways at almost a right-angle to the head. Twisted stumps jerked spastically where arms and shoulders should have been. Below what passed for a chest, the body ended, in a collection of clear pipes visibly pumping fluids between the apparition and the metal turntable on which it perched.

Wood felt his stomach convulse. It was not so much from the creature's appearance, but the malaise of the air itself. He shuddered uncontrollably.

'So,' frothed the voice. 'Not, perhaps, as bad as you feared. But bad enough.'

'I … I'm sorry.'

Tom's voice rose in a choking splutter. 'Do not patronise me with your pity! Do you think I would expect not to generate revulsion in others, when I generate infinite disgust in myself?'

Wood swayed in silence. The eyes continued staring: impassively, but so very terribly. Wood felt that he was being sized up in some way. It felt like being devoured.

The mouth flap trembled and dripped. Tom rotated silently on his plinth towards Hazel.

'Hazel, I am pleased for you. My dear Wood, you must be a remarkable young man to hold the interest and devotion of one so special. I hope for a time when much happiness may come of it.'

There was a pause which seemed curiously like a sigh.

'I, alas, will not be here to see that. But my hopes and aspirations go with you both. A time of great change and loss is upon us. There is work which must be done. Unwilling as you may be, young ones, to embrace the judgement of an unfeeling cosmos, you will find that much of this burden falls at your feet.'

Wood glanced at Hazel. Frowning, she silently shook her head.

'Wood: you must return to your spacecraft and make the modifications you have been planning. I cannot overstress the importance of this. You must complete them within the next

Haven month and a half. When the time comes, you will know what you must do.'

Though he was too distracted by his situation to pay proper attention, Wood was startled. He found the words branded on his memory.

'Hazel, dearest child. Please, you must remember this: when the time comes, return to Haven. I beg of you both, remember this! Changes are coming.'

The writhing of the creature's body intensified, and then was still. Hazel's frowned intensified. 'What changes?

'You will know when the time comes.'

Tom became silent and motionless but for the twitching of his mouth-flap. The feeling in the air increased until it was positively hostile.

AS HE STUMBLED after Hazel back down the dark confines of the tunnel, tension and nausea drained from Wood's body like poisoned blood. By the time they reached the cave entrance, the feeling was like awaking from a bad dream. They scurried, blinking, into dim sunlight percolating through low clouds.

'Short meeting.'

Hazel heaved aside the door of the SEV, and he shivered.

Hazel … 'Sorry, but what the *hell* was that all about?'

She clambered up into the cabin without responding and strapped herself in as the lifting fan began to hum, building to a crescendo as Wood jumped up beside her. Hazel flung the SEV from the landing pad without waiting for him to close the door.

Skimming the treetops, they breasted an outcrop. Hazel only visibly relaxed when Tom's cave had disappeared from sight.

'Conversations with Tom tend to be like that,' she breathed, with a shudder. She took a deep breath and blew it out very slowly. 'You need to see them in the context of this predictive ability of his. The IQ system can't be used to measure his intellect: it'd be like trying to measure the speed of light with a ruler.

'You and I perceive only one instant of time – one point along our worldline – at once.' *Tom doesn't suffer such restrictions.* 'His past, present and future are contemporaneous. You might think that would make him omniscient, but things are …

complicated. Worldlines are actually like a fantastically intricate tree, with a selection process governing possible futures. Tom can apparently see which of an infinite number of possible futures are most likely, but not which will happen. Or has already happened, from his point of view.'

The spindly tops of taller trees zipped past on either side as Wood processed this – or tried to. Presently, Hazel shook her head.

'But I'm puzzled why he was so insistent about you getting your ship fixed up,' she went on. 'And that talk of "changes" and "when the time comes" …' Her fingers tightened around the joywheel. 'Time for what? Why does he have to be so *cryptic* all the time!'

She watched the forest roll past in nervous silence, eyes dark.

I'm really worried, she admitted eventually, half to herself. 'The way he was talking, he expects to die – soon. Changes!' she spat. 'Amber's light, if everything's about to go down the shithole, then why, in the name of the Great Mother, can't he just damn well come out with it and say so?'

22

FUNNY BACTERIAL COUNTS

RANDAL BRIGHTSTONE SAT in his favourite swing chair cradling a mug of sweet-smelling green tea. Fingering his balding head, he propped his feet on the lowest rail of the veranda, mulling over the day's findings at the laboratory, wondering what they might mean.

It was all quite bizarre. He'd repeated the cultures several times, just to be certain. Five repeats, in all. The isolation unit had been functioning perfectly, as far as it was possible to tell.

He'd racked his brain to pinpoint possible sources of contamination. He was buggered if he could think of a single one.

He bared his teeth, exasperated.

There was, he realised with dismay, only one thing for it. He would need to gather more samples, being particularly rigorous with the methodology this time, just to be sure. He would video everything and ask some of Haven's other biologists to review his methods.

He had a strong and dispiriting feeling that this would only generate the same results.

A nearby noise intruded on his introspection. He looked up from the patch of leaf litter he'd been unwittingly scrutinising to see his life partner dismounting one of the town's little two-seater electric buggies. The buggy towed a wooden trailer weighed down with bales of creamy wool from the town's herd of vicuñas, which roamed the foothill meadows of the Snowfires at the back of Juniper township.

She called to him, and walked round to the trailer, shouldering a bundle with much exaggerated puffing. He waved absently back.

'You could at least help,' she complained as she trod heavily up the steps. Randal grunted, and stomped down to the trailer as

Willow dumped her bundle on the veranda by the old loom. He hoisted a bale silently on to one shoulder, and then, single-handed, a second on to the other. She gave him a quizzical look, shielding her eyes from sunlight filtering through the trees.

'Anything wrong, love? You seem distracted.'

'Not really,' he muttered. He walked with some difficulty up the steps and dumped his bales beside the first.

'Willy-waver,' growled Willow, returning for another bale. 'You're not twenty any more, you know. You'll do yourself a mischief.' Randal's nose wrinkled. Slightly breathless from the exertion, he put his hands on his hips, exaggerating his paunch.

'I don't know. It's just …' He moistened his lips. 'I got some funny bacterial counts at the lab. It's weird. I was doing a plate count of soil samples. Must have got contaminated somehow. A real nuisance – the whole batch, hundreds of the things, from all over Carolsland. For the monitoring programme. They're the ones I spent the last four weeks collating.'

'How annoying,' Willow called out, hefting another bale and hoisting it more awkwardly over a shoulder. 'The whole batch?' She squinted. 'That sounds unlikely. What d'you mean, funny counts?' She began negotiating the steps.

'It's probably nothing.' He gazed at where the wall met the dusty floorboards. 'Counts were generally well within expected ranges … except for this thing I don't think I've even seen before, at least, not in the wild. Outwardly bacilliform, but very primitive. A cyanobacterium.' He pursed his lips and peered for a few moments off into the trees. 'As I say, probably just contamination.'

Willow dropped her bale with a puff. 'From where, though? You say you haven't seen it before.'

'Hmm.'

He ran his tongue over his lower teeth, probing their crooked edges.

'Darling … could you spare a couple of days? I think I should run the tests again. Hose down the drones just to be sure and send 'em off for a batch of new samples. Go out and take some manually too. I'd like your gene ecologist's input, if that's okay.'

She blinked at this. 'Sure, love. I've a batch of jerseys to do, but I guess clothes can wait.'

'I think this is important enough to take precedence anyway,' said Randal, suddenly convinced that this was not sloppy lab procedure on his part. Willow, he saw, had quickly picked up on his change of mood.

'What do you think it is?'

'That's what we have to find out. I don't see any point in alerting anyone else. At least, not yet.'

23

NOT ENTIRELY COMPATIBLE

WOOD PEERED PAST the rising and falling of Hazel's midriff, through the control room's selectively transparent hull, and into hyperspace. Its discomfiting blankness was framed by the edge of the freight pallet, whose strangely organic look was shared by most modern structures engineered to be both strong and light.

After a few moments, he turned his gaze back to Hazel. She was wearing briefs and one of the T-shirts the Havenners had given him, which was slightly too small for her. Her bare legs hung over the shaggy armrest from her comfortable sprawl in his lap. They were sturdy legs, shapely and tanned, with scars here and there. *Like the rest of her.* Covering them was a down of brown hairs, which, like most Haven women he'd seen, she hadn't depilated. The smell of her so close was making his head spin.

He ran a palm down her shin, causing her to murmur sleepily and nuzzle against his shoulder. Besides the shape of her face and her curvaceous solidity, there was a natural curl to her expressive lips which he found entrancing. Even groggy and nauseated from his sterilisation 'hangover' as Hazel had described it – unpleasant, but less so than his original infection with microorganisms – he felt things leap inside him every time he looked at her.

It was three days since Tumbleweed had returned the pair of them to Gamma station. Wood had found the ecosphere unexpectedly claustrophobic after months on a planet. So excited had Tink been at Wood's return that, breaking almost every local traffic rule, he'd flown *Oscar* in mad loops around the structure's docking bay, causing consternation amongst the station's human and org inhabitants as the lumbering machine, a quarter of the size of the fragile ecosphere itself, created dancing shadows around the translucent interior like some monstrous demented moth.

On entering the control room, minutes had passed before anything could be got out of the AI but ecstatic gibberish. Hazel had found this wonderful. *He's like a puppy!*

After introductions, Tink had greeted her with embarrassing formality. 'Are you a female, a woman, a lady?'

'I am. Yes.'

'You're covered up. Could you please remove your clothing so I can see your body? I've studied Wood's and the things he likes doing with parts of it. Can I see yours now too?'

Wood had watched from Hazel's eyes as he turned almost purple. Hazel had just laughed. She'd even kicked off her clothes as the AI had asked, providing a balletic twirl before Tink's control room pickup. Wood had watched with every bit as much interest as the machine.

'That's all you're getting.'

'Your body looks very nice. I prefer it to Wood's, which is too thin and lumpy. I like your breasts a lot. Perhaps I should be a woman?' The AI's avatar gyrated suddenly feminine hips within a skirt worthy of a strip bar, its face still terribly male.

'Tink!' wailed Wood, hands clasped over his eyes.

'Just what we need: a machine with a gender crisis.' *Oh Woody, he's lovely!*

(Groan) *Now, don't go getting all maternal on me.*

Tink had greeted the news of their intent to marry with an unexpected lack of reaction. 'Does that mean you'll both be living in *Oscar* now, then?'

For a while afterwards, Wood had been very quiet.

The Havenners operated two large and very old Panspacial interstellar tugs. Each was shaped like a fat bullet, with powerful thrusters at the four points of the compass held on stout arms which also supported the enormous TFG hoop. The immense coupling at each tug's rear was designed to trail a snake of cargo pallets. The captain of the *Happy Lugger*, the stained workhorse currently speeding them through hyperspace, was a colourful character of mysterious origins by the name of Pilong Watana. According to Hazel, he hadn't left his beloved tug for more than two days at a time in a quarter century.

'Doesn't he get lonely?'

She pulled a face. *Doesn't seem to.* 'He has friends in every port of call. Mostly lady friends – he's quite notorious. Some tag along on a regular basis.' *Often in twos or threes.*

And you wonder why he never leaves his tug?

Pilong had deftly used the Happy Lugger's arsenal of manipulative arms to manoeuvre the wrecked stern of the confederation cruiser *Born to Destroy* into an open cargo pallet, where grapples and containment fields clamped it into place and secured any loose debris. He'd offered to do the same for *Oscar*. Bristling, Wood had responded by squeezing his vessel between the decks of the second pallet with a speed and careless ease Hazel found both highly impressive and very irritating.

Boys. Idiots, the lot of you.

'Light load this.' Pilong beamed down at them from the control room's main screen, his eyes glimpses of white in skin almost as dark as his beard. Their conversation was being transmitted on tight beam. 'Have you there in no time. Biggest I ever had was ninety pallets big as the one you're in, all twisting and rattling away. Needed thirty clip-on TFGs to make the jump. Slowing down was hairy as hell, let me tell you. Right, I'm hitching you up in a minute, so no more uncle Pilong I'm afraid. Tons of privacy for you to do anything you fancy.'

He'd laughed a great booming, evil cackle, and his face was replaced by a view of the rear of the tug; a dirty four-pointed star against the blackness. It slipped out of sight beyond the first pallet and reversed towards it, leaving just a protruding thruster leg visible. *Dirty old man*, Hazel had said in a good mental impression of a growl. A faint boom was transmitted through the hull as the tug linked with its payload. Almost instantly, light had speared from the tip of the visible leg, and the stars began to shift.

Three days into their journey now, they were due to make their first jump back into realspace, near a planet called Terra Nova. 'Got to stop and fill my baby up,' Pilong had told them, reappearing on the screen without warning.

And there was me thinking we were stopping to refuel.

Wood had been nonplussed for a moment, but then laughed.

THE MOST DISTANT of Haven's small network of supportive and defensive 'outpost' planets and stations, Terra Nova was a mottled brown ball of rock and dust whose atmosphere had long ago fled into space, leaving relict polar caps of frozen carbon dioxide. In a magnification of its drab plains, Wood could see clusters of shiny droplets catching the sunlight.

Environment domes, Hazel explained. *We call them endomes. They grow vegetables there, and even have some trees.* 'That's our main decoy,' she said aloud. 'The hope is, and it's a vain one I imagine, that the Pukes will find it first and be satisfied they've found Haven.'

There were three, longer, jumps to come, and Wood was already restless. It surprised him how acutely he missed the trees, open skies, and the wind on his face. It somehow felt as though he missed them for all of his previous life as well. He wanted to make up for lost time.

And yet, here he was, heading in precisely the wrong direction.

So do you really think it'll work? Hazel was looking up at his face, her head raised sleepily from his shoulder. Feeling his brooding thoughts, she'd asked mainly to distract him.

'Oh yes.' Face brightening, he peered into hers. He wasn't handsome in the classic, masculine mould – his nose wasn't prominent enough, his face dominated by his liquid blue eyes. 'Cute' was how her peers might have described him, now that he'd recovered from his earlier emaciation. When one of his sudden grins appeared, however, it was like sunlight through rainclouds. This and his diminutive leanness kept making her want to embrace him. To *protect* him. He flushed, experiencing a moment of vertigo, not used yet to this constant feedback; of experiencing conversations and interactions from both perspectives at once, and seeing his own face respond. *It should work*, he went on, rubbing an arm. 'I haven't done, or … um, orchestrated anything practical before in anything except simulations. But I spent quite a bit of my time at schooltech working on sims of drive units and hyperspacial field generators. I'm fairly sure it'll work.'

Hazel was less convinced. She grasped his hand. Felt resistance but drew his forearm gently towards her and kissed the scars. *And if you're wrong?*

He twitched, looking distractedly at his arm, wanting to cover it up. A shrug. *Same as with any prototype, I suppose.*

No. Don't hide. This is part of you. 'Which is?' she asked, aloud.

He nibbled his lip, his mind for a moment darting in bewildering directions with equally bewildering speed. She'd never been in a mind like this. Half the time, it was quite impossible for her to keep track. 'It'll require very fine tuning,' he said. 'Which we can only do by simulation. If the Thomson Field isn't integrated properly …'

'Yes?'

'… We could find ourselves somewhere very strange.'

Strange?

Strange, yes. 'And not entirely compatible with, um, our continued existence.' *At least, not in a conscious or recognisable state.*

24

COSMIC SHIT-SHOVELLING

IN THE INTENSE LIGHT of a young red star, the Orbital Self-Contained Asteroid Refinery hung, blood-red, against the stars, encased in the gridwork of a purpose-built construction rig. Six thousand kilometres below, the crimson and plum plains of the Freelancer colony world of Nugget rotated imperceptibly as a smaller, yet otherwise similar, rig was manoeuvred with utmost precision behind the first.

The squashed buckets of the mining vessel's old main thruster were gone. In its place, a massively reinforced new articulated mount grasped at space like an expectant hand.

Construction drones and manned heavy-duty manipulators buzzed in a small organised swarm around the amputation as the smaller rig drew inexorably closer. Finally, after a period of hesitation, the two frameworks met, docking clamps fusing them into a single unit; the new thruster – several hundred times more potent than the old, fitted with sophisticated clamshells which could deflect the thrust forwards, and ludicrously oversized in relation to the ship it was unwillingly thrust upon – slotting perfectly into the awaiting joint.

The swarm descended, welding and fusing, disrupting and resetting sub molecular glue which would bind the structure in bonds only the universe's most extreme forces could break.

Hugging the perimeter of the industrial complex's observation bubble was a semicircular bar top served by high stools. Lounging chairs occupied the room's centre, with brochure terminals scattered on shiny coffee tables between plates of nibbles and cans of beer. Bathed by the red glare from outside, Wood occupied his stool, toying with a cocktail, his face set in the mask it adopted when he was stressed.

His anxiety was understandable, Hazel thought. If Tom was to be believed, some important part of the future of her people and their charges hinged on the rusty theoretical knowledge of an academically frustrated undergraduate.

'Phase one over,' he murmured as sparks fanned into space from the join between *Oscar* and its new propulsion unit. 'More or less. In eight cycles.' He stuck out his bottom lip. 'Pretty efficient, these Lancers of yours.'

Amidst a quiet crowd of technicians overseeing the process from behind the panoramic viewing window in the neighbouring control room, Lorn Navotna was smiling to himself, having overheard the remark. It was true, he was thinking. He was fucking good at what he did. As was everyone in Nugget. Sufficiently so to have caused skirmishes with neighbouring colonies who were suffering as a result.

'Unfortunately,' Wood went on, 'the hard part comes next. I was wondering how to solve the problem of leaving the TFG ring exposed on the outside of the hull.' Unexpectedly, his face lit up. 'Then I realised – why bother? Why not put it inside?'

'But … they have to be on the outside. Don't they?'

Wood shot a glance at Nugget's chief astroengineer, who was watching from an eye-corner as he manipulated an army of interface fields. Packed with information, at least a hundred of the coloured bubbles were suspended in a floor-to-ceiling holoscreen showing the busy construction rig.

'Hey, don't mind me,' chirped Lorn, a smile cleaving his ochre face as his hands darted around the screen. 'I'm not interested in your ship. S'far as I'm concerned, you're paying us – and handsomely too, I might add – so we'll do what you want, no questions asked. If you *did* ask me though,' heavy eyebrows pushed slightly together as he waved a hand at his screen, 'I'd say you were wasting your money on an antiquated bucket of bolts like that – and, hell, that thruster?' He shook his head. 'Ain't even gonna to ask. Gonna space all your fuel in seconds, that thing is. But customer knows best, as always.' He gave a sly wink, and returned to his bubbles.

'Thank you *so* much,' purred Hazel, turning back to Wood and pushing her dark glasses back up her nose. *You were saying?*

I was about to say that the actual process of translation between hyperspace and truespace is pretty brutal and inefficient. There's little finesse or even understanding involved, beyond calibrating the form and output of the field. The only reason TFGs are invariably external, where they're horribly exposed to all kinds of damage, is that that's where they work most efficiently.

Concentrating, he built Hazel a series of graphic diagrams which somehow showed her the whole of *Oscar*, inside and out, at the same time. Hazel realised, with a pang of envy she couldn't quite hide, that they were better than what she might have constructed, with a lifetime's practice. Feeling the pride and pleasure behind them, her envy twisted into a pang of feelings for him so strong that it was all she could do not to embrace him.

The energy drain is so enormous, he went on, *most ships can only carry fuel for three moderate jumps in and out of hyperspace. With their fields damped by layers of toughened hull material, all but the largest would struggle to make even one jump.* Oscar *doesn't have that problem. All I need to do is compensate for the Thomson field being distorted and weakened by thicker layers of matter.*

Yes, she said, brightening. 'I see.'

Navotna frowned at the sudden remark.

The spinning hoop containing the generators will still need to be not far below the surface, so it might constitute a weak point, but it'll be infinitely better than having it outside. The generators from the cruiser will be far more powerful than we'll really need anyway, so they should cope just fine.

Hazel took his hands, pressed her nose and forehead to his, and looked at him in a way which made him feel very wobbly.

Genius partner.

He looked, and felt, acutely surprised and embarrassed. *Not your partner yet.*

There was a loud cough. Lorn came striding out of the control room, rubbing his hands together. 'You'll be pleased to know we've finished the job, more or less,' he said, as they pulled apart. 'They're just tidying up bits and bods now. Before we leave for the next part though, I want a word with you.'

He came confidentially close and looked seriously between the two of them.

'My friends, that wreck you brought in was a Panspacial Mark Eight Eraser-Class fast cruiser. One singularly lethal death machine. According to our sources, the Pekkers never lost one before. Not in accidents, not in combat, nothing.' His eyes narrowed. 'Where the fuck did you find it?'

Wood opened his mouth to speak but thought better of it. *It's Okay*, Hazel told him. *He'll be impressed. Lancers are well into recreational drugs: he'll probably send you away with a hamper of them.*

But what if IPEC hear of it? I'm sure the Lancers aren't the only ones with spies.

Of course not. They'll make the connection anyway. But why would they link it with us?

Despite her reassurance, he both felt her unease and shared her intuition of matters beginning to slide out of control. Smoothing his hands along the sleeves covering his arms, he looked at his feet.

'I didn't exactly find it. It found me.'

The other man's face darkened.

'Don't worry,' he added hastily. 'It was a long, long way from here. I, um, rammed it. At the time I didn't think I had any choice.'

'I don't believe you,' said Lorn, flatly.

Wood looked at him and shrugged.

'What … you mean, in *that* thing?' the engineer jabbed an incredulous thumb in the direction of *Oscar*'s half-hidden outline. Wood smiled weakly and shrugged again. 'Mister, I ought to be either dressing you down for some spectacularly cosmic shit shovelling, or …'

He regarded the younger man in a perplexed, almost agonised manner. Wood was trying not to convey anything in his face. For a moment, Hazel was with him back in *Oscar*'s control room, watching a legless, baking corpse drift in terrible detail past the cabin.

Not your fault. You saved us.

No answer.

'Well I'm damned. Well I'm *damned*.' Having failed to notice Hazel's involuntary spasm, Lorn clapped Wood on the shoulder. 'This colony lost more than five thousand to them and their hellish incursions over the years. That's why we relocated so far out. I tell you, if you can prove to us what you just said, you might just get this refit on the house!'

Yeah, Hazel said, pushing her sunglasses up her nose. *And other fairy stories.*

25

PERIOD PAINS

IT WAS OBVIOUS TO OLEA that the long voyage, which had somehow contrived to be both tedious nerve-shredding, was nearly over. There were hints of body language which, in anyone else, would have been routine.

For Jo, they were extravagant.

He would tap fingernails on the console, staring out of the window as if imagining a different view. He sat straighter in his chair, and when he caressed her it was as though restraining some flamboyant urge. His eyes seemed to shine. The last leg through hyperspace had been a long one, and, while they'd found ways to pass the time, Jo's quietly vented restlessness had grown palpable. *Nearly home!*

'Prepare for hyperspace exit, one minute,' said the starship's blandly smooth voice.

'So, is this actually Haven now?' Curled sideways in the co-pilot's chair, Olea couldn't help smiling at his suppressed fidgeting. 'If it's not, I'm afraid I might to have to scrape you off the ceiling before we get there.'

He gave her a slightly sharp look, as though unaccustomed to his thoughts being so transparent, or being spoken to in this manner – and, while not actively hostile, ambiguous in his feelings about it. 'No,' he said, 'I'm afraid this is as far as we're allowed without a medical. This is where you get your inoculations.'

She gulped. 'The little creatures?'

He nodded, a sadistic little quirk to his mouth vying with concern in his eyes. 'Don't worry unduly. I won't lie, it's rotten for a couple of tendays, but it's fine after that. I had to be completely sterilised before I left, so I'll need to go through the same rigmarole. We can suffer in synchrony.' His brow furrowed. 'What's the matter?'

Jesus, fuck! 'Uh … nothing.' Her face burned. 'I need the toilet. Excuse me.'

'But we're entering real space in –' he glanced at the countdown. 'Fifteen seconds! Is it that desperate? You *really* don't want to leave hyperspace on the toilet.'

'Sorry.'

Extracting herself from the chair, she almost ran to the shower and toilet cubicle.

JO WATCHED IN SURPRISE as Olea sprinted to the rear of the cabin, flinging aside the toilet door and pushing through it in such haste that she careened off the frame. The gossamer-light door slammed shut. He listened for a moment, then swivelled his seat to face forwards again as the strange blankness outside began to twist. Stars and blackness were wrung out of it like water from a cloth, accompanied by that interminable, directionless yanking sensation which not even the most advanced inertial suppression could eliminate.

Ahead, a bright star appeared against dark dust clouds veining an instantly familiar lilac nebula. *Trene's Veil*. A magnification showed the crescent of a planet with the slowly shifting spark of Alpha Station just visible against its night side.

Despite himself, Jo heaved a sigh of relief which seemed to involve his entire body. He collapsed back into the seat, a smile leaking through as some of the tension of the past few weeks began to ebb, leaving him exhausted.

He rubbed his eyes. When he looked at his fingers, he was surprised to see that they were wet.

STAGGERING INTO THE CUBICLE, clutching her abdomen, Olea shoved the door closed as she tore down her knickers, sat on the toilet seat which obligingly unfolded, and braced herself against the soft wall pad behind it.

What's happening! What is happening to me?

The pain had come on suddenly, so intensely that she wanted to scream. It was like a skewer inside her. Like period pain, but worse than she'd ever experienced. She wanted to cry out for help, or just for an end to the pain – but what could Jo do? In some obscurely shameful way, she felt that complaining to him would be letting him down.

She clenched her teeth, eyes screwed so tightly shut that she saw patterns, trying to control her breathing. She barely registered the hyperspace jump when it came. She relaxed her bladder. Felt it drain. She thought for a moment that she'd felt movement between her legs, but the pain departed with the last drops of urine, replaced by a dull ache.

Olea breathed several deep, slow breaths until she was sure she felt better.

She stood, dizzily, and examined herself. A thin trail of dark blood was dripping down her thigh. She sat back down. Pressed the sanitiser button. Felt the deliciously soothing spray of astringently-scented cleansing agents. She tried to calculate when her next period was due. Then she remembered.

It wasn't, of course. Unless …

Unless those idiot doctors fucked up.

She sat there for a moment and scowled. Then she shuffled to the bathroom dispensary, her knickers trailing from one ankle, and ordered a panty liner.

Christ.

Would be just my kind of luck.

She hesitated briefly at the door, pondering what to tell Jo. Her personal problems were unlikely something he'd want to be bothered with right now. She pictured the spark in his eyes replaced by worry.

Her hormones were probably just shaken up after being on the run for several tendays. Often, it was only after the source of stress was gone that the body reacted badly.

'FEEL BETTER?' Jo asked her, brushing a hand down her arm as she sat back beside him. Olea nodded. Then she shook her head.

'Don't know what's up with me lately. Probably all the excitement.'

He studied her. She could feel sweat on her forehead. She gazed defensively back.

'You're probably right,' he said, though his eyes didn't leave hers. 'I feel completely spent myself. All the same …' creases appeared between his eyebrows, 'you look terribly pale.'

'I'm okay.' When he still wouldn't look away, she glared. 'I'm *sure*.'

The speakers crackled to life. 'Calling unidentified vessel! Identify yourself on tight beam, repeat tight beam, immediately, repeat *immediately*.' The voice's accent was very strong, similar to Jo's, but much thicker. It was male, high-pitched, and sounded close to panic.

Jo touched the console.

'This is Jo Fox. Pass sequence Macropus rufus zero-four-four, zed-eight-six-five-alpha. Priority docking order, make ready medical lab for two persons, prepare to receive and despatch priority communications immediately, repeat immediately.'

There was a short silence.

'*Professor?*'

Animated voices began babbling in the background. Olea could just make out the words 'really him?' She smiled to herself.

'Professor,' said the first voice, sounding incalculably relieved. 'It's good to have you back.'

'It's good to *be* back.' A grin spread until it stretched almost between Jo's ears. 'You've no idea how much. I recognise that voice. Who are you?'

'Me? ... oh, I'm Amon. Amon Kachutwalla.' Jo considered for a moment.

'The elephants. How's the project going?'

'It's going well, Professor, quite well.' The man sounded like a delighted child. 'While you were gone ...' there was a hiatus, after which the voice sounded closer to the pickup, 'we released the first Indian elephant into Sampsonia. She died, sad to say, but we are learning where we went wrong, and we have two more to be released soon.'

'That's promising news. I'll see you shortly and you can tell me more.'

'Yes Professor! I look forward to it.'

A hollowed-out forty-kilometre nugget of crater-pocked rock, Alpha Station was, according to Jo, both the largest space station operated by the Havenners and the oldest, having provided the bulk of the raw minerals used for their early expansion. It revolved lazily around a non-rotating central spindle whose exposed end resembled a tarnished bottle top. Manoeuvring thrusters thumping, the starship brought them smoothly towards a rectangular door. Olea watched as low sunlight caught environment domes on the cratered planet below, making them shine like drops of oil.

The door yawned, engulfing them. Though the station was minuscule compared to the deep-space complexes and refuelling stations they'd visited on their dash across the confederation, the port's dim interior was quietly impressive.

'Looks almost derelict,' she commented, eyeing empty bays sliding past and rows of docking booms grasping at the vacuum like hands. They looked part-finished, as though needing spacecraft to complete them.

'It was our most important asset for more than a century, and Terra Two – the planet we're orbiting – was where most of our people lived. It's run by a skeleton crew these days. Now that we're self-sufficient, the focus of our society is a long way from here. Alpha Station's really just a staging post now.'

The ship slowed and there was a muffled thump as the docking arm connected. A small crowd of colourfully-dressed people was gathering within the environment bubble on the dock outside. As the scene became stationary, Olea's eye lit on something green and alien-looking attached to one of the docking ports.

'Jo?' Clutching his arm, she pointed towards the strange object. 'Jo … please tell me you know what the hell that … *thing* is over there?'

'Ah.' He smiled, thinly. 'Some things will take a lot of explanation. For now, though, I'm very tired.' It was true: his eyelids seemed to be trying to close of their own volition. 'Remind me when we're settled in, and I'll arrange access to a library for you later, if you like.'

26

DOWNFALL

MODERN MACHINES were built with one thing in mind: to be easy to use.

Unfortunately, this philosophy did not extend to the poor mugs who had to maintain the wretched things. Probably, thought Beam, darkly, because the idiots designing, and buying, and using them, were almost never the ones who had look after them. If the people who ordered them also had to maintain them, transport engineering might have evolved very differently, and maintenance technicians might have kept their nerves, their looks and their hair a good bit longer.

Twisted sideways on both knees, with one arm braced in a highly unnatural position behind him, Beam Marlin used his free hand to close and reseal the narrow access hatch to the chamber enclosing the starship's reactor, having physically checked the plasma column's regulation unit. Like every such system, this one was self-diagnosing – even self-healing, to an extent – but, also like every such system, its thinker was both obstinately dedicated and hideously complicated, and therefore (like most highly strung intellects) not above making the occasional blazingly obvious oversight.

A thorough inspection and service was what he'd been told, and that's what Beam was determined to provide. The fact that this was the ship in which *the Professor* had escaped the clutches of the Pukes – from Earth, no less – made it less of a chore. As he squirmed backwards in his claustrophobic burrow and closed the reactor chamber's cowl of shielding, he even found himself smiling.

Contorting, he turned his attention to the power conduits for the field generators, using his little touchpad to order a blanket check of the complex maze of circuits involved in field manipulation. The ship was not exactly factory spec, he reflected, which didn't make his job any easier. Humming a tune by one of Haven's currently popular crop of young singers, he waited on his back for a few minutes while the diagnostic programs completed their simulations.

'That's your innards, Professor,' he mused aloud, when the results were to his satisfaction. 'Now for the outside.'

Strictly speaking, this was the wrong way around, but the least unpleasant part of a task was always better left until last. Whistling now, he unsealed the outer maintenance hatchway with a code from his terminal and squeezed gracelessly back through it on to the bay's echoing maintenance deck. The warden's instructions had been to check for mites, or mite holes. There were not likely to be any, he'd been assured. The Professor had seen to this, in his usual thorough manner. It was just a routine check.

From the footwell of the giant maintenance waldo which hung from a rail in the bay's convex ceiling, he began running a scanner methodically over the starship's upper surface, looking for the tell-tale burrows left by the miniature spybots.

'Nothing,' he murmured contentedly after fifteen minutes of painstaking sweeping. He continued whistling: a 7/8 Balkan jazz tune this time, by Beyond the Veil, his favourite local band, from Terra Two. Beam had been in a good mood even before the Prof's arrival. Just three days ago his daughter had given birth to a baby boy – three weeks early but doing fine – and although he'd been unable to make the birth, he'd been given leave to travel to see her tomorrow. The arm set him down on the deck once more and he continued on foot, tracing the scanner contentedly over the starship's travel-soiled underside.

'Okay, what have we here?'

Bleeping softly, the scanner was flashing a question mark on its little popup screen.

He zoomed in on the offending area, which was targeted by a flashing red square. Finally, the device highlighted the subject of its query using a small, flashing circle, just above and to one side of the left main landing leg.

He squinted at the spot, but could see nothing, and double checked the scanner to be sure.

It still wasn't happy.

Beam scratched his stubbly chin. On impulse, he brushed dust away from the offending spot then stared it, slowly bringing his head down in an arc until his cheek was pressed against the ship's dirty, but flawlessly smooth surface.

There, picked out by the distorted reflections of the bay as he looked across the surface of the hull, was a scarcely visible depression.

Beam sucked his teeth. He wasn't whistling now. It definitely wasn't a mite hole, although it was almost small enough. He didn't know *what* it was. Yet he knew intuitively that it should not be there.

An old repair? It was possible, he mused, that it was a product of one of the performance-enhancing modifications The Professor had made to his ship. Or perhaps the repaired site of a micrometeorite impact?

He called up detailed specifications and an interactive plan of the ship's model. It was a Hyundai Solar Corona, according to the station grid. The customisation work, he was relieved to see, was on file as well. After a brief set of queries the plans confirmed that, even with the described modifications, there was no pre-existing structural reason for the imperfection. He wondered briefly if quality control could explain it. According to the computer, Hyundai was a prestige marque, so that seemed doubly unlikely.

Intensely involved now, Beam sent a wheeled drone to fetch an ultrasound scanner.

Scratching his chin distractedly, he paced as he waited. Alarm bells were sounding loudly in his head. *No sense telling anyone quite yet.* A few seconds later the drone scuttled up to him, clutching the handheld device in one outstretched claw. He plugged it into his touchpad, then placed its two contacts against the hull either side of the depression.

Slowly, generated from ultrasounds of a frequency which could make even the subatomically-bastardised material of the ship's hull vibrate, a 3D picture built up of the hull's internal structure. It did little to lessen his perplexity.

One thing, however, was much clearer. He was sure that all was not well.

'FOUR MONTHS!' exclaimed Amon Kachutwalla, with feeling, 'and already I am looking forward to getting back to Mahogany Bay. That's on Haven, miss Olea – and you should see the

Jacaranda trees at this time of year! The town is alive with purple, and the scent of a thousand blooms. My son, Durrell, will have started school now. I miss my family, but it is not considered sensible to bring whole families this close to the edge of our little part of the universe. And so, I must be content with pictures, and the messages on the missile which comes for us here each week. Oh – my Rachel! How I wish that it is already four months time.'

For a moment, the look in the thirty-year-old man's dark eyes made Olea yearn for something about which she could feel so strongly. Then she glanced at Jo, who was lounging in the futon opposite, his modest yet somehow imposing frame framed by a big viewport spattered with stars. Listening to Amon, he was staring just as distantly into his alcohol glass.

They'd been on Alpha Station something like five Renascido days now. Half that time seemed to have been spent in sleep so complete that she didn't even remember going to bed. The station was an intriguing place: shabby, but clean, with odd little homely flourishes using materials she didn't recognise. Paintings were everywhere – almost entirely impressionistic, for reasons Amon had told her were more to do with security than artistic expression. Some of them were excellent. Others, given equal pride of place, were utterly childish, and she'd laughed when Jo had explained that they were, indeed, by children.

It was her first experience of spin-induced gravity. It still made her a little queasy. All the people she'd met had been embarrassingly deferential to Jo – Jesus would have enjoyed little more adoration, she thought. To her, they'd been polite. Other than Amon and a half-dozen others, however, they'd also been wary, their eyes a little too wide, their smiles strained. Some of them looked openly from her to Jo, as though silently questioning his wisdom in bringing her here.

She didn't blame them one bit.

Toying with her own glass, she tried to imagine what being without Jo would now be like.

He'd stolen from her the entire world she knew, replacing it irrevocably with one that was entirely strange, and not a little forbidding. What he'd done to her could be seen as appalling – for motives she'd yet fully to understand and had begun to suspect she never would.

And yet, she found herself thinking that her decision to go with him had, after all, been the right one.

As if he had *known*.

She was still waiting for the guilt to kick in. Guilt at abandoning her friends, her employers. Her dismal excuse for a family. It had failed to materialise.

Fuck them.

She'd been experimenting with this thought, trying it on for size. The truth was, it felt liberating. She'd had a great deal of time to think over the past few tendays. Time to view her previous life from the outside. She'd been dismayed to find little evidence that she'd truly be missed by anyone. Work would simply hire some other artist desperate for recognition. Dad would be just fine with his pension, his bridge club and his old pals from work. For more than a decade now, he'd not once visited or suggested meeting her. Any contact with him had been her doing.

And as for Randa ...

Well, her son had always had a knack of adapting his contacts to his prospects. His washed-up mother, he'd made silently but abundantly clear, remained on his contacts list out of obligation and a vague sense of pity. As years wore on it had seemed ever more that she shared genes with him and nothing else.

Her one twinge of real regret was Natalia. Even then, it was obvious in retrospect that her days as Natalia's best friend had been numbered. *Since I met Costos, things have moved up. I just want you to look at where you're going.*

Well, she'd done that. And now she was here, with the galaxy's most wanted man. *And I wonder what you'd make of that, Natalia my dear?*

In her short time aboard Alpha Station, she'd relaxed considerably – and not just compared to her journey on Jo's starship. Beneath their nervousness, the people she'd met seemed warm and straightforward. At her request, she'd been lent a primitive easel, and already found herself at the core of a tiny but enthusiastic amateur artists' group. Like Amon, all worked in the 'sterile' half of the space station, which handled Havenners bound for, or returning from, Lancer space. To her relief, given what she now knew of microorganisms, the decontamination procedures seemed exacting.

Tomorrow her course of inoculations was due to begin. Perversely, the thought thrilled her.

It felt like an initiation.

But what of the future? How would she occupy and support herself, now that she was finally here, among the Havenners? She had no idea what lay in store, yet found that, for perhaps the first time since she was a child, she didn't much care. She'd find something to do. Somewhere to be. It would be enough. She'd manage.

Was that naive?

Jo had offered to build her a treehouse. She hadn't known what one of those was, so he'd explained.

It was, quite literally, a small house, built out of wood in the branches of a living tree.

The thought made her heart beat faster. She wasn't sure what it would involve, or how practical it might be, but a treehouse sounded like the most magical thing she'd ever heard.

'This is Beam Marlin, technical, urgently calling Head Warden Amon Katch …' the voice on the intercom tripped over the name in its headlong rush. 'Sod this for a bucket of worms – Ame, are you there?'

Amon jabbed a finger at the device he wore strapped to his wrist. 'Go ahead Beamer.'

The voice was breathless. 'I was servicing the Prof's ship, doing a routine inspection. Couldn't find any mites, but …' there was a pause. 'This might sound stupid, but there was a carefully refilled tunnel just under three centimetres in diameter leading from the …' Another hesitation. 'The recycling tank of the toilet? To the outside of the ship. I want to think I'm paranoid, but I've quite a bad feeling about this.'

Jo sat slowly upright. His eyes narrowed, then grew wide. He raised his own wristwatch to his mouth as his stare swung on to Olea. 'The *toilet?* Are you sure? Definitely the toilet?'

'Professor? Yes – yes, I am.'

Olea stared numbly at the two faces now staring at her: one brown and puzzled, the other almost white with horror.

Jo sprang to his feet.

'Evacuate Alpha Station,' he roared. '*Immediately!* Full emergency protocols.' His voice was like a physical force. 'Evacuate Terra Nova as well, the whole planet – this is a general withdrawal from this solar system. Arm the station bombs, destroy everything. Send an encrypted message to Haven telling them we're compromised. *NOW!* You've all got five minutes to get off the station before I set off the damn bombs myself.'

His gaze fell back upon Olea like molten steel. He thrust out a damning finger.

'And get a sick bay on a ship ready to examine ... *her!*'

'What by the Great Mother's armpit-hair is going on?' protested Amon, though he raised his wrist back to his mouth as he sprang to his feet. 'You heard the Professor – evacuation order! Everyone *shift*. This is for real, guys, repeat: this is real. Auto-destruct in five and counting – whether you're out or not.'

Striding for the nearest door, he continued to pour orders into the intercom, which echoed his voice a fraction of a second later as a deafening cascade of noise. A piercing, unsettling scream began. It seemed to come from all sides. Its intensity went beyond mere noise, bypassing the conscious part of Olea's brain, instructing her legs to run.

But her legs wouldn't move. All she could do was stare through the viewport into space, head shaking.

No. No! What was happening? She didn't understand. Didn't *want* to understand.

Then, even as she was watching it, the area of space she was staring at changed.

Olea cried out as a vast, concave wall completely filled the viewing port, blotting out the stars. Blotched by shrinking phantoms of darkness, its surface seemed to squirm, like a film of translucent oil. In a corner of her vision she was conscious of Jo and Amon following her terrified gaze. She saw their knees buckle.

Recovering, Amon sprinted wildly for the door, shouting into his watch. Jo just knelt on the carpet where he'd fallen.

'No,' he cried, hands clawed. 'Please, not like this. Not *now!*'

He sprang up and advanced on Olea as though to intending to tear her apart. His eyes were seething pits.

'I should have known,' he growled. 'Oh hell, I should have known!'

Olea shook. Her eyes were transfixed by his. Her mouth worked to try, somehow, to explain, but no sounds came out of it.

Sorry! she mouthed. *I'm so sorry.*

An almost subliminal vibration began. It scythed into Olea's head, severing what remaining control she had over her body. She felt her bowels and bladder vent. Jo was staggering now, eyes rolling, shrieking as a wet patch spread from his groin.

'Bastards – *it's too soon!*'

Though his legs tottered, he somehow kept his feet, bellowing in fury. Olea felt the weight of her limbs drag her to the floor. Even her mind felt as though it was being crushed by gravity. Jo continued to lurch around like a drunken dancer, head clamped between his hands as though it was bursting. He staggered to the wooden chair Amon had occupied, and grasped it in his claws, spraying crimson spittle.

There was a distant boom. A stronger vibration ran through the station. Jo was hurled to the floor. He lay there, immobile, an arm trapped beneath his chest, eyes twitching. Sounds of distant explosions pervaded Olea's numbed brain. Then a much nearer boom rumbled through the station's broad corridors.

There were running footsteps. The staccato thump of a weapon, and a short scream.

Jo lurched from the floor. Eyes now hard and hideous, he hurled himself forward, seizing the chair, and – impossibly – raising it above his head. Olea's eyeballs felt glued into her skull. As he lunged beyond her vision, she couldn't make them follow him.

There was a gunshot. Then a clatter, and the sound of breaking wood.

A thump. A screech of pain and surprise.

Another gunshot.

Jo hurtled back into view, his head thudding into the floor, legs flipping and twisting through the air above him. He came to rest on his back in a tangle of his own limbs, a gleaming hole the size of a soup plate burned in the front of his shirt.

Olea wanted to scream. She tried, but nothing would come. Jo's body sighed. His head lolled towards her, eyes locking on to her own.

Jo! Jo!

He mouthed something, but she couldn't tell what it was. She ached to reach out to him, to hold his dying body against her as she waited for the end, but she couldn't even move her eyes away from his. They just stared at her, accusing. Hollowed out by the knowledge of her betrayal; his failure.

Jo! I didn't know! I didn't!

'Calter,' growled an oddly bland voice. 'That's him, you waste of air. If you've killed him …'

Spluttering noises. 'He … he was trying to kill me!'

'An aim with which I empathise. Perhaps I should finish the job?'

'I didn't know it was him.' The voice was thick with shock. 'Just saw some mad Freak coming at me with a chair. Everyone was meant to be out of action for Chrissake!' A gasp. 'So much for this fancy new nerve suppresser.'

There were barely heard noises. Then: 'Get on with it!'

'God, there's bones sticking out of my chest! Oh fuck, there's bones sticking out of my fucking chest!' Moaning. 'I think my wrist's broken.'

'Apply your suppressants, idiot.'

'Don't talk … to me that way you piece of shit – I'm a naval officer!'

'Act like one. Are you stable?'

Silence. 'Yes.'

'Then see to Fox.' There was a pause. 'That's her.'

The owner of the voice filled Olea's field of vision as he knelt down on all fours, blocking Olea's view of Jo. He brought his oddly plain face close to hers, peering into her frozen eyes through the domed mask of his grey isolation suit.

'I suppose you'll be disposing of her, now she's done her job.' The words of the unseen man dripped disgust. The man in front of her turned towards the voice.

'Those were the orders.'

'Whose?'

The man laughed, standing up as he backed away, eyes maintaining the same blankly casual expression as he focused on Olea again. She saw that he was holding a gun. Its muzzle rose towards her.

Please! Please!

Olea screamed, but, again, no sound came. She wanted at least to shut her eyes. Inside, she bucked and thrashed, powerless even to look away as the weapon was pointed directly at her. She felt her eyes welling. Between the man's legs, she could see Jo's eyes still fixed on hers.

Light blazed from the mouth of the weapon.

She felt a sting across her chest. Little more than a hard slap. It didn't feel like pain, and for a long moment she thought that everything would be alright; that somehow the shot had simply grazed her. But her mind was becoming sluggish and clouded, and Jo's horrified eyes were growing distant, and soon, with the smell of burning in her nostrils, she knew with terrible certainty that everything would not be alright after all.

A bright tunnel was closing about her, pushing all that she had been into the darkness where Jo lay. She struggled to prevent it from slipping beyond reach, but the harder she tried, the more remote and unimportant it seemed.

In the distance, two strangely clothed tall men bent down and dragged Jo's broken body away.

PART
TWO

27

BLOOD

LISSA RAINSTORM, Willow and Randal's next door neighbour from the small red-painted cabin two hundred metres back into the forest, had stopped by for a drink with four salmon from the lake dangling over a shoulder from the spear she'd used to catch them.

Water and blood trickled down the toned, bark-coloured skin of her back into the waist knot of her yellow and green sarong. Willow had promised to join Randal in the lab an hour ago, but Lissa's somewhat unilateral conversations gathered a momentum which was near-impossible to deflect. And so Lissa had talked, and Willow had sipped herbal tea and listened politely until she'd become sufficiently restless for her hints to be blunt enough for even Lissa to notice.

'Dear me, I'm terribly sorry, is that the time?' babbled Lissa, 'And you having said you were just off to the lab, and that was likely an hour ago – dear me, I won't keep you waiting any more; have a salmon.'

Willow watched the little woman scuttle away over the grass, dreadlocks a-bob, calling to the imprinted ducks which followed her in a line towards her house. She carried Lissa's salmon to the kitchen portion of the main room and placed it in an earthenware dish. The fish stared back with a glazed, silvery eye, and she was struck by the uncomfortable irony that mainstream consumerism had created blanket veganism while the ostensibly compassionate idealists were often carnivores. The dish was far too small. The salmon's head and tail drooped over the ends and would barely fit in the fridge. She experimented with various orientations and shelves but could still barely close the door. *Should really be gutted,* she thought.

She would have to tend to it later.

She rinsed her hands at the sink, drying them on the seat of her jeans as she strode down the front steps of the veranda. She followed the main path near the reed-studded lakeshore, bearing away up the mossy, stone-paved track which climbed the short hill to the research centre.

There were enclosures, demarcated by near-invisible monomolecular netting, from which raptors glowered at her passage. Fowl pecked, and pumas and lynxes prowled, awaiting freedom after almost half a millennium. Behind the enclosures, the building itself was visible as a row of windows in an overgrown grassy bank capped with a large skylight bubble and a retractable mast bristling with instruments and communications antennae.

Willow followed the path to the wooden door hidden at the building's near end. Closing the door behind her she strode down steps into a long corridor, brightly lit from skylights. Doors and passages branched off left and right, but she knew where she was going.

Lab 23b. Bacteriology. The 'Bug Room'. Taking a lab coat from one of the hooks outside, Willow pushed through the door as she pulled it on, inhaling strong smells of antiseptic.

'Ran?' She called out.

'Ran?'

The main lab was empty. In the sample storage room at the far end a light was on, yellowing the crack under the door. This was where Randal had set up his terminal, complaining of lack of privacy.

Even before she reached the door, Willow knew that something was wrong.

'Randal?'

She hastened her footsteps. She was about to reach for the handle of the door, when it turned. The door was wrenched open and a pair of bleary eyes blinked at her as if in surprise.

'It's you,' observed Randal.

'Congratulations, you idiot.' She had a hand over her heart, nerves more jangled than she wanted to admit. 'After only twenty-nine years you can recognise your own partner?'

'I wish you'd been here.'

She already regretted her sarcasm. His face was tight with worry. 'What is it love? What's wrong?'

She advanced towards him, but he backed away, emphatically shaking his head.

'Will …' He swallowed. 'I think we're in a whole heap of trouble.'

A heartbeat. 'The samples?'

Randal nodded. 'It wasn't contamination, Will. There was no mistake. Except … since those first samples were taken, there's a thousand times more of these bacteria, and their numbers are increasing like there's no tomorrow. I don't understand what's happening, and I don't know what we can do about it, but … Well, we've got to *warn* everyone.'

He hesitated.

'Before we do, though, could you give a blood sample?'

Willow's eyes widened. 'Blood?'

'Just do it Will. Please.'

She searched his face, but he looked away. Then her gaze fell to his arm. The sleeves of his lab coat and his maroon hemp top were, as usual, rolled up above the elbow.

In the crook of one elbow was a small dressing.

Her eyes snapped back to his, and this time he did not look away. Feeling a little strange, Willow raised her sleeve as Randal went to fetch a syringe.

28

CHESS

OSCAR SLIPPED SILENTLY from blood-red sunlight into the cool illumination of the Lancer industrial complex's cavernous dock. Wood seemed relaxed and quietly exuberant.

Occupying the newly installed co-pilot's seat, Hazel felt relieved more than anything. The morphable seat was considerably more modern, supportive, and safe than Wood's, but he'd stubbornly refused to have his ridiculous furry throne upgraded beyond retrofitting the pedals to control what he insisted on calling 'the brakes': the new thruster's clamshell reverser.

At least he'd conceded to having the seat – and the rest of the cabin – thoroughly cleaned.

The trials had passed better than either of them had dared to hope. The only significant problem had been the inability of the cabin's inertial suppressers to shield its occupants from the full range of bone-crushing G-forces *Oscar* could now induce. Fortunately, injuries had been limited to bruising, and it was something easily rectifiable with a generator upgrade.

As Wood had predicted, *Oscar*'s apparently inexhaustible power-source meant that hyperspace jumps could be made without waiting for the Thomson field generators to recharge: something which, on a normal starship, took from minutes to hours. The spacecraft (no, she reminded herself, it was now *a starship*) could make jump after successive jump, indefinitely, waiting only long enough for 'Mrs Blob', Tink's slaved thinker, to fix their position and plot the next jump.

'What I think you could call a success,' Wood enthused from his couch. 'Do you realise we're already as quick off the blocks as a courier missile? Over a long burn, *Oscar* could probably break the manned speed record! I don't think there's any doubt it's the fastest mining vehicle there's ever been.'

195

Above and below the now largely redundant hydrogen scoop, Navotna's team had installed two huge disrupter cannons, which retracted into rotating blisters. Two hundred metres long, as ugly as sin, and able to punch through more than a kilometre of solid rock from orbit (something Novotna had gleefully demonstrated), each could be rotated through slightly more than a hemisphere, leaving no blind spots. At Tink's insistence, Wood had ordered them hardwired to *Oscar*'s grid, leaving the AI in sole control. 'You've got to give me *something* to do,' Tink had complained.

'But Tink … you never asked before!'

'I'm asking now, aren't I?'

Within the innermost layer of hull, either side of the lengthy corridor to *Oscar*'s main airlock, the Nuggets had also installed a pair of very modern two-person lifepods, each with its own high-G launch tube. Essentially miniature starships, each was fitted with a powerful distress beacon, a tiny courier missile, and its own miniature TFG capable of a single twist in and out of hyperspace.

Hazel and Wood exited the main airlock and crossed the pontoon where *Oscar* was docked. By they'd entered the gravtrain on the far side, Wood was in an oddly sombre mood. Minutes later, as they left the gravtrain terminus deep in the complex's busy workshop area, Hazel's one-sided attempts at conversation began to falter.

Wood?

He pursed his lips, and breathed out, hard.

Wood, what's wrong?

'I was thinking …'

He stopped suddenly and stood perfectly still, eyes glazed, like a statue. Hazel waited for an explanation. Boiler-suited passers-by eyed him curiously.

'This is all very impressive,' he began, coming to life again. '*Oscar*, I mean. But seriously, if you're relying on *Oscar* … Against the I. P. E. C.?' He shook his head. 'I mean, Hazel –'

'We're not defenceless. Not by a long shot.'

'If this single vessel is enough to make a serious difference … then I hate to say it, but you *are* as good as defenceless. Even if it were invulnerable, which it's nothing like, it can't be everywhere at once. And I'm not sure *Oscar* would be a match even for one of their big battlecruisers. Have you any idea of the field power those things can generate? Or how many nuclear missiles they pack? Three big nukes would take this complex apart. A direct hit from just one would probably be curtains for *Oscar*.

'And what if they send fortresses?' he went on, hand-waving now. 'I don't know much about those, as they're pretty secret – but they're the biggest hyperspace-capable structures ever made, and Panspacial seem to have found a way to put the TFGs inside their hulls. Exactly like *Oscar*, and probably for the same reason: power to spare. TFGs on other ships are weak spots. As far as I know, fortresses don't *have* weak spots.'

They left the lift and marched in subdued silence down the narrow corridor to Navotna's office. The door iris was open, and they went in. Navotna beamed, but his smile faded when he saw their glum faces.

'Uh, everything okay?'

'Yeah,' breezed Wood, managing a smile. 'No problem.'

'Everything we could have expected and more,' added Hazel. 'We can't thank you enough.'

Novotna's look darkened. 'Fuck over more Pecker warships, that'll be thanks enough.' He brightened. 'I tell you though, we'd be quite interested to know what you have powering that thing. You obviously have something very special in there. Something new? A prototype?' His eyebrows drew together. 'Though why you'd stick it in that crock of shit is beyond my comprehension. Is it a prototype testbed?'

He peered solicitously between Hazel and Wood. Hazel shook her head.

'I guarantee we can negotiate a very attractive deal,' Novotna went on. He was rubbing his palms together. 'I can safely say we'd be interested in investing heavily in its development potential. We could probably quadruple your effective budget – and offer facilities and a workforce you're unlikely to find elsewhere. I'll bet we can quarter your pre-production phase. We can be very flexible.'

'We can't sell it to you,' Hazel told him. *Literally, you fuckwit.* 'Even a share. I'm sorry.'

Lorn gave them both a searching look, in which his frustration was clear.

'There's a courier waiting for you,' he began, with a resigned shrug. 'It's so tightly wrapped in boobytraps that none of the guys would go near it. We don't want this thing lying around, so we'd like you to take it to your ship as soon as possible. It's on a dolly, so you just need to collect it.'

Wood felt Hazel's sudden apprehension, with no need for telepathy.

'Lorn,' she said. 'Thanks for your help, as always. I think we'll be leaving very shortly, but we need one extra thing very urgently – within the next hour, if possible. A cabin inertial suppressor, with a very high output. Is that possible?'

His smile reappeared, and he clapped his hands. 'Of course! Anything's possible. For a price.'

'The ore's in the second pallet. There's eighty thousand tons more than we'd agreed, which you should find will cover the generator.'

Novotna bowed. 'Listen, it's no problem for us to install it, but if you're really pressed … These things are modular, and literally install themselves. Child of six could do it.'

He's right, Wood confirmed. 'I'll set a drone to do it,' he said aloud.

'Well, if you're in that much of a hurry, guess I'll be seeing you. The best of luck.' Lorn's eyes flicked warily between them. 'Look,' he said, 'we've had a good relationship with your lot for a long time. I really hope you change your minds about that power plant. The fact is, we could really do with something like that here. I'm certain we can offer something which'll be mutually beneficial?'

'THEY SEEM A STRAIGHTFORWARD BUNCH,' Wood remarked, stepping over the lip of the control room door with the courier missile's angular, black message module cradled gingerly in his arms. Its booby traps were still armed, and it belatedly struck Hazel that it hadn't been checked for radiation. 'Lorn's lot. Quite trustworthy.' He glanced at her. 'Don't you think?'

She didn't respond.

'Certainly know what they're doing,' he mumbled, laying the module beside the control console. 'We need to get a proper interface fixed up for these missiles.' *Damn. Should have done it while we were here. Idiot.*

It was understandable, thought Hazel, but he really did do an awful lot of talking to himself. He raised his eyebrows.

'Didn't you think they were okay? The Nuggets? Hi Tink! back again!'

'Pretty much out for themselves.'

Wood treated her to a frown. 'Hazel, most people *are* out for themselves. They were way more helpful than they needed to be.'

'Oh, sure. In the interests of future trade.'

'Jesus! And I thought I was cynical.'

No, love, you are one of the most charmingly, dangerously naive people I know. She masked the thought. Wood was glowering now.

'Could you not try just taking people on face value for once instead of looking for ulterior motives?'

What? Hazel put her hands on her hips and stared at him. 'If the survival of everything you held dear had depended for centuries on an awareness of hidden motives, you might be just a bit more cynical.'

'Lucky you've had something to hold dear, then, isn't it?'

'Fucking … Wood! I will not get into an argument over … over *this!*'

'I didn't start it!'

'You asked the question. If you might not like the answer, don't ask.'

Having scrolled excited greetings across the main screen since their arrival to no avail, Tink had taken to waving his persona's arms around and cycling all available screens between clashing colours. When this failed to attract attention, the avatar produced a gigantic megaphone.

'OI!' boomed the intercom, at a decibel level which made the cabin's human occupants clap hands to their ears. '*Thank* you. What's the message?'

'I have no idea,' Wood declared hotly. He shoved the module into the recess of a portable terminal which had been bonded to the floor back at Gamma station for the purpose. Hazel carefully tapped a long code into the terminal's screen.

'From your obvious tension,' said Tink, 'I gather you're not expecting good news. Your code is cleared, Hazel, the safeguards are deactivated. I've pulled the message off it. D'you want me to run it?'

'No,' snapped Wood. 'We can see it perfectly at the moment.'

'Has anyone told you you're a sarc …'

'Just play the effing recording!'

The hunched back of Tink's sulking persona was replaced by the head and shoulders of Dorrin Porro. The expression in her eyes was so grave that for a moment Wood didn't recognise her.

'Hazel, Wood, Tink,' she began, with obvious urgency. 'I have important news which effects us all. We have received an intelligence report, weeks ago by the time you receive this. It appears that IPEC intelligence knows, or at least suspects, Haven's location to within a volume of perhaps a billion cubic light years. That's a large volume, but one which is sparsely populated with viable planetary systems. The message was sent by the Professor himself from IPEC space in the vicinity of old Earth.'

'*The* Professor?'

Hazel silenced Wood with a feeling he found unpleasantly like his brain being given a slap.

'I won't go into details, but the org which brought the information was injured during the journey and forced to recuperate in the atmosphere of a heavily populated planet: an adventure in itself. It has taken months to reach us. We believe IPEC fortresses will sweep the area thoroughly until they find us, and that it's likely that IPEC will launch a full offensive soon, if they haven't done so already.'

Age seemed to steal across Dorrin's face as she spoke. She paused, and the silence seemed to echo: Hazel's own heartbeat, transmogrified by her altered, slowed-down state of awareness.

'We have yet to choose a course of action,' Dorrin continued. 'In the meantime, for the first time in our history, the state of emergency has been stepped up to Full Alert. The *Comhairle* will have met by the time you receive this, and we can only hope that some course of action can be agreed. I fear our options are limited. I cannot at this moment see that the future holds much that is good, but we must live in hope, and believe in ourselves.'

Dorrin pursed her lips, laying one hand over the other on the table before her. Her eyes wavered. 'Wood and Tink. I'm deeply sorry to spring this on you so soon. Please believe me: no one expected events to move so fast. We are assuming the modifications to your vessel have progressed to plan and are near completion. Please return to Gamma Station as soon as you can, all of you. You'll be fully briefed there. Take utmost care – not just of confrontation, but of leading IPEC to us. Their starships could be anywhere now. Act as you think best, but please remember, you're worth more to us alive than dead.

'Our hopes go with you, and we beseech fate that you reach us safely before the confederation does. Good luck, all of you.'

The screen returned to its default systems status displays.

Shocked silence.

'One million square light years means something in the order of five hundred planetary systems,' Tink observed after a few moments. 'A small fleet of those IPEC fortress-things could make a thorough search within one hundred and fifty days.'

Tact, Wood reflected, was something Tink would have to work on.

THEY SET OFF IMMEDIATELY for Alpha Station and Terra Two, which Hazel had said was the nearest of the Haven controlled solar systems. 'It's en route, and we can get an update there.'

Wood cradled her head in his arm, stroking the nut-scented dense hair spread across his chest as they stared at the sleeping-room's ceiling, lost in combined and separate thoughts.

Hyperspace fled outside.

Some time later, he interrupted the silence. Speaking felt unwelcome and uncouth, like swearing in church. Even so, he wanted words for a while.

'Hazel?'

Mmm?

'What Dorrin said … That the message – that org – came from the Professor.' He moistened gummy lips. 'Not *that* Professor, surely?'

Hazel breathed sleepily before she answered, finding words a laborious form of communication. 'The Professor, mhmm. That one.'

'But I thought … I thought he was this sort of Saviour figure in Haven's history. Like Jesus, or something.'

A little smile. He felt her head move against his chest, nodding. Pre-empting his next question, she murmured 'He's five centuries old. Don't ask me how. He's looked much the same since our records began. He's secretive. Nobody knows much about him.'

Contemplative silence.

I met him once, Hazel said. 'I often wonder what effect it had on my life.' *I was six – Haven years.* 'I was walking along by the lake, and suddenly … he was there, in front of me. Then he crouched down, looked directly into my eyes.' *Never spoke a word.* 'He … took my hand, and then he said directly to me –' *Hazel, I want to show you something.*

'And then he showed me the Earth.'

As she spoke, Wood saw in her face a kind of rapture. It stirred in him something which felt like jealousy.

Everything, she said. *Just like I was there. He didn't ask, no preamble: he just showed me, like he knew it would fill me up and I would understand.* 'It was so real, Wood! Like actually … *being* there. And there was such sadness.' *More grief, and sadness, and pain than I had thought anyone could ever feel.* 'I don't know how long I was just standing there.'

As she spoke, her eyes faded to fragile ice-blue.

'Anyway,' she continued, gathering herself, *he disappeared seven years ago without a word to anyone.* 'He's like that. A law unto himself, which has got some people's backs up. The rules he laid down in the beginning are those we still follow.' *When it comes down to it, he's responsible for everything we have.*

Wood was frowning. 'What is he?'

Hazel turned her head questioningly towards him.

'Well, I mean, he can't be human. Not conventionally anyway. If he's hundreds of years old. And, to have done all that …'

At first, she was annoyed. Then, wondering why the question had annoyed her, thoughtful. *He had a job to do. Maybe the only way he could do it was to stay alive.* 'Willpower is a very potent force. Deceptively so.'

Wood compressed his lips. 'Surely it's not *that* potent?'

Perhaps, she admitted. 'But you're still wrong. Ultimately, I think he's just a clever, determined man, who, for whatever reason, has had five centuries of experience to fall back on.'

They didn't speak after that. There was no need. They just curled contentedly into each other, without and within, until Wood's guilt at his neglect of their non-organic companion began to intrude. They wandered to the control room, where Hazel introduced her companions to chess.

The two novices began roughly level, but after five games, Tink started to beat Wood consistently.

'Lack of interest,' was Wood's defence. 'Can we play something else, now?'

Tink claimed, with Hazel's support, that this was 'a load of fat, hairy bollocks.' By the time he'd begun to beat Hazel, Tink had developed an enthusiasm for the game which bordered on obsession.

Light years passed, somewhere else.

29

HARD TIMES

'OLEA?'

He was suspended in redness. Redness which was on fire.

For a while he was completely disorientated. Then an image came to him. Of terrified, staring eyes and a smoking, awful hole punched through the centre of a woman's chest.

Olea!

Everything became breathtakingly clear. Olea was dead, and everything he and his people had worked for half a millennium to achieve would soon follow.

All because of the hormonal failings of a man too old to justify being alive.

Carol.

Olea.

Both now, because of him.

He grew confused again, thinking the two women were the same. Their faces became a single, unclear face. Yet there was another presence too. One with the sadness of an autumn sky, and eyes of many colours.

Why are you here? he asked it.

I'm sorry, the presence said. *I've failed you.*

Then it slipped away.

'PROFESSOR JOSEY MATLOW FOX?'

A sharp smell of antiseptic. A voice, somewhere. Soft. Intrusive.

'Professor?'

Silence.

'I know you can hear me, Professor.'

His mouth was numb. There was something wrong with it. He felt his tongue probe.

Missing teeth.

The teeth are missing!

'Sorry, Professor. Yes, we found all the poison teeth. Couldn't have you pegging out on us prematurely, now, could we?'

He felt his eyes open. It was as though fingers had reached under his eyelids and pulled them up. A face was above his own. Gradually, his vision cleared. He could focus on nothing but the face's eyes.

They were like polished stones.

With effort, Jo tore his gaze away and raised his head.

'That's enough.' A firm, deep voice. One used to authority. Subtly dulled, as though by intercom transmission. 'I'm on my way. Use restraint. Is that clear?'

He was looking through something transparent. It was like a film just beyond his eyes. *A containment field*, he thought. *Probably, given the circumstances, an isolation bubble.*

Beyond it, softly luminous white walls merged with a grey floor. A table hovering nearby bore surgical-looking implements which he couldn't clearly make out. Their presence worried him. His chest felt tight. He tried moving a hand to it, but, like the rest of his body, found his arms gently and completely restrained.

'Who are you?' The exertion of the words left him gasping.

'Ah, Professor Fox. Jo. Good to have you back in the land of the living. I must apologise for your,' a licking of lips, '*accident*.' Most regrettable. However, good fortune prevailed, and you are still with us. We saved much of your lung, you will be pleased to hear, although some of your ribs are now plastic.'

'Who are you,' he lisped, more carefully this time. 'Where am I?'

'Who I am is unimportant for the moment.' The man's voice was smooth and high pitched. It dripped superior amusement. 'But I wish you to remember it anyway.'

The face came so close to Jo's that their noses almost touched through the bubble.

'I am Satan.'

A genuine fruitcake, thought Jo. This understanding only increased his fear. The man was smiling in a way which made his neck-hairs prickle.

'Where we are, you already know. We are orbiting the planet you so kindly led us to. Would you like to see it? Go on,' he cajoled. 'You know you want to.'

Jo knew what he would see, but he had to anyway. Swallowing, he nodded. His couch tilted until he was almost standing. The wall he was facing became either a window or, more likely, a holoscreen. Outside, portions of Alpha Station's broken shell shed chunks of themselves and clouds of dust and gases into space under a bombardment of disrupter weapons. On the planet below, the shiny droplets of the endomes were bursting into glowing clouds. Smoke fanned high into the thin atmosphere.

Fox closed his eyes. 'Haven,' he murmured.

'Naughty,' chided the man. 'We know that planet is not Haven. You are going to tell us where that is. We will find it anyway, of course, and soon. But we would welcome … ah, a hastened end to the proceedings.'

'Olea …?'

'Ah, yes, poor Olea. A cutey, wasn't she?' The man sighed. 'Olea didn't realise she was working for us. She had a little trip to the doctor which I suspect she didn't tell you about. Feminine problems, you know the kind of thing. Embarrassing. We took the opportunity to, shall we say, find a solution to our mutual advantage? Well, not so much to hers, as things transpired.'

'Tell me what you bastards did to her!' Jo clamped his eyes on his captors, before pains in his chest sent him into a coughing fit.

'Dear me,' said the man evenly, eyes unwavering. 'Such *terrible* reservoirs of anger.'

He tutted and waited patiently until Jo had regained control.

'Well,' he said, eyes rolling, 'if you really must know. We were aware of where you'd gone to ground – is that a sufficiently archaic term? – quite some time before your somewhat precipitous departure, but you would have been of limited value to us if we had just grabbed you then and there. That really would have been a wasted opportunity, would it not? And besides, I must confess you were commendably thorough in your operations. Admirably *ruthless*.' The man nodded appreciatively. 'No point us going in all guns blazing if your precious data goes A. D. and you commit hara-kiri, is there? So, we had a problem. How to put a trace on you in a way, or a place, that you were unlikely to detect.'

Backing off, the man spread his hands. Jo noticed for the first time that he was wearing a white surgeon's coat. That, and the antiseptic smell, worried him.

'So! Enter miss Olea Hudril. Heaven could have sent her. You were a fool you know – you and that tree. Anyway, did Ms Hudril ever tell you the reason she only had one child, and so early? It must have crossed your mind to ask – quite unusual amongst upwardly mobile women. No? But then, dear me, love tends to blind one to the obvious, doesn't it?'

'How would you know?'

'Now, now. That's unbecoming. Olea, it seems, had a medical condition. "Uterine fibrosis", I believe is the clinical term. Precludes natural child gestation in many cases. Unusual in one so young. The condition was not very advanced when we selected her – she had been medicated for years, I believe – but we took the liberty of making certain additions to her water and other supplies to help it along. And so, your dear Olea went to hospital, where we took the opportunity to replace her uterus with something more *useful*. You wouldn't have found out, I don't think. The materials were chosen to mimic the properties of the tissues they replaced very closely. Did she have a medical, at your space-station here? Ah, I thought so.' He shook his head. 'Geniuses, those people.

'So, anyway, one way or another, we turned up the pressure until you felt obliged to leave poor old Planet Earth. We already had a fair estimate of which bit of space you were all hiding in, but this sweep searching is such a frustrating, costly business.

'We were hoping you might go all the way to Haven,' he went on, 'but you mentioned the phrase "medical examination". So, rather than risk detection, Miss Hudril's new uterus quickly turns itself into a miniature factory. She develops an urge to …' he coughed, '"use the bathroom", and out pops a tiny machine, a bit like a mite. Of course, this is an unusually capable mite – I mean, consider the design brief. It has to leave your ship undetected, without leaving an obvious hole, and travel an unprecedentedly long way through space for such a tiny thing. It was more like a starship, really, and I believe some genuine ground-breaking was necessary to achieve it. Then it jumps to where we've been waiting, not so very far from here, and turns on its beacon.' He clapped his hands together. 'All rather neat, don't you think?'

'Unless you're Olea Hudril.'

'But I am not.'

Beaming, the man turned away from the couch and began striding with a curious, stiff gait around Jo's upended couch and isolation bubble, hands at his back. Jo searched for a glimmer of hope. This time there really seemed to be none. And something at the back of his mind was filling him with even more dread than his immediate predicament. Some oversight he'd made. Something fundamental.

Try as he might, he couldn't pin it down.

A chime sounded, and the man who calling himself Satan turned. He seemed irritated. The door opened, and into the room strode a pair of armed mechanoids like chest-high, four-legged spiders, followed by two battle-suited guards. A man and a woman, wearing strange, over-large helmets, the guards stood aside for two men wearing the uniforms of naval officers, although something about them struck Jo as not entirely naval.

The commodore (if Jo read his pips right) was a burly, bald, brown-skinned man with eyes glinting from deep folds below his brows. He moved into the room like a cat, his presence instantly making him the room's focus. His taller first officer was an altogether different proposition. Hard eyes peered uncompromisingly from beneath a solid, pink brow. His walk and bearing were powerful yet mechanical. If Jo knew anything about people, he had a sadistic streak a kilometre wide.

'We meet at last,' said the commodore. He took a moment to appraise Jo from his head to his feet and up again as he stopped, hands at his back, before the upended couch. 'I had been wondering what kind of man you were. Now I see that you are just a man.

'Forgive me,' said Jo, 'you have me at a disadvantage.' He forced his gaze down towards his restraining couch. 'Apart from the obvious.'

A wry curl came to the commodore's lips. 'Commodore Aral Nikumi. In command of the Interplanetary Economic Confederation Navy fortress *Violator*. A distasteful name, but, in the circumstances, accurate.'

'Sorry you feel that way. Aral Nikumi seems a benign enough name to me.'

This caused an involuntary noise from one of the guards, but Aral Nikumi ignored him. 'I am also an officer of the Special Branch of IPEC's Joint State Security Service, and a less well-known division developed because of *you*. You will forgive me if we don't shake hands.'

Nikumi held Jo's level gaze.

'I must apologise for what happened to Ms Hudril. Had I known, I would have prevented it.'

'Blaming your shortcomings on a subordinate? Exactly what I'd want in a leader.'

Nikumi's eyes lowered, just for a second. 'A fair point. What happened to Olea was … regrettable. As, in fact, is this whole business.'

'Indeed. Such a pity we can't agree just to coexist.'

'I don't seriously believe you're that naive.'

Jo smiled coldly.

'We would be in a position to reward you quite highly for a certain set of co-ordinates,' Nikumi told him. 'I am authorised to offer you custodianship of one of our more profitable mining planets. There would be restrictions on your freedom of course. But I think it's a reasonable offer.' A pause. 'That's more than most people dream of.'

Jo blinked. 'We were discussing naivety. Even if I believed you, until a few tendays ago my wealth was sufficient to buy a hundred of your planets. Do you honestly think I'd destroy all I've tried so long to achieve for less? Do you think I could be *bought*, when, to me, being able to sit in the shade of a tree is worth more than the sum total of that twisted world of yours?'

'But the difference, Professor Fox, is that then you were a free man. Which you will never be again.' Nikumi raised his eyebrows, and then nodded. 'I must admit to a weakness for romantics. And for nostalgia. During the past five years, I have come to know a great deal about you.'

'You should know me better. My motives are neither nostalgic nor romantic. It's pragmatism. Have you not extrapolated current health trends? The impression of booming health over the past five centuries is misleading: it's caused by the mixing of human gene pools. Geneticists call it "hybrid vigour", and its effects are fading. Build the models. You don't have all the historical data, but I think you have enough to see that you've perhaps a century before the die-off gains momentum. You might self-perpetuate as machines, but you've cut off even that avenue by banning AI research and cybernetics, haven't you? Is that a world you want?'

'And what makes you think you have the answer?'

'It worked before. For millions of years.'

'It nearly destroyed us.'

'*Greed* nearly destroyed you. As it will destroy you ultimately.'

Nikumi regarded him pityingly. 'Now you just sound like a religious zealot.'

'Have you met James Marcell?'

Nikumi stiffened.

'You realise, of course, that your so-called "free society", including your JSSS, is orchestrated largely to provide for the personal whims of people like James Marcell. He and Jesus Hussain have dinner together. Now, who do you suppose is in who's pocket? Please don't take my word for it. It's all there in your own records, if you know where to look.'

The commander clearly hadn't expected this. Jo allowed a corner of his mouth to rise.

'I take it you're no fan of Marcell either.'

'What I think of Marcell is irrelevant. No system is perfect. Regardless of who controls what, the arrangement is for the greater good. I'll admit that I came here hating you and your people. Now I appreciate that you are merely a misguided cultist exploiting malleable people who need a god to follow.'

'At least I've never executed or tortured innocent people for my aims.'

'No?' Nikumi's mouth curled in a sneer. 'Yet you have blackmailed others into doing your dirty work, at the cost of their own, and others', lives. You have schemed and manipulated. You have employed the sickest of murderers and indulged their perversions. You have driven businesses to ruin for your own aims, causing untold grief and hardship. You have murdered state security officers. You fool yourself, "Professor", if you believe that just because your finger isn't touching the trigger which kills, you can somehow avoid responsibility.'

Something was still nagging him. Something bad. 'These actions were all reactive.'

'They were morally bankrupt. Your list of illegal activities is so long only a thinker could memorise it.'

'Is the same not true of Special Branch?'

'Enough! Professor, I did not come to bandy words. I came to see for myself the cause of all this uproar. I was led to believe that you were a lunatic. I think that was to underestimate you, likely for the peace of mind of those you have been scaring witless for the past few decades. And that makes you even more dangerous.'

There was the slightest shake of the man's head. 'Why must you persist in clinging to this vestige of mankind's past? We left it behind for excellent reasons, I wish you could accept that. We *evolved*.' Nikumi set his jaw, eyes hardening. 'But I waste my breath. No, I was under no illusions. I was required to make the offer, but I'd have been astonished, not to mention deeply suspicious, had you had made anything of it.

'Now,' he went on, 'I have my orders. They are to extract the co-ordinates from you, at any cost. I hope you will appreciate, Professor, that although it troubles my conscience –'

'I can just *feel* your pain.'

'Trust me, I'll live with it. We both know what hangs on our deriving those coordinates. I hope you will make it easy for us. If not, we both forfeit needlessly.'

'You think your loss is my concern?'

'Be silent.' Nikumi turned his head towards the man who'd called himself Satan, with an expression of unflinching revulsion. 'Professor, you have already met our *associate* here. He will be conducting the interrogation. I strongly advise you not to piss him off.'

Something seemed to pass between the two men. Jo thought that the strange man in the laboratory coat looked perturbed. 'Advise me the moment you have the location,' hissed Nikumi. 'We can work on less important details afterwards.'

Then he strode out, his first officer casting a gloating look over his shoulder at Jo as he followed.

The two guards and the mechanoids stepped backwards after them, and the door sealed itself shut.

JO AND THE STRANGE MAN regarded each other.

'So nice to be alone,' said the man. 'Just the two of us, now. Together.'

He treated Jo to a ghastly grin. It was salacious, almost tender. Filled with creeping dread by the look in his captor's eyes, Jo searched for a quip, but rejected the impulse.

The eyes narrowed.

'I have been through a lot of preparation for this, Mister Fox. It has been my duty to know you. It is not conceit when I say that I already know you better than you know yourself.'

Then you're even more delusional than I gave you credit for, thought Jo. What was wrong with all this? He saw the face again. A familiar one, from years ago – but the more he struggled to focus on it, the more it slipped away.

'To tell you the truth,' the man was telling him, 'I was resentful of being dragged out here. Away from my routine. It's so easy, is it not, to allow oneself to wallow. There's comfort in repetition. Given long enough, tedium comes to seem like a friend.' Fastidiously, he began smoothing his lab-coat sleeves. His movements were oddly precise. 'So base, this desire for comfort. So *corrosive*. Such an insidious tool for those who understand the power of its application. Because comfort, after all, is relative.

'That was when I began thinking. I have always dreamed of travel among the stars.' He came closer. 'And then, there you were, my sweet. The legendary Josey Matlow Fox. No – ultimately, I would not have missed this chance for any promise of *comfort* in the world. It has been my business to know you as well as anyone has ever done, Professor Fox. And now I shall know you perfectly. Inside and out.'

A small, twisted smile.

'No irony intended.'

IT WAS A WOMAN'S FACE. A face lined and gaunt with years and worry, but with eyes … *bright, changeling eyes*. Could it have been his mind which turned them to emeralds when they looked on him? Did they shine for his single act of compassion, or for the person behind it?

So easy to ask such questions after the chance is gone.

Jill. There was too much pain there already to risk burdening you with mine.

He finds her face above his own. He's on a table, in a cabin. *His* cabin. She's wearing her serious smile, eyes a shade bluer now as she looks down on him.

Josey! she is chiding, and despite himself, he likes the sound of the name when formed by her mouth. *Try and relax! I can't do this with all this clutter jamming your head. How can you* live *in here? It's a fucking mess!*

He thinks to say something but does as she tells him. She's close enough for him to smell her strongly. He wants to reach up, to embrace her, but doesn't – hoping (or thinking he hopes) that she does not know; cannot feel.

A little better, she says. *Look, I'll help you. Don't worry: the only effect of this you'll ever notice is if you're ever captured and interrogated against your will.* A rueful smile. *And by then you won't notice because you'll have forgotten anyway. I can make it quite specific. If there's anything you'd rather not forget …*

A nice thought. 'No. No one must never be able to find Haven through me.'

'Very well Josey,' she says, aloud this time. 'Watch my eyes. See their colour, their shape.'

Their colour. He drowns in their colour.

'See how deep they are, like a deep sea …'

Jill no! This can't be happening! You said it was foolproof! You said only a telepath …

Forgive me. Her eyes are ice-blue now. *I've failed you, when you needed me most. I'm so sorry. My daughter and I were the last. That's what I always thought.*

Oh God, he screams, *help me!*

JO TRIED to clear his mind of anything which might betray him. He needed a diversion. *Anything.*

Looking up, he was relieved to find Satan apparently still lost in his monologue.

'Do you have savings?' he interrupted, managing a veneer of calm. The other man squinted, suspiciously.

'Why, whatever do you mean by that?'

'I presume these bastards are actually *paying* you. Despite what you are to them. You know? To maintain the illusion. To keep you tame. Have you saved, and saved, or invested your earnings somewhere? Bonds perhaps? Equities? Oh, I'll bet you have. The fruits of your life's work, busily gaining value – though I'm sure there's always been some excuse whenever you've wanted direct access. Are your details safely in the files of some bank or building society on Renascido?' He forced a chuckle. 'I'd imagine you've quite a sum stashed away on the Grid by now, for the hiring of your unique talents.'

The man stared blankly. 'I have been adequately rewarded for what I do. I have enough to guarantee myself a comfortable …' he tailed off.

'Ah, but here's the thing. You don't. Not any more.'

The other man's face darkened.

'What do you mean? Tell me what you mean by that!'

Jo looked, hard, into his eyes. *It's all in here*, he said, without moving his mouth. *You tell me.*

Then he laughed. Satan paled. His mouth opened.

'You … you *can't* have!'

'How can you serve these murderers,' Jo exclaimed, 'after the way your kind has been treated? How can you ignore your memories of their suffering? It's the same people, Satan – or whatever your name was before they twisted you into what you are now. *The same fucking people!*'

'No,' Satan blurted. He seemed about to be sick. 'You *can't* have. That would be insane! The whole CCG? Impossible! Trillions of people would be utterly ruined! That would …' his brow knotted itself in disbelief. 'Doing such a thing would cut the jugular of the entire transworld economy. You … you might as well let off nuclear bombs!'

'Join us!' Jo cried. 'It's not too late. We'll give you a home. There are others like you there. We'll make a place for you. You could be *happy*. Can you remember that – happy? Do you even know what it feels like?'

Purple-faced, Satan tore at his eyes. 'There, damn you!' Coloured lenses fell to the floor. In their place, his irises glared like hot coals. 'You –' Words seemed to fail him, but Jo felt his fury like a scalding wind between his his ears. 'It is you who are the fool!' Spittle drizzled on the shield before Jo's face. 'What you have done will incur the wrath of *billions*, and their revenge on your tribe of freaks will be worse than –'

Again, he seemed to lose the power of speech. He clenched his fists, then seemed to regain control, his anger equally bright, but colder.

'Can you *imagine* what these people will do to you when the find out? They will tear you limb from limb! They will torture you for eternity, and every one of your followers.'

He brought his face hard up against the isolation screen.

'But I'm going to play with you first. I deserve my fun for what you've taken from me. I am going to indulge my most lurid whims with you until your heart splits in two and your mind explodes.'

Breathing heavily, he drew back. Still staring, he raised an arm to the table drone, which slid smoothly between them. Arranged on it were an assortment of Scalpels, hooks, corkscrews, syringes, electrodes. Small saws …

'You are going to die, Josey Fox. But not until you have suffered, and not before you have seen everything you value die before your eyes, which I will allow you to keep for that purpose. You might like to know that that tinpot soldier Nikumi ordered me not to torture you physically. Well, *fuck* him. He's replaceable – and besides … I can do whatever I like! These fools,' he rotated a finger at the ceiling, 'still think a few robots will offer you, or them, protection from me? Well, perhaps they might, if I hadn't got in the heads of their programmers first.' He snorted. 'In any case – I could not care less. You will be my opus, Josey Fox, my legacy. With you, I will have achieved a genuinely new level of artistry in agony and depravity.'

He indicated the tools laid out on the table.

'State of the art equipment, once upon a time. Crude compared to modern instruments, of course. But that's just a hobby of mine. For my work, I also use tools of a far more sophisticated nature. My dissecting is far deeper and more precise.'

Leaning close again, he tapped his head with a forefinger.

Yes, Professor. You are about to understand what it means to be truly vivisected. Mentally and physically, at the same time. Laid bare, probed and mangled in places and ways more plentiful and painful than you can possibly imagine. The beast within me – my perversion, if you like – wants gore, and blood, and glistening organs exposed: palpable evidence of pain. Mutilation: the flesh's memory of torture.

'However, the beast within the human soul does not understand – cannot perceive – the exquisite delicacy of the mind, or the scale and scope of the damage which may be inflicted there. Physical pain and physical damage are methods of the less evolved. I operate on an altogether higher plane.'

He brought his face closer still, so that his eyes hovered centimetres from Jo's. Jo should have felt his breath, but the screen prevented it. 'You are about to discover that plane, Professor. You will remember my name.'

I will be your God.

Jo tried to keep his eyes on those of the other man. 'I don't, of course,' he croaked, 'know the co-ordinates. No one does. For this reason.'

Satan pulled back. 'Oh, I guessed that. That should not stop me being thorough, though, should it? Oh – and thoroughly enjoying myself while I'm about it, at your very considerable expense.'

With a command, Satan opened a channel to the Bridge.

'Message from Satan to Nikumi. Fox has sabotaged the Central Communications Grid on Renascido. You won't get a message off in time. It's already happened.'

Jo felt something malign stalk through intimate, private places, like stealthy footfalls on stairs in ancient films he'd seen a long, long time ago. Something inside him was already screaming.

'Cancel the isolation screen.'

He willed himself to die.

30

COLLAPSE

JESS COULDN'T REMEMBER having eaten so well in his life.

He certainly couldn't remember anything quite like this. It had been quite a shock to start with. He'd emerged that morning from his doss within one of the city's giant street-level air ducts only to find that the world had gone mad.

Now that the initial bombardment of vehicle accidents had abated, the skies were almost empty of traffic. Nothing moved in the air above him but the occasional police or military vehicle. There were none of the tourists who peered and poked about the street floor with their recording drones and their weird clothes and weirder questions. Simply a lot of other basement people milling about in the burning wreckage, staring in the same confused way Jess imagined he was doing. All the endless, frantic activity in the upper levels, which he'd assumed to be as much an unchanging part of the world he lived in as the streets themselves, had simply ceased.

Except for the rain.

He had no other word to describe it. The rain had been falling since early morning, and it made walking anywhere but the centre of the streetfloor a risky activity. The only sound to break the eerie and unfamiliar near-silence, except for bursts of distant gunshots, was the irregular drum of clothed flesh hitting concrete.

It sounded like a downpour of wet sacks.

Executive types mostly, he thought, judging by the smartly severe suits they wore. Also, mostly men. He wondered what that meant. They littered the street floors, crumpled and scattered in irregular but growing piles. As well as expensive jewellery, and shoes, and (so far, inert) terminals, Jess had forty suits now, all stockpiled in his lair. All expensive ones, he could tell. Most soaked with blood, but he'd find somewhere to wash that off.

His friend Winch had said it had something to do with the communications grid. Winch had worked in something to do with communication, so he knew about these things. The grid had shut down – something it had never done before, apparently – and now none of the Wall People knew what to do because all of their money was either gone, or they just couldn't use any of it. That was why people were jumping out of windows, Winch had said.

Jess sighed, wishing he was clever like Winch so that he could really understand what he talked about in those long, rambling speeches of his; understand what went on up in those endless, cold walls.

Now he'd begun to think about Winch, Jess realised that he hadn't seen him since early morning. *Wouldn't put it past the turd to get himself squashed*, he thought. *Leaving me on my own would be just like the selfish old git*. He busied himself undressing another corpse. A good, lean one this. No fat. And he wouldn't even have to fight anyone for it. He began to saw with his scrap-iron knife, biting an untidy wound into the man's thigh. The blunt edge began grating against bone, and he intensified his efforts, beginning to sweat.

He'd already gorged himself that morning, but he'd make a cache for himself next to his suits over in the air duct before the others, the ones who roamed in gangs, took all the best pickings. Something for when the rain stopped and hard times returned, as he knew they would.

'SON OF A WHORE!'

The enigmatic, outdated courier missile had been delivered to the heavily shielded and armoured holding bay reserved for unsolicited communications more than twenty-three hours ago. Since then it had languished in quarantine, waiting to be picked apart by expendable bots looking for mites, malicious parasites, boobytraps and other dangers.

Now that Lorn Novotna finally came to look at its downloaded message, he wished it had been opened a lot sooner.

'Fucking hell!'

Dour, pinch-faced Dale Panovich, with whom Novotna was jointly responsible for the technical supervision of Nugget's astroengineering operations, looked up from a screen which mocked him with dismaying expanses of spreadsheet. Along with Novotna, Panovich was also a colony councillor and trustee. Bookkeeping was something he made little secret of feeling was beneath him. 'What?' he snapped, rubbing his shiny scalp in irritation.

'This courier …'

'*Which* courier? We get any number of the little shits.'

Novotna raised a hand. 'Will you just *shut up* for a minute, and let me listen? In fact, why don't you listen too.' He leaned forwards in his seat, bringing his face closer, focused on the mysterious video. It had been captured in a small, metal-walled room, which looked like an airlock, apparently in zero-G. The speaker was an oddly ageless man, with a fan of long, silver-grey hair.

Novotna had never heard of the name he'd given, nor the colony he claimed to represent. Yet, as the man spoke, he found his mouth hanging open.

'Dale, you really should see this.'

Looking up, he found Panovich already leaning over his shoulder, squinting at the two-dimensional image in the holoscreen.

'What did I miss?'

Novotna swiped the pause icon. 'This guy, whoever he is, claims the IPEC economy's going down. Not some unspecified time in the future, either – he's saying it'll be happening as we read this. Claims he's had the same message relayed to other Lancer colonies all over the shop.'

Panovich grunted. 'You're actually wasting time listening to this wanker?'

'Says he can prove it.'

'They always do.'

'This seems different. He's given details. Listen!' He swiped resume.

'Because of this move,' continued the sonorous voice, 'it is almost certain that martial law will be declared by core IPEC governments. Given the primacy of these worlds, this may be applied to all governments. To contain the situation, there will be demands for IPEC's naval and other armed forces presently active within Lancer and outer IPEC territories to be redirected to the core worlds to police civil unrest there and distribute supplies. This will leave territory presently under IPEC control in an unprecedented state of vulnerability. Think of it. A well-equipped, *coordinated* Lancer offensive could retake the outer IPEC worlds. Without bloodshed, and virtually unopposed …'

'Open a comms channel to colony central,' Novotna barked into his hand implant. He swore under his breath. 'We've already lost almost a cycle.' Panovich looked pained.

'You're getting ahead of yourself.'

'I don't know, I'm getting a funny feeling about this. The figures he's given seem just too damn real. He's sent us *models* of the collapse, for the Madonna's sake. Even if the guy turns out to be another crank, this needs following up. 'Cause if he isn't, this could be exactly what we've all been waiting for.'

'He's a terrorist.'

'Your point? That's exactly what IPEC thinks of *us*.' The comms chime sounded. 'Denis Aschev's office.'

A hologram appeared over Novotna's desk showing the head and shoulders of the mayor's hard-eyed, shaven-headed young secretary.

'Goldie, it's Lorn Novotna. I need you to do something, urgently. Get couriers prepped for all our contacts. Include any in Pekkerland we can reach directly without blowing their cover.'

'All of them?'

'All of them.'

'Blimey. Express?'

'As fast and direct as possible. We'll need to act quickly.'

'I'll need to clear this with Den first.'

'I'm not asking you to *send* them, Goldie. Just to make sure we've enough that aren't assigned to other things, and fuel them.'

Her hands twitched as she manipulated her terminal interface. 'I'll need to pull some off other schedules.'

'Do it. Until there's a consensus, I'll take responsibility. Put the cost on my tab for now. Get the council to meet in half an hour.' Seeing her expression, he said, 'Yes, half an hour. Oh, and I've a Pekker Joint State Security file I need authenticated ASAP. It's the most wanted list of their Special Branch.'

'How did we get that?'

'It was sent to us. If the sender's to be believed, by the number one on that list. His name is Josey Matlow Fox. After you've done the other stuff, I want you to pull out any information we have on him.'

Goldie Chrpova nodded resignedly. 'Okay, send it over.' Her eyes dipped to her screen. 'But half the council are on sleep shift.'

'Then wake them!'

31

SOME KIND OF PLAN

'SOMETHING'S WRONG,' Hazel said, urgently. 'I can feel it. Turn the ship away.'

Wood stared at her for just a second. During the long arc of their approach to Terra Two, her bright mood had inexplicably deteriorated into agitation. In the past half-hour she'd been acting sufficiently strangely for him to ask several times if she was okay.

She'd replied only that she wasn't sure.

He flipped the bulky spacecraft on its axis and stamped, hard, on the thruster pedals. Hot plasma scythed across the vacuum in a blinding tail which soon preceded the backwards-plummeting vessel by more than a thousand kilometres.

'Plot us a new orbit,' he snapped at Tink. 'Magnify the rear view. Show us the planet.'

Oscar's two human occupants examined what the sensors revealed in aghast silence. The sun had risen past the limb of Terra Two, throwing a widening crescent of the planet into bright daylight. Against the night side, clearly visible now that its orbit had brought it into sunlight, was what looked like a streak of dust. Tails of smoke and their shadows streaked what was visible of the planet's dusky plains.

Tink's avatar had produced its binoculars again. 'I don't think we're going to Alpha Station any more,' he said, deadpan. 'Not if the data I have for its orbit is accurate.'

'I don't like this,' Wood fretted, eyes darting between space beyond the hull and the screens. 'Something here's not right.' *Apart from the blindingly obvious*. 'Where's whatever did this?' He gnawed his lip. 'Tink … is the mass of that debris what you'd expect given your details of Alpha Station?'

'That's funny.' Tink sounded surprised. 'Not only is it apparently one and a half times the expected mass, but it's behaving very oddly.'

'Something else is there.' *Something big.* 'Shit. They must be manipulating the debris with fields or something to hide themselves so well. And I just did the equivalent of setting off a beacon telling them where we are.' He swallowed loudly. 'Okay. What the hell do we do now?'

'Turn this thing around,' Hazel demanded. 'Get us into a low orbit. Get closer, if you can.'

'But … we've no idea yet even what we're dealing with, Hazel. Whatever's hiding in there – whatever did *that* – is not your average light cruiser!'

'Turn it around!' she screamed.

Wood looked for a moment into her fiercely tearful eyes. Even now, there were times when Hazel scared him. He eased off the thruster and began pulling on the joystick, only to find that Tink was already changing their trajectory. The stars began to shift.

'We should jump out of here as soon as possible,' he muttered. 'There's nothing we can do here. They're buggered! They're all dead!' He gestured at the screen. '*Look*, for God's sake!'

Hazel silenced him with an angry chop of her hand. Her eyes had the glazed look which meant she was searching for something using her ability. 'They may have prisoners', she murmured, moving her head around as though listening for faint sounds. Wood watched, his frustration building.

'Oh,' she breathed after what felt like several minutes. Her eyebrows came up. 'Ahh …'

Her entire body went rigid. She rose up on her toes with staring, agonised eyes, veins standing in her face, the tendons in her neck raised like cords.

'*Nooo!*' she screeched, and hurled herself to the floor, striking her head heavily. Twisting on to her back, she thrashed and spasmed as though in a fit, only the whites of her eyes showing.

She began clawing at them with her fingernails.

'Hazel!'

Leaping free of his seat, Wood slammed his body down on top of her. He tried to grasp her flailing arms but was totally defeated by her insane strength. Arms spread for balance, he tried to suppress her using his weight.

It wasn't enough. She was bucking madly, screaming incoherent sounds. 'Shit. Hazel! Tink – help me somehow, she's uncontrollable! *Uugh!*'

She'd driven a flailing elbow into his jugular.

'Fuck, Tink, get a drone! Get a … *uungh* … drone to hold her down!' Spraying blood from her mouth, she drove her knee at his groin with bone-crunching force. He barely squeezed his legs together in time. Straining every muscle, he managed to trap one of her arms, then punched her as hard as he could across the face. Her struggles weakened. He hit her again, leaving her cheek crimson. She sagged, staring sightlessly.

Wood lay over her, tearing for breath, as the drone trundled into the room on its gravity field, tentacles extended. 'You're a little late!' he yelled. 'Christ, I hope I didn't hit her too hard. I'll get her down to medical, you just get us out of here.' His neck where she'd caught him was beginning to hurt like hell.

'No,' protested a weak voice.

Raising himself, he looked down into wandering, pained eyes.

'Hazel.' He raised her head from the floor, and his tone hardened. 'What d'you mean "no"? There's no "no" about it. We're leaving.'

'Can't,' she said thickly, probing an eye-socket with trembling fingers. It was bleeding. Sitting, she spat a mouthful of blood and tenderly fingered her tongue. 'It was *him*, Wood. The Professor. There's an IPEC mobile fortress. I don't know how, but they have another telepath aboard. He's got around the hypnotic screening. He's …'

Her eyes glazed. She shuddered.

'He knows so much – we can't leave him, Wood. We *can't!*'

Wood was scowling now as he picked himself up. 'The Professor? You're absolutely sure it was the Professor?'

'Of course I'm sure! How could I not be fucking sure?'

'Okay, okay!'

Her expression softened. 'Woody, he's in *agony*.' She screwed her eyes shut, squeezing clear droplets from their corners. She grabbed Wood's proffered arm, lurched to her feet, and flung herself into the pilot's seat.

'Hey! What –'

'Tink, get ready to attack them.' Tink's avatar's eyes bulged. 'Pardon?'

'Hazel,' Wood barked. 'Calm down.'

'Don't you fucking tell me to "calm down". No one should suffer like that. And the Prof knows more than any of us. What he knows could destroy everything!'

'*Hazel!*' Braced against the console, Wood rubbed his face, trying to force his thoughts into some kind of order. 'Tink, what kind of chance do we have against a fortress?'

'How should I know? However, they are appallingly big, and frankly terrifying.'

He gaped. 'Fat use you are! I'm asking what you think we should *do.*'

'Go away, very fast?' Hazel glared. The animation looked nervous. 'On second thoughts, I agree with Hazel.'

Wood scoffed, folding his arms. 'And why's that, so suddenly?'

'Because it's waiting here for a *reason*,' Hazel yelled at him. 'Wood, I know you're afraid, but can't you see what's riding on this?'

His arms fell to his sides.

'Great,' he huffed after a moment. 'Just great. Hazel, get out of my chair.'

She happily obliged.

'Right.' Tilting the joystick as he strapped himself in, Wood experimented with deep breathing. It didn't help. 'Insane,' he muttered, stomping his toes on the thruster pedals. 'Well, I think all we can do is try and ram holes in it. If it'll let us.'

'No!' Reaching across from her seat, Hazel tugged his arm. 'You can't do that.' Ahead, the planet's crescent was growing visibly. 'We must get the Professor back.'

'How?' demanded Wood. He was gesticulating. 'Exactly how would you achieve this?'

'I'm sorry, I don't know. I just don't know – but we've got to try!'

He threw up his hands. 'Well, apparently I'm just the sodding driver here. If anyone has any bright ideas, I'll just do what I'm told.'

'Can we reason with them?' asked Tink. 'Could we ask them to hand The Professor to us?'

'Of course not!' Hazel cried. 'If they know we know they have him, they'll kill him!'

Wood rolled his eyes. 'Oh, this just gets better.'

'Converging objects,' warned Tink. 'Four. I think they're nuclear missiles.'

'Oh … *shit.*' Wood turned to Hazel. 'Still happy doing this?'

They stared together at the rapidly closing blips on the screen.

'Convergence time, thirty-nine seconds. Hazel … Er, I'm kind of starting to agree with Wood. Quite strongly, in fact –'

'See if you can get them with the cannon,' Wood cut in.

'The cannon's not terribly precise. At this range, the speed of light –'

'Try! Strafe round them. Try and narrow the … ah, spread I think it's called?'

'Spread? You mean, like cheez?'

'No – what? Look it up in the library!'

In external views on a screen, four fat, black muzzles erupted from their armoured fairings. Rotating, they seemed to join themselves to the growing planet ahead by rips in space through which light shone. The light-slashes continued every fraction of a second, the minute corrections Tink made for each burst invisible to his human companions.

'Convergence nine seconds. Help! What shall I do?'

Wood's breath seemed lodged in his throat. 'Are our defensive fields up?'

'Not …'

'*Get them up!*' he gasped. 'Kinetic deflectors too, everything! Try to use the furnace fields as they close. Some kind of … pulse or field that'll hurt them. Gravity waves or something! I don't know – think!'

There was a brief barrage of flashes from where *Oscar*'s disrupter beams converged. Three balls of heavily hull-filtered light blossomed majestically.

'One still closing!'

Two pairs of human eyes and several hundred electronic ones stared silently ahead. Tink made a strange gibbering noise. There was another flash – intense even through Wood's eyelids as he closed them – and then a strange feeling of concussion, like the tolling of some vast, distant bell.

The floor trembled.

Then the planet was filling the control room's viewing bubble – huge, and round, and growing improbably fast; murky brown clouds of pulverised rock spreading through its thin, clear atmosphere where *Oscar*'s guns had inadvertently raked its surface.

'Yugga aiii!' said Tink, or something equally random.

In response to Wood's feet, the clamshells of *Oscar*'s new reverser diverted the thruster's searing exhaust forward, pressing him and Hazel against their restraints. The remains of Alpha Station swelled quickly from a speck to a nebula of dust, rubble, and larger chunks of rock and shinier debris swirling in a loose orbit about itself.

He stood *Oscar* on its tail for the final intense burn to match orbit with the debris cloud.

As the violently decelerating starship arced closer, something pointed and symmetrical began slicing out of the cloud like a scalpel cutting through paper. Within minutes, most of an enormous, pinched cube had emerged from the remains.

It was like a conjuring trick. The cube was as big as the cloud of debris which had been hiding it.

Divide and Rule-class, breathed Hazel. *Oh, Great Mother.*

'Well, whatever it is, it's rapidly scaring me shitless.'

'I'm firing at it with the cannon,' yapped Tink, 'Tell me to stop if you think it's a bad idea.'

Flipping *Oscar* through another quarter-turn, Wood applied the thruster so that the cube, its defence fields sparkling as they absorbed *Oscar*'s cannon fire, grew dead ahead.

This is insane, he thought, again, as the immense shape began to loom.

Space on all sides came alive in a storm of light. The onslaught was bewildering in its ferocity. There were pulses and flashes. Streaks seemed to skewer *Oscar* from all sides, curving crazily into space where *Oscar*'s fields deflected them. 'We can't sustain this,' objected Tink. 'We're heating up! I've retracted the cannon to protect them.'

With a flick of his wrist, Wood began powering *Oscar* away in a steep arc.

What are you doing? Hazel.

'This won't work.'

'But …'

'Hazel, *this will not work!*' Fresh flashes blossomed in space around the ship as dispersed matter from Alpha Station turned to energy against *Oscar*'s shields. Weapon strikes rumbled against the aft hull. Wood was sweating as though in a fever: this was utterly different from dodging asteroids. The last few seconds had felt like falling into a caved-in planet. A planet which fought back. 'I am not going near *that* again without some kind of plan.'

From Tink's excellent diagrams, he could see that the immense vessel measured more than a hundred kilometres along each side.

What options could they possibly have against a weapon on such a scale? Confronting it was ludicrous. There was no obvious weakness: even ignoring its insanely powerfully defensive fields and armament, its armour was likely a hundred metres thick and full of smart nanotech. He couldn't even guess how he might disable its Thomson Field Generator, or generators, wherever it – or they – proved to be.

As if that wasn't enough, they were seriously hoping somehow to find, and then rescue, a single person from *inside* the thing. Someone whose whereabouts they couldn't even guess. Amongst a crew whose number was probably well into six figures …

Then it struck him that the object's very size might offer an opportunity. As he slewed *Oscar* around once more, a mad idea had begun to form. Before he could act on it, however, he and Hazel both found themselves completely paralysed.

As quickly as it came, the paralysis faded to a sensation of lethargy.

'What was that?' gasped Hazel and Wood in unison.

'Nerve weapon, I think,' said Tink. 'Blocked it. Are you functional?'

'Yes,' Wood assured him. *Crap, what next?* 'Good work. Quick, Tink: the fortress will have self-sealing bulkheads, won't it? And emergency fields and pressure doors and stuff, in case of breaches in the hull?'

'I don't have that information. Their fields are blocking my scans and attempts to access their grid. Ten more nukes are closing. What should I do?'

'Quickly: could you access their grid from inside the fortress.'

228

'I think so,' said Tink, sceptically. 'Er, those nukes are closing awfully fast.'

Hazel stared at Wood, eyes widening as his thoughts became apparent to her. 'You're crazy.'

'This entire situation is crazy!'

'Nukes,' squeaked Tink. 'Nukes anyone? Hey, listen!'

But Wood was not listening. He was flipping the ship through the rest of its turn to face the fortress once more.

'*NUUUUKES!*'

A point of light swelled to engulf everything in a painfully brilliant maelstrom of light. The storm seemed to go on, and on. The ship shuddered and rumbled. Hazel swore under her breath. 'Eeek!' yelped Tink. 'Yikes! Hudda-erble!'

Then they were through, and the fortress was growing with increasing speed until it filled the view on all sides but behind, like an impossible cliff. The bombardment resumed.

'Tink,' urged Wood, oddly calm now. 'Remember *Born to Destroy*? I want the same thing from you now, but bigger. Don't hold back.' The light of impinging beam weapons became so intense that the fortress was almost hidden. Knowing what was coming, Wood found himself utterly unable to breathe.

Hazel raised an arm to shield her eyes.

The impact, when it came, was so violent that the agony of her arm almost tearing itself from her shoulder seared across Wood's brain, her cry swallowed by the groans of stressed materials and a screeching, thundering cacophony transmitted through *Oscar*'s flexible hull.

A drone which had been anchored to the floor by its grapples ricocheted from the back of Wood's chair and splintered against the transparent control room wall.

32

BREAKING AND ENTERING

JO FOX'S FACE was fixed in a silent scream. A stalactite of crimson drool hung from his caved-in mouth. His blood-filled eyes twitched unseeingly, like the death throes of one of the insects he and his people had taken such pains to resurrect.

It had been with great disappointment that Satan had withdrawn his razor-edged telepathic probes.

It had just been getting interesting. Such a mind! Such depth, such perception. So uniquely, wonderfully *twisted*. He'd carefully rubbed at all the parts which hurt, all the tortured and guilty memories, and pared away all else until little but torment remained, swollen and raw and bleeding like the satisfying amounts of flesh he'd simultaneously exposed.

It had been a struggle to start with, and for his trouble, Satan had installed some highly unpleasant sensations and memories of his own devising. So much new information! And Fox, it transpired, had been lying. He knew – and was perhaps the only person who knew – the exact co-ordinates of the planet Haven.

And yet, somehow, he was still holding tightly to that knowledge. He'd buried it at his very core, and a lot of further mental flaying and dismemberment was going to be necessary to retrieve it.

Fox would suffer multiply for his stubbornness.

The red alert had not been unexpected, and Satan had continued, unconcerned. Then he'd felt the unfamiliar light footsteps through his own synaptic corridors, and he'd been suddenly afraid.

And Fox had smiled. A tiny, crooked, ghastly smile, but a smile nonetheless.

Unnerved and puzzled, Satan had called the command deck on the intercom.

'An approaching vessel.' Aral Nikumi never made any attempt to disguise his loathing, knowing there was no point, and disinclined even to try. Satan couldn't help admiring him for that. 'It matches records of an obsolete mining vessel implicated in the loss of one of our cruisers eleven tendays ago.'

'You have taken measures?'

Nikumi's response had been withering. 'Get off this channel. I'll notify you when it's been destroyed.'

'Thank you *so* much.'

The face darkened further, then disappeared. Satan considered briefly whether a brief vandalistic excursion around the commander's head was worth the fallout he knew it would bring. He decided against it.

One day, though, Nikumi. And soon.

Sitting in the interrogation room's lone plastic seat, he tried to home in on the source of the intrusion. He'd felt strongly that it came from the approaching vessel, so he wormed his extrasensory fingers into the void around *Violator*. He felt the faintest vibration, as though the fortress was beginning to move. He turned on the intercom.

'Commodore, what is happening?'

Nikumi whirled to face him. Behind the commodore, bridge personnel were locked into their virtual reality worlds. Satan did not have to probe anyone to sense their consternation.

'We're at battle stations,' thundered Aral Nikumi. 'I don't give a fuck whose protection you're under, you smear of shit, I'll execute you myself if you disturb me again.' He turned to bark orders, refocusing on his own, unseen, sensurround.

Satan frowned. He reached out again … and this time quickly found his quarry. The presences were closing, extremely fast. There was a young male, with a very odd taste to his mental makeup, and something else that he could neither identify nor understand. And … A *telepath!* The female was a telepath!

After all this time.

The revelation detonated an explosion of clashing emotions. For a moment he was so overwhelmed that he found tears streaming down his face. He longed to meet her, to *share* with her. Suddenly his isolation seemed unendurable.

But the same time, it was clear that she meant to kill him.

Her hatred was like nothing he'd experienced. It was blindingly focused, breathtaking. A searing heat like a plasma-bolt through his skull. He found himself afraid.

But what can they do? What do they possibly hope to achieve? He was near the heart of one of the IPEC navy's biggest and most powerful weapons – a weapon considered by some to be invulnerable – and they had only one small ship. A ship that was a virtual museum exhibit. Built, apparently, for mining.

Yet, the male seemed sure of himself. He believed that they could succeed. Satan rose and paced about, concentrating. In contrast to the hot fire of the female telepath, the young man's anger was cool. Ice cool.

He knew exactly what he was doing.

'Commodore,' he screamed, opening a link to the command deck. 'They're going to ram us! They're coming inside!'

The command decks were in turmoil.

'Nerve weapons are being jammed, Sir.'

Satan dived into Nikumi's head, staring through his eyes as the commodore rose from his seat, mouth open, transfixed by his personal projection of surrounding space. There was a maelstrom of flashes as the fortress's missiles detonated, and a portion space became peppered with brilliant, expanding spheres. A hush descended.

Then, out of the resultant glowing cloud, rushed something which grew and grew: two intensifying points of light against a dark, expanding shape at whose heart was a hellish red glow.

'Impossible.' Nikumi. 'Everything that thing does should be impossible!'

Then the shape was gone.

Silence in the command room. Wide-eyed uniformed officers looked between each other. The floor began to tremble. Then it lurched, making officers grab seats and consoles for support.

'It's inside, it's inside!' babbled Waranika, clutching her console. 'That *thing* is inside *Violator*.' She whirled in her seat to face the commodore. 'Sir, we haven't simmed this scenario. What do we do now?'

Ironic. We've been violated.

Blood draining from his face, Nikumi was wondering what, indeed, they could do now.

ABRUPTLY, THE NOISE CEASED. Wood twitched his wrist, flipping the ship backwards, and slammed both feet back down on the pedals. A jolt went through the cabin as *Oscar* ploughed, tail-first, into something unseen. His view was almost completely obscured by smoke or dust outside.

'Tink: fix that drone to something before it kills one of us! Try filtering the view or something so I can see through whatever's outside. Damage?'

'We've lost visual on two sensor pods, and I now have an insight of what it means to "shit" oneself. We're inside a large space. Vacuum, except for debris we brought in.'

Two sensor pods? That's it? Wood could scarcely believe his ears.

'Ease off the thruster, Wood – we're almost stationary. Let me, I can see.'

Reluctantly ungluing his hands from the controls, Wood glanced at Hazel. Face ashen, she was clutching her shoulder. *I'm okay*, she told him. The control room screens transformed into an external view built up from sonar, radar and EM wavelengths not absorbed by the smoke. Debris was everywhere, much of it glowing intensely white in the false image. The strange light made the ranks of huge warships docked inside the fortress ghostly.

'I'm in the fortress's command grid,' said Tink. 'Its name, apparently, is *Violator*.

Delightful. 'Don't get infected.'

'But they can't touch me. I can *see* all their software, and just squash it. You're forgetting, I'm not a thinker.'

'Don't get complacent. Where are we?'

'The main dock: it's sixty-two kilometres long. The atmosphere's escaping from damaged fields and doors on neighbouring floors. The smoke should clear soon. Rooms and corridors in undamaged sections of the fortress are now all sealed on emergency lockdown. Professor Josey Matlow Fox is the only listed captive, and the only logged survivor from Alpha Station or the planet. He's being interrogated on level one hundred and two, room six-three-six.'

Wood felt Hazel tense. 'Guide me,' he said. 'Can you disable those ships with the cannon?'

An antique rifle materialised in Tink's hands. The bombardment began.

Yearning for something to occupy her, Hazel stared about as smoke was sucked into the star-studded vacuum beyond the ruptured hull. The huge battlecruiser they'd clipped on their blind deceleration was spraying molten debris across the hangar, glowing red in the gloom where *Oscar*'s thruster had raked across it.

Oscar began strafing the immense chamber with sizzling beams, the shining spheres of its twin furnaces casting shifting shadows as it turned. Explosions bloomed in weird shapes as burning atmospheres and explosively vaporised materials, confined erratically by failing containment fields, burst into the vacuum. Crammed together, unable properly to deploy their defences, warships of all sizes began disintegrating under the bombardment, ejecting chunks of themselves and clouds of molten globules into the growing chaos. Two flattened oval destroyers, each five kilometres long, lifted from their docks only to collide. They ploughed as one into the facing bulkhead, smashing their streamlined noses flat, pouring yet more debris into the melee.

Between broken weaponry and disintegrating fighter craft, minute flailing figures were drifting in increasing numbers towards the star-filled hole where, only seconds ago, part of the fortress's hull had been. Some clung to more massive objects to try and prevent themselves being dragged into space, but soon even warships were drifting towards the hole like crumpled paper aeroplanes. Hazel watched their struggle with a gleam in her eye, her hatred momentarily so overwhelming that she'd rather have killed them all herself.

Oblivious to the bedlam it had created, the hulk whirled once more above the equipment bay floor, and purposefully faced a heavily buttressed wall peppered with the lights of observation windows. Behind the windows, figures wrestled with sealed doorways, or stared at the weapon now ominously facing them. A line of armed munitions drones wheeled and scuttled on to a nearby docking platform only to be obliterated by the careering stern section of a light cruiser.

Unconfined by gravity, flames licked like living things along a wall of the hangar, bathing the carnage bright orange.

DUFFY EAGLEBERGER had been en route to taking command of the Battlecruiser *Eat Dirt*, one of three to be left patrolling the enemy planet as *Violator* sped away for reinforcements, when what she at first mistook for a meteor had burst into the dock, bringing with it a convincing impression of hell.

Through a storm of debris, she watched with failing vision as the twin globes at the front of the thing shone with white fury, and light belched from its monstrous rotating tail, eating an expanding incandescent bowl into the far wall of the dock.

The shape shot forwards, and the wall it had faced dissolved in an explosion which deluged further molten debris around the dock, annihilating much of the surviving machinery assembled on the marshalling platforms. Then it was gone. Deeper inside. A weird, flickering cloud fanned out from the gaping hole the monstrous machine had left; evidence of the havoc it was wreaking, unseen, on the other side.

The air Duffy had held in her bursting lungs escaped in an involuntary sigh. She was astonished to find that, as well as most of the walkway she'd been standing on, her shoulder and seven-year-old regrown arm had disappeared, along with one of her legs below the knee.

When did that happen? She hadn't felt a thing.

Her remaining fingers slipped from the railing she was clutching, and she felt herself lifted, *so gently*, from the deck to join the growing tornado of debris spewing into space.

BULKHEAD AFTER BULKHEAD dissolved in dazzling explosions of tortured matter. Scrabbling human figures soared as hurricanes of escaping air sucked them from floors or chairs, tossing them amidst clouds of colliding, spinning and disintegrating furniture, hand-weapons, robots, machinery and other debris into the wake of the terrible machine. Grasping anything solid, some of the tiny figures were pathetically firing handguns before they died. After the carnage of Alpha Station, Wood had felt little initially, but *now* ...

Fear drove him on.

'We need to go up for level one hundred and two,' said Tink, with curious neutrality.

'Straight up?' Another wall dissolved into molten spray and vapour.

'Follow my plot.'

NIKUMI SURVEYED the skyrocketing catalogue of damage in consternation. The casualty toll was climbing faster than he could keep track. 'What does Nervecentral suggest?'

Jeetwa's image appeared before him. 'Sending fighters up the hole it's left, Sir. Our larger ships are disabled or blocked in, but we have at least a hundred serviceable fighters. This will be difficult: the fighters can't take the punishment the larger ships can, and it's chaos in there, full of debris. Clearing it will take time, and casualties will be considerable.'

'Casualties *are* considerable. Do it Jeetwa, now. We have visual on it, yet?'

'No Sir. This situation is unprecedented. Any sensors in position long enough to get a fix on the thing end up melted. There is no existing strategy to cope with this eventuality.'

'*Not* what I want to hear. Do we know what it's doing?'

'It's burrowing through our structure, creating havoc.'

'Random?'

'It seems to have a purpose.'

'Will it go for the reactors?'

'Holy fuck.'

'I want feedback, gentlemen!'

'Wait!' Waranika. 'I've visual on them *inside* fuel chamber nine.'

'Empty?'

'Yes.'

'Thank Christ. Now track them! I want to know how fast this weapon is going, and how long we'll have if it decides to go for the reactors.'

SLEWING *OSCAR* TO A HALT, Wood rotated the machine inside the enormous empty chamber they'd just entered. 'What's this?'

'Fuel tank for the main reactors.' *Empty*, thought Wood. *Maybe that's good. Maybe that means they've come a long way*. He toed the throttle pedal and they burst into an identical, equally empty chamber above. 'Track fifteen degrees left to miss the reactors.'

'I'll save them for the way out.'

Oscar burst through the next wall diagonally. The continuous inferno of the next seconds signified that they'd entered an area of smaller divisions.

'Crew's quarters,' said Tink.

Wood wanted to vomit. He longed to escape; to run away somewhere. It didn't matter where. Just anywhere but here. To wait for the end if need be. Survival's price was too high.

'Stop!' Tink cried, seconds later. Smoke and debris quickly cleared, revealing floor levels which *Oscar* had exposed in a neat cross-section as though the ship had burrowed through one of the honeycombs made by Haven's bees.

'What next?' Wood asked. He was breathing heavily. He hadn't thought beyond this stage.

'The interrogation room will be airtight. If we are very careful, we can whittle away the surrounding structure and use a docking extension to link up with it.'

'That's brilliant, Tink.'

'Hurry,' Hazel urged through her teeth. 'I think the telepath's realised what's happening. He knows what we're going to try. I might be able to stop him …' Her mouth opened as an unseen battle began. 'Shit. Going to be a struggle. Just do what you have to.'

Her face twisted in a snarl. Wood stared at her. Then, as quickly and as gently as he could, he began to manoeuvre *Oscar*'s cumbersome hulk into position.

33

TERRIBLY WRONG

SATAN PACED in increasing alarm.

The intercom was dead. He could still feel the guards outside. They were beginning to panic. The floor was trembling more violently now, and noises from outside had grown from distant, muffled booming to a deafening fusillade of sound. The screen by the door showed that the only way in or out of the room had been sealed shut by the fortress grid.

He was trapped.

Not only that, they were coming, soon. And it was unquestionably *him* they were after, though he still failed to grasp how they expected to reach him, here in the heart of a massively protected warship. He needed to find the co-ordinates of Haven, he realised – and quickly. If anything was to happen to him, then he'd at least make sure that others suffered for it.

Then he understood.

I don't believe this.

The audacity of what his pursuers planned was breathtaking.

Dispensing with his instruments, he plunged once again into the deeply wounded mind of his patient. There was no time for delicacy now. He cut deeper, hacking at the mental barriers Fox still managed to raise against him. The man was losing coherence and identity, forgetting who he was and why he was fighting.

Just as it seemed that he was finally about to break through, Satan felt an unexpected, fierce sense of pressure, and suddenly the emphasis was changed. He was now defending his own mental sanctity from the combined wills of what remained of Fox, and someone else.

The telepath!

He tumbled, gasping, to the hard floor, hands spread for support. The floor shook violently beneath him. It was scorching hot where he touched it, but he barely noticed as he fought to escape the corner he'd backed himself into, feeling his defences buckle against the ferocity of the onslaught. He was faintly aware of the stench of burning skin. Shapes, images, destructive commands were hurled at him like hammer blows, making his head spin, killing brain cells.

With a violent effort he withdrew, and lay, panting, on the bucking floor. His trousers, he noticed vaguely, were smoking. As were his hands. Something inside his head – he couldn't tell what, exactly – felt soft and vague, like flesh bruised beyond the point of recovery. The cacophony from outside was now ear-splitting: tortured materials screaming, booming, clattering like a flood of garbage descending a chute, and a thunderous background roar. He clamped hands over his ears. What was going *on* out there?

Then it all stopped.

He reached out but could no longer sense the guards. There was the sound of grating metal, and a hollow clank which made the room resonate like a bell. An eerie silence descended.

They were coming in.

Gripped now with fear, Satan pulled his stolen sidearm from its holster. Retreating to the corner nearest the door, he instructed the room's interactive furniture module to form a high, solid table in front of him. Light danced behind his eyes: she'd found him again, smashing against his mind like blows of an axe. He pushed her back, but her fury was terrifying. He clutched his head. He'd never felt anything like this. It was like being eaten alive from within.

There was a sound. A sharp smell. The door began to smoke. A bright, red line travelled purposefully around it until it formed a circle. Something pushed the detached sheet of door material into the room, where it landed with a clang.

Satan raised his pistol with trembling hands. He was straining to see through the blade-like shapes slashing into his perceptual framework. Doubting his accuracy, he adjusted the setting to maximum spread.

Something was at the door. Something shiny.

A piece of reflective metal on a pole.

He roared with effort and fired. Metal and pole dissolved into vapour and molten gobbets, along with much of the surface of the door. He felt the pressure slacken a little and blinked, allowing himself a small flush of triumph. Then a pressure suited figure hurtled through the hole and skidded across the floor.

Roaring once more, he fired into it, again and again, until only charred fabric remained.

He cried out in triumph.

Only then did he notice the small, flame-haired figure standing in the room, feet braced pugnaciously apart, not far from the hole in the door.

Instantly, everything in the room seemed to focus on her eyes. Orbs of crimson, they bored into him like surgical lasers.

Her!

Satan stared. He was completely frozen. The air around the woman seemed to crackle. An arm was held behind her, over her shoulder. She was tensing.

Screaming, he swung the gun round. As her arm came up and forward, she screamed herself, in a way that was beyond sound. His mind seemed to melt before it; ice before a furnace.

The gun fired. Then it slipped from his fingers as he raised hands to his head and *something* punched into his chest, lifting him off his feet, hurling him into the wall.

His knees buckled. Braced against the wall, he looked down and was puzzled by what he saw. A dirty bar of metal was protruding from the lapel of his white operating coat, central to a thin corona of dark red. He grasped the protruding part. Tried to pull it free. It *worried* him sticking out like that. It wouldn't move; he could feel it wedged between bones inside.

He blinked at the young woman he knew was called Hazel.

What have you done?

The flame haired girl was staring in the direction of Josey Fox. Derangement was in her eyes. With terrible purpose they swung back towards him, and the look in them loosened his bowels.

I haven't finished yet, hissed her voice in his head.

The blows began again: relentless, spiked clubs of palpable force which pummelled his mind into a bloody mess. He pitched on to his knees, collapsing against the corner as one of his legs gave way completely. Some part of him, he knew, had just been destroyed.

'Stop,' he managed to mumble. He could no longer feel half of his face, and could barely form the word. Thoughts wandering, he began to ramble, one eye half-closed, the other staring fixedly at Hazel, who stood over him, snarling and shaking, veins standing, her streaming eyes now screwed tightly shut.

'LOCATED THEM: they're in the same sector as the prisoner. And Satan.' This was Jeetwa again.

'At least they've spared the reactors.' Nikumi knew he was missing something. 'How did they know where the prisoner was?'

'Their thinker sequestrated our grid.'

How did things suddenly get like this? he wondered, knowing that the thought was perilously close to self-pity. 'But that doesn't explain …' *Never mind, concentrate!* 'How is the pursuit?'

'Twenty kilometres, advancing.' Kettering this time. 'Thirty Firefuries up there. We lost eight to debris.' As Kettering spoke, Nikumi watched in glorious 3D as another of the shard-like fast attack craft was crushed against the lethally jagged wall of the tunnel by a molten gobbet. 'Make that nine. They're clearing the way using bond disrupters.'

'ETA?'

'Five minutes,' said Waranika.

Too long. 'Evacuate that area as best you can.' He saw that the damaged battlecruisers *Merciless* and *Scum Killer* were predicting operational status within eight and ten minutes. They'd have no option but to destroy what remained of the hangar portal from the inside. 'Atmosphere?'

'We've lost a lot, but we're stable.'

'How long would that thing take to breach the reactors?'

'Based on their progress so far, Nervecentral reckons three minutes.'

Mother of God. 'Keep on it. Send in a smart nuke.'

A startled pause. 'Sir?'

'Do it!'

'We can't evacuate anywhere except the bridge – the fortress won't let us! It's telling us its structural integrity depends on keeping all doors closed.'

'Send the nuke, Lieutenant! Send it, or leave your position for someone who will.'

WOOD SPRINTED to the airlock.

The concertina-like extension of *Oscar*'s outer door had sealed itself to the outside of the room where the Professor was supposedly being held. Stealing up to the room's exposed door, he tried to quieten his breathing. Keeping to one side, afraid to peer in, he strained for sounds coming through the hole Hazel had cut. Its edges were still smoking.

All he could hear from inside was ragged breathing and what sounded like whimpering.

He edged closer. There was a disquieting, thick smell behind the sharpness of the smoke. Despite the apparent calm, the air seemed somehow sick with violence. He couldn't see anything without risking revealing himself.

Scalp prickling, he gathered himself, grimaced, and took a few deep, short breaths.

Then he threw himself head-first through the hole, the way he'd seen police officers do in holovids.

A Morphtec table was nearby. He hit the floor hands-first. Rolling awkwardly on one shoulder, he could sense Hazel to his right, and what might have been another man in a corner to his left. Completing his roll, he managed to scramble behind the table, keeping Hazel at his back.

His eyes widened as he peeped over the top and saw the bloodstained instruments strewn over it.

Hazel?

No answer. He ducked down again, listened, and then peered more determinedly over the top. His attention was grabbed not by Hazel or the figure in the corner, but what he saw to his right.

Strapped to a tilted board inside an isolation bubble, and spread over two large surgical tables, was what remained of Professor Josey Fox.

The man had been eviscerated. His entrails were pinned to one of the tables in an artistic arrangement of bows and knots, which an assortment of plastic drip bags had dyed different colours. Full of something luminously green, similar tubes vanished into his liver and small orifices torn all over the rest of his body. His scrotum was vastly expanded and lit from within like a green lampshade; his ribcage spread open, lungs pinned aside with clamps, revealing his heart, still beating in the harsh white light. With three fingers missing, one forearm was skewered inside a vat of something which seemed to be dissolving it. The inverted skin which had been flayed from it was stretched over his other arm like a wet, crimson glove.

But the worst thing ... Propped in a kind of tripod on the nearest table was the top of a human cranium, now a convenient container for an assortment of blood-caked knives, skewers and hooks. In its place, optic filaments sprouted like silver hair from purple-grey cerebral folds. The front of the creature's brain wore what Wood at first took to be a crude tiara. With a jolt, he realised that it was formed by the protruding cusps of the man's own extracted teeth.

Clutching his mouth, he collapsed to his knees behind the table. *Don't think. Don't think. You didn't see that!* Stomach convulsing, he forced himself to look at the other man; the one slumped in the corner. He didn't seem an immediate threat, with a metal bar sticking out of his chest, crimson bubbling from his mouth, and irises which seemed to have disappeared inside his head. Merely the echoes of whatever Hazel was doing to him were making Wood's skin crawl. *Hazel?*

He looked up at her face. Froze.

'Hazel!' he cried, if anything more aghast at the relish in Hazel's eyes than what had been done to Josey Fox. 'Stop it – you've won!'

Jumping up, he pulled at her arm. She seemed not to notice. 'Hazel. *Stop.*'

Again, he found himself hitting her around the face – in his horror much harder than intended. She spun into the wall and her victim relaxed with a sigh. The man crumpled forward on to his side, half his oddly plain features twitching, one eye gazing fixedly at Hazel.

Crouched against the wall as though about to attack him, Hazel regarded Wood with diamond-hard, mauve eyes, wiping a droplet of blood from a corner of her mouth.

'Hazel.' He was backing away. 'It had to stop. It *had* to! He won't bother us any more.'

Still looking at Wood in a way which made him shiver, Hazel stood up. Without a word, she approached the bubble enclosing the couch the Professor was fastened to and looked into what remained of his face.

'Get out of there, now.' Tink's voice, relayed from a battered drone now hovering at the hole in the door. 'They're sending things up the tunnel we made. I don't know what they are, but I really think we should leave. Two of their battlecruisers are coming online too.'

'We're coming!' Wood yelled. Hazel stomped across the room and stood over the twitching body of Fox's torturer. She pointed at Fox.

'How do you deactivate the couch?'

'Please miss,' the man slurred, 'don't hurt us miss; please miss, please don't hurt us, please.'

'*How do you deactivate the couch?*' She came a step nearer.

'Please, miss. Don't hurt me!'

'HOW?' Hazel screamed, kicking him in the stomach. The thud was sickening. Satan grunted and writhed, vomiting a dark slick along the floor. Wood put a hand to his face. This was all so *wrong*.

Then he remembered the gun.

'Don't hurt me!' the man gasped, his good eye swivelling. 'Don't hurt me don't hurt me don't hurt me don't hurt …' The words tailed away into mumbling.

There was a gunshot. Jumping, Hazel turned to see Wood pocketing the man's pistol. The leg supporting the Professor's couch sparked and smoked, the bubble of its field gone. Trailing a fat red smear, the Professor's body sagged to the floor in dreadful silence, the pins holding his lungs aside and the clamps spreading his chest open ripping chunks from his obscenely trailing lungs.

Wood watched in horror. '*Fuck!*'

'Help me,' Hazel ordered, rushing to the Professor and getting an arm behind him.

'But what do you want us to do? His … guts are all over the place! His head …!'

A look of madness entered Hazel's eyes. She tore at her hair, screaming, then grasped the Professor's lungs and began stuffing them into his chest cavity. Blood ran down her arms.

'Help me, hurry! We'll lose him!'

As far as Wood could see, he was already lost. He dithered, then began hauling up soft armfuls of multicoloured guts, tearing them off their retaining pins, struggling to force them between flaps of skin and internal membrane into the Professor's almost empty body cavity.

'They won't go in! Ah God, they won't go in unless they're folded neatly!' He was on the verge of losing his mind. The Professor was making awful smacking noises with his lips and toothless gums. 'Which one of these tubes was his air? He'll suffocate!'

'Tink! Can you float The Professor out?'

'It'll take a minute to arrange.'

Hazel stooped to pick Fox up.

'But his guts,' Wood protested. 'His brain'll spill out on the floor! Those fibres …'

Hazel seized the guts from Wood and tried to ram them into the Professor's body using her arms and stomach. 'Use the tubing – *tie* them!'

Wood pulled some of the tubing from the couch, spilling green fluid across the floor. Having wrapped it twice around Fox's torso, he fiddled ineffectually with the knot.

'Just carry them, Wood!' She tore the fibre optics from their socket in the neighbouring surgical drone, grasped the top of the Professor's skull, emptied the instruments it contained on to the floor, and placed it carefully over his exposed brain.

The forehead was hairy. It was back to front.

Hazel shrieked in despair. Ripping another tube from the couch, she wound it over the top of his head and around his chin, tying it with shaking, gore-caked fingers in a bow next to his cheek.

Face a white mask, she picked up the twitching body up as though it were hollow and strode to the hole in the door, leaving Wood scurrying behind attempting to bundle lengths of slippery multicoloured intestine up in his arms.

Hazel stepped through. Wood flung his armful into the space beyond and followed.

FRYING IN HIS OWN BLOOD and vomit, Satan lay on the smoking floor. He listened to his breathing and the clank as the airlock disconnected, and then the rush of air pouring out through the hole in the door into the flickering light beyond.

He was no longer entirely sure who he was, or what was happening to him. It was certainly a mystery why his skin felt so tight; why he was sliding sideways, or where the ferocious wind was coming from.

Had someone left a door open? *Fools.*

The only thing that really mattered was that those horrible people had gone. Now, perhaps, he could be alone for a bit.

He liked being alone. He had to, really. He remembered that he'd been alone a lot, although he could no longer remember when. Seeing other people together – laughing, touching; sharing – had always made him angry and uncomfortable. People meant pain, with their needles, and their horrible machines, and their *examinations*. It was why he liked to hurt them back.

It really was better to he alone.

Perhaps he would just go to sleep. He certainly felt sleepy. Or … no, that wasn't exactly it. He felt sort of … cold – but, despite the pain, warm and snug at the same time, if that made any sense. The feeling frightened him a little. He felt there was something about it that he should know was bad.

Perhaps it would come back to him.

'CLOSING OBJECTS around the first bend,' warned Tink. 'Under power. Many more following.'

Hazel was in the sleeping room putting Fox in the surgery. Wood prayed she had everything fixed down. 'We'll go another way. Hazel,' he bellowed, 'hold on to something!'

In the rear-view HUD screen, Fox's torture chamber protruded like a stump into the cavern *Oscar* had excavated around it. As Wood halted the ship's rotation, a tiny figure in white pirouetted out of the circular hole in the doorway amid a shower of furniture and sparkling smaller items. On all sides was a chaos of twisted materials and colliding debris. Down the tunnel, something was moving. A beam of orange light seared out. It struck *Oscar* close to the control room in a plume of vaporised hull material.

'Missile incoming! That's crazy – it's got a nuclear warhead!'

Wood pushed hard against the pedals. The wall ahead disintegrated. They burst through, leaving more debris ricocheting around the now red-glowing empty chamber behind.

'Still closing!' A diagram showed the progress of the missile: a dark cone picking its way through the debris of the tunnel. 'We won't kill it in here – certainly not if it's behind us.'

'Will our thruster torch take it out?'

'I think it's intelligent enough to avoid it.'

'Reactors.' Wood realised he was shaking. 'Where are they? Quick!'

'Right thirty degrees, up seven.' Tink displayed the target's direction as a cross on the main screen's orientational grid. 'The reaction core is heavily shielded. That thing's gaining fast.'

'Give us everything.'

Wood pulled at the joystick, doing his best to grind the tips of the thruster pedals into the floor. *Oscar* ripped through wall after wall, faster and faster, the ship jarring at each contact.

Seeing their retreat, the missile tore through the bombardment of hot debris after them, every circuit of its focussed little thinker straining to plot the fastest possible course.

34

CALCULATED DEMONSTRATION

'REACTORS!' bellowed Waranika. 'ETA eleven secs!'

A chill shot inwards from Nikumi's skin. 'Abandon ship! Everyone for yourselves!'

Even as he fully realised what he'd just screamed, Aral Nikumi was sprinting for the red-lit emergency gravtrain portal which snapped open in the sphere of stars a few metres from him. He seized Jeetwa and threw him ahead. As the emergency klaxon began howling, the two were already diving into the portal's circular opening, closely followed by Kettering.

A burst of savage acceleration made his vertebrae crackle. In close formation, the three were soon flashing through a dark tunnel at more than four hundred metres per second. Lights zipped past too fast to separate. *If they've damaged the gravtrain …*

Well, then he would never know.

How could a machine move through solid material like that? And so fast?

After an equally punishing deceleration, the three were spat into the collection field of a bare, cylindrical cabin. To Nikumi's amazement, according to the display of his implant, barely nine seconds had elapsed since he'd given the command to abandon ship. There was a thump, and the mechanical screaming noise of a spacecraft launching at around twenty-five Gs. Five of which were transmitted to the occupants.

'The others,' gasped Jeetwa.

'Were too late,' breathed Nikumi. 'Maybe some in other tubes. Might be too late ourselves.'

He couldn't believe it. It was inconceivable.

He'd just lost *Violator*.

THERE WAS A JOLT significantly more violent than the rest, and light crowded the control room, swiftly darkened by the hull's smart filtering. There was a deafening rubbing sound as *Oscar* catapulted through the other side of the reactor chamber, glowing matter flickering and bubbling just metres from where Wood was sitting.

Seconds later, his bizarre starship burst through the thick outer skin of the fortress and out into open space, shrouded in glowing ionised gases, trailing vaporising molten slag like a meteor hitting an atmosphere.

'We lost the missile.'

Wood took a shuddering intake of air. In the rear-view display, the squashed cube began squirting searchlight beams of superheated gases from the two holes punched in its tough exterior shell. Slowly at first, it started to spin. A hundred smaller cracks and weaknesses opened up one by one, spewing out the enormous structure's corrupted contents in smaller jets at different angles. Gradually it rotated faster, and faster, until it was spinning like a top, drifting and whirling inexorably down towards the thin atmosphere of the planet.

'Escaping ship,' warned Tink.

Wood frowned. 'Alone?' Warnings were lighting up all over the console. He didn't dare look too closely.

'Just one. Designed for speed, quite small. It's pulling away at twenty-three Gs.' The central screen showed a magnification of the vessel: a stubby cylindrical frame ninety metres in length containing a large hydrogen reservoir with a huge thruster on the stern, pouring hot particles into the vacuum in a brilliant five hundred-kilometre tail.

We can't let it go, Hazel told him, from the sleeping room.

'Is it armed, Tink?'

'I can see two small missiles with radioactive signatures.'

'Can we catch it?'

'Just. Wood, we've sustained damage.'

'I know. Just hold it together a little longer.'

NIKUMI, KETTERING AND JEETWA had arranged themselves in semi-comfortable positions with the aid of voice-activated fields in the emergency escape courier. The playback of their escape when they'd activated the little vessel's sensurrounds had been hair-raising. The explosion of the reactor, and the subsequent chain reaction involving all other fuels, flammable gases and secondary reactors on board, had overtaken them fractionally before they'd reached open space. They'd narrowly avoided large chunks of debris in the disintegrating launch tube ahead of them.

'Jesus fucking Christ,' hissed Kettering. 'It's coming after us, Commodore.'

In the view astern, just above the spinning shell of *Violator*, twin pinpricks of light could clearly be seen. They grew larger and wider apart as they watched.

'What *is* that thing? Physics doesn't seem to apply to it!'

Nikumi examined options. They were severely limited. No other escape ships had been detected: the onboard thinker seemed convinced that he, Kettering, Jeetwa were the sole survivors. The enemy vessel was closing fast – and twisting into hyperspace this close to a planet was not just risky, it was suicide. Nothing but a missile should have been able to outrun a naval warship officer's escape courier.

He studied the courier's inventory. Enough food, water and air for sixty days. Two nuclear missiles. Nothing else.

Using his implant, he fired both missiles. The three men watched with growing tension as they arced towards the approaching craft.

'BOTH NUKES FIRED. Shall I ...'

'Guide them into the scoop. Damp them.'

'*What?* I don't know if *Oscar* can withstand that.'

'Try! It's important, Tink. Trust me.'

'MISSILES CLOSING,' murmured Jeetwa, unnecessarily. Strained from shock and the escape vessel's continuing acceleration, his face brightened slightly. 'If that thing was going to react, they're leaving it very late. Maybe we damaged it? Three ... two ... *Yes!*'

Magnified by the courier's sensors, the missiles zipped down the open throat of the machine and detonated. There was a blinding flash. Momentarily, the twin globes on the machine's front glowed as brightly as the distant sun.

Then it was still coming at them.

'Holy shit,' breathed Jeetwa. He was beginning to shake. 'Shit. Did you *see* that?'

'We all saw that,' muttered Kettering. Nikumi let out a resigned sigh. The machine's dark mouth was approaching, its booms seeming to spread on either side of the courier like encompassing arms. The vessel twitched. They were in a gravity lasso.

'Options, gentlemen?'

Kettering gave him a fierce stare. 'We wait for capture. Redline the reactor. Take the bastards with us.'

'You've just seen their nicely calculated little demonstration involving two genuine warheads. Nice gesture, but how much good do you think that's going to do?'

'We can try.'

'We would fail.'

Kettering's fists were clenched. 'We can't let these monsters get away with this!'

No. We can't. Though he hid it better, Nikumi was also enraged. Well, he thought – they would bide their time and see what avenues presented themselves. *Violator. My God.* A total of almost two hundred thousand good people, including the crews of the auxiliaries …

A shadow crept over the sensors until everything was black. Astern, the remains of Inter Planetary Economic Confederate Navy Divide and Rule-class Fortress *Violator* spun, ever faster, down towards the thin atmosphere of the Freaks' hideout.

In a few hours there would be a new crater on the planet's drab plains.

35

'SCREW YOU'

HE SHOULD HAVE seen it coming. The uncomfortable truth was that he'd grown complacent in his old age. He'd seriously underestimated both his enemy's cunning and his ruthlessness. Not to mention his anal retentiveness and paranoia.

And yet, even if he *had* seen it coming, the mechanisms Fox had installed were unlikely to have been cleanly eradicated. The best that could have been hoped for was damage limitation. It pained him to admit it, but the man had always had them over a barrel, in ways no-one had suspected. Only a sage could have predicted his masterstroke.

What fucking irony, that he'd used the heart of their own system against them.

Marcell rested his temples between his fingers. The planet below was mostly dark today, echoing his mood. For the first time in centuries, the light of the reflectors had ceased to shine on the city, which was visible only as a dim orange gridwork. Instead, it spelled the words 'SCREW YOU,' in bright letters across the plain of low cloud west of the city.

A light on his desk screen caught his attention. He gave the go ahead with a wave of his hand. 'Yes,' he snarled. 'Ah, JH. I hope you're bringing some good news.'

'It's chaos, James.' The Supreme Chief of Special Services had aged a good ten years since Marcell had last seen him. His flinty eyes were dulled, yellowed, and encircled by puffy rings. 'The scale and depth of this is unprecedented. Ructions, right across the board – and the ripples are spreading through the confederation as fast as couriers can fly. The finances of civilians, corporations – everything – are wiped clean. The only entities with anything left are those with their own private grids or physically isolated storage, but they're rare. Besides, even some of those have been wiped, and with the grid itself down their credit's worthless anyway.

'Nobody knows who owns what, anywhere. No one can *buy* anything. It's estimated that point five percent of Renascido's population has already self-euthanised, and the rest is either cowering and waiting for starvation or helping to tear the place up. The rioting itself has killed millions and is tying up the army and emergency services which should be distributing emergency food handouts and aid. Everything was controlled by the Grid. *Everything*, James. The contingency plans just did not cover a manmade disaster this fundamental.'

Jesus Hussain shook his head. 'With all the streetblock thinkers down, an estimated twelve percent of the surviving population can't even be reached without cutting into buildings with debonders. News won't have reached Paradise yet, but the military bases it *has* reached are in a state of near-mutiny. Even commanding officers are refusing to work until pay can be guaranteed. And with the bottom having fallen out of the economy, even if there wasn't the problem of how to physically to pay them, we now have nothing to pay them *with*.'

Marcell held the bridge of his nose between a thumb and forefinger. 'What's your worst-case scenario.'

Hussain puffed out his cheeks. 'The end of the I.P.E.C.? It's becoming difficult to see how the transworld economy will survive the shockwaves without major changes.'

Marcell was speechless. The enemy's action was simply breathtaking. What he'd perpetrated was quite simply the most catastrophic act of vandalism in history.

Well, if he'd wanted enemies, he had made them with a vengeance. 'All this just to sabotage a single offensive?' He ground his teeth. '*Against one infested little planet?*'

'He may well have succeeded, James. This puts us in an extremely difficult, not to say vulnerable, position. A move our tactical thinkers agree Fox is likely to make next, if he has not already done so, is broadcasting our economic woes, and our intention to send our navy away on an invasion, to the Lancers. They'll be watching us closely now. He's playing this like a game of chess. We can't move the fleet against him without the Lancers sweeping into the gap and helping themselves to some of our prize assets. And I can't see that they *won't* react, given an opportunity like that.'

'Tiny Mind agrees,' conceded Marcell in a monotone.

'We're looking at triage, James. We cannot hope to defend the outer perimeter in the circumstances.'

Marcell gave the comment a cursory nod. 'Is Troubleshooter ready?'

'The last communications from Panspacial say it's fully operational, although the test programme has another three months to run.'

'Tests?' he spluttered. 'Launch it immediately! Launch the fucking fleet!' The other man showed signs of losing his composure.

'James,' he replied, rubbing face forehead. 'It's not that simple! Have you not been listening? The economy is crashing – and this crash is spreading to the fringes of the IPEC as we speak, as fast as information can travel. By the time such an order arrives, credit will be worthless. How will people be paid? Who do you think will fight or work without prospects of pay?'

Marcell rose from his seat, fists clenched. 'J. H., I find this intolerable. I do not accept that that little *fuck* has us beaten. I don't seriously think you do either.'

'We are looking at options,' agreed Hussain, grimly. 'They are being discussed, and I'm afraid the matter may soon be beyond our control. The house of representatives is voting on the effective quarantine of Paradise and the withholding of information from all military personnel there, along with those involved with Troubleshooter, so that the fleet can be employed before word of this can stop the operation in its tracks.

'With martial law now imposed, we're considering giving the military legal rights to loot our own colonies and operations. Which they may well do anyway – and the threat of a coup cannot be ruled out. Ironically, the threat from the Lancers might prove enough to fire up and reunify both our military and civilian populations. Unfortunately, that's likely to be directed at the Lancers, and not the Freaks.'

What a mess. Turning from Hussain, James Marcell rotated his seat, took a deep breath, and stared through the window wall at the dark planet below. The words 'SCREW YOU' greeted him. His knuckles popped.

'JH, we have to find a way to sell the Freaks as the main problem. Damn it, grant all ranking officers a proportionate share of Unicorp's assets. Just burn this wretched planet!'

'I will pass on your suggestion. But it's *out of our hands now*, James. Ironic, isn't it? How, when the crunch comes, your puppets unexpectedly develop a life of their own. And don't be too sure of Unicorp's assets. You may have everything locked down in that fancy grid of yours, but if the market itself is gone it may benefit you little. Like I said, we're looking at triage. The emergency delegations met an hour ago, and the majority vote was that the outlying third of Confederate space should be sacrificed to the Lancers.'

'Sacrificed?' He could scarcely believe his ears. 'Almost half of the Confederate worlds, just *handed over* to the Lancers?'

'Yes James, handed over. Remember, however, these are comparatively lightly populated planets –'

'And increasingly our most reliable mineral sources! Quite apart from the direct losses to the economy, have you any *idea* of the tactical power this will hand to the Lancers? Especially if they're united by Fox into some kind of crusade! We need to expand to survive. A few years down the line, they might be able to squeeze us out entirely!'

'As you're so fond of saying, James: first things first. We cannot hope to patrol the outer regions in the circumstances, even if we halve the fleet we had hoped to send to Haven. Sending what we planned is simply no longer an option. It will make us too vulnerable.'

Marcell grasped the edge of the desktop and glared into the eyes of Hussain's image. 'Get them before they can do anything else,' he screamed. 'Whatever you need of Unicorp's assets are at your disposal. *Just get them!*'

Creasing into a very irritated frown, Hussain's face flicked abruptly out of the air. Marcell sat in his chair, breathing hard.

Fury took him. He rose, kicking the chair away. Then he took an antique driving iron from its clip on the wall and began single-mindedly smashing his collection comprising every single one of the world's remaining Ming vases into small fragments.

Damn them all. The damage they'd done already was enough to justify turning them and their miserable little planet to slag a million times over. Suddenly he wanted to be there; to watch it happen. He wanted to see Fox's face as he watched his infernal creation boil.

He would watch the recordings of it. That would have to suffice. In the meantime, he knew that his life now had a single purpose.

He would not rest until he'd seen the Freaks utterly exterminated, like the infernal, crawling, backward little parasites they were.

36

MONSTER

WOOD STARED at the slatted metal ceiling. He was so tired that he felt sick, but sleep was somewhere chaos and fear awaited. He was still buzzing with adrenaline.

He propped himself on an elbow and studied the profile of the man who occupied the surgery's skeletal couch, above him at waist level by the far wall.

The surgery had returned his internal organs to their natural places and repaired them as far as it was able. It had painstakingly extracted the cables from his brain, neutralised the toxins the telepath had used, encouraged regeneration of damaged and missing tissues and body parts, fused the top of his skull in place, and glued his flesh and skin back together. A red seam encircled the man's otherwise unlined shaven head just above his brow. He seemed to be sleeping. His sunken eyes were closed, his ageless, once more human face was calm – perhaps unnaturally so. Occasionally the features would tense, and there would be a small twitch, or the eyebrows would raise as though in surprise or alarm.

Wood wondered if he'd ever be able to meet the man he'd heard so much about. Whether he still existed.

He pushed aside his blanket and walked, barefoot, to his seat in the control room, rubbing prickly eyes with his palms. Hazel was still in the co-pilot's seat, her arm in a sling, staring blankly at hyperspace. The fact that she could stare at it at all said a lot about her state of mind. She didn't seem to register his arrival.

He studied her shapely ears and pointed chin, the scarred bump on the bridge of her nose and her high forehead. Mats of curled hair hung before her face. Her eyes were a haunted blue. He'd thought he had known her.

Now, he wasn't so sure.

He lay back in the pilot's seat and stared beyond the transparent hull. With nothing to hold his attention, it quickly became uncomfortable. He returned his attention to Hazel. He opened his mouth to speak, but lacked the necessary momentum, and instead examined the switches and interactive displays of the console.

Before he could give himself the chance to back out again, he said 'Hazel, is he going to be all right? The Professor.'

She seemed not to hear, but as he was about to repeat the question, her gaze dipped to the hands clasped in her lap.

'I don't know. Physically, the surgery is patching him up well, and he should make at least a partial recovery. What was done to him was done skilfully, to cause the maximum trauma while keeping him alive. Mentally –'

She shut her eyes.

'That man did horrific things. I don't know how much he's been damaged yet, or even what's left.'

Gloomy silence resumed. According to Tink, the systems of the IPEC fortress had logged the launch of a message by courier not long after its arrival at Alpha Station. Though the content of the message wasn't known, it was bound for a military base called Area X, using a string of deep-space relay stations the fortress had laid behind it in interstellar space. IPEC would soon know approximately where Haven was.

'He kept saying that this has all happened "too soon",' Hazel said, abruptly. 'That's all I can get out of him.' She shifted her injured shoulder with a grimace. 'When he wakes, I'll see if I can start untangling the knots, and sorting out what's real and what that monster put in there.'

Wood vented a restrained sigh, watching his feet brush the control pedals. Memories of the previous day were like snatches of a nightmare. *Oscar* was damaged, though not disastrously: mostly burned-out sensors, ducts clogged with resolidified debris, and stress fractures in layers of the hull. Tink was supervising the repair programme and had promised that the ship would be largely recovered by their return to Haven. He'd even claimed to be modifying the composition of the hulls to provide more elasticity.

'Never, ever, pull that stunt with the scoop again,' the AI had told him with uncharacteristic bluntness.

There had, at least, been no trouble from the captives in the scoop. Tink had crippled their thinker, shut down the reactor, fried all their vessel's sensors and even melted the escape craft's thrusters shut to make sure they couldn't cause mischief. Hazel had wanted *Oscar* to digest the vessel and its occupants as fusion fuel. Wood had eventually managed to talk her out of it, feeling that more than enough blood was on his hands for one day. He'd just killed enough people to populate a city.

He wasn't sure what kind of monster that made him. Worse, he had a terrible suspicion he was going to be called upon to do the same thing again.

'Wood.' Hazel's soft, throaty voice interrupted his introspection. As he turned his head she looked briefly into his eyes. Then her own eyes darted away again, darkening to pools of onyx. 'Wood I …'

She stalled, struggling to find words for what she needed to say.

'Thank you for stopping me.' The corners of her mouth were arched downwards. 'It wasn't good. Not good at all.'

Shrugging, he managed to meet her gaze only by squinting. 'I had to stop you.'

'I know. I was …' She pressed the heels of her hands into her eyes and began to shake. Gently at first, then harder and harder. 'Wood, please forgive me. I am so sorry!'

Wood slipped out of his seat. He bent down and put his arms about her shoulders, pressing her face into his chest. The front of his shirt was soon soaked.

I wish I could do that. He kept the thought to himself.

Slowly, hesitantly at first, their minds found comfort in each other again.

ENVIOUS OF THIS CAPACITY for emotional release, Tink watched the two humans in silence. He couldn't even lose himself in work the way his companions seemed to: his capacity for introspection remained undimmed regardless of how busily the parts of the ship which served as his arms and legs, eyes and ears were operating.

The events of a few hours ago troubled him deeply.

For most of his short life, two things had terrified him above all else: the concept of death and being alone. Wood's extended absence on Haven had distressed Tink more than he would ever let his friend know.

Having analysed his thoughts and feelings on such matters at length, he'd concluded that what he cared about were things which affected him directly. That meant Wood, and now Hazel, and finding somewhere he could exist without persecution. These things were now all inextricably mixed up with the fate of the planet Haven, and so he'd agreed to help with whatever was needed to make Haven and its inhabitants safe.

That had been the case until yesterday.

Now, his synapse-analogues seethed with images of the mayhem he'd helped instigate – each of whose casualties he assumed to be a unique person capable of feelings much like Wood's or his own – and he was just confused, and worried by the ambiguity of human, and his own, concepts of the value of individual lives.

Meanwhile, his bodily appendages were busy restructuring, rebonding, checking, cleaning and unclogging. In an attempt to distract himself, he'd even decided to give the outer hull a makeover. The task barely begun, he'd sent a dedicated sensor drone outside, operating on what Wood might have called a 'hunch'.

He couldn't recall having one of these before – not one so important, anyway – and was quietly excited despite his otherwise brooding thoughts.

The drone drifted from the airlock. Beginning with the main thruster, it began a systematic, infinitely patient sweep of *Oscar*'s exterior, slaving other, less specialised drones to its control. From the tip of the main drive to the furnaces, the little flotilla corkscrewed steadily over the hull, mapping every millimetre of the scored, blackened surface and areas of silver-grey and yellow which the drones doing the scrubbing, polishing, repairing and strengthening had so far uncovered.

It wasn't long before his suspicions were confirmed. One of the drones found a small hole a couple of centimetres wide. Hours old, if spectrographic readings were any evidence.

Then the drones found another

And another.

The ship was infested with mites.

Tink allowed the drones to continue until he was sure that none had been missed. He even sent them inside the scoop to scan the IPEC escape vessel.

He had formed, then followed up, an important intuitive thought!

Despite the fear generated by the discovery, the knowledge of what he'd done – by himself – was exhilarating, and he revelled in it until the issue of what he should do about it began to intrude. *Oscar* could not emerge from hyperspace with the mites still in their burrows.

Ask Wood. He'll know what to do.

From his monitors he could see that Wood and Hazel were still deep in some mental conversation. Their vital signs were steadily calming down, and he found himself very reluctant to disturb them.

Perhaps he could deal with it himself?

The prospect was daunting. And yet, he had the required knowledge, surely? All he had to do was formulate a solution, based upon available facts, and implement it …

But what if you're wrong? What if something terrible happens?

The AI sifted through the library and modelled outcomes from a long list of possible solutions. He found himself rejecting one after another. Then, eventually, he hit on one which, no matter how he looked at it, seemed to bear no obviously fatal flaws.

He got the Mrs Blob to examine the solution independently, and it seemed to confirm his opinion. Which, unfortunately, was useful only if his appraisal of the facts had been correct, and he possessed all the necessary facts in the first place.

He hesitated, terrified of basing such drastic action on his own judgement of an imperfect dataset, wondering yet again how Wood and Hazel managed to make split second decisions with such apparent confidence. What if he woke the mites up, and they escaped?

What if he blew *Oscar* to bits because he'd overlooked some flaw, or some critical aspect of the vessel's design?

Perhaps, it occurred to him, confidence was simply a state of self-deception. Perhaps humans continuously deluded themselves that their actions would always be beneficial, or that it didn't matter if they weren't.

Perhaps *delusion* was the secret!

He would delude himself, he decided. He would pretend, for now, that his solution was the right one. If it proved to be so, then perhaps he could delude himself again when a similar a situation arose. The self-deception might become easier, then easier still the time after that. That way, once sufficiently deluded, perhaps he could pilot *Oscar* with the extraordinary ease that Wood did.

Allowing himself no time to ponder further, Tink focused the manipulation fields of the furnaces against the surface of *Oscar*'s hull and steadily ramped up the output. The vessel began resonating with vibrations too small for even its most acute sensors to detect directly. The calculating part of him which had begun life as the ship's thinker had supplied a mental map of where it predicted the vibrations would be amplified, and where they'd be damped by the structural pattern of the hull. As an afterthought, he applied less intense vibrations to the surface of the little IPEC ship. Its occupants would be alarmed, but that couldn't be helped. He'd envelope it in a stasis field if its hull seemed in danger of a breach.

Ignoring the dominating part of his mind which demanded certainty, Tink watched anxiously as temperatures rose quickly to thousands of degrees. Incandescent islands grew in dark seas of relative coolness where vibrations cancelled each other out, leaving sensitive parts of the vessel unscathed. His drones registered tiny plumes issuing from each burrow as the devices inside evaporated, their gases sparkling strangely as they drifted beyond the protection of the Thomson Field. The dense, dead outer hull began flowing into the holes, entombing the mites' stubborn diamond skeletons.

I did it! It was me! I did it!

Tink wound the furnaces back down, surveying the sealed burrows just to be certain, yearning to tell Wood all about what he'd just done. He already knew, ultimately, that he would not. Wood had enough on his mind.

The drones returned to their repairs and cleaning as the ship radiated its excess heat into hyperspace.

'HE'S TALKING.'

Wood was striding listlessly around the control room, as he'd been doing for much of the past two days. The surprise and relief Hazel saw in his face were genuine.

'That's great news. From what you were saying, I thought he was going to be a vegetable.'

So did I. 'I don't know how he survived at all, I really don't. He's in a lot of pain. I think he always will be. Because I'm a telepath myself, it's possible for me to undo much of what that man did, but there are still … wounds and amputations. Distortions. He's badly screwed up.' *I doubt he'll ever be the person he was.*

Wood absorbed this. 'What did he say?'

She smiled, and it felt like his own, personal sunrise. Not being fully in contact with her for almost a day now had felt like amputation. Her sling was off, and he hugged her ferociously. Looked up into a pair of electric green eyes.

'He says thanks,' she said, aloud. 'I explained about you and Tink and the ship. He wants to meet you both.' *No, not now, he's very fragile.* 'He needs time to try and … "collect everything" were his words.' Her eyes fell. 'He's a remarkable man.'

She sank into the nearby pilot's seat, suddenly drained. 'He wants us to remove some of his ribs. Says they were replaced on the fortress, and that spy devices could be hidden in them. He also wants us to take him direct to Haven, along with the captives. I said this wasn't allowed, but he said he made the rule, so he could override it.' *It's possible that he could have been reprogrammed in some way to act for them. I don't get the impression that's happened, but I could be wrong.*

Her brow crinkled. 'He was still talking about it being too late, saying we must "make time", or something like that. He wasn't making much sense, and …' she sighed. 'Well, I'm not sure we should be doing what he says.'

She looked up for a moment into Wood's eyes, as if seeking an answer there.

'He says we have to evacuate, Wood. From the Freelancer colonies, the stations and planets – everywhere. He says everyone must come to Haven as soon as possible.' She shook her head. 'That's crazy! Surely what we should be doing is getting everything and everyone *away* from Haven and fighting, if we have to, as far from it as possible?'

'Perhaps he has a plan.' Catching Hazel's look, he said, 'There must be *some* kind of plan?'

'But Dorrin and Zhelkar would know! And I'd have found out by now.' Wood rubbed thoughtfully at his bottom lip.

'So, do you think his judgement is impaired?'

She shrugged, suddenly tearful again. 'I don't know!' Her eyes searched the floor. 'But you're right. I had the impression of some long-term arrangement of some kind. I just couldn't find out what it was. It's as if he used every last fragment of will to protect this one bit of information. It's about the only thing in there left unscathed.' She made a sound halfway between a grunt and a sigh. 'What I did pick up, though, was something about a weapon. A "doomsday weapon". He tried to block me, but I tricked him into revealing it. I don't know what he meant, but I'm afraid, Wood.' *Very, very afraid.* 'This little skirmish we've had is just the beginning.'

Looking grimly out into the blankness outside the ship, Wood pushed his fingers along her scalp, wanting to give comfort, needing it badly himself. He felt a hand slide on top of his. 'Well,' he murmured, 'I suppose what we urgently need to decide is: do we trust him and do as he says?'

Hazel bowed her head. After a while, she nodded. Wood puffed out his cheeks.

'Tink? What about you? This has to be unanimous.'

37

EVACUATION

THE EVACUATION had already begun. Space around the two-spoked wheel of Haven Station, languidly turning above brilliant stormclouds, was busy with small shapes. Either arriving from other planets or space stations or beginning their plunge from orbit into Haven's turbulent atmosphere, some were bright and flashing as they caught the sun. Others had the duller sheen of orgs.

Wood had spent several frustrating days at Gamma Station after Jo Fox was pounced upon by the ecosphere's quartet of horrified healers, who'd supplemented the surgery's repairs with more up-to date facilities, grafts of speed-cloned skin, and medications derived from some of the plants growing on Haven.

Their prognosis was promising. Given time he might even walk again, they'd said, although his left side would remain palsied.

Despite weak protestations Jo had been forced to undergo counselling. He'd refused the prescribed two months' rest, and when it became clear that he couldn't escape the attentions of the horde of surgeons and health specialists who'd flocked to the station from all over Haven, had demanded that their therapies begin immediately.

Despite the risks, the consensus was that his recovery would be much faster and more complete with healthy colonies of personal microbes, so, on the fourth day, following an accelerated course of immunisations, they'd allowed his reinfection. Hazel visited him hourly as he used an eye-operated holo-interface to monitor the retreat to Haven from his wheelchair-cum-sickbed.

Thousands of tiny non-sentient surveillance pods, or 'sniffers' – part machine, part vegetable – were being scattered throughout Haven's system of planets and out into Freelancer space. They would jump back to Haven with any news. The Havenners' – apparently considerable – stock of virtually undetectable Lancer-developed nuclear smart mines was to be scattered throughout the Haven's Gate, Walnut, Terra Two, and Terra Nova solar systems.

The three captives had generated such cold hatred amongst the population of Haven's Gate when news of Jo's torture had leaked out that Wood found himself almost sorry for them. Tink had regurgitated their unrecognisably mangled vessel into a loose orbit around Gamma Station, from where a drone was launched to bore into the cabin and inject it with a full complement of Haven microbes.

The following day, a faint mayday had been received from the vessel, and an armed isolation team was sent in. Hazel had wanted to be amongst them, but both she and Wood were all but forbidden from doing so by Dorrin, who'd just arrived from Haven. The team had gleefully reported scraping up the hollow-eyed, green-hued officers from pools of their own excreta. They'd been capable of little resistance. Hazel had spent time with each of them. The subject was one she refused to talk about, and Wood wondered what their fate would be.

He'd heard they'd been inoculated, and was glad. There had been enough killing.

Since leaving Haven's Gate, Jo had just reclined in his wheelchair in Wood's bedroom as though sleeping, clucked over by Indora Hibiscus and her beefy, blue-eyed young apprentice (and toy-boy, according to Hazel), Cam Riverrunner. Wood had slept in the control room, Hazel spending hours with Jo, locked in silent dialogue. Often, she'd come to Wood with a puffy, wet face, embracing him desperately, and he'd held her, and done his best to comfort her, and then she'd gone back to Jo again with determination in her face and resignation in her eyes.

Now they were in orbit around Haven, waiting.

Wood surveyed the bustling space station. 'We're meant to wait for a tight-beam message,' Hazel told him wearily, answering his unspoken question. The past week had drained her of her usual energy. *They know we're coming.*

He still didn't like this. '*Oscar* is only a spacecraft, Hazel. We have antigrav, but that's for sub-orbital use. It's not really equipped for manoeuvring in an atmosphere or landing on anything. Let alone a planet with full gravity.'

'The gravity's only 9.4,' Tink interjected from his customary deck-chair, hands locked behind his head. '*Oscar*'s easily strong enough to support itself, and the centre of gravity's well towards the stern, so it won't tip forwards on to the furnaces as soon as the antigrav's off. We'll need a hard surface though, or we'll sink into it.'

Wood pulled a thoroughly sceptical face. 'If you're sure.'

'Yes, Wood, I'm *sure*.'

He nibbled his lip, wondering what it was about Tink which seemed different today. Then he noticed that Hazel was angling her head, first to one side and then the other, as though straining to hear some faint noise. He watched with interest.

After a minute or so of this, she became completely immobile. Then she began moving her head from side to side again.

'Is anything wrong?' he asked, with a frown.

Hazel didn't answer immediately. Eventually she said 'I'm not sure. I thought …'

She tailed off and concentrated again.

'I can *feel* something.'

Wood blinked. 'Like what?'

She ran her small, round tongue across her upper lip. 'I'm not sure,' she ventured at length, eyes narrowing. 'I really don't know. It's quite faint, but –'

She shook her head.

'I don't know. I need a rest. It's like some kind of background noise. Perhaps I'm just tired.'

THE MESSAGE was delivered by the tight-beamed hologram of an intense young woman who said how good it was to see them safe and asked tearfully how the Professor was. As they sank towards the boiling clouds on antigrav, *Oscar* began trailing fat plumes of steam. Feathers of Cirrus fled past.

A minute later, they broke through a shallow ceiling of mid-level clouds, falling through the plane of clear air below into boiling cumulus. Eventually *Oscar* levelled off below a glowering sky, thundering eastwards barely a hundred metres from ocean. Drizzle formed orange shrouds of steam around the furnaces, whose light reflected off dark, scudding waves.

'These clouds!' enthused Tink, standing on a virtual plinth and waving his arms like a demented conductor. 'Equilibrium formations of dihydrogen oxide suspended in crystalline, gaseous and droplet form. A sunlight-powered dynamic circulatory system of evaporation and condensation. Cool!' he added, destroying the effect completely.

The rocky coast of Hades Island grew on the dim horizon. 'Is it always like this here?' Wood grumbled, studying the dismal ceiling.

'At this time of year. The winter's cooler, but calmer.'

The floor of the cavern was considerably more crowded than on Wood's first visit. As he guided *Oscar* carefully down the entrance tunnel, he could just make out figures swarming like microbes between the tiny buildings and parked aircraft and spacecraft below. As he'd predicted, while *Oscar*'s antigrav field was easily capable of supporting its weight, the hulking spacecraft felt alarmingly unstable, with an enthusiasm for rolling unexpectedly sideways which he was keen not to explore.

He gingerly nestled *Oscar* into a barely adequate space between two large orgs. Once the hull had ceased its vocal protestations at being subject to such unreasonable structural loadings, he breathed a sigh of deep relief.

Immediately he felt a babble of anxious queries. *How is the health of The Professor?*

We have heard of your amazing rescue. Are you healthy?

How is Hazel?

Is it true that you have Puke-people captive?

He quickly tired of the well-meant, but trying, inquisition. *Why not just ask the Professor how he is?* he suggested, testily. He wanted nothing more than to fall asleep under a tree.

There were shuffling sounds from behind in the corridor. Hazel and Wood turned towards them in unison. The Professor was clinging to the edge of the doorway with a bandaged, incomplete paw, his cadaverous face creased by a ghastly smile.

'Professor!' Hazel cried out, in surprise as much as alarm.

'Not bad … progress, all … considered.' The man's face was growing more corpse-like by the second. She rushed over and grabbed him beneath an arm.

'Where are the healers?' she yelled down the corridor, then turned on him, grimacing at the red line around his skull. 'You shouldn't be on your feet – the top of your head might come off!'

He began sagging, cheeks white as sun-bleached branches.

Wood had been watching in horror, fully expecting the man to fall and his brains to spill out. The image as he peeped over Satan's torture table came flooding back. 'The chair,' Hazel was shouting, supporting Jo by the armpits, but Wood was already out of the room. Dashing into his sleeping room, he returned moments later pushing the wheelchair at a run and half-throwing it over the sill of the control room door.

''M not an invalid,' slurred Jo feebly as Hazel hoisted him into the chair's embrace. He slumped there looking terribly dejected.

Yes, you are. Hazel's voice in his mind was firm. Somehow, Wood could hear it too. *Listen, I think no less of you than I always have – than all of us have – but you'll do whatever it is you have to better if you accept the fact that you are, for now, an invalid.* 'Where the Mother is Indora?' she snapped, looking around.

Knew your mother, Jo said, with a sickly grin. *Brought her here. Was a lot like you. Couldn't tell her … couldn't tell her, you see, because everything I care for dies. She died anyway. I'm so sorry. For Haven, too. I'm so very sorry.*

Wood looked into the man's ravaged face, and what he saw there was reflected in Hazel's.

'Come on,' he said gently, laying a hand on Hazel's shoulder. 'I'm sure the others are somewhere. Tink: I'll see you as soon as I can. I promise.' He chewed his lips. 'You be alright on your own?'

'I suppose.' Back turned, the AI's persona stared across dunes of purple sand, drawing on a thin cigarette.

'See if you can get to know any of the orgs. They'd all love to talk to you, but your mind is apparently a real bummer to read. You'll have to help them.'

In the corridor, they met Indora and Cam. Both were flustered and profusely apologetic. From what Hazel could glean from their confused story, Jo had somehow tricked them, against their better judgement, into leaving him alone while they went off on some nebulous errand. This news caused Hazel's face to tighten.

Still think he has it together? Wood asked as the two fussed over a weakly protesting Jo.

She didn't answer.

Oscar had sunk a good twenty metres into the ground, but the door of the lowest airlock was still higher than that above the landing bay. Although spacecraft and other vehicles thronged the cavern like bees, the cool air outside was surprisingly quiet. The smell he now knew was caused by fungal spores was comforting, somehow.

As the five peered out, a ground vehicle approached trailing a cloud of dust, a gantry concertinaing upwards from its rear.

The driver backed his machine towards the hull and a sizeable platform drew level with the airlock floor. Hazel pushed the wheelchair containing Jo Fox's – now resignedly sessile – figure on to it. Once everyone was aboard, the platform returned swiftly to ground level. The driver gestured at the low buildings in the distance, and, with a whir of electric motors, sped off towards them.

Looking behind as he gripped the platform rail, Wood watched *Oscar* retreat. The machine looked ridiculous, towering over the orgs and almost everything else like a sensibly sized atmospheric vessel which had crashed in a field of vegetables. Tink had done a superb job of restoring it, bless his house-proud socks. He doubted that the starship had been presented so well in all the years since its launch. Its hull gleamed, and with its restored stripes of black and yellow chevrons, it looked almost smart. It certainly did not look like something to get on the wrong side of.

Turning away, he wondered how he might ever reconcile being with Tink and being on Haven. *There has to be some way of making him fully mobile*, he thought. *A robot body or something.*

But would that be what the AI wanted? It dawned on him that he was being terribly presumptuous, and that his knowledge of his closest friend was at best superficial.

It was a problem he sensed he was going to have to face up to in the not-too-distant future.

Indora and Cam were staring at Jo as if afraid to take their eyes off him. Jo had his eyes closed. He at least looked considerably better with most of his teeth back in his mouth. Wood glanced at Hazel. She was behaving oddly again, angling her head as though trying to pinpoint the direction of some distant sound, with an expression of deepening puzzlement.

Hazel? Their communication was so natural now, he didn't have to attract her attention. *What is it? Is it the same thing?*

I don't know. She was frowning. *I really don't know what it is. It feels like something's here.*

Here?

On Haven. Something that wasn't here when we left. A lengthy pause. 'I'm sorry,' she said aloud, 'I have no idea at all.' *Please: this is worrying me, and I must concentrate for answers.*

The vehicle swerved to an abrupt halt at the main entrance of the cavern's largest building. Cam pushed Jo's chair down the sloped edge of the platform, and the driver motored off again at high speed, waving and calling over his shoulder.

THE WAREHOUSE-LIKE LOBBY of the coordination centre was almost filled with featherweight silicon crates crammed with equipment and foodstuffs salvaged from the outer planets. A recording of classical cello music played in the background. Jo weakly raised a bandage at the young woman currently supervising the row of terminal screens there as his chair was wheeled in.

'Aspen, isn't it?'

Where is everybody? asked Wood's voice in Hazel's perception. Apart from this one person, the place seemed empty.

Organising.

The woman did a double-take and stepped back in shock, gaping at Jo's missing fingers and the red line around his shaven head. 'Aspen Sunrise, yes!' She leaned forward, squinting as her eyes welled up. 'Professor, is that really you? What happened? I heard you'd been rescued by the ...' her eyes lit upon Wood and she tailed off. 'I've heard terrible things. I didn't know how much to believe, but now I see that you really are ... injured.'

'I was lucky,' Jo replied curtly. 'Unlike the fourteen thousand others who were in the Terra Two system.'

Aspen swallowed. Though clearly alarmed at their patient's activity, Indora and Cam seemed too reverential to protest.

'Now Aspen, I need your help, quickly. I need something fast.' He turned his head with difficulty towards Hazel and Wood. 'Can either of you fly an SEV? As you can appreciate, I won't be piloting anything, at the moment.'

After a hesitation, Hazel nodded.

'Thank you.' He manoeuvred his attention back to Aspen with an involuntary grimace which caused Indora and Cam to twitch in unison. 'Fast, three person.'

Aspen wiped her eyes with a sleeve. 'As it's a state of emergency, Professor, why not take the ramjet on pad fifteen? It's old, but reliable, and it's hypersonic. I presume that under the circumstances tearing up the troposphere won't be such a sin? We keep it flight-ready for emergencies. I don't think the exhaust is heat-camouflaged, but with all these spacecraft incoming, we're not silent any more anyway.'

'Good girl. Hazel?'

Since leaving *Oscar*, the man everyone had almost written off as being beyond recovery had subtly and thoroughly taken charge without anyone realising. Hazel stared at him. His face was deathly pale, and one eyelid was drooping, but his eyes gleamed, as though this small bit of action had reignited something in them. His words were still slurred, but his voice, little more than a croak during the journey on *Oscar*, had regained some of its familiar command. 'It's a few years since my last sims,' she said, 'but I don't foresee a problem.'

'Professor,' ventured Aspen. 'Why have we risked blowing our cover by bringing nonorgs here? Why is everyone coming to Haven?'

Suddenly Jo seemed once more just a crippled old man.

'Aspen,' he began in little more than a whisper. 'I'll tell everyone as soon as I can.' Hazel couldn't stop herself picking up the words he'd left unspoken: *Though I'm afraid that when I do, many will wish I hadn't.*

38

CRISPY

WOOD PACED along the shore of Juniper Lake.

Occasionally, he swam in it.

It was seven days now since Hazel had left for Tom's cave. The Professor had ordered her to fly him there, alone, barely twenty minutes after their arrival in Juniper, and Wood had been told – in a way which, while polite, left no scope for argument – that he was not coming.

Rumour had it that the three captured IPEC officers were still being held on Haven Station, but would be brought down to Haven later today.

The Havenners' reaction to the men was, Wood thought, curious. As commanding officer of the destroyed fortress, it was widely known that one of them was directly responsible for the deaths of thousands of their fellows and was, at the very least, partly culpable for Jo's torture and mutilation. Yet what the Havenners showed towards the captives had, so far, been nothing more overt than a kind of inwardly focused rage. Jo had half-expected the officers to be torn apart by vengeful mobs. He began to see that this was unlikely.

It was the first time that he'd been without Hazel for more than a few hours since their first meeting, months ago. Her absence felt as though part of him had been physically ripped out. He couldn't function; couldn't concentrate on the most mundane tasks. Not that concentration would have been easy anyway. Most of Juniper had lost family or friends in the attack on Terra Two, and every day there were commemorative tree-planting ceremonies in cherished spots in nearby woods or on neighbouring islands.

Wood felt unable to attend. He didn't know whether his presence was wanted or expected. The town was full of people he didn't recognise, most of them wandering about in a similar daze to his own. Juniper had come to feel almost crowded. There was an atmosphere of tension, even foreboding. All the evacuees had stories to tell. Rumours spread and became exaggerated. The fact that none were worse than the truth made his knowledge, and Jo's request that he discuss none of it, unbearable.

Sidling along the lakeshore path, he found himself at the Brightstones' cabin. He stood on the veranda, hands in pockets, gazing at the clothes machine. A reddish spider was entombing a butterfly in a cocoon of threads in a web strung between the machine's body and its manipulating arms.

This place is cruel. A selection process governs everything here.

He knocked on the open door and went in.

Editions of the Juniper Echo were scattered across the floor where a stack had toppled from the tree-trunk coffee table. Unwashed mugs and cups had sprouted everywhere like a crop of colourful fruit, muddy footprints were all over the rug and floorboards, and dirty washing littered the furniture.

For a moment, he thought he was in the wrong house.

He called out, but no-one answered. He was about to leave when he heard voices, then footsteps on the stairs.

'... Nonsense I ever heard in my puff.' It was a gruff voice that he recognised immediately. Less familiarly, it sounded angry. An equally distinctive female one said something he couldn't quite make out. 'Of *course* it's important,' continued the first. 'And were not exactly going anywhere, are we? You and I won't be involved in any fighting, if it comes to that, unless we take the fastest pilot's course anyone's ever seen. We might as well do *something.*'

There were shuffling footsteps and a gap of unintelligible conversation.

'By the Great Mother's frigging fanny, maybe he is five hundred years old, maybe he is a genius, but he's also an arrogant pain in the brown eye!'

Randal Brightstone appeared in the doorway, red faced and scowling. Behind him, Willow looked worried and drawn. Seeing Wood, Randal treated him to a cursory smile.

'Son, it's good to see you safely back.'

Willow pushed forward and put her arms tightly around him. 'We heard what happened,' she said, into his ear. 'We're so glad you're here. What you did was heroic.' She shook her head.

'I think everyone in the town knew someone on Alpha Station or Terra Two.' An intake of breath. 'It's so awful.'

'Poor lad probably wants to forget it,' said Randal a little sharply. His partner released Wood, who could feel his face burning, and wiped her eye.

'Well, we're just glad you're safe.' For a while no one seemed to know what to say. Randal broke the awkward silence.

'Can I ask you a question, son?'

'Ran, no!'

Randal ignored this, and she looked away, hands on her hips. 'If you discovered that your planet was suddenly crawling with bacteria – of a kind which weren't there before – what would your reaction be? Would *concern* strike you as a natural response, followed by a desire to find out what the cause is, and what the implications and risks are?'

Wood looked between the Brightstones in confusion. 'I'm sorry?'

'Bacteria. One kind. In everything, and I mean everything! The soil, the plants, the animals – me, Willow and almost certainly everyone else here. The air even. The rocks, all the way down to as far as we've drilled, which is over five kilometres! Everywhere! On every part of every continent.'

Wood wasn't taking this in. 'What – you mean, like a ...' what was the word? 'A *plague?*' Randal threw up his hands.

'Could be! Could very well be! We don't know, do we! They don't seem to be doing active *harm* – not yet, at least. But their sheer number, their sheer biomass, is enough to give me the screaming willies.' He poked a finger at Wood. 'And I'll tell you something else; the weirdest part. The only close phenotypic match we've found for them so far is the bacteria in the orgs. It's baffling. We've never found bacteria quite like these living free before.' Randal was quivering with frustration. 'And now that Professor has gone and told – told, mind you! – Zhelkar and Dorrin that Willow and me aren't to continue our research. Without explanation, without a by-your-leave. I mean, apart from it being totally out of order for anyone to fling their weight around like that, we don't have he faintest idea what we're *dealing* with here!'

From his expression, Randal seemed to be looking to Wood for support, or even an answer. 'Randal!' snapped Willow.

'You're being impossible! Both of you sit down and have a drink.'

Randal's expression didn't change. Wood pulled a face.

'Perhaps he doesn't think it's important right now?'

'Then why's he not *telling* us? I mean, this is frightening! If what we've found in our sampling is representative, then the amount of organic matter bound up in these things is already considerably greater than all other life on the planet put together – and from what we've been able to tell, their numbers are doubling every few hours. I don't mind telling you that I'm scared shitless. I'm as scared of this now as I am of the confederation!'

Wood felt very set upon. The last two weeks had all been a bit much. He put up his hands. 'Listen – no offence, but I think I'll just … I need to be by myself for a bit.'

He pashed past them and out of the door.

'Damn you,' hissed Willow, behind him 'You've driven him away! He's such a nice boy. I was going to see if he wanted dinner with us this evening.'

'*Dinner?*' exploded Randal. 'Why is no-one taking this seriously? You prepared the cultures yourself, for Amber's sake! I tell you Will, something very serious indeed is going on, and I've a good mind to say sod the restrictions, and just do the research anyway.'

Willow voice was aghast. 'Randal, please – don't even think that way. No one has broken the Code of Trust since before we were born.'

'That we know of. And anyway,' Randal growled as Wood fled down the path, 'we keep being told this isn't a dictatorship. Perhaps it's time someone did.'

THIN SMOKE CURLED SKYWARDS between pine needles, carrying with it scents of resinous wood and corn fritters. The Firedomes once more lived up to their name: forested ridges tinged with the first rusty hues of the season Havenners called *Foghar*, glowing against the deepening evening sky. Birds called. In the distance a wolf began its elemental conversation, its mournful howls echoing across the still waters of Juniper Lake.

Wood shivered.

He added another log to the fire. Beside his beached canoe, an otter regarded him with casual interest before going about its business, vanishing into the glittering water with barely a ripple. He sighed, lay back on his blanket in the pine needles, rested his head against his sack of clothing and closed his eyes.

Quiet, methodical splashes. Not the faint ripples on the beach, but louder, and more distant.

He opened his eyes. A canoe was approaching, towing thin lines through the reflection of sunset oranges, the brassy blue of the clear sky, and the greens of the forested shore beyond. He smiled.

You were a long time.

He was in there for ages. *Days. I got back only half an hour ago.* A pause. *I came straight here.*

Raising the hem of her pine-green sarong, Hazel stepped, barefooted, from the open topped-canoe into the water and hauled the canoe up on to the beach. Wood rose to meet her and they embraced. Her smell after so long apart made him giddy.

Lips began to explore. They found that they were starting to move against each other. Gently at first, then with urgency.

Eyes locked on his, Hazel began to undo her waistknot.

ROLLED UP IN a blanket, they lay beside the fire, content for a while to listen to the evening sounds of the lake and the forest.

What I felt before, Hazel began as night came on, reluctant to break the spell, *it's growing – I can feel it. The nearest thing I can liken it to is background noise. It has no form or shape that I can identify, but it feels like it's everywhere. If it gets much worse, I'm going to have difficulty communicating. Are those sausages burnt?*

Wood sat up and cursed as he tipped the blackened sausages and fritters from the frying pan on to a wooden plate. 'Arse, not again.' He proffered the plate at Hazel.

'Don't worry, I like them like that.' She speared a sausage with a small stick. The air was getting chilly. Wrapping his part of the blanket around his shoulders, Wood held a fritter up on a fork, and blew on it.

I was talking to Randal Brightstone today, he said, as he waited for the fritter to cool. *You might find this interesting.* 'Says he's found something strange. He was ranting about it.'

Ranting? Hazel wrinkled her nose, most attractively, Wood thought. 'That doesn't sound like the Randal we all know and love.' It was unclear whether or not this was sarcasm.

He says the Professor found out and effectively ordered Zhelkar and Dorrin to get him to bury the study.

She slid a hand under the blanket and gave his testicles a squeeze. He squeaked in surprise. *Woody, petal, get to the point. You're beating around the bush. It's unbecoming.*

'Well,' he grinned, taking a bite from his fritter, then breathing out a plume of steam. 'Hah – 'scoose me. Hooh!' he flapped a hand in front of his mouth. 'Says all these – hoo! – bacteria have suddenly appeared, and are multiplying …' he swallowed, *well, very fast. Apparently, everything has them, even the rocks a long way underground.* 'I don't really know anything about bacteria, and it didn't strike me as particularly weirder than anything else around here, until he mentioned that they are "a close phenotypic match", were the words he used, for the bacteria in the orgs.'

He had Hazel's attention now. He watched her eyes widen, fading to what, in the firelight, looked like mustard-yellow: a colour he couldn't recall having seen in them before. *Which … are physically indistinguishable from the bacteria that are part of me.*

Coincidence?

Hazel thoughtfully prodded her chin. Then she took a deep breath and let it out slowly, controlling its escape with her lips.

There's to be a meeting in the town hall in two days time, she said. 'The Professor's going to make a big speech which is to be piped live all over Haven. Perhaps we'll find out something then. If not … I don't think Randal would keep quiet.' *Neither will I.*

'Haven't you, er, ah, probed him? The Professor.'

Hazel chewed on a mouthful and swallowed it. 'If he knows, it's buried very deep.' *But to be honest I don't think he does. Not clearly, anyway.* 'I don't know whether the hypnotic screening worked partially when he was captured. He could have forgotten.' She pursed her lips and shrugged. *I just don't know.*

Delicate planes of mist hung over the water, mimicking the colours of the afterglow on the mountains. Wood sighed.

'It's all too fast,' he said, aware his expression had become one of pain. *No time. It's not fair.*

Hazel brushed his neck with her fingers. *Wood.*

I have this terrible feeling that we haven't long left together.

278

She looked into the fire.

'Let's get married,' he said, turning to her suddenly. 'Tomorrow. Grab the chance while we've got it. Before the meeting. Before we *know.*'

She studied his intense, eager eyes. 'You know that we would never … That *I* will never have children. I'm sorry … but, it's not something I'll debate.'

I know.

'Telepathy dies with me.'

'Hazel … I'm not even sure I *can* father children. After being in a supernova, my genes are …' *kind of crispy.*

She smiled. The smile became a grin. 'We could get the town hall for a dance or if it rains. Have a big bonfire … Yes! In fact, it might be just what everyone needs to get them out of the dumps.'

Laughing, she gazed out over the lake, and Wood saw that she was picturing the scene she described.

'We should choose a name,' she said. 'It's our tradition for intendeds to choose a name for themselves.' *Something symbolising the days leading up to the marriage.* 'Not everyone does – there are people who've kept the last names of their mothers or fathers since their ancestors left the Earth.' *But I'd like to do it.* She looked up at the early stars. 'I hope Dorrin can conduct the ceremony. She'll be very busy.'

Besides Haven's defence coordinator, Dorrin was Juniper's *Fear-Treòrachaidh*, or sky lady: one of a sisterhood of ceremonial custodians whom Hazel had described as 'odd-job women for pomp and ceremony'. Organised religion was something Havenners frowned upon. 'Gods,' Dorrin had told Wood, 'have a nasty habit of justifying their followers to do whatever they want. Most of humanity's worst crimes have been committed in the names of gods or prophets.'

She wanted me to be her apprentice, Hazel was saying. *Was disappointed when I didn't want to, for one reason or another. I don't even know who she's chosen instead. But I want Dorrin to do it.*

She turned to Wood again, eyes gleaming.

'Yes, let's do it. Give me a name, Wood. Hazel is all I have.' *Give me a name that I can share with you.*

39

THE WEDDING

IN THE EVENT, they didn't have to use the hall.

The sky was clear, and the *Foghar* afternoon crisp, but warm. Over the course of an hour, several hundred people from all over Juniper and the town's hinterland had descended on the largest beach of Emerald Lake.

Five amphibious SEVs, painted in themes ranging from abstract knotwork to colourful creatures from the imaginations of the town's children, had set to work shuttling back and forth between Juniper and the lakeshore, depositing fresh revellers a dozen at a time. There was an atmosphere of devil-may-care. A little over twenty of those present knew Hazel well. Most attended partly out of curiosity, keen to see the telepath's unexpected marriage to the offworlder they'd heard so much about.

All had come determined to enjoy the occasion, and to forget.

Waiting nervously by the water's edge, dizzy from the vile but intoxicating drinks people kept pressing into his hands, Wood found himself teased and cajoled by Sander and his apparently inexhaustible supply of friends. He was even teased by Berry, who, until now, had seemed flatly to dislike him. In the background a four-piece band of instruments he now recognised as a guitar, bouzouki, bòdhran and border-pipes played utterly unfamiliar rhythmical tunes on the sand, almost drowned by chattering voices and laughter. He couldn't conceal his surprise when Sander introduced his partner Stephanie: slender and immensely tall, with eyes as glacially blue as Sander's and immaculately plaited platinum blonde hair.

'Um, pleased to meet you, Mrs Leafdance,' he stammered, looking up at least thirty centimetres into her perfectly proportioned face (or at least at her chin), drawing titters from the encircling audience.

'Please, just Steph.' Her voice was lustrous and low. 'It's good to meet you too, Wood McCorkindale. I've heard a lot about you. Largely from Sandy, but I've been stationed on Beta Station these past four months.' She tilted her head elegantly. 'You seem surprised?'

When Wood spoke, his own voice seemed dull and jarring. 'No! Well, um, I ...' He glanced desperately at Stephanie's partner. Sander was wearing a week's patchy stubble, the same threadbare trousers, and a smart lapel-less jacket embroidered with emerald-green intertwined vines. Despite the valiant effort, the jacket made his appearance somehow even more disreputable. 'It just came as a shock ... a *surprise* to ... find that Sander was, er ...'

'Married?'

Sander's perennial grin collapsed with the majesty of a condemned building. Laughter erupted on all sides. Wood felt himself flushing furiously.

'Thanks very much!' Sander spluttered, looking wounded.

'He has a point,' Stephanie told him. 'You always were the most indescribable clart.' She leaned towards Wood. She was the only woman he'd met here who wore perfume. 'I've tried to change his ways,' she whispered loudly, 'but even now, he hardly ever washes his –'

'Steph!' howled Sander, lunging towards her. More hilarity.

'I mean, can you imagine it?' Steph said, evading her partners' attempts to gag her by using Wood as a shield. 'I hope you'll show your partner more decorum.'

At this, a section of the crowd, with great gusto, burst into song:

For he's got no falarum, no Diddle-i-arum,
He's got no falarum, hey diddle-i-ay!
He's got no falarum, he's lost his decorum
'Maids, when you're young, never wed and old man.'

Sander continued to dance around Wood, yelling at Steph over the top of his head. 'You know what they say about glass houses?'

'Meaning?' she enquired primly. A smaller group of the crowd were continuing the song as an impromptu choral group. Their voices and harmonies were quite good.

'... *When he took me to bed,*
'*He lay there as he were DEAD!*
'*Maids, when you're young, never wed an old man ...*'

'What,' began Sander evenly, still dancing around Wood, 'if I were to use the phrase "teenage affinity for phallic vegetables".'

There was a chorus of '*Oooh!*'

'Hey!'

His gaze swept the enclosing group. 'Some things don't change. And you all just thought we ate healthily?'

'Sander! You ... *disgrace!*' By this stage the gathering circle of faces represented a mix of puzzlement and hilarity. A few onlookers seemed in danger of bladder problems. Stephanie was not to be downplayed. 'More of that, sunshine, and I'll circulate some fascinating images I discovered from *your* late teens.'

Sander's face fell again. Several of the congregation were by this point clutching themselves. 'What do you mean? What images?'

'Mmm, what could I mean?' Stephanie cradled her chin. 'What if I were to form a sentence containing the words "Sander", "virginity" and "vicuña".'

'What?' cried Sander. 'Absolute bollocks!' He seemed quite irate.

'You have no secrets from me, Sander Leafdance.'

'Bitch! You ... contemptible slut! I can't *believe* you're suggesting to all our friends here that that was my first time!'

Someone Wood didn't recognise waved a hand feebly from the foetal position he'd adopted at Wood's feet. 'Make them stop.'

'That vicuña left with a big smile on its face, let me tell you.'

'I'll bet it did.' She held a hand up, finger and thumb a few millimetres apart. 'Vicuñas are very small.'

While Wood suspected that this typically Haven formula of humour, and much of the ensuing mirth, was partly for show, it soon had everyone in the right mood. A wooden pail of disgustingly soft brown apples appeared, and in no time the contents had been liberally redistributed all over the clothes and faces of most of those present. He managed to escape by hiding behind a juniper bush.

Slightly alarmed at the chaos, he'd begun to wonder where Hazel was when a dull roar made itself felt over the hubbub. Gradually the clowning and banter was replaced by apprehensive murmuring. Stephanie and Sander, Wood noticed, were nowhere to be seen.

He cautiously approached Berry, who was standing a few metres back from the throng with a strange half-smile on his lips. The serious, black-haired man peered down at Wood with an unreadable, not entirely friendly expression. Berry had never been someone he felt comfortable around. 'Do you know what's happening?' Wood asked him.

'Think you're about to discover who your best man is.'

Wood eyed him uncertainly, standing on tiptoe to try and see over the heads of the tall crowd. All were looking across the lake. The roar was now a mesmerising thunder. Still, he could see nothing. The ground began to shake. Birds flew out of the forest in alarm as standing waves appeared on the water. People were looking about with expressions ranging from knowingness to puzzlement and fear.

A shadow fell over them.

Whirling around, Wood found his vision filled by a darkness which blotted out first the sun, and then the entire sky.

Most of the crowd screamed. Some staggered or fell. From the direction of Juniper, a gunmetal-dark ceiling slid over the lake until the sun returned, blinding after its unnatural eclipse. The immense shape rotated majestically over the lake, in defiance of gravity, attitude thrusters blowing its surface into froth and steam. A strong smell like ozone wafted over the beach.

Clapping his hands together, Wood whooped above the deafening thunder. 'Tink! Tink's my best man! *Ha ha!*' Then he put his fingers in his ears, like everyone else.

Oscar slid sideways towards the crowd. Wood found himself in involuntarily retreat with the others towards the forest. It felt like being fallen on by a skyscraper.

With amazing delicacy, the spaceship rolled on its side, lowering itself towards the sand, stopping only as it brushed treetops at either end of the beach. The crowd were cringing as one: all the spectators could see was a curved roof suspended over them where the sky had been. Trees thrashed in the downdraught.

Then an oval of illumination appeared in the darkness, and a small figure hurtled from it towards the beach.

The crowd gasped.

At the last second, barely a dozen metres from where Wood stood gaping, the figure seemed to slow. It rebounded almost to the height of the hatchway in a flurry of emerald fabric, coming to rest several oscillations later, bobbing upside down, its dress inside out, six metres above the sand.

A cheer went up, audible even above the thunder. Sander appeared at Wood's side, grinning as usual.

'You know what you're asking for, yet?' he bellowed into Wood's ear.

'I'm rapidly finding out!'

Dangling from a thin elastic line by what seemed to be a towel tied around her ankles, Hazel was lowered, dishevelled and beaming ecstatically, into the arms of Stephanie and Berry, who flipped her to her bare feet. Stephanie restored her ruffled hair, adjusted its inlay of small white flowers, and helped to reshape her dress. It was simple, green, elegant, and precisely Hazel.

Slowly, either flirtatiously or bashfully, he couldn't tell, she raised her eyes towards Wood. They matched her dress. Then she smiled at him, and it was like his own personal dawn. He smiled back helplessly, feeling light-headed and strange. The cleaned and polished trapezoid of one of Tink's drones lowered itself on its antigrav field to the sand between them. Slowly at first, but with gathering speed, the looming presence overhead heaved itself away until *Oscar* was only a speck in the sky, soon vanishing altogether.

In the following silence geese descended, honking, on to the lake. The drone floated towards Hazel and took her hand in one of its clawed, whip-like tentacles. Something small was clasped in the other.

'You look *maaarvelous*,' crowed Tink's voice. 'Sex on a stick.'

Hazel gave the machine a solid kick. 'Cheeky monkey. Who did you learn *that* from? Anyway, you're just saying that.'

'I admit I lack judgement in these matters. By the idiot look on his face though, and his drooling, Wood thinks you look marvellous.'

Hazel snorted, leaning closer. 'Poor boy would think I looked good covered in goat manure.'

'Tink,' cried Wood, finally finding his voice. 'How come you can fly like that? And how come the drone? I thought transmissions here were forbidden?'

'Practice,' said the drone, mysteriously. 'The transmissions rule has been repealed. The Professor said so.'

Radiating calm like an energy field, Dorrin Porro emerged from the crowd to conduct the service. The mood immediately became serious, but electric. She wore her long, still raven-dark hair in tresses woven with brown and white bird feathers and forest flowers in clusters of pink and blue. About her shoulders hung hoops of larger flowers, each hoop a different shade, interspersed with others of woven grasses which hung almost to the hem of her shapeless, brown gown. Her face was daubed with paint in parallel stripes of red, white and yellow on her reddish-brown skin, her eyes glinting within their deep wrinkles.

Her partner, Wood couldn't help noticing, was nowhere to be seen.

She raised her arms, palms to the sky.

'Brothers and sisters beneath the cold, empty stars, we gather here today in this place of life to celebrate the riches of our world, Haven, and the joining in love of two cherished children of the Daughter of the Earth Mother, who have been blessed with her gift in such abundance. I speak of the dear child of Juniper who is known to us, her family of friends, as Hazel — and the one named Wood McCorkindale, whom fortune has brought to us from a far-off, less blessed place to share, at last, in the eternal dance.'

It was a curious ceremony, thought Wood. In some ways it felt cobbled together: a deity-free version of a Christian service. Gradually, however, he felt himself caught up in Dorrin's undeniable storytelling power. He was within touching distance of Hazel now, with the *Fear-Treòrachaidh* to his right and Tink's drone between the three of them. As Dorrin's chanting washed over him, the world seemed to melt away but for Hazel's mesmeric eyes. The teeming life which, through her, he could feel throbbing everywhere around seemed like a piece of dark, long-forgotten music in which the two of them were a small, bright part.

'So now, here beneath the sky, let these trees bear witness, as they have for eons untold, to the joining of two kindred minds. The great wheel comes full circle –' Dorrin drew arcs with her hands, eyes raised to the sky, 'birth, life, death, renewal. So it has been since the beginning; so we hold the hope in our hearts, in these times of trouble and uncertainty, that it may always be. For the love that our heart-brother and heart-sister have found in each other shall live forever in us, and in our children, and our children's children; renewing, recycling. Growing and fading. But never dying, as long as the eternal circle is complete.'

The words and the occasion were doubly poignant now. Like many of the onlookers, Dorrin wept openly as she spoke, her hands darting and weaving in accompaniment to her words as though conducting elemental forces.

'Children, equal with all living things in the eyes of the Earth mother, proclaim in our witness now! Do you, Hazel, love this man, Wood McCorkindale.'

'Yes. I do.' *Yes!*

'What was that?' scoffed Dorrin, head tilting. 'We can't hear you. Shout it so that the rocks will hear you and remember!'

It was all part of the tradition of the ceremony, but Hazel embraced it with typical gusto. '*YES!*' She screamed. 'Yes, I love him, I love him! I cannot live without him!' A chorus of cheering and wolf-calls erupted from the congregation. Several near the front clutched themselves, miming vomiting – for which they received cuffings and less physical rebuffs from some of the others. Despite grinning so much that it hurt, Wood could see through Hazel that his face was flushed almost purple.

'And you, Wood McCorkindale, whose kindness and bravery has so recently blessed us, and who we welcome with great gladness as our own: do you love this woman, Hazel?'

'Yes,' he mumbled.

Dorrin cupped a hand expectantly to her ear.

'YES, *YES!*' he thundered, surprising just about everyone with how loud his voice was when he chose to use it. 'Ah, I can't express this too well … frankly I love her so much I could shit myself.'

There was complete silence. Then another chorus of cheers, wolf-calls and whistles erupted, even louder this time, dying down only after what seemed like an age.

So much you could "shit" yourself?
Aah, sorry! Nerves. Never was much of a poet.
That is quite an understatement.
Believe me, it takes a lot of love to make me shit myself.
What in Amber's name have I let myself in for?

'Then,' cried Dorrin, glancing at Wood a little strangely, 'take these seeds as a token of your love, and plant them in each others name!'

The crowd pulled boisterously aside, leaving an alley from which hands beckoned them towards the back of the beach. A slow handclap began. Hazel took a shiny, green acorn from the drone. Wood followed her example, taking a smooth, brown chestnut, embarrassed now, and feeling suddenly overwhelmed, wondering what to do next.

Take my acorn hand in your empty hand, you nitwit, and my empty hand in your chestnut hand.

He did as instructed and they walked slowly up the human isle towards the edge of the forest, arms crossed between them, hands clasped. They reached the wide clearing they'd chosen and turned to face Dorrin who stood, fingers interlocked in front of her, looking slowly from one to the other. The handclapping, Wood realised, had stopped.

'Have you chosen a name for yourselves?'

Say 'we have'.

Wood coughed. 'We have,' he said, in time with Hazel.

'Then, tell it now.'

Hazel smiled, and swallowed, suddenly choked up. 'We …' she began, and stalled. Tears were coursing down her face. 'We have chosen the name of Starsong.'

Dorrin nodded. '"Starsong". A good name. Tell us the reason you have chosen it.'

Hazel was overcome for many seconds before she spoke. 'We have chosen this name because, whatever our own fate may be … what remains certain is that …' she swallowed, 'the silent song of the stars shall continue long after Haven itself has passed beyond memory.'

An electric hush descended. Hazel kissed her acorn. Then she bent and placed it reverently in the shallow hole which had been dug for it. Having paused for her eyes to leak all over the exposed sandy soil, she replaced the plug of damp turf over it. Wood hesitated, and then did likewise, placing his chestnut in his own hole a couple of metres away. Hazel beckoned to him, and they stood between the two holes facing Dorrin again, hands clasped, Wood wiping away his own unexpected tears with the back of his free hand, smiling so much that his cheek muscles ached.

Hazel. I've never been so happy.

She snuffled, smiling down at him. *You'll need a change of underwear, then.* He grimaced.

I've an odd premonition that's something I'm not going to be allowed to forget.

Oh, you're so right. It's going to be legendary!

'So now,' began Dorrin once more, 'may these trees you have planted in the sustaining soil grow strongly. May they flourish and flower as a symbol of your love, so that future children of the Great Mother may gather beneath their branches and your love shall live on, enriching us all, long after Haven has taken your goodness back into her soil. Our hopes and wishes live on in you, as your love shall live on in us.

'Wood and Hazel Starsong: you are life-partners in the silent witness of the trees. Have a long and happy life … and to that end, remember your duties to each other. Contentment comes from sex at least three times a week, unless you have a medical or psychological condition – and never for less than an hour!'

They kissed, almost oblivious to the huge cheer erupting around them, and the circle of struggling bodies closing around them. Still holding her, Wood found himself lifted unceremoniously from his feet.

'No!' Hazel was screaming, lost in the uproar. *'Don't!'*

Wood shot her a puzzled look as she was torn from his arms and borne off beside him on a forest of raised arms. This was a part of the ceremony he hadn't been told about.

Fuck! The Lake!

He thrashed for a bit, only eliciting fresh taunts and wolf-calling from below, then laughed and flung himself back into the supporting hands. The congregation waded in past their waists and he was still smiling as he was hurled, like a sack of potatoes, into breathtakingly cold water. He surfaced disorientated and spluttering. The mob was splashing as one back to the shore, cackling and joking, largely at his and Hazel's expense.

He felt something on his leg. Hazel's red, puffy-eyed face erupted, grinning from ear to ear, from the surface in front of him, framed with bedraggled hair and limply hanging flower stems.

Kiss me, then.

Absolutely.

AS LIGHT FADED from the day, Jo watched the party from his wheelchair by the tree beneath which he'd watched the wedding itself.

Despair still smothered him. If anything, it was intensified by the merrymaking on the beach. The music – diving and weaving melodies on stringed instruments and squeezeboxes, underscored by cross-rhythms from didgeridoos and various kinds of skin drum – drifted clearly up to his solitarily vantage. The shadows felt all the more chill in contrast to the firelight below.

Groups of eight were engaged in a whirling dance which seemed to involve using partners' feet to injure bystanders, bowling lines of clapping onlookers awaiting their turn to the sand, causing much hilarity. Wood's awkward enthusiasm and Hazel's lithe energy were conspicuous as they took their turn.

Looking on, he saw himself and Carol. It was always Carol he saw like this. Whenever he saw Olea, she was alone on a metal floor with a smoking hole blown through her chest, staring at him in terror as she died. He shuddered, screwing his eyes tightly shut.

What had Olea been? Had he tried to make her Carol in his mind? Thoughts of her only brought confusion.

Poor Olea.

There were great chasms in his memory now, in which dark things lurked. Other parts of his life seemed amplified. Carol, he recalled, had asked him once to marry her. He'd told her (so arrogantly!) that he thought things were fine as they were. He watched the young couple below, dancing and whirling, round and round, gazing helplessly into each other's eyes as he and Carol must once have done.

He could conceivably forgive himself both for Carol and Olea if it had been worth it. Individual lives were, after all, insignificant in the scheme of things. But now ... Surely it was all too late? So many interminable decades – *centuries* – of pain, suffering and death. The life of his home planet and its guardians nonetheless surviving, against all the odds stacked against them.

And now, because of him – because of his weakness, his *hubris* – it seemed that, after all this time, they were to be just a couple of days too late.

He cried out at the rising moon, the sound drowned by the revelry below.

40

ALARM

SURROUNDED BY SILENT, wall-spanning flatscreens, Zhelkar Porro sat in the comfortable lean-to backroom tacked on to the back of his cabin.

He sorely wished he was at the wedding party. Sighing, he put the book he was largely failing to read down on the desk and rubbed prickly eyes. Written by a twenty-eight-year-old author from Juniper – a girl he saw around frequently but knew only to exchange pleasantries with – the book was a routine spy story. An IPEC agent had undergone plastic surgery to become the double of a Juniper man killed in a raid on a Freelancer colony.

It had started off promisingly, but by halfway through it was clear that the spy character would never be more than a two-dimensional zealot and xenophobe.

Zhelkar seized the book again and hurled it, pages fluttering, through the open window. He stared after the book and scratched his head.

Where did that come from?

Maybe, he thought, the money-worshippers really were like that. Perhaps that was why he couldn't read the book – because he knew that the unpalatable picture it painted was essentially true, and it robbed him of hope. He could no longer see any kind of future.

It had been clear for a long time that the best Haven could hope for was to forestall its invasion. Suppressing that knowledge had eaten at him for half his life. Yet Jo had, as far as he could see, made no plans for an evacuation. No fleet of arkships had been built; all he seemed to have done was monitor the situation and talk with Tom. Now that the invasion was imminent, they were marooned. The only way Haven or any of its inhabitants were ever going to escape from this desperate situation was teleportation.

He beat his fist against the wooden table. *Damn them all! Xenophobes the lot of them.* 'Rot in whatever hell you believe in,' he cried at the window.

He rose from his chair, and paced round the room, feeling slightly mad. Delinquent thoughts and urges kept entering his mind. It struck him that he could take a chainsaw and cut his cabin into portions. He could set fire to his neighbour's homes or urinate on their furniture or their feet. It wouldn't make the slightest bit of difference: the world was about to end. He knew it in his bones – he was just awaiting confirmation.

He wandered outside.

The town felt deserted. Half the population had gone to Hazel and Wood's wedding, and of those who remained, most were couples or less traditional unions enjoying quiet moments together in their homes while there was time. He wished terribly that he were at Emerald Lake with Dorrin, or that she were here with him. She'd be at the party, putting on a brave face as was expected, as was her way. Tidemaker's face was full, drifting between tasselled branches like a big, pink cheese. He stared at it, wishing he'd enjoyed the luxury of being born a century earlier when everyone was full of such optimism, wishing he didn't have to be amongst those who would see it all end.

He picked up a handful of leaf-litter. Held it to his nose and breathed. How, he wondered, could anyone live without such things as the smell of decaying vegetation in their nostrils? It had always mystified him. Perhaps, he thought, offworlders would wonder how Havenners could cope without their xenomorphic furniture systems? How they could choose to live with frequently getting ill; the risk of dying, even …

He breathed in again and thought of Randal's bacteria. He didn't doubt for a moment that it was true. Their explosive spread seemed unconnected with anything else that was going on, and yet its speed and magnitude suggested a process, or even a purpose. It was the sole aspect of current circumstances whose outcome did not seem obvious, and as such he found that it inspired him, curiously, with hope.

And Fox had told them all to play it down …

The more Zhelkar thought about this, the more he agreed with Randal that something unspoken was going on.

He wandered back to the backroom, almost stumbling as he saw the message alert on the screen. He sat down and had to steady himself with a hand on the desk as he tapped in the report request.

The report was sent from Haven station. It had been relayed by courier from the only surviving 'sniffer' surveillance pod in the Terra Two system. It had taken four precious hours to arrive.

What Zhelkar saw when the recording began made him temporarily stop breathing.

THE ALARM SOUNDED in every one of the six hundred and fifty-two permanent settlements of Haven. At Juniper, the sun was well up, although it had yet to rise sufficiently above the treetops to warm the lakeshore, when the thunderous drumming assaulted the clear morning air, sending waterfowl flapping in clouds up from the lake.

Hazel and Wood had spent what remained of the night together in a woollen blanket, a short walk along the shore of Emerald Lake from where the bonfire sent sparks into the sky long into the early hours. Woken by sunlight, they'd made love again and enjoyed an invigorating wash in the lake. Someone thoughtful had left a small SEV behind for them.

As it dropped through the trees of the town twenty minutes later, everyone was already streaming along the lakeshore path in the direction of the town hall.

Hazel threw her partner a worried look. Something had happened: the meeting had been scheduled for the afternoon. She manoeuvred the aircraft down into a space between a tree and a larger SEV in which figures, obviously having spent the night there, could be seen rubbing eyes and nursing their heads.

She opened the door, winced at the full force of Juniper's drum alert, and shut it again, quickly.

My love, I've a feeling we were lucky to marry when we did.

They joined the bewildered crowd in its march to the town hall. By far the largest building in the town, its steep, photovoltaic-painted roof was the only one to rise through the tree canopy, its automated drum-tower (now mercifully silent) clearing the tallest branches. Supported by artfully carved wooden pillars, its eaves overhung broad wooden verandas on all sides.

People milled around. All ages, from babies slung in scarves on the backs of parents or honorary or actual aunts and uncles, to leather-faced women with grey plaits, jeans and floral blouses and white-haired men wearing shorts or sarongs and hats adorned with fishing tackle. A few leaned on walking sticks or sat in wheelchairs. All queued haphazardly on the verandas and the steps and paths which led to them. Doors in the sides of the hall and the double one at the front, above which a circular stained-glass window depicted a tree in blossom, were all open. The queues filed through in hushed silence.

Wood had never been in the building before. It proved quietly impressive: an echoing, rectangular room rising to a wooden ceiling whose curved beams were carved with vines and animals. Gape-mouthed frogs, chisel-toothed porcupines, paddle-tailed beavers and startled hares gazed on the crowd from chunky crosspieces. The air smelled of old wood. Above the stage and the lectern at the far end, in an expanse of pine carved in intricate knotwork, was a second stained-glass window, through which shone beams of sunlight. This one, however, was predominantly blue and white: a planet, seen from space. Wood initially took it to be Haven – the colours were right, and it had an ocean, landmasses, and icecaps. But the shape of Haven was now fixed in his mind's eye, and the continents were very different.

He sat beside Hazel on a wooden chair near the front. Scanning behind as the rows filled up, he caught sight of Sander, Stephanie and Berry, sitting together two rows away. Berry gave him a flick of the eyebrows but did not smile. Sander and Stephanie were talking in whispers. Everywhere, faces were set and apprehensive.

Soon the seating was full. Late arrivals sat or squatted in the aisles and below the stage or organised themselves into ranks standing around the perimeter with the smallest at the front. The hall had begun to feel crowded. With chairs still grating on floorboards, Jo Fox was wheeled to the lectern by a grim-faced Zhelkar Porro. He looked crooked, ashen and frail. A murmur arose as many got their first view of the shadow of the seemingly invincible figure they'd known.

Jo spoke to Zhelkar, who nodded in Wood and Hazel's direction. They continued talking, Zhelkar nodding occasionally.

Finally, everyone had settled, and only cooing doves in the eaves outside broke the silence.

Zhelkar walked to his seat at the side of the stage and entered something into the terminal there. Jo coughed and addressed his audience in a quiet voice cracked with effort or emotion.

'Fellow guardians of Haven.' The words were slurred, but clear enough. Another cough. 'My appearance may come as a shock to some of you, although Haven's state-of-the-art communications system will doubtless have informed most of you.'

There was a murmur of very strained laughter. *He means gossip*, Hazel explained, for Wood's benefit. Again Jo coughed, raising the bandaged remains of his hand to his chest.

'As most of you are probably aware, I've been away from Haven for nearly eight years. What I've been doing in that time may be more of a mystery, which I now aim to dispel.

'To do so, however, I must first explain some things which I've made a great effort to keep hidden from you. I'm not entirely alone in this conspiracy. Zhelkar and Dorrin Porro have been confidantes for some time, although some of what I'm about to say will be news to them too. I hope that once you've heard it, you'll forgive my deceit, if only for preserving your peace of mind.'

Jo paused and scanned the audience of open faces.

'It's been clear to me for a long time, and has, I'm sure, occurred at some time or other to many of you, that Haven cannot remain hidden for ever. While I made every attempt to find a planet as suitable, as remote, and inconspicuous as possible, our proximity, cosmically speaking, to space controlled by the Interplanetary Economic Confederation has, from the beginning, made our discovery inevitable.

'This was a conundrum which gave me sleepless nights in the early days. I'd envisaged a hideaway: a last sanctuary, where remnants of the Earth Mother's once mighty profusion of life could flourish, safe forever from those who destroy what they cannot use or own. As time went on, however, and the Interplanetary Economic Confederation formed and grew, the naiveté of my concept became apparent. Our secrecy could be only a stop-gap measure. Ultimately, we *would* be found.

'I'm sorry to tell you that day is now upon us.'

Through Hazel, Wood saw faces watching screens in towns, villages and recolonisation and research stations around the planet, all stunned and silent. In Juniper Town Hall, some were not so restrained. There was a swell of angry voices.

'What are you telling us Professor?' On his feet, the speaker was Randal Brightstone. 'That we need to pack up and start all over again? This is our *home!* I can't believe we were never told all of this.'

'Randal – Randal Brightstone, please.' Jo raised a pacifying hand, an action which seemed to cause him pain. The hubbub died and Randal, though still red-faced, fell silent. 'All I ask, for now, is that you listen to what I have to say. Then anyone who still has anger towards me, or questions they'd like answered, can have their say.'

Randal glared, but reseated himself. After a respectful pause, Jo continued.

'Nearly a century ago now, I stumbled across one of the last surviving products of IPEC's "blue-sky" genetic and biological research programme. This terribly deformed young man made me an offer. He told me he would put his genius at my service in exchange for the isolation which his extraordinary mind required to range freely. He craved a purpose with which to occupy himself but despised those who were his creators and captors. I freed him. I brought him here. You know him by the name he asked us to use: Tom.'

There were murmurs from around the hall.

'Many of you have queried the purpose to which Tom has put his intellect. Some have wondered why he is here at all. Though it saddens me to think that anyone or any*thing* should have to justify their existence on any grounds *whatsoever* – I believe some of you forget that a core tenet of the Code of Trust is that we do not base our treatment of other beings on their perceived value to ourselves –' he paused to let this sink in, eyes sweeping the hall in a manner which made some of the crowd look shiftily at the floor, '– The arrival of Tom is perhaps the single most important event that Haven has witnessed. Since he was brought here, Tom has been trying to save us.'

The silence seemed to deepen. Seven hundred thousand pairs of eyes around Haven were fixed expectantly on Jo Fox.

'Haven is building its own defence. The process was begun decades ago, and its fruition is imminent.'

Randal's eyes were now wide. The Professor was looking directly at him as he said this.

'That's why you have all been recalled here, to Haven. We are committed to this course of action. Nothing can now stop what Tom and I have begun.

'As to the charge of withholding information – from you, whom I should have held in firm trust – I can only plead guilty. We've had spies before. I hope you can appreciate that if this had become common knowledge, and IPEC had come to hear of it, then their actions may have been carried out with considerably more urgency. I know I ask a very great deal, but for now I ask you to put your trust in Tom. And in my judgement.

'What I can tell you is that the culmination of the defensive process will carry a risk. Should its completion prove successful, however, then that will be a day of which legends are written! From that day, we'll be *invulnerable* – it's no exaggeration to say that the might of the confederation will become irrelevant. From that day, we'll no longer need to concern ourselves with people whose ambitions are incompatible with our own. For the first time in history, Haven will be truly our ours.

'Think of what that means.' He moved his good arm. 'IPEC has hung like a cloud over every one of you, and everything you have achieved, since you were born. We've lived under the threat not simply of losing everything we hold dear, but of those things *ceasing to exist*. Soon, fate willing, that will be over, allowing every one of us the chance, finally, to live for life's sake. Truly to enjoy what your forebearers began here.

'In short, we will be free. Forever.'

Not a sound could be heard in the hall but the cooing of doves. Jo grew sombre.

'The original plan was for the process to be completed in a little less than two months time. Following my recent audiences with Tom, at the expense of a degree of extra risk, Tom has managed to move things forward. Completion is now estimated in one hundred and five hours' time. That's a little over five days.' Members of the audience looked at each other. Jo Fox swallowed, visibly. 'Unfortunately, even this may now be too late.'

A rumble of voices rose into a clamour of questions, astonished cries and shouting. Jo raised a hand awkwardly to silence them.

'Please, please,' he urged, the soft authority in his voice quenching much of the dissent. 'I am sorry … I have only so much strength.'

There were still angry cries. 'This is lunacy!'

'If anyone here, or listening to this broadcast, does not think they can trust Tom, or for that matter, me,' countered Jo in a sterner tone, 'perhaps they can they suggest a workable alternative?'

Quiet resumed. Jo sighed. He looked like a wizened old man.

'Tom predicted at the beginning that the time available would be barely enough,' he went on. 'Because of this, eight years ago I decided to return to IPEC – in fact, to Renascido, the remains of the Earth herself. A long time ago, when I still had influence within what was to become IPEC, in one of my better moments of foresight I began embedding within Renascido's embryonic Central Communications Grid, in whose construction I was involved, a series of sabotage mechanisms.

'The aim of my recent visit was to establish whether military and other developments warranted the drastic step of awakening these mechanisms – something which could be done only within Renascido. By freezing economic activity at the nerve-centre of the Interplanetary Economic Confederation at the right moment, I'd hoped to disrupt their economy in ways which would cripple their ability to launch an offensive at us.'

He twitched and lowered his eyes.

'It appears that I've been, at best, partially successful – and I regret to say that …' he hesitated, eyes haunted, 'I have been responsible, through an error of judgement, for accelerating the process of our discovery. It was only through the remarkable bravery of an outsider – Wood McCorkindale – his companion Tink, and our own Hazel from Juniper, that Haven's precise location was not revealed. To them I owe – we all owe – a heart-debt which can never be repaid.'

He remained silent for several seconds, staring at his trembling, mutilated hand. A ripple of whispering travelled around the hall. Necks and eyes strained for a look at Hazel and Wood.

'The confederation has a new weapon,' Jo told them. 'I learned of it through high-security information channels in Renascido's Central Communications Grid. Its name is "Troubleshooter". I tried, but failed, to discover its exact nature. However, it is clearly a massive engineering project. Such a weapon seems unnecessary for use against us alone. I believe that it was ultimately intended for use against the Freelancers, who are collectively many times stronger than us. Such a large weapon could quickly and efficiently dispose of entire Lancer operations.'

Was intended? thought Wood in alarm. *Why's he using the past tense?* Hazel shot him a startled look. Jo swept hollow eyes over the seated crowd once more.

'In the past few hours,' he continued, 'there have been … developments. The weapon has been used. It is my painful duty to tell you, my fellow Havenners, that the invasion has begun.'

The lights dimmed as a dark screen slid silently up the wood-panelled backwall of the hall. An image formed. A collective gasp arose as the audience realised what they were looking at.

'This is the planet Terra Two,' said Jo, voice as dry as death now, raising his more usable arm as he turned his chair half towards the glowing red sphere. Occasional small prominences erupted from the planet's incandescent new atmosphere. Darker patches showed against the intensely red magma which now formed its surface. Sensing the dread pervading the room, small children began to wail.

'We received this picture from one of our sniffers, this morning, at five Juniper time. Terra Two's surface temperature is now on average more than one-point-six thousand degrees centigrade. We don't understand yet what could generate enough energy to do this, but fusion reaction on a vast scale seems the only likely candidate.'

He turned his wheelchair to face them all.

'My friends –' He paused, in tense silence for many long seconds, eyes beginning another slow sweep. 'We are all here on Haven – we are blessed with this world to enjoy – because of the efforts of your ancestors, who spent, and in many cases sacrificed, their lives making all you see around you possible. We cannot let their efforts be in vain. Wherever humankind has travelled between the stars, he has so far found no life but that of Mother Earth. All that remains is here. On Haven.'

He scanned the faces before him. Many listeners were now staring into space or cradling their heads.

'We need a little over five days. Terra Two is five days away by hyperspace, by the fastest route. We have weapons, but I won't sugar coat it: we are outmatched, potentially by orders of magnitude. Yet we need time. We must delay the arrival of what is certain to be a large fleet.'

Wood gaped at Hazel. *Please tell me he's not talking about attacking the IPEC fleet?* Jo ran his gaze over them all yet again, eyes full of the knowledge that what he was about to say was the greatest iniquity.

'We have four hundred and thirty non-organic spacecraft capable of bearing weapons and serving a useful purpose in battle,' he began. 'However, we must use the important tactical advantages that wormhole travel affords us. We can choose our battlefield. That means that all non-organics we use will have to be transported there by orgs. The orgs can transport a maximum of two hundred and ninety-six nonorgs.

'We therefore need five hundred and forty-two people to man the spacecraft which are to be sent to intercept and delay the approaching force, or forces, before they can reach Haven, and four hundred and fifty more for the vessels which will be held in reserve guarding Haven itself.

'I won't mislead you. It's unlikely that those in the interception fleet will ever return to Haven. Even so, all the orgs not currently undergoing fission have already volunteered, and I feel this reflects on them as ...' his voice began breaking up 'as a ... a race it is an honour for us to call our friends. Their capacity for fear is, if anything, more acute than our own. Yet not one showed any hesitation.'

Jo fell silent, as though pausing for breath after an exhausting task.

'There will be a callup over the Net,' he continued eventually, quieter now. 'All over the age of eighteen who want to volunteer may do so. It will obviously be important to use the best pilots. If there's a surplus of volunteers, then numbers will be filtered according to ability and experience.

'It speaks volumes of you, my *friends*, that I am not concerned there will be a shortage of volunteers. My wish that I could be there with you is second only to the wish that this invasion were merely the imagining of a paranoid old man. I've lived far longer than anyone has a right to ... and I would far rather die than see a single one of you fail to return. In my present condition, I would be a hindrance.'

Looking utterly broken, he went on: 'The rollcall will be at three this afternoon, Juniper Mean Time, to allow everyone time to talk things over with families and friends. Those chosen will make their way immediately to Hades by transport already organised, and will he briefed there.

'I would like to say that ... whatever the, the future may hold,' Jo's throat made an odd, strangled sound, 'it has been a privilege to be amongst you. And ... if there is any justice in the ... world, you will all ... all come ...'

For a moment, his blinking eyes filled with what looked like madness, his mouth working noiselessly. Several hundred thousand pairs of eyes watched, spellbound. They had never seen anything less than utter composure from the man.

His hunted eyes turned desperately towards Zhelkar. Looking shocked, Zhelkar seemed to hesitate, and then rushed awkwardly over. Jo coughed something into his ear and was wheeled away with undignified haste.

The audience stared at the empty stage in consternated silence.

41

SOMEONE ELSE

'I REALLY THINK we are alone. I haven't seen anyone for hours. They must all be away at a meeting or something.'

The Havenners, as their captors called themselves, had put the three surviving officers in a cabin hidden amongst the tree-organisms some distance from the lake. Insubstantial lacy nets called 'cobwebs' festooned its corners, their centres patrolled by multiply-legged dark creatures which, though small, were the stuff of nightmares. They seemed to be using the nets to capture and eat some of the other small creatures which fluttered around the light or scuttled over the floor and the walls.

The cabin lacked furniture of any kind. Meals had been brought to them ready-cooked by a taciturn, very tall, thirty-something man who'd introduced himself as Berry. There were no facilities except a sink and a staggeringly pungent toilet in which excreta just dropped into a pit, with a wooden hot-tub outside which someone had filled from a hose. The three had slept in blankets on the floor. There was no lock, nor bars on the window.

Aral Nikumi walked to the window, lip curling in distaste at the grime and the little corpses stuck to it with cobwebs. He took the edge of the blind – a contrivance of plant-stems and string – from Jeetwa, who stood respectfully aside. Through the gap between the blind and the window frame, he could clearly see the dark ramjet about four hundred metres away between widely spaced tree trunks. His implant would have told him the exact distance, but the Freaks had found a way to disable its tactical functions.

'They must be pretty sure of themselves.' To Kettering the entire situation was still unbelievable. 'No guards, nothing.'

Nikumi repositioned his foul-smelling nappy. It needed cleaning and was chafing his assortment of pustules and rashes.

'They believe they hold two aces. This mind-worm thing, and our infection.'

'We've got to *try*,' Kettering growled. 'We can't just sit here.'

'Sitting here is an option.' Nikumi replaced the blind and looked between the others. 'One we should consider carefully. The fleet should already be following up our message.'

'And then what?' demanded Kettering. 'Their stated aim will be to turn this hellhole into slag. You're kidding yourself if you think there'll be a rescue mission just for us.' Teeth showing, he rubbed his concave midriff. 'Now we're infected, we're as good as dead anyway.'

'They said they have ways to uninfect us. And they must have. Otherwise Fox would never have been able to live for years in Renascido undetected. To find him, we'd simply have needed to follow the epidemics.'

Kettering clenched his fists and glowered. The strangeness of the world in which they found themselves captive, and the privations they'd been forced to endure, had hit him hardest. 'And how, in our circumstances, are we going to persuade them to uninfect us? Hasn't it struck you that's why our prison doesn't have bars?'

Nikumi was thoughtful for a while.

'Alright, Kettering,' he said eventually. 'We will try. If only to speed up this place's destruction.'

'But this mind-worm of theirs,' Jeetwa interjected, his long face drawn with illness and worry. 'If what they said is true, we could even end up brainwashed into piloting against our own fleet! I don't mind dying if it means we can bring them down – but I won't have that.' He looked thoughtful for a moment.

'I have to confess, though, these people aren't quite what I expected. I'm finding it very hard to get any real handle on them.'

During the previous twenty-four hours the three captives had, to their surprise, had the run of the haphazard little town. On the pretext of intelligence-gathering they'd stalked around feeling paranoid and increasingly dazed. They'd even been given access to the library, although the terminals there had been limited to a small range of access commands to prevent tampering. Nikumi and Jeetwa, to Kettering's undisguised disgust, had spent much of their time since cramming as much library information into their processor-augmented craniums as time would allow. Wherever they went, townspeople – even children – had acknowledged the officers' presence by silently avoiding them. Only occasional looks and glances betrayed the anger and fear running just below the surface.

'Being honest, I expected to wake up with my head in a jar.'

'This isn't what anyone expected, Jeetwa,' Nikumi told him. 'Just remember that everything we see will be what they want us to. We have no idea what these people are really like, or what their motives towards us currently are.' He felt his nostrils flare. 'Kettering is right, we have to escape. In view of what they've told us however, I cannot risk all three of us.'

Kettering began pulling pieces of dried plant-stem off the ends of the blind. Two long, one short. As he clenched them in his palm with the tops sticking out, Jeetwa put out a hand to stop him. 'That won't be necessary.'

Kettering glanced at Nikumi, who raised his eyebrows. 'Jeetwa?'

'Look, sir, I'm trained to sit in an armoured cube a hundred klicks wide and process information. I'm not cut out for this situation. We have no concrete reason to suspect they're bluffing about what they've done to our heads. Of the three of us, I'm most expendable.'

Nikumi gave the officer a searching look. Then he grasped Jeetwa's shoulder and peered through the blind again. He grunted, still unwilling on an instinctual level to believe what he was seeing. 'Still seems clear. Are you certain you can fly that thing?'

'Shouldn't be that different from some of my naval college sims,' Jeetwa replied nervously. 'What's more, I think it's equipped for orbital operation. But I haven't seen any signs of armament.' He frowned. 'In fact, I haven't seen weapons at all since that thing murdered *Violator*. It's almost as though they don't have any.'

'Never mind, try whatever you can – it may be possible for you to commandeer a spacecraft somehow. But I do not expect miracles, Jeetwa. Your priority is to broadcast the message. In the Freaks' position I would be very stealthy about my communications, so you might need to modify their tight-beam transmission hardware for broadcasting. Or even build your own transmitter.'

Jeetwa fingered his lips. 'Should be relatively straightforward. I imagine their equipment is primitive.'

'Don't fall into that trap. Some of what I've seen here is very sophisticated. It's not that they lack technology. They just seem to use it selectively.'

'Sir.'

'A broadcast from the atmosphere should be enough. If you find some way to commandeer and repurpose a courier missile, so much the better. Unless we hear from you, and you can devise some reliable way to get us out, we'll sit tight and wait until another opportunity presents itself.'

Kettering picked up one of the sturdy sticks he'd been sharpening with a shard of broken ceramic and handed it to Jeetwa. One of the few things he'd learnt from the library was how to produce a potent nerve poison by sun-drying the sap of one of the local plants. The stick's point was coated in dark residue.

'If you run into trouble.'

Jeetwa smiled thinly, pushing his hand away. 'That won't be necessary.'

THE DOOR OF THE bizarre little shed-like building creaked closed behind him. Taking a deep breath, trying not to be distracted by the insane value of what he was walking on, Jeetwa clumped furtively across the wooden floorboards and down the steps.

Think relaxed.

Instantly, he tensed. Two Freaks, both men, were making their way through the woods between him and the lakeshore. Just his luck! The first people they'd seen here for over two hours.

Without once looking his way, they continued in the opposite direction, hand in hand. Soon they were lost amongst the trees.

He moved on, stumbling over stones covered in spongy green mats and tentacular structures grown from the base of what he now knew to be trees. Every step was uneven; each part of this bizarre landscape designed with utter indifference to physical or psychological human need. It was like wandering through the nightmare of a disturbed child. There were things moving, and crawling, everywhere. Even inside him, now, they'd said. *Sick, sick.* The thought made him shiver and gag. *Got to get out of here …*

He was perhaps halfway to the sleek black ramjet. Despite his training, his thoughts had become focussed on it to the exclusion of almost everything else. He felt his step quicken, along with his breathing. He tripped on an exposed woody tentacle and fell to his hands and knees.

Shit.

A movement caught his eye. A hand-sized orange creature with front teeth like chisels and a tail like a bottle brush looked down on him with glinting eyes, like a furry sculpture on the side of a green-furred tree. Its tail swished suddenly, making him start.

He stumbled to his feet, wiping black-stained hands on his trousers.

Perhaps twenty metres to go. *Come on, come on …*

He looked behind him. The hand-holding couple were nowhere to be seen. The whole place seemed deserted.

Didn't these people know anything about security?

In his urgency, he'd considerably underestimated the distance to the ramjet. As he entered the clearing, he saw that there was easily thirty metres still to go. His feet thumped against the short grass, skidding in the soft faeces of one of the large, long-necked fluffy creatures which watched him approach.

Jesus Christ. Almost there …

Dripping sweat, squinting into suddenly bright sunlight, Jeetwa scurried beneath the fat, forward-swept wing of a childishly-painted smaller aircraft and palmed the entry pad on the ramjet's side. A hatch hissed open. He pulled himself through.

Panting for breath, he began strapping himself in using the primitive webbing arrangement of the seat. He scanned the instruments and displays for familiar landmarks. A joystick and throttle and thrust-vector levers were the main controls. There was a big red button helpfully marked IGNITION. Lift-off looked simple enough. Landing would be trickier, but that was a street to be crossed when – and if – he came to it.

He fingered a switch-pad to prewarm the old antigrav generators, and heard their rising whine. *Too loud!* Someone was bound to hear. Through the tree trunks he could just make out the grim cabin where the other officers were hiding.

This was crazy! There was still no-one around.

He waved at the others, willing them to see him. There was no reason now, he thought, why all three of them couldn't all escape. He beckoned them towards the ramjet.

'*Come on,*' he breathed, as though by whispering loudly they would hear. What were their names? The officers?

Jeetwa froze, mid wave.

He couldn't remember their names.

He looked around him, confused, and annoyed. Now, of all times, he wished he had a better memory for names. Now that he came to think of it, he wasn't even sure why he'd come to the ramjet in the first place.

Through the trees, he could see two men running like commandos, yet both with a faint but curious waddle, towards the clearing. Their clothing was entirely grey or black but for some kind of red insignia on the shoulders. A uniform. As they drew close, they began gesturing frantically. He powered the generators back down and, with one arm, swung the door up.

'Can I help you?'

'Jeetwa,' hissed Kettering, panting. 'Stop fucking about! Let us in.'

Jeetwa's eyes narrowed. 'I think you're mistaking me for someone else. Come to think of it … I don't recall seeing you two around here before.'

Whoever this pair were, they were behaving very suspiciously. And both looked terribly unhealthy. Diseased, even.

After a brief internal debate, he pressed the alarm on the console.

'*SHIT!*'

Kettering launched a flying kick at the side of the ramjet, hitting it with a solid thud. He fell on the grass.

'Hey, steady on!' cried Jeetwa.

Nikumi stared silently at the ground.

'Let's kill him.' Kettering was advancing menacingly towards the cockpit. 'Those bastards, they've brainwashed him. He told us he'd rather die than be used by them.'

Jeetwa paled. 'Help!' He screamed, slamming the cockpit door. Kettering banged his fist against the pad and then against the window. Jeetwa flinched back, eyes wide, speaking urgently into a hidden microphone.

'Enough,' Nikumi said quietly, seizing his first officer's wrist. 'This won't get us anywhere. He's gone. He knew what might happen.'

'Motherfucking bastards.' Kettering was shaking. He turned in the direction of the town's vague centre. 'I hope you all burn!' he shrieked into the air, fists waving. 'I hope you die, screaming, in the inferno we're going to make of this vile pit of yours, and then burn forever in hell, you perverted fucking freaks of nature!'

As if from nowhere, an audience had begun to assemble around the strange tableau. Brightly clothed people were converging on the scene from all over the forest, looking on with tight, wary faces. None were obviously armed. This only inflamed Kettering's rage and terror. A military problem he could deal with, but not this.

As the crowd grew, an unfamiliar plump, black-haired woman stepped forward and moved towards the ramjet. Though she was relatively short, her presence suggested a leader of some kind. She halted a couple of metres before Nikumi and looked him impassively in the eye. Her gaze was formidable.

Nikumi stared levelly back.

She walked calmly to the ramjet's door and opened it.

'Come now, Jeetwa,' she said, raising a hand to help him down. 'I'm sorry about these men. They are outsiders, and full of anger. We'll make sure they stay away from you until you get more of your memory back, my dear.'

Jeetwa looked uncertainly between her face and the proffered hand, then fearfully back at the red-faced Kettering. He allowed her to help him from the cockpit on to the grass, where he clung to her shoulder like a scared little boy.

Kettering watched the woman, with her infuriating air of aloofness, lead what had once been Tactical Officer Jeetwa off to a life of Freak servility.

Rage twisted his face, turning it purple.

He sprinted at the departing woman's back, drawing the sharpened stick from his sleeve. Hearing the enraged yell, the crowd cried out as one as they saw the strange man pounding over the grass towards their leader, arm raised, holding something sharp. The woman began to turn, but everyone watching knew that she wouldn't be quick enough.

There was a swishing noise, followed by a thump.

Kettering whirled around like a top. He fell to the ground, clutching his shoulder and screaming hoarsely. Forty centimetres of wooden stick capped with feathery red fins was sticking out of him.

'One down, just fifteen hundred billion to go,' chirped a wizened little woman with an improbable shock of tangled brown hair, fitting another blade-tipped stick to the tensioned cord of her impossibly primitive weapon.

'That'll do, Lissa.' The plump woman gave the shooter a sharp look, then inspected the figure writhing on the ground. She raised her eyes to Nikumi's.

'Do we have an understanding now?' she inquired, mildly.

Nikumi glared at her, then at Kettering's thrashing.

He ground his teeth and nodded.

42

VOLUNTEERS

HAZEL FOUND Wood by the lake.

He was sitting with his feet buried in the warm, golden-pink sand, staring at the ripples as though they'd hypnotised him. She hesitated, then sat and leaned against him, knees drawn up under her chin, head propped on his shoulder. Painfully skinny when she'd met him, his frame had filled out, and lean muscles now covered his slender bones. Well on their way to adulthood, a late brood of moorhen chicks foraged by themselves amongst the lilypads and other waterweeds, seeming strangely subdued and silent.

'I didn't volunteer,' murmured Wood, after a while.

I know.

He could feel her unasked question boiling below the surface of effected calm.

'I didn't see the point. I'll have to go anyway, won't I?' For a few moments, there was only the soft slap of ripples on the shore.

'Haven would have the best chance if you did.'

You used me. You and Haven. You used me from the beginning.

A breeze ruffled the water; tiny rippling sounds became momentarily more frantic. Smells of pine wafted past on the wind. Hazel noticed for the first time what had been troubling her. There was no birdsong. Even the crickets had ceased their chirping. The dragonflies and smaller insects which usually darted and skimmed over the surface of the lake were gone. It was as if Haven held its breath, waiting.

'I was told to win you over if necessary,' she said. 'I didn't have to. I just brought you here. You did the rest yourself. I never planned on falling in love.'

Wood picked up a pebble and threw it into the water with a plop. 'And if it wasn't for *Oscar*? What then?' He could feel her tense beside him.

'Then …' she sighed. 'I'd have wiped the parts of your memory which recalled anything to do with us, and we'd have either brought you to a Freelancer colony or released you in Federation space.' She looked away. When she spoke, her voice was strained. 'Wood … I thought you knew all this.'

Wood made no comment. He just raised his knees, crossed his arms on top of them, and laid his chin on his forearms.

I'll go with you, Hazel said.

'With me?'

'In *Oscar*.'

'And what would be the point in that?' He hurled a handful of sand down the beach. 'Other than me, it only needs Tink – who, incidentally, you're all completely taking for granted in all of this – to operate the thing, so what exactly would that achieve?'

'I wasn't chosen. The list is out, and I wasn't on it. I don't know why – I expected to be. I'm a good enough pilot. I thought I was needed to coordinate everything. But now … no-one will lose out if I go with you.'

'But that's *pointless*, Hazel. You know we'll probably not be coming back.'

He heard her swallow. 'That's why I want to go.'

Wood opened his mouth to say something more, but the words died before he could speak them. His arms went around her fiercely, and sudden tears dampened her hair.

'Damn it all Hazel,' he hissed. 'I was just beginning to live. I'd give anything for just two more days.'

THE LEAFDANCE'S HOUSE was an almost perfect model of dynamic equilibrium. Food would be spilt, clothes and bits of machinery and electronics would be left strewn around any one of the four wood-panelled rooms; dirty crockery would accumulate in the sink and on the battered folding table – mostly a result of the entropic agent that was Sander Leafdance. The chaos would be continuously restored to order by Stephanie Leafdance, only to be replaced by disorder equally fast.

Stephanie had long ago learned to accept this as one of the less endearing traits of her partner, which he – by and large – made up for in other ways. She wasn't above the occasional tirade, however, which Sander generally ignored with his usual equanimity.

Berry stepped over a pair of discarded trousers which lay crumpled in the front doorway like a casualty of war. Beyond, books lay scattered amongst dirty mugs and pieces of what looked like a photovoltaic regulator. 'Get out of that chair, you pig,' he heard, bringing a brief smile to his lips. 'Dammit, I am *not* your bloody slave! Clean up yourself for a change. I cannot live in a place which looks like a typhoon hit it.'

'Yes, darling,' came the bored reply. Berry winced.

'Damn you!' There was a slap and a startled grunt. 'Just you tidy up, right now – no, don't give me that look, I mean it! Take these –' there was the sound of breaking crockery '– and tidy all this crap away – or you might as well not bother about coming back.'

There was a stunned silence. Then: 'Hon, we shouldn't be arguing about this! I've only got two hours left.' The voice sounded terribly hurt.

'And wouldn't it have been nice to spend them in something that wasn't like the inside of a compost heap?'

There was the sound of bitter sobbing. Berry felt his shoulders slump. He clamped his lips between his teeth, counted to three, and rapped his knuckles against the inside of the door.

'Hullo?' he ventured. 'Sander, Steph. It's me.'

He heard cautious footsteps. A face he'd never seen before appeared in the doorway to the living room. It was Sander's, but without any traces of humour.

'Berry … I …' Sander studied Berry's moccasins, then his eyes rose again with a pained expression. 'Come in, come in.'

He led the way into the living room, stepping over dirty cups. Stephanie was sitting, puffy-eyed, on the futon. She managed a weak smile as Berry entered. 'Cuppa?' asked Sander, gesturing at the sink. Berry raised a hand.

'No, thanks. Don't know what I'd catch,' he added, lamely, eyeing piled cups and dishes. Fragments of porcelain littered the top of one of the bookcases and the adjacent floor. He looked at Stephanie. 'How d'you put up with him, Steph?'

She just looked tearful. Berry dithered. Then, looking at Sander, he said 'I wasn't called up.'

Sander's expression didn't change.

'That's good, Bez. I'm pleased.'

Berry turned away. Watched golden aspen leaves bob in the sunlight beyond the window. Listened to their rustle. *Leafdance*, he thought, closing his eyes. *Sander and Stephanie Leafdance.*

'I've no family,' he said. He turned back to face them. 'Unless I count you two. No sense seeing you split up.'

Sander frowned. Then his mouth dropped open. 'What are you saying?' Stephanie was looking alarmed.

'If I go, Sander, you can stay.'

'No!' cried Stephanie, vigorously shaking her head. Sander nodded wildly in agreement with her.

'Not an option, Bez. The choice was made fairly. I took the draw the same as you. I've about the same experience and skill as you; my number came up, yours didn't.' He shrugged, toeing aside a book. 'That's really all there is to say about it.'

Berry folded his arms and turned to the window once more. 'I expected a fight, Sandy. You've been a good friend to me. The best. You, me. Hazel … We were inseparable, weren't we? For a while. Do you remember?'

His stomach churned as he looked into Sander's eyes. Sander nodded, warily at first, then with conviction. 'They'll probably still be talking about us in a hundred years.'

'Do you remember that time we stirred … chilli juice –?'

'– Into the pots of Juniper's stock of thrush cream.' Sander's eyes glinted. 'Seemed so unfair at the time, the way everyone automatically just knew it was us.'

'Even though they'd no evidence.'

'Worth it, though.' He snorted. 'All those terribly serious, responsible ladies waddling around like they'd ridden from Timberlake on horseback.'

Berry turned back to the window. 'Hazel's going,' he said. 'Told me a few minutes ago.' He scanned the sill's collection of dead flies and wasps. 'You two have each other.'

He turned again to find Sander and Stephanie both looking in agony at the floor. 'Berry please stop this,' gasped Sander. 'It isn't doing any good. Just stop it!'

'Shut up. Listen.'

'Berry! Just *think* for a moment, you fool – if you didn't come back …' He tailed off, helplessly. Berry looked him directly in the eye.

'I'd imagine,' he said, moving towards the woodstove, 'you could live with it, you self-centred mule, more easily than Steph could without you.' Making sure the action was hidden by his legs, he used his left hand to pull the heavy iron fire-poker from its rack, keeping it tight against his thigh.

Sander looked stunned. Stephanie had her eyes closed. No-one spoke for several seconds.

'Berry, I know you're trying to help. But this is … it's not …

Berry nodded, feeling that a question had been answered. He steeled himself. 'Sorry,' he said, moving forward. Badly miscalculated. I'll leave you in peace.'

He stretched out his right hand.

'Berry –' Sander hissed, shaking it by reflex. He got no further. Pulling Sander off balance be his wrist Berry brought the shaft of the poker down on his extended hand with all the force he could muster.

Sander screamed. Berry had a glimpse of a fist filling his vision –

– and then he was sitting dizzily on the floor, propped against the – fortunately unlit – stove with a scything pain in his mouth. Tasting blood, he dabbed at his nose and mouth. Stephany was looming over him with a broom-handle raised above her head. Sander was on the futon, white-faced, staring at a hand which was already swelling up like a puffball.

'*Get out*,' shrieked Stepanie. 'What do you think you're doing, you maniac?'

'Mother, you throw a mean punch.' Berry staggered to his feet, eyes locked on Sander. 'Lefthanded, too.' His front teeth wobbled as he explored them with a finger and thumb.

'Berry,' protested Sander, 'to use a Puke term, what the absolute *fuck?*'

'Able-bodied pilots only,' he mumbled, making unsteadily for the door. 'Looks like a nasty break, that. Take days to heal properly.' He sighed. He'd imagined he'd feel better, but now the deed was done, he just felt sore and unutterably sad. Turning, he saw Sander slumped, defeated. Still clutching her broom, Stephanie was crying.

'This is messed up,' said Sander, eyes also brimming, clutching his hair and shaking his head.

'If I come back, Sandy, I'll make this up to you any way you want. But if you choose to waste even a day on some self-pitying guilt wallow, I'll never forgive you. Spend your time on something useful. Like occasionally trying to clean after yourself for the woman who loves you.' He wiped blood on his trousers. 'Now, got to go. Said I'd help prepare the fleet. Not much time. Better get that hand looked at – you don't want it to set wrong. You two take care.'

He heard boards creak as Sander rose but had already turned away through the door. The Leafdances followed him on to the veranda and watched in silence as he walked away between the trees towards the main SEV pad.

43

FURIES

'YOU ASKED TO SEE ME?'

Nikumi forced himself to look down at the twisted figure in the wheelchair. Fox was staring expressionlessly over the big lake towards a series of low islands infested with trees. Beside him was a flat-topped, knee-high stump where one of the organisms had been severed near its base. Green stuff was growing on it, along with something brown and shaped disturbingly like ears.

Behind the wheelchair, the elderly man he knew as Zhelkar Porro studied Nikumi with hard eyes. Fox dismissed the man with a raised hand and a nod. Porro's eyes lingered on Nikumi's a moment longer, then he shook his head and stalked off into the trees.

Nikumi watched him go.

'You're wondering why none of you have been lynched, yet,' observed Fox, mildly. One side of his mouth didn't seem to be moving properly. 'One of the advantages of being able to select one's followers. There's an inherited component to violent tendencies, and a feedback between an individual's experiences and the genetically expressed behaviour of their grandchildren, passed on via sperm. Even I've been surprised how peaceable my people are, if you want the truth. Not that they won't defend their planet to the death, of course. Please, sit down. There's a flask of jasmine tea by my wheelchair, if you'd like a drink.'

Nikumi offered no sign of complying.

'Commodore Nikumi. If any of us had a mind to kill you, no matter how stealthily, surely we'd have done so already?'

Nikumi remained motionless. Then he stepped forward, picked up the flask and poured some of the steaming contents into its screw-on cap. Having inspected the stump on which he was clearly intended to sit, he brought his nose close to it and sniffed. Convincing himself that nothing immediately fatal was likely to emerge from it, he lowered his backside on to it and inhaled the vapour coming off his drink.

The smell was unfamiliar, but not unpleasant.

'There was a leader of a doomed empire on pre-Eden Renascido,' he observed. 'Adolf Hitler, I believe he was called. He espoused similar methods, if your library is to be believed. History was less than kind to him.'

Fox smiled. 'As your society's historians will, doubtless, be to me. Who knows, Commodore, perhaps they'll make you a saint? Which would be ironic, given the number of people you've killed, and the methods you employ – or allow – for the extraction of information.'

Nikumi turned his eyes back to the water. 'History will record you as the greatest mass-murderer of all time. Or do you not count terrorism as murder? Whether people are driven to suicide or killed by a bullet, the result is the same.'

'Despite the moral ambiguity of the service you work for, you think of yourself a man of principle, Nikumi.' It wasn't phrased as a question. Nikumi inspected his cup.

'No system is perfect.'

'I appreciate you saying that.' Fox raised a shaking, maimed limb at the lake. 'Take this, for example. Not perfect by a long shot. There's death here. Unnecessary suffering. Ugliness and pettiness. Yet there's also compassion. Indescribable beauty. A viable future. The possibility of something greater.' He coughed, stifling a grimace, and fixed Nikumi's gaze with his own. It remained imposing with control of only half his face. 'What are your impressions, Nikumi? Go on, I'm intrigued. You must realise you've nothing to lose by telling me the truth.'

'I don't understand your world. It means nothing to me.'

A nod. 'Does it repulse you?'

'Sometimes.'

'And the people? What's your impression of them?'

'They seem,' he pursed his lips, 'like people.'

'Fanatical?'

'Less so than I'd imagined.'

'Do they seem miserable?'

There was quite a long pause. 'They seem content enough.' As he spoke, it struck Nikumi that this was true. It was no act, if he was the judge of people he'd trained to be. What he'd observed had felt complicated, and human, and real. 'From what I've seen.'

Fox nodded. 'You know, I believe they are. Not always of course, for which I'm largely to blame – but broadly content, yes. It's comforting to hear an outsider say that, because after a while it gets difficult to take a step back.'

Nikumi felt his lip curling. 'And when your acolytes decide they want something different from the vision you've prescribed? When kids get tempted by the shiny trinkets IPEC has to offer? What then? Reprogramming? Incarceration? Public executions?'

The cripple raised an eyebrow. 'A valid point. And I can hardly claim moral high ground when I learned the power of peer pressure from your corporate overlords.' Nikumi did his best not to show surprise. 'I can only state my relief that such a situation hasn't yet arisen. Though I think you overestimate the capacity for boredom of youngsters who have an entire planet to run wild in.'

'And what did you imagine was going to happen when you are dead? Or did you intend to play God for ever?'

'Heavens, no.' A crooked smile. 'Nature will have to take its chances again. My role has been simply to provide a bridge across an impasse.' The man spoke without apparent irony. 'Who knows what the future holds? But I do know that when I'm gone it'll be my people's choice whether, given the facts of what went wrong the last time, they screw up their second chance.'

My people. Nikumi looked back at his cup. Vapour rising from its contents was clearly visible in the low sunlight. Fox gazed at a skyline of distant mountains.

'We will win eventually,' Nikumi told him. 'Against our decline. We don't want disease – of any kind. I believe that in the end we will defeat it.'

'I hope you do.' Again, Nikumi was surprised. 'I mean it. Though don't hold much hope of humanity surviving in isolation for long, at least not in its present, limited form. Life likes complexity and strives towards it. And it's tenacious. You may find the Purges less complete than you've been led to believe.'

Nikumi stiffened.

'Look underground, Commodore. Beneath the oceans and within the deepest caves or the rocks themselves, where your viruses and disinfectants could never reach.' The ancient smiled lopsidedly, one eye looking sad. 'Oh, I wouldn't worry about it – not for millennia at least. Possibly not until Renascido gets swallowed by the sun. The Purges were more than thorough enough: any surviving organisms are likely to be exclusively deep-benthic or subterranean, and no immediate threat. Diseases require close genetic or trophic links to bridge species. That's how domesticating animals gave us most of our infectious diseases, and why genetic modification helped spread so many diseases and immunities between previously unrelated lifeforms despite mankind's best efforts at control.'

Nikumi was unsure whether his racing pulse was because of Fox's astonishing claim, or simply because the rug had once more been pulled from under him. He concentrated on keeping his expression neutral.

'Some of our bioextrapolists,' Fox continued, 'have interesting views of life's importance in the cosmos. The field's barely a century old and relies on mathematical constructs we've been able to explore only using the fuzzy processing of our most recent organically-based quantum thinkers. But if they're right, life is not a "thing", or even an end point. It's a phase of matter and energy in response to entropy, as fundamental to the cosmos as the big bang or the separation of universal forces.

'Its existence in quantity may govern the future of the cooling universe, as a precursor to the next entropic phase: sentience. By sentience I don't mean the self-awareness of a few animated bags of salty water like you or me. I mean awareness becoming a property of the universe itself. Ultimately, life, and the sentience which springs from it, may offer an escape from the lingering cosmic death which our theoreticians call the Flatline. Call it "transcendence", if you like. However, as our understanding becomes more advanced, our models increasingly agree on one thing.'

Nikumi found himself confronted with the full unrestrained force of Fox's stare.

'In terms of worldlines, life spreads – *crystallises* – across the universe from a single point.'

As the significance of the statement sank in, Nikumi found pieces of the Freaks' baffling motivational jigsaw finally slotting into place. It was, in a very real sense, a religion. Yet, once again, this created further questions. The timescales involved in such thinking were inhuman. What was promised wasn't even salvation on a personal level, but the salvation of descendants surely millions or even billions of years in the future.

'Which brings me,' continued Fox, 'indirectly, to the proposal I want to make to you, Commodore. One I hope you will take in good faith. In a very short period of time, there is going to be a bloodbath.'

He gestured feebly in the direction of the town.

'My people will fight like furies to save this world. I imagine your navy will have seen nothing like it – and, as you've experienced, things will be far from one-sided. We will hurt your navy and your society, deeply. None of us here want that. We understand your fear of disease, and we don't blame anyone alive now, with perhaps one exception, for what was done centuries before you were even born.'

'An exception. You mean James Marcell?'

'You're better informed than I'd hoped. All we want, be it right or wrong from your perspective, is the chance to survive as you see us. Nothing more, nothing less. Not to have that chance is something we all find unthinkable.'

He turned back to Nikumi, his eyes penetrating. 'As I'm sure you're aware, a battlefleet comprising more than half IPEC's navy is approaching. However, in a little under six days from now, we believe we will have reached a solution to both our problem and yours.'

Fox lowered his eyes and, rather awkwardly, handed Nikumi a small terminal, whose screen dutifully unfolded.

'In six days.'

The screen showed a video. Nikumi studied it at first with scepticism, then with increasingly bulging eyes. He fixed Fox with a wondering stare.

'My first thought,' he said, 'is that this proves you are insane.'

No response.

'You seriously think you can achieve this?'

'We will certainly try.' A shrug. 'I always was an optimist.'

'Do *they* know?' Nikumi darted his eyes in the direction of the town. Jo ignored the question.

'I'm asking for a little more than half a tenday, Nikumi. Six days, to avoid the waste, one way or another, of millions of human lives and what remains of the irreplaceable life of an entire world. Perhaps the only life there will ever be.'

It was Nikumi's turn not to respond.

'What I propose is this. We'll thoroughly sterilise both you and Commander Kettering, using the methods your own people developed for the Purges. You know we can do this: it's required of our spies before every operation within Lancer or confederation space, and you should know from Green Section records that there's never been any kind of outbreak.'

'Recorded,' Nikumi pointed out.

'You'll be given one of our interstellar-capable ships to intercept the approaching fleet. All we ask in return is that you inform the admiral in charge of the fleet of our request.'

He digested this. 'Which is?'

'We ask for a ceasefire until one hundred and seventy standard hours from now. After that time, should your forces consider us still to be a threat, we'll offer our unconditional surrender. One hundred and seventy hours, then surrender. The killing must stop, Commodore. Of course, I have no guarantee you would do what you promise, but as a man who I believe is, at heart, honourable, I'm hoping you'll at least try.'

Nikumi stared at his cup. He sniffed it again, suspiciously, then took a sip. It tasted bitter at first, and was rather tepid, but he decided that he might come to like it if he had to.

'There are scientists in IPEC who expect us all be dead in a few centuries,' he said, quietly. 'Some people seem convinced you have an answer, though that seems a fairy-tale to me.' He titled his head. 'Do you have an answer?'

Fox's gaze dipped for a moment. 'We do,' he said. 'Though even if it were possible for your lot to adopt, it's something I doubt most would ever accept.'

'Why not?'

'Because your society already rejected it.' He spread his hands. '*This* is the answer, Commodore. Everything you see around you on Haven; everything you and your people fear. It's about life and death. Cooperation, very harsh forms of competition, and changes over which we have no control. It's about accepting our nature as a small part of something much bigger, which doesn't have our personal interests at heart. A kidney will die not long after its host body does.

'Your society, Commodore Nikumi, is that kidney. Its body died – was *killed* – three centuries ago. There may be other answers available to you, technological methods of life support. But if so, they're likely to involve radical changes regarding what it even means to be human, and you're resisting even those. You need to start looking for them quickly.'

Fox seemed to be finished. Nikumi set the cup down on the leaf litter. After a short pause, he stood up.

'I'll consider your proposal,' he said. 'Is that all?'

Fox hesitated, then nodded.

'You will have an answer in two hours.'

44

STIRRING SPEECH

THE SEV SETTLED in a haze of dust on to the terraced cavern floor. Wood trailed Hazel outside. They found Aspen Sunrise jogging towards them from the largest building, calling out 'Come on, you're the last to arrive.'

She bustled them through the entrance and down spiral stairs to the underground level below, where she beckoned them through a double wooden door.

The semicircular auditorium beyond was dimly lit. Eyes adjusting, Wood began to make out faces on the figures inside. All were talking and eyeing the latecomers, some smiling at Hazel. Recognising Berry, she nodded at him, unsurprised to find him here despite not having been called up. Hovering above the lowest row was a battered trapezoid box, whose status light returned Wood's wave with an electronic wink.

The drone dropped down to meet him. Soon Tink was enthusing about his attempts to communicate with the orgs. Although both sides evidently found the process challenging, there was now enough mental traffic that the AI was clearly enjoying all the attention he was receiving.

After a hurried reunion, the drone floated up towards the ceiling leaving Wood to slip into a second-row seat beside Hazel, who was kneeling to chat with Berry in the row behind. Several in the room had apparently completed their exodus from Lancer colonies only in the last few hours. Twenty-five intelligence operatives remained unaccounted for: a subject no one was keen to talk about.

The middle-aged woman beside Wood introduced herself with a smile and a gentle, dry handshake. 'Dora Acacia, from Yelloo.'

'Wood McCorkindale,' he replied. 'From, er, Juniper. Sorry, I keep forgetting, I'm Wood *Starsong* now.' He winced. 'Sounds a bit embarrassing now that I tell someone else.'

Her smile was a white crescent in skin that blended with the shadows. 'Oh, I know who *you* are. I doubt there's anyone on the planet doesn't by now.'

Wood was glad the dimness hid the flush he felt. He struggled for something to say. 'So are, I mean – is everyone here … are you all trained as – in, ah, space combat?'

She gave a little laugh. 'Dear me, no, I doubt any of us've fired a weapon before! Apart from rifles, maybe, and bows or crossbows.' Wood stared at her. 'But we certainly know how to fly – and everyone's been involved in species re-establishment, which I'm told requires qualities similar to what we need now. Don't worry, we've plenty experience fighting losing battles!'

This encouraged a drizzle of slightly hollow laughter from nearby. Wood found his hair stirring. Suddenly all attention was on the unmistakable figure of Zhelkar Porro, who pushed a blanket-wrapped, wheelchair-bound figure to one end of the large projection table at the centre of the stage before seating himself behind it. Sensing Wood's turmoil, Hazel bubbled up in his head.

Wood?

God, Hazel. IPEC'll have troops and pilots who've spent their lives training. They have state of the art weapons, including something no one's even identified yet – all coordinated by insanely sophisticated thinkers which have nothing to do but plan how to use all of this to dispose of nuisances like us in the most efficient manner possible! (Images of Havenners naively brandishing bows and arrows evaporating in thermonuclear explosions).

We're in a stronger position than you think. Listen to Zhelkar.

Sighing, Wood turned his attention to the white-bearded figure who was prodding the controls of the projector table. 'Whose idea was it, lurking in darkness like this?' Zhelkar muttered. Suddenly the room was bright, leaving its occupants squinting and covering their eyes. There was the briefest eye contact between Zhelkar and Jo.

'Okay,' began Zhelkar. 'You all know why we're here. To begin with, no one should underestimate the importance of this briefing. We face a force vastly superior in size and armament.'

Lacking a handscreen, or even a watch, he peered at the auditorium's clock.

'By now, Commodore Nikumi should be in Haven Station beginning his sterilisation for what we *hope* will be an attempt to buy us the time we need. While we obviously hope he is successful, it would be unrealistic to depend on that avenue. Assuming we must fight, our only chance against such odds is spectacular coordination combined with surprise. I should say at the beginning that we can't possibly hope to defeat the invasion. Our aim must be to delay them for as long as is necessary.

'We have four trump cards,' he went on, and held up an index finger. 'Firstly, the orgs' ability to travel interstellar distances almost instantaneously – and there are tactical tricks we can employ using this, which I'll come to later.' A second finger joined the first. 'Secondly, we have the org disrupters, with their specialised bacterial batteries. We don't know precisely how these will perform in a battle situation, or how they will compare with the enemy weapons, but they are potentially very potent.' A third finger came up. 'Thirdly, we can communicate over interstellar distances in real-time, in ways the invaders should be unable to intercept or jam – again, more of which later.' Another finger appeared. 'And fourthly, we have the remarkable mining vessel you have all now heard about.'

What are these org disrupters he's talking about?

A bulbous green shape appeared in Wood's mind's eye. He could see it from every side – externally it seemed similar to any other org, if fatter – but at the same time he could visualise the lobes of spongy, bacteria-packed living tissue which occupied much of the internal volume of the creature. *Same principles as wormhole travel,* Hazel explained, *but employed destructively. To use wormholes, orgs must preserve a volume of gently curved space to pass through – which is far more difficult than it sounds. Structured matter can't exist if a gravitational gradient is too high.*

Spaghettification near black holes?

Exactly. Disrupters can churn the spacetime membrane into violent localised distortions, something like expanding a froth of dead-end wormholes up to supermolecular scales. The volume affected is only tens of cubic metres, but it can be targeted very precisely – within solid objects. The gradients get so high that matter can degenerate into particles as small as quarks. Exothermically, she added, unnecessarily.

Accompanying her commentary, images and diagrams streamed into Wood's head. As the implications sank in, he felt a burst of unexpected hope. *The fleet's defence fields will be no protection! How many orgs have adapted themselves like this?*

Twenty-three.

Shit.

'I want you all to familiarise yourselves with each other,' Zhelkar was saying. 'A few of you may not have met before, so introduce yourselves. Start at the back.'

The tired-looking, pink, mid-thirties silvery-blonde woman at the door side of the back row coughed, and said nervously 'I'm Ivy Clearwater, from Weddell Bay … in New Antarctica. Please forgive me if I seem a little out of it. I got the message while I was undercover. I got back yesterday.'

'No apologies required,' Zhelkar assured her.

The dapper young tan-skinned man next to her was more confident. 'Perry Skyview, from Acacia. No exciting spy stories, I'm afraid.' Next was Moonbeam Cherone, from Hollytree in Carolsland: a big-eyed, short-haired, earth-brown woman who looked a few years older than Wood and flashed a relaxed, bucktoothed smile. A few seats along, Tooni Snow was a dour-looking man with skin as black as his beard, who spent most of his time at the Ice Edge research station in New Antarctica, where pine forests met the vast southern ice-cap.

First in the next row was Berry. He sat alongside the curiously named Bee Chee-chee from Palmtop, one of a chain of volcanic islands off the tropical southern coast of Carolsland: a strange-looking woman in her twenties with hair like copper wire and eyes and skin so pale they were almost colourless. Beside Wood, Dora Acacia beamed her bright-eyed smile as she spoke. Her hometown was the largest in the island-continent of Durrellsland, which stretched in a ribbon from the frozen southern seas to the northern hemisphere. After Wood and Hazel came Shane Summersea: a dark-haired man nearly as pale as Bee Chee-chee with the height and slender build of a low gravity adaptee. He glanced shiftily at Hazel as he spoke.

Next to Summersea, Beetle Matula, also from Durrellsland, seemed so diminutive and mouse-like that Wood found himself smiling – until hearing that she'd also just returned from deep cover on a Lancer colony. Havenners seemed to view age as an abstract property, and he found hers difficult to place. Last to introduce herself was the woman who'd ushered them in: Aspen Sunrise, tall, imposing, and self assured. Born on Alpha Station, she said with grim passion, but based now in the settlement of Cedar on the western seaboard of the continent of Novasia.

The motley group wore anything from garish knitted cardigans and hats to T-shirts decorated with slogans such as 'Speciologists do it with phenotypes $>(1/n)x3c/\Delta+q$ generations removed'. Wood was finding them very hard to take seriously.

Yet they were, apparently, deadly serious. They were planning, in a matter of hours, to engage in battle perhaps the biggest war armada ever assembled, and almost certainly die in the process. He didn't know whether to laugh or cry.

'Also present,' began Zhelkar, 'is someone who should be less shy about introducing himself. Tink —' he gestured at the floating drone in a way which suggested that a position nearer the floor would be more appropriate, '— has said that he would like us to refer to him — and, yes, he does consider himself male — as a silicon-based person, and as such we should regard him. He is operating this drone by tight-beam from orbit. His actual mind resides in the vessel, which I shall refer to as "*Oscar*" —' there were smiles at this, '— which made the frankly astonishing rescue of Professor Fox from Alpha Station.'

Nodding, Jo Fox clapped what remained of his hands. The others followed. The drone twitched, as though nervous. 'Hello,' it said, as the applause died, drifting silently to the front of the auditorium beside Zhelkar. Zhelkar patted the top of the box, making the drone wobble.

'Tink, I hope you feel that you are among friends here. Not to say admirers. You have a contribution to make which is at least as great as anyone else's. As far as everyone is concerned, you're one of us. Is that okay?' he added, when there was no response.

'Okay.'

The drone floated upwards two metres and returned to its dormant state. Wood noticed Hazel smirking. *He's even shier than you, my love.*

'Now to your roles,' continued Zhelkar, facing the auditorium. 'The thirteen in this room will lead the interception force. There will be five semi-autonomous groups, each comprising standard and disrupting orgs — who, by the way, are listening in on this meeting – and nonorgs armed with beam weapons, railguns and most of our supply of fusion missiles. The reasons for this will become clear.

'Hazel, for anyone here who isn't aware, is telepathic. Her role is crucial. She will allow us to coordinate the different groups with a low risk of our communications being interfered with or blocked.'

I've been set up, Hazel murmured between Wood's ears.

Guess that makes two of us.

'I say low risk, as it is conceivable that they will have a telepath working for them. We already encountered one working for the I.P.E.C., who has now been … um,' Zhelkar faltered, 'ah, *neutralised*.'

The image of a skewered, white-coated figure flashed across Wood's mind, the terror in the man's eyes contrasting with the look in Hazel's as she destroyed him. He felt her hand squeeze his.

'Hazel, who knows the situation better than any of us, considers it unlikely that there are more, but we can't rule it out. While we cannot rely entirely on this method of communication, it should offer a crucial advantage as we cannot hope to compete with the signal jammers the Pukes will use against us. As most of you are doubtless aware, jamming, viral incursions, EM pulse weapons and other forms of electronic warfare are pretty much the only reason for sending human pilots into space warfare. Any signal can be blocked, any thinker corrupted. Consequently, while our vessels will carry hardened versions of our latest semi-organic thinkers, which we hope may prove tough nuts for IPEC's binary systems to crack, all are being rebuilt with overrides for direct manual control using robust fibre-op circuitry.

'Hazel will therefore oversee the operation from *Oscar*. This is a compromise: while the vessel is by far the most potent and durable nonorg we have, for that reason it is likely to be singled out for attack. The orgs will assist where possible in coordinating the attacking groups telepathically, but they are too few to be spared for a communications role. They will be in the thick of it, and likely to be scared and distracted. Ivy Clearwater will therefore be secondary coordinator should anything … make this necessary. However, it is important to understand that the beginning of the battle is when coordination will be paramount. The first seconds will be crucial in dictating the outcome.'

Zhelkar tapped something into his terminal on the projector table. 'Before you on your seatback screens are the groups of leaders I put together. If you feel you will work more efficiently with someone else, please say now.'

He scanned the semicircle of faces.

'Good. Ivy and Perry: you will lead the largest group, which will include the disrupters and our own signal jammers. Our heavy artillery unit, if you like. Moonbeam, Bee and Tooni, you will lead the group whose primary task is to defend our heavy artillery and orgs which lack defences of their own. You will have smart mines, cluster missiles, some nukes, railguns and beam weapons. In the last few days, we have also developed and tested a defence against beam weapons, which is being manufactured and should be ready before you leave. It scatters clouds of tiny mirrors which should deflect or diffuse incoming particle beams and confuse missile targeting systems. This shouldn't limit your own ability to use particle beams, as the mirrors will keep their non-reflective sides towards you.

'Aspen and Shane will lead one of the two main strike forces – Strike Group One – and Berry and Beetle will lead Strike Group Two. These will harry the invasion force from close range, draw fire away from the artillery, and employ armour-piercing nukes. The fifth, much smaller force, Strike Group Three, will be led by Wood, Tink and Hazel in *Oscar*.

'You will be briefed in detail later, but the idea is for a small group of Type-22s,' the room dimmed and a spacecraft like a flattened, stretched egg with an oversized nozzle at the back rotated above the projection table, incongruously huge, gape-mouthed missiles sprouting from pylons spaced equally around the broadest part of its hull, '– which have been fitted, as you see, with ten state-of-the-art Lancer-supplied guided nukes each – to follow under the cover of *Oscar*'s defensive shields then break out to deliver their payloads. Each missile has defence-shield negating technology which I don't pretend to understand, but I'm told at least matches IPEC's own, and is armed with ten anti-missile missiles and a hundred anti-anti-missile missiles. Your aim is simply to get within the invading fleet as a tight unit, then split up and inflict as much damage as possible.'

The spacecraft disappeared. 'Surprise is our greatest asset,' Zhelkar told them. 'We are confident the Pukes are unaware of the full capabilities of the orgs – and even if they are, as I mentioned before, their ability both to travel and to transport our nonorgs between star systems almost instantaneously will still be in our favour. The small size of our ships may even be an advantage: those we will face are the size they are primarily because of the need to be self-sufficient over long distances and timescales. We have no such problem, and we're confident the orgs can pinpoint and destroy the defensive shield generators of a good dozen Fortresses and battlecruisers before a counterattack is launched. A well-placed nuke could then destroy a big battlecruiser or cripple a fortress. One missile: the same as would be needed to destroy one of our smallest ships, and a Puke battlecruiser is a target a thousand times the size. Looked at this way, things start to seem less one-sided.

'Also remember: your task is simply to prevent these vessels reaching hyperspace, for which you need only cripple their Thomson Field Generators.'

A pinched cube appeared above the table. Causing an outbreak of drawn breaths, it flensed itself as it rotated, revealing internal structure.

'As you can see, the most recent Divide and Rule-class fortresses are unique in the layout of their TFGs. A separate generator ring lies beneath the outer hull of each of the six external faces. Our intelligence suggests that a fortress can function with up to four of these knocked out. This will make them tough nuts to crack but will not protect them from our disrupters.

Zhelkar peered round the semicircle. When he began again, his voice was lower. 'I'm afraid we still don't know the exact nature of the invading force, and so must prepare for the worst scenario. From early surveillance reports, there may be a total of thirty-eight operational fortresses capable of reaching Haven's outer systems as we speak.'

A murmur of dismay went around the room.

'Most are likely to be outfitted as mobile ports, or carriers, each storing up to three battlecruisers, nine cruisers, twenty-odd frigates, gunships and missile ships, or combinations of these. I regret that since the intensification of Confederal action within Freelancer space, our intelligence has been … patchy.'

'Try non-existent.' The voice belonged to Aspen Sunrise. Zhelkar glanced at her sharply.

'We can expect up to around eighty battlecruisers, which are much the most heavily armed of the known Puke arsenal in terms of outright firepower.'

Bristling with huge railguns and disrupter cannon, the streamlined shape now revolving above the table could have been designed to instil fear.

'We can also expect around one hundred and twenty cruisers and a larger number of frigates. Missile ships and gunships operated from the carrier fortresses are likely to be in excess of,' he hesitated, 'two thousand. These will not be hyperspace-capable. Rather than launch them immediately after twisting back to truespace, the Pukes may feel confident enough to rely upon missiles launched from their larger ships to handle our initial, hopefully unexpected, attack. Another key task of the org disrupters will be disabling the ability of the fortresses to launch these vessels. There is no point going over this in detail now: you will study each model of vessel, their strengths and weaknesses, numbers, and modes of employment later.'

Zhelkar met the gaze of each of the small audience. 'Much depends upon the confederation's perception of us. If they expect a walkover, they are unlikely to waste the prodigious expense of unnecessary firepower, particularly given the likelihood of a Lancer invasion of IPEC space following the Professor's tip-off.

'I personally think, and I gather that both Tom and the Professor agree?' he turned to the wheelchair-bound figure opposite, who nodded, 'that we can expect a fleet of two-thirds of the worst scenario. However – and this is by far the greatest area of uncertainty, as well as the biggest threat – this is without considering the new weapon, the effects of which you have all seen.'

'It would be unwise to speculate regarding its nature at this stage,' Jo cut in, quietly, his speech noticeably slurred. 'While it's clearly extremely powerful, it's not necessarily reason to feel hopeless. From information I was able to gather in my recent trip to the confederation, it's likely to be untested, and may have problems or weaknesses. It's also very large, and probably unwieldy. No matter how effectively it destroys planets, it could be a liability in a battle. And remember – all you need to do for it to be entirely ineffective is delay it.'

Is that all? Wood stared at Hazel, but she was focused on Jo.

'Indeed,' continued Zhelkar, 'this weapon's most important impact may be psychological. We must not let it terrorise us. That is what they want.'

Pausing, Zhelkar cleared his throat.

'So, to our actual plan. Our intercepting fleet will orbit Haven in battle-readiness and await the go-ahead, which will be given the moment a sniffer returns with the location of the invading fleet. Whatever system they arrive in, they will need to reorient, regroup, and prepare for the next twist to hyperspace. Even if no immediate offensive action is planned, they are expected to spend between four and six hours over this.

'That is when we hit them.'

He ran his hand through the air over the table. It shivered into darkness which spawned points of light: mostly yellows and reds, one crimson and far brighter than the others, one white, towing a banner of silvery and purple illumination spotted with diffuse sparks. The scene rotated slowly.

'Trene's Veil,' he said, producing an extendible pointer and thrusting it into the glowing band. 'To orient you: Goliath.' He pointed to the bright red light. 'This green star is Limetree. Haven is here.' A small yellow light to one side, orbited by a speck of green, began flashing a blue halo. 'And Haven's Gate and Gamma Station are here.' He indicated a yellow dot and its rapidly circling fleck of pale blue, which flashed a green halo.

'As you see, the manned star system nearest to a straight line between us and Terra Two, which the presumed Troubleshooter weapon has destroyed, is Haven's Gate. It's also our closest neighbour – excluding Firebrand, which has only gas giants. While Beta Station and Walnut are closer to Terra Two than Haven, Tom predicts they will be ignored, along with the Firebrand system. The Pukes know what they're looking for.

'Haven's Gate,' he continued, jabbing his pointer, 'is just thirteen-point-five lightyears from Haven. That's roughly ten hours by hyperspace. However, we believe – we *hope* – that Trene's veil, which lies directly between us and Terra Two, will divert the fleet first to the Primrose system and Terra Nova. Primrose, as you should know, has four planets outwardly suitable for habitation – it may appear a more tempting target

332

than Haven. Tom predicts the Pukes will be sufficiently sure of themselves to conduct a mopping-up operation, sweeping through our occupied planetary systems as they find them, rather than making sure they find Haven first.

'So –' another yellow star became circled, this time in a purple halo, '– here is the Primrose system and Terra Nova. Thirty-one lightyears from Haven's Gate. If they go to Terra Nova first, then their next move is likely to be the twenty-hour hop to Haven's Gate, moving onwards to Haven after that.

'The most likely volumes for hyperspace exits in both the Primrose and Haven's Gate systems have been seeded with millions of smart proximity mines. The Lancers' most recent, they are stealthy and destructive, but we do not know how effective they will be. If our predictions are correct, the invasion should arrive at the Primrose system in –' he studied the clock, 'around thirty-seven hours time, perhaps less. When that time comes, many questions will be answered. I want all of you ready for rapid assimilation of new facts at that time, and rapid action.'

If Zhelkar attempted to hide the deep breath he took, he made a poor job of it.

'Now, to details,' he said. 'The present aim is to meet the enemy at Haven's Gate.' There were raised eyebrows at this, and worried faces. 'I know it's terribly close to us. But we must trade the increased risks as they draw closer against the possibility they will pause along the way. Remember, they should be unaware they are working against the clock, and that Haven's defence mechanism will be ready soon. Whatever that proves to be.' He looked away from Jo as he said this, his frustration clear. 'Understand, however, that we cannot fight a sustained battle, and the more our fleet is extended from Haven, the more vulnerable we are.'

He turned back to the projection. 'Now, once surveillance pods have returned to report the invasion's arrival at Haven's Gate, the fleet will connect there in just two groups.' Coloured plots appeared. 'For any of you who have never taken part in this process, the orgs will position themselves around the nonorgs and use a combined aura to transport all the ships and orgs in each group at once.'

The diagram of stars transformed into a cluster of spacecraft surrounded by a spiralling shell of orgs, the whole assemblage suddenly sucking itself out of existence.

'It's more efficient than pairing you individually and will minimise draining of the orgs' battery organs. After your arrival at Haven's Gate, circumstances are unlikely to permit the coordination necessary to achieve this again, so I'm afraid organising your escape will be up to you. Strike Groups One and Two will go in one cluster. The artillery group, artillery defence and *Oscar*'s attack group will go in the other, the disrupters playing a part in transporting you.

'The moment you arrive, hopefully taking the invasion force by surprise, the disrupters will begin softening up the carrier fortresses and – if possible – the secret weapon, which remains the main area of uncertainty despite also being the primary target. Battlecruisers and non-carrier fortresses will obviously need to be tackled as well. We hope that ignorance of our abilities may mean their smaller vessels remain berthed inside the fortresses after their twist out of hyperspace.

'Make no mistake about what you face. Once your presence is noted, you will be confronted with a sustained barrage of nuclear missiles. You may be swamped. The most effective action of the strike squadrons is likely to be to get in close as soon as possible, release weapons quickly, then retreat. If orgs and nonorgs stay in close alliance, it may be possible to wormhole from one part of the battlefield to another, or away from the scene entirely, then back again – although this could be achieved only a few times before the orgs become exhausted. However, once a smart missile has decided it is after you, it may be your only option.

'Wood, Tink: your task is to engage, and hopefully destroy, enemy targets at close range, as that seems to be *Oscar*'s forte. I realise it's a lot to ask, but you must do your best to safeguard your squadron, who will be defenceless without you until you are within the fleet.

'Finally, I would like to say this. This is not a suicide mission. It would be naive to hope that you will all return, but with luck most of you shall. Fighting may prove unnecessary if the invasion proceeds more slowly than feared, or Nikumi is successful. I would also like to point out that the selection of those in this room was not random. You were cited as people others in the interception force would most like to follow. By that,' he raised his eyes to Tink's drone, 'I mean all fourteen of you.'

Zhelkar retracted his pointer and held it behind his back. 'I'm afraid this will likely be the penultimate briefing. I want you to study the packages waiting on your terminals very carefully. Make use of every available moment on the simulations. Before that however, there is a recording of this meeting for your groups. You each have a couple of hours in which to familiarise yourselves with your tasks and to coordinate your group members into cohesive teams. You will find the simulations realistic. Work solidly at them: from now on, every minute counts.

'Now, I think the Professor has something to say to you.'

The figure in the wheelchair nodded, but then said 'Please: Jo. For once, my name is just Jo. I regret that due to other urgent commitments, this is being recorded for those not here. I shall keep it short.'

He drew himself up as much as he was able.

'Tarnished as our reputation may be amongst any beings with the wisdom to judge us, you do your species proud. You've volunteered to fight not for yourselves, or even for something you believe to be "right", or "best", because of some exclusive ideology. You've chosen to fight for something you believe deserves to exist simply because of its own intrinsic worth; because the universe would be an incomparably lesser place without it. You fight ... because you want to believe that somewhere in this empty universe there will always be such wonders – such miracles – as bees, spreading life flower to flower; as earthworms, tunnelling through living soil. Trees, spreading their leaves against the sun. These are the things we fight for. Because they and their descendants deserve to outlast the petty wants of any individual, or individual society.

'We have shown here on Haven, this once barren rock, what we can do. It's people like you who made it possible. We provided the Earth Mother with a chance: the tiniest chance she needed to come to good again, which nonetheless was denied by our cousins. It was a chance she seized with both hands – and look what has become of it! One day, here on Haven, she will recreate the swarming oceans, and the herd-filled savannahs, and the proud, teeming forests which made the Earth unique.

'Likewise, here we have the tiniest chance to make good. We will seize it, and, I believe, we shall succeed. Good luck, every one of you.'

A stirring speech.

Wood didn't project the thought.

45

THE KILLER

FEELING HAZEL'S brush against his concentration, Wood put *Oscar*'s furnaces into a feedback loop. After a few seconds of alarms and warnings, it ripped the vessel apart in a spectacular explosion.

'Sorry guys,' he grunted into the pickup of his helmet, still straining against residual G-forces. 'Be back in a sec. Carry on like I've been knocked out. Simone, over to you.'

During the past four days it had dawned on Wood that, since *Oscar*'s arrival on Haven, he and Tink had attracted a kind of following. Their folk-hero status was not, Hazel had noted, something he'd been sluggish to exploit.

He halted the spinning of the simulation bubble containing his seat, locked it to its pedestal and removed his bulky VR helmet as the containing field dropped and the gravity generators deactivated. Hazel forced an odd-looking smile as she strode towards him into the chamber where the simulation had been set up.

Hi-G manoeuvres, he explained. *In case of inertial suppressor failure. Or in case we need to push Oscar beyond what the suppressor can manage.*

Would we survive an inertial suppressor failure?

Um ...

'How's it going?' she asked, aloud.

'Well, actually. My group ...' he gestured at the six bubbles gyrating in their own suspensor fields, their occupants straining vocally under simulated G-forces as they focussed on their virtual worlds, 'the teamwork is amazing! We're at a level I wouldn't have thought possible in three days. I'm starting to think we might have a slim chance, though I wish Simone Morningdew had been leader instead of me.' His smile faded.

Really not sure I'm cut out for this, Hazel. I wish you could be down here with us.

Then he noticed her face.

What's wrong? he demanded, leaping down and seizing her hands.

'Terra Nova. It …' They became aware of other bubbles coming to a stop and the occupants removing their helmets. Soon a row of anxious expressions was turned in their direction.

'The weapon?'

She nodded. 'We've seen the fleet they've sent.'

A pause. 'How bad?'

For a moment her mouth moved noiselessly. 'It's best you see the probe's recording. Everyone in all strike and defence groups is to attend.'

TERRA NOVA hung against the stars, its mottled plains of ochre and brown revolving serenely towards its segment of nightside darkness. Empty endomes occasionally caught the sun, betraying themselves by glints and flashes. Feathery swirls of cloud projected faint shadows.

Flashes appeared. The view zoomed in towards a segment of the planet. Omega Station was clearly visible as a tiny cartwheel rotating against the speeding plains.

There were more and more flashes. Then expanding, dissipating coronas, central to which dark objects of small but widely varying sizes began appearing. Largest and most recognisable, dwarfing the distant Omega Station in the vastly magnified view, were dark, indented cubes.

Shape after shape appeared until space was peppered with them.

Terra Nova began to expand as the fleet organised itself. The warships swung ponderously about in formation and, thrust torches spearing brightly behind them, began accelerating towards the planet, the sniffer's view zooming in to keep pace. Sparks began igniting among the tiny shapes. There were sharper flashes. A chaos of lights flickered and streaked around the fleet. Intense blobs of brilliance bloomed, momentarily outshining the combined thrusters of half IPEC's navy. As they waned, a handful of the smaller shapes were left behind.

Our mines, thought Wood. His pulse was thudding.

Almost in unison, the torches went dark as the ships of the remaining fleet turned on their tails. The coordination was eerie. Light lanced out towards the planet as they commenced deceleration. Omega Station seemed to skim just above the plains, still expanding as the view continued its inexorable, slow magnification. Without warning, it was engulfed in a dazzling, expanding sphere which darkened everything else as the sensor's exposure compensated. The brilliance took more than a minute to fade, revealing outwards-spinning arc-shaped fragments tearing themselves apart in smaller explosions.

Zhelkar broke the grim silence. 'We can see thirty-two fortresses, of which at least twenty are carriers for their fleet. This means we can only guess at the size of the rest of the fleet, although the smaller ships you see – forty battlecruisers and sixty-five cruisers – should account for most of the larger vessels. I'll be honest, we had hoped these vessels would be berthed in the fortresses for hyperspace travel. Their deployment before the twist to the Primrose system suggests that they view the threat of resistance seriously. We must presume that all gunships and missile ships are still inside the fortresses and battlecruisers, as none are visible.

'Of the warships deployed, our mines have put ten cruisers out of action, damaged four, and significantly damaged one battlecruiser and a fortress.'

The fleet was splitting into three. Composed of cruisers and the much larger battlecruisers, the smaller two groups accelerated wastefully, the bright spikes of their thruster-plumes spearing almost perpendicularly away from Terra Nova as the ships dived in power-orbits around opposite sides of the planet. Terra Nova seemed to shrink as the remaining group – mostly the huge fortresses – turned their braking manoeuvre into acceleration back towards the distantly orbiting sniffer, whose sensor reduced its magnification to keep pace until the planet's entire sunlit semicircle was again visible.

'The weapon will emerge from hyperspace once the fleet has had time to mop up around the planet,' commented Zhelkar. 'We assume that is what they are currently doing.'

After several more minutes, dark flecks could be seen growing against the planet's bright limb. On the night side, gleams of sunlight reflected off similarly approaching hulls.

Gradually, the fleet began to reassemble, putting ever more distance between itself and the planet.

Then, with majestic slowness, a narrow arc of light appeared above the dark limb of Terra Nova, fading as it expanded into the void. A murmur of consternation turned to gasps of fear as it dawned on the audience what they were seeing.

The arc was part of an expanding circle. A hyperspace-exit corona.

Impossibly, it was expanding *behind* the planet.

Then a sliver of ghostly brightness appeared above Terra Nova's thin atmosphere. It thickened steadily into a crescent. Feeling Hazel's alarm as sharply as his own, Wood found his mouth hanging open. What the hell were they looking at? Something was creeping over the horizon like an impossible rising sun.

As the apparition rose, the view zoomed towards it. Features became visible. Its surface was divided by dark lines into polyhedral cells, some of which were darkly infilled. As the crescent became a semicircle, a featureless circular area, defined by a ring of elongated, filled-in cells, emerged from behind the planet, glowing with the same corpse-light as the rest.

The pupil of a sickly eyeball the size of a world.

The viewpoint changed. Terra Nova appeared against the stars as a bright little semicircle. Seen in profile, the ghastly eyeball could now be seen to be a long way from the planet its pupil was focused on.

'This is from the second of our three sniffers covering Terra Two,' said Zhelkar, his voice sounding strained. 'The *object* –' he spat the word as though what it described was an affront, 'is fractionally over fourteen thousand kilometres in diameter. To put that in perspective, Terra Nova's is eleven.' Wood was fairly sure that what no one needed right now was perspective. 'Its mass is fifty-six percent of Terra Nova's. We are seeing the two almost side-on. The object is currently ninety-two planetary diameters from Terra Nova.'

That distance was closing visibly. Terra Nova rotated serenely, unconcerned at its fate. 'At this point,' Zhelkar went on, 'the gravitational pull of the object is causing tidal stress. We cannot see evidence of this yet, because Terra Nova is a world without crustal activity, but the planet has stretched measurably, and its orbit is being perturbed.'

The appalled silence deepened as the implications for a world like Haven, with thin crustal plates floating on plastic magma, sank in. The effect of such nearby mass on Haven's orbit was likely to make the planet uninhabitable by itself. As the similarly-sized, yet very different, bodies drew together, the view zoomed in, keeping pace.

'The separation is now thirty-two planetary diameters. Gravitational stress is causing local subsurface melting on Terra Nova,' continued Zhelkar. 'Fissures have opened, allowing magma to surface.'

Flecks of reddish light were visible on the dark side.

'While the object has also measurably distorted, its surface seems to be flexible. It is rotating the circular structure, which we believe to be a forcefield lens, into position. The lens-structure is five hundred and ninety kilometres in diameter.'

Spikes of light the length of continents stabbed at angles from some of the dark patches on the object's surface. Directional thrusters, Wood presumed. Almost imperceptibly, the eyeball's pupil turned until it was locked on to the planet. After a few minutes, the cells comprising the thing's surface began to darken, while its pupil grew brighter.

When most of the object had darkened almost to black, a blinding pencil of light extruded from the pupil towards Terra Nova, lighting up the world's dark side, connecting the two bodies like the bar of an asymmetrical dumbbell.

Around the column of whatever was pouring into it, Terra Nova's night side began to glow: first blood-red, then orange, through to yellow-white as the luminous area inexorably expanded. The sunlit side continued its serene rotation apparently unblemished.

A sheet of cloud began to spread away from the terminator until the sunlit half of the world was pearly white. It was short-lived. After a few more minutes, spots of clear air ate like acid into the cloud-sheet until the skies were largely clear again. Imperceptibly at first, darker areas of the plains seemed to shift, peppered by expanding lighter areas. Streamer-like high clouds formed, curling and growing thicker by the minute, coalescing until the corrupting landscape was sheathed in a second skin, duller and greyer this time, unbroken but for the luminosity of the planet's night side.

Once more, the clouds began to evaporate. They were replaced by a glow which was apparent even in sunlight, its irregular honeycomb of darker lines – presumably demarcating convection cells of rising magma – crudely mimicking the skin of the planet's destroyer. Abruptly, the bar of light split from the sphere which had created it, dropping like a glowing rod into Terra Nova's boiling remains.

The screen went dark.

Zhelkar faced the ensuing silence. There defiance in his eyes, but he looked haunted. When he spoke again, his voice seemed to echo.

'We believe the weapon is a star, confined under intense pressure within an elastic web of gravitational and other fields. That beam we just saw is essentially an immense laser. The dark areas on the object's surface are likely to house machinery including generators and amplifiers for the confining fields. The structure almost certainly has defensive shields, for which available power is likely to be …' he licked his lips, 'considerable.

'Do not lose heart,' he went on, raising his hands. 'The fact that the Pukes' conventional fleet not only arrived first, but is present at all, suggests the weapon could be vulnerable. Other than the lens, our sniffers were unable to find signs of weaponry on the object's surface. There is a possibility that portions of the confining fields can be knocked out, in which case Strangefruit predicts that the trapped star would eject itself under its own pressure, destroying the weapon. Also, as you have seen, the whole structure must orientate for firing. This takes time.

Zhelkar pulled a handkerchief from his pocket and blew his nose. 'I will not mislead you. Our initial reaction is that things are worse than feared. We must not let this cloud our sense of purpose. Our belief that this may be as much a psychological weapon as a strategic one still applies. Physically, the Pukes could achieve as much useful damage, at less cost, with bombs.'

Then why don't you *sound convinced?* Wood didn't need to look around to tell that others were thinking the same.

'However, we may have to adapt our objectives. Revised briefings have been compiled for you, and updates and refinements to strategy will be sent to your training pods.

Remember, if anyone at all any has suggestions or valid points to make, please do so via Strangefruit.'

His gaze scrambled around the surrounding faces as though trying to negotiate a feared obstacle. 'The invasion fleet has already left the Primrose system. This means we must prepare to fight. As predicted, the main fleet twisted to hyperspace ahead of the weapon, which is being escorted by a force of five fortresses and twenty battlecruisers. The ETA of the main fleet at Haven's Gate is …' he looked up at the auditorium clock, 'a little more than twenty-two hours.

'You have fifteen hours left on Haven. After that, you will need to wait in your assigned ships in orbit near Haven Station. Use the time wisely. Become as familiar as you can with your roles, the strategy, and your group-mates. Above all, get some sleep, even a couple of hours. You won't be at your best if you're tired.

'This will be the last time I speak to you in person before you go. The spirit of the Earth Mother, and the love and hopes of everyone remaining on Haven, go with you.'

Zhelkar hurried from the auditorium like a tired old man. Hazel stared at the empty doorway long after he'd gone.

She'd already said her goodbyes, but for Zhelkar and Dorrin especially, it was not enough.

'TINK?'

'Wood! That was terrible! That huge machine …'

'I know, I know. We need to find somewhere to talk.'

'Why can't we talk here?'

'Too many people.'

'Why is that a …? Oh.'

'Follow me.'

'You don't want even Hazel to hear us?'

'*Shhh!* This'll do. Quick, in here.'

'Wood, this is a cupboard.'

'Well spotted. Oh.'

'A very *small* cupboard.'

'Shit. Okay, come over here. Maybe this one. That's better. Well, okay, it's still a bit tight. Close the door. No – squeeze behind me. Here, I'll do it. You on tight beam?'

'Of course I'm on tight beam.'

'Good. That's good.'

'Wood, you're behaving out of character. It's very dark in here. I can see you only on infrared. It's highly unattractive.'

'Tink … I don't know how to say this.'

'Forming the words using your mouth might be a start.'

'Comedian. If we stay here to the end, we aren't going to make it out of this alive.'

'This cupboard?'

'No, not the cupboard, you idiot! Given the choice between everything that's about to happen and being in a fucking cupboard, which do you think I'm likely to be talking about?'

'Oh. But then … What are you suggesting?'

'However this all pans out, the only thing I'm reasonably sure of is that it won't be the way anyone here has planned. Before long, I'm afraid we're going to have to make some very hard decisions, really quickly. That's why I think we need to talk them through. Privately.'

'Are you saying what I think –?'

'Just listen!'

'I'm listening.'

'Good. Oh hell, Tink. This isn't going to be easy …'

46

SUICIDE

CLOUDS and glittering seas rolled past a couple of thousand kilometres below. Across them were sprinkled a motley assortment of spacecraft and spacefaring creatures, waiting in a slightly lower orbit.

Among the largest and most distinctive were the bulbous disrupter orgs, their bellies swollen with great batteries of spacetime-bending bacteria. Also instantly recognisable were the once-graceful Havenner-designed Type-22s, bastardised by absurd pylons to which ten fat missiles half the length of the ships themselves were incongruously fixed.

There were sixty-two Lancer-built light cruisers. Much the largest of Haven's fleet, these were fat cylinders a little under a kilometre long, blistered with retracted clusters of weapons and sensors. All but six bristled with around a hundred nuclear missiles each, attached with similar crudity. The rest served as propulsion units for Haven's Lancer-inspired signal jammers, whose fragile spherical housings were as large as the ships they were mounted on.

The most common shapes were squat, ugly and inefficient but very heavily armed gunships which dated right back to the Freelancer Wars. Also numerous were the little spearheads of the fast and manoeuvrable Terra-Nova built Type-24 interceptors: little more than self-propelled disrupter cannons each with four nukes, a pilot, and ten minutes' operational time at full thrust. According to Hazel, they'd never been used in anger.

Wood chewed fingernails already bitten to the quick. He was glad he didn't have a knife: he was developing a strong urge, missing for months now, to cut himself. Every few seconds the voice of another org would bubble up in his head, seeking reassurance, confused by the increasingly numbing mental interference originating from the planet below. Hazel had warned him of this, and of how important it was to be tolerant and supportive. A morale crash amongst the fleet of jittery creatures would be disastrous.

'They're not the only ones who need reassurance,' he'd muttered.

In the hours since Zhelkar's war briefing, Hazel had seemed drugged. What she felt from Haven had grown from background noise to a white noise scream which all-but overwhelmed her telepathic functions. It was like being painfully crippled: enough residual contact with her had leaked through to give Wood an idea of what she was enduring. She yearned to escape the din, yet couldn't bear the thought of leaving Haven, perhaps for the last time. Wood felt her presence slowly diminish, like a drawn-out amputation.

No sign of the invading fleet had been reported. Its arrival in the Primrose system was already almost four hours overdue. Might they escape having to fight? The war between hope and fear was agonising. Hazel was massaging her temples in a futile attempt to relieve the discomfort.

'What're the names of our team again?' she mumbled.

'Pardon?'

'Our team members. Their names.'

Wood let out an impatient huff. 'You should know this.' Realising how unreasonable he was being, he took a measured breath, went behind her seat and put his arms around her shoulders, nuzzling his stubbly cheek against her smooth one.

'You okay?'

She turned to meet his gaze. 'Not really. But I should be once we're clear of Haven.'

'You're the most important person we've got. You need to keep us in contact.'

'I'm painfully aware of that.'

He raised her chin, studied her for a moment. Kissed her forehead and then her lips, fingers pushing into her hair. A tingle shot through him as she returned the kiss. She smelled amazing. His eyes lingered on the ridge where her nose had been broken. He kissed that too. It occurred to him that he'd never asked her the story behind it.

'I'll send a request for them to introduce themselves properly,' he said, returning reluctantly to his seat. 'They're in the 22s right behind us.' He gestured at six sunlit shapes filling the control room's aft view screen. The nose of each was painted with cartoon shark's teeth. 'Got that Tink?'

'Yeah, yeah. Let muggins do it.' Having absorbed Haven's entire library with sponge-like ease, Tink was sulking in his deckchair wearing the battledress of a warrior from a part of ancient Earth apparently called the Highlands. He offhandedly doffed his weird blue, bird-feathered hat. 'They're online now.' Views of the spaceships were replaced by six anxious faces.

'Simone here.' The speaker was a wide-eyed young woman with freckles, brown skin, strikingly slanted eyes and an explosion of coppery hair. Though Wood had never asked her age, he doubted she could have been more than twenty.

'Thought I needed some kind of, er, lieutenant,' he explained to Hazel, feeling oddly defensive. 'Hi Simone.' She returned his smile nervously. 'How's everyone bearing up?'

'Wishing we could fucking get on with it,' growled a scowling, equally striking young man. *Simone's brother*, Wood told Hazel mentally, forgetting she couldn't hear.

'Fallin,' snapped Simone, in full elder sister mode. 'You're doing no one any good being like that.'

'So, court-martial me.'

'Fallin!'

'My mistake. We don't have a court-martial. We don't even have a proper *navy*.'

'Fallin, this isn't fair on anyone. You volunteered, remember?'

A snort. 'And that means I have to fucking enjoy it?'

Wood forced a laugh. Fallin muttered something and looked away from his screen. Simone sighed.

'We're bearing up okay I suppose,' she said, resignedly. 'Nerves, really. Fallin's more forthright with his feelings than the rest of us. Perhaps he's right letting off steam.'

'I expect everyone feels the same. You're all coping better than the orgs. They've been a handful since we were planetside – I've had a dozen trying to get inside my skull at once. It's giving me a headache.' He took a controlling breath. 'Listen, ah, I just realised you haven't been introduced to Hazel yet. Sorry about that. I gather none of you have actually met her before.'

A thumbnail appeared, showing that Tink had put Hazel's face on their screens. Forcing a smile, Hazel a raised hand.

'And you're a telepath?' asked Fallin. '*The* telepath?'

Wood winced but was surprised when Hazel only gave a weary nod. 'Though I'm not "'pathing" too well at the moment. Haven's interfering.'

'Yeah.' Fallin's eyes were wide. 'I felt it too, before we left. Can even feel it up here now. It's like the air is kind of, I don't know – *charged*.'

Five other heads nodded agreement. The palpable sense of energy building around the planet was giving them an unexpected confidence. Fallin's face lit up as he turned towards the reflective clouds.

'I wonder what's going on down there? I know a couple of physics wonks who reckon Haven's developing its own defence shield, using gravity waves. Maybe it'll kick out a massive gravity pulse and splat any Pukers who get close.'

'Perhaps it will,' agreed Hazel. 'Anyway, I'm thirty-one, and from Juniper, in Carolsland.' Wood stared. He'd never actually asked her age. Hazel gave him a wry look and leaned towards him. 'Haven years are shorter than IPEC standard, remember?'

He grinned. *Not by much.*

After a brief exchange between the six on the monitors, Simone spoke again. 'Well, Hazel, I'm Simone Morningdew – twenty-four next Tuesday. I'm from Beartree, just over the mountains from you. Kinda surprised we never met before.'

'Perhaps we can remedy that when this is over.'

'I'll drink to that.' Simone raised an imaginary glass. 'As I think I heard Wood mention, I now have the dubious honour of leading this bunch.' Hazel's support was important to Wood, and he saw her beginning to appreciate his choice of Simone, whose maturity seemed to be growing with every word. 'This is Nilo Perez.'

Nilo courteously dipped his head, pulling gaunt olive features into a smile which made his grave brown eyes come alive. 'I only wish the circumstances were different.'

'No argument from me there,' replied Hazel.

'Nilo's my wing-man,' Simone explained, 'and will watch my back all the way in.'

'With limpetlike tenacity.'

'He's … thirty-eight? Thirty-nine –?'

Nilo nodded. 'Thereabouts.'

'– And from Boojum in Durrellsland. The next pair will be led by Fallin.' Scowling Fallin put his thumbs in his ears, stuck out his tongue and waggled his fingers. 'My parents claim he's part of my family. I presume they mean taxonomic family, though I can't imagine what species.'

'Screw you, Sis.'

'He's twenty, though you'd never think it, and,' she continued in an exaggerated whisper, 'has a huge chip on his shoulder about a sister who's better at everything than he is.'

'Refer to my previous statement, with the following amplification.' He cranked a middle finger into the air using an imaginary winch. Simone blew him a kiss.

Wood had worried that trouble was brewing, but with the exception of Nilo, who clearly found all this very irritating, everyone including Fallin was now smiling. It was the distraction they needed, and Simone was exploiting it beautifully.

'Next, Jorge Songbird is the unfortunate who'll have to trail the recipient of all the wrong parts of my parents' genes.'

A pale young man, his blonde ponytail spread in a comical zero-G fan over the helmet seal of his black pressure suit, nodded timidly.

'He's twenty-four, and though you might think butter wouldn't melt in his mouth, spends his life with Fallin making life in Beartree hell for everyone else.'

'How?' Fallin again. 'Like, people can't take a joke?'

'Fallin … stuffing an old lady's salmon supper with live earthworms is not a joke.'

There were hoots of laughter from a deeply wrinkled, grey-bearded man.

'The man who seems to think frightening old ladies to within a centimetre of their lives so hilarious,' continued Simone, 'is Michael Bernard. One Mother of an old-fashioned name for someone who thinks he's still twelve.

'One Mother of an old-fashioned guy,' he replied, with a snort of pride. 'You young lot have forgotten how to have fun.'

'As you may have gathered, Mike is – physically, at least – ancient. He's seventy-one.'

'Only as old as you feel, young lady.'

'And how old do you feel?'

'Ninety,' he groaned, as the others rewarded him with barks of laughter.

'No wonder,' commented the fiftyish woman who was the only one yet unnamed. 'Wasted most of his wretched existence in a cave, eating juniper berries.' More laughter, even from Nilo. Jorg and Fallin mimed gagging.

'Don't knock what you haven't tried, darlin'. Two bowel movements like clockwork every day for thirty years.'

'Moving *swiftly* on,' Simone cut in, 'last, but by no means first, is Janno Silverbee – who's an expert on Mike's digestion because, for reasons known only to herself, and probably best kept that way, she is his partner. How old are you, Janno?'

'Mind your own buggering business.' More hilarity.

'Two couples,' Hazel said brightly. 'Wood and I were married a week ago.' Fallin rolled his eyes.

'Is there *anyone* who doesn't know that?' Simone was scratching her head.

'We could make this a couples only outing. Nilo darling, how about it? We could draw up one of those marriage-lease things Pukes use.'

'Only if you make me your slave' said Nilo, unexpectedly. 'I require maltreatment.'

'Delighted! I'll bring my riding crop. That leaves you two, Jorge and Fallin. Ever experimented with the home team? I hear there's lots to recommend it.'

'Fuck off,' suggested Fallin. 'Seriously.'

The conversation seemed self-sustaining. Wood excused himself and Hazel and closed the channel. The Havenners' capacity for humour under pressure wasn't shared by the occupants of *Oscar*. Hazel seemed deeply preoccupied. He was about to ask what was eating her when she blurted 'Wood, what do you think of the plan?'

He looked at her blankly. 'The plan?'

A pause. 'I'm having second thoughts.'

This was the last thing he'd expected. Especially now. For a moment, all he could do was stare. 'It was devised by far better tacticians than us. Do we know enough to speculate?'

She chewed her lip. 'I don't know.'

'I thought Tom was this all-seeing mega-genius.'

'He's not infallible, Wood. Besides, I'm not convinced Tom had anything to do with this.' She gestured at the fleet scattered above the clouds. 'I think he's wrapped up in whatever's happening to Haven. I've the feeling whatever he's doing involves considerably more than just thinking about it.'

Wood scratched his head. 'Then who drew up the plans?'

'Zhelkar and Dorrin, heading the elected emergency council with input from our relatively limited thinker network. You see why I'm worried? None of them have experienced real battles in space. I'll bet they're using old archive data from the Freelancer wars and the odd Puke hit-and-run raid to build their models. It's not *like* that any more,' she cried. 'I just can't see how we can delay the arrival of the weapon for long enough. Either we'll defeat them, and they'll retreat, or they'll defeat *us*. Either way, the ultimate outcome will likely be decided as soon as the first missiles are fired – in which case it can only go in their favour.'

Wood began to say something but thought better of it. He clamped his teeth together. 'Like they said, any suggestions are welcome.'

'But I don't *have* any better suggestions!' She lashed a foot at the console so hard that it left a slowly fading dent.

'Hey!'

'I think I see what Hazel means,' ventured Tink. 'Whichever way it goes, I can't see the battle lasting long enough to buy enough time. The only way we can delay them significantly will be to disable the Troubleshooter weapon, or to damage enough of their fleet to force them to wait as one unit while repairs are made.'

'Brilliant!' Wood exploded. 'And where the hell does that leave us?' He shook his head. 'But ... maybe that was the agenda all along – maybe Zhelkar and Dorrin thought we might *panic* slightly if any of us knew we actually had to defeat a force a hundred times bigger than us!' He flapped his hands. '*Fuck*. Well, what the hell do we do now? Should we *tell* anyone?'

'It changes nothing,' Hazel said.

'How? This is suicide!'

Her mouth was a tight line. 'I can't believe Zhelkar and Dorrin would do that to us. We'll all give everything we've got, whatever happens. And besides,' she added. 'We're forgetting Nikumi.'

Wood gave Hazel, then Tink, a long, hard look. 'You honestly think he has a hope of persuading them? Even if he actually *tries?*'

Hazel did not answer.

351

47

SOUND THE DRUMS

THE SEV HUMMED through wind-whipped air a few metres from the wave crests. Neither the Professor nor Zhelkar spoke. Each was wrapped in his own thoughts.

They'd never been exactly on close terms, reflected Zhelkar, watching the almost inconceivably older man from a corner of his eye. Apart from the visible injuries, and the shortness of his hair and beard, Jo Fox looked much like Zhelkar's memories of the man from when Zhelkar had been an awestruck young boy.

He wondered whether Jo Fox had ever been on close terms with anyone.

A storm was brewing inland over the Rock Thunder Range. Towering cumulus with sunlit summits: a wall of convective violence seemingly frozen in the air.

Lightning flickered between columns of rising cloud.

Zhelkar glanced at the shapes scudding over the waves in the rear-view screen. Ten of them: the final evacuation of Hades. Whatever was to happen to Haven in twenty-three hours' time was expected to strain the planet's crust. An empty magma chamber beneath a not-long-extinct volcano was not an advisable place to be.

The truth was that there were few sensible places to be. Jo had warned that, whatever happened, Haven was in for a rough ride.

The aircraft bobbed upwards. A rocky headland zipped by beneath, then salt-lashed grassland and temperate forest. Zhelkar let his eyes play over the forest's shades of green, red, orange and brown. A dark ceiling blotted out the sun as the ground rose and the frozen wave of the storm rolled overhead.

Headlights sprang to life on the shapes behind.

He saw Dorrin's round face, still young beyond her years. Eyes gleaming, her hair still black as the night sky. At once the SEV seemed terribly slow.

Darkness deepened as they climbed. Sheets of rain lashed the windscreen. The wiper-blade was a blur of motion, slashing back and forth between its parallel grooves. His thoughts turned to Hazel. He saw her as she'd come to his childless family twenty-five years ago. Unapproachable, dangerous. Eyes full of inconsolable grief and pain. Lying on her adopted bed on their veranda, staring out at the lake.

Then, later. He was wet, in a doorway. His house. For some reason, the incident was engraved in his memory with perfect clarity. There was a bucket. A puddle. Not water: it smelled too much. A face bursting with impish mischief, running off with young Sander and Berry. He'd vowed to flay them all alive. They'd just laughed.

Like a punch in the stomach it dawned on him fully that he would almost certainly never see her again.

Guilt consumed him. He shouldn't be cowering down here. He should be up there, fighting, with them! What right did *he* have to send them all off to die? That his name had not been picked had made no difference.

But, then, he was old, and more fragile even than he looked. Perhaps it was excusable. No one but Dorrin and Juniper's doctors knew about his heart condition or his cancer.

He tried consoling himself with the thought that someone more capable was in his place now. It didn't work. The light aircraft bucked in a downdraught as the rain intensified. Lightning flashed. *Storms really are beautiful*, he thought. *Elemental power epitomised*. Jo remained silent, but for a moment his troubled face seemed to clear slightly.

The ride over the pass was a rough one. Zhelkar was almost thankful when they at last broke into bright sunshine, crossing the River Therese beneath a clean-washed sky of crystal blue. Sinking low, Amber glinted off the river's convoluted loops and giant ox-bows. Great herds of long-antlered elk moved in water-meadows which shone like glass.

'A beautiful day,' said Jo.

He said nothing more during the journey through low cloud filling the Crystal River Canyon, up over the moors above the canyon's head, and down into the Juniper Basin, which was basking in the sunshine of a mid-*Foghar* evening. Opening the SEV's door, Zhelkar unfolded Jo's wheelchair and helped him into it, pushing him on to the waiting wooden lift platform. As Jo was lowered to the ground, Zhelkar made his way carefully down the SEV's extended steps, then pushed Jo towards the crowd which had gathered in expected silence.

Looking tense, Randal Brightstone stepped forward to greet them. 'How are things going?'

'To plan,' Zhelkar answered brusquely. 'Everyone must be at the town hall in a quarter of an hour. We need to evacuate the town up to Summertop. Make sure everyone knows.'

Randal's eyebrows went up.

'There may be earthquakes, trees falling, floods,' Zhelkar explained. 'We can only guess. Juniper's barely kilometres from an active fault-line. Summertop should be the safest place.'

'I'll sound the drums,' called Randal over his shoulder as he ran off in the direction of the hall.

48

HOPE

DESPITE A COOL BREEZE and clear skies, there was a heaviness in the air which stifled energy and oppressed spirits. The hike up the path from Juniper seemed endless. There was no birdsong, and no one saw any birds. There didn't even seem to be insects. No sound broke the eerie silence but for the rumble of cascades and the scuff of shoes against turf and rocks.

Sander jiggled aching shoulders beneath the straps of a rucksack which contained his sleeping bag, a week's rations for several people, and data drives containing some of Juniper's irreplaceable library files. The *Foghar* sunshine was warm, and he was sweating.

Beneath its cast, the hand Berry had shattered with a poker ached and itched. He still didn't fully understand what had happened. He felt raw. *Betrayed.* Undeniably relieved, while simultaneously intolerably guilty at his relief and so worried about his errant friend that often he felt sick. The whole mess ate at him like caustic soda. How much better it would have been had the idiot let fate run its course. He appreciated why he'd done it. He supposed he might have done something similar in his position. And yet …

Well, he didn't know yet what to think. He was still processing.

Turning, he studied the long procession straggling up the slope below. Laden with a similar load, Stephanie returned his smile hesitantly as she joined him.

They were above the tree line now. The colourful train of people wove through the band of scrub back into the pines. A thousand metres lower, Juniper Lake reflected tiny cumulus like a mirror.

Everyone carried something. Most had rucksacks of food, sleeping bags and lightweight tents. Many bore larger burdens of books, portable terminals or data cards and gene-banks – even pots of seedlings and cages containing the more portable creatures from the reintroduction pens. Some carried wide-eyed children and babies on shoulders, or in papooses or scarves made from hemp or silk. Children, grimly determined, carried loads as large as themselves.

'Should we wait for the others?' Stephanie suggested.

'Don't see why. Everyone knows where we're going.'

They set off more slowly, savouring the meadows of late alpine flowers; the skyline of white-splashed peaks; the sky's graduation from cobalt-blue at the zenith to copper-grey at the toothy horizon. Sander reached out his uninjured paw and Stephanie took it, smiling again, though her eyes were clouded. Hand in hand, they continued at their own perfectly matched, long-legged pace, arriving at the elevated meadow which formed the summit of Summertop half an hour later, long before anyone else.

From here, on the continental divide, it was possible to see all the way down to the Crystal River Canyon in the east. Above its vertiginous notch in the distance, thunderclouds rose high and white above the Rock Thunders, obscuring their summits.

They eased their packs to the ground with moans of relief. Sander rolled his shoulders. He looked around and grinned.

'I think we've around ten minutes to ourselves.'

It took Stephanie a few moments to understand. 'Sander.' Hands went to her hips. 'You're incorrigible!'

'Steph …?'

For a moment, she was downcast, and he could tell that she was thinking the same as he was – that it might be their last ever opportunity. Then her expression became wolfish. Without warning, she leapt on him, wrapping her legs around his waist, kicking his knees from under him with her heels and knocking him – grunting in alarm – to the grass, smothering his lips with hers.

'Mmm – *ow!* My arm.'

He struggled, but felt his eyelids begin to droop. His arms flopped back in the grass. 'Don't ever stop surprising me,' he mumbled around the kiss, fingers curling around the edges of her shoulder-blades.

'Shut up.' Stephanie emphasised the order by biting his lips together. 'You have just one purpose in life for the next few minutes.'

'Shit. Just occurred to me that we haven't … That is, you're not …?'

'No.'

'Did you bring any …?'

'Forget it. We're wasting time. Now, will you help me off with these trousers off, or what?'

DORRIN GLANCED at her partner. Staring at his screen, Zhelkar was smoothing the tip of his pointed beard between his fingers. Beside him, in his wheelchair before the largest screen, Jo was lost in thoughts as enigmatic as they'd always been.

She studied the subterranean research centre's cheerless slate floor, trying to imagine the trees and cabins on the surface close by. Juniper's once-welcoming homes would all be empty by now.

Her attention returned to the array of hastily rigged flatscreens. They decorated three walls of the room like enormous tiles, surrounding the central holoprojector which would simulate the confrontation's progress as information became available, updated by a relay of sniffers and orglets cycling continuously between Haven and Haven's Gate.

Half the screens showed the waiting interception fleet: twin clusters of dark specks against the clouds of Haven. Others showed the slacker scatter of the defence fleet.

She beseeched fate that they never had to use either. Though a candle of hope still flickered, she felt in her bones that it was forlorn.

'They're coordinating themselves well,' she ventured, to break the leaden silence. 'I'm pleasantly surprised by their discipline.' Zhelkar nodded, grateful for the distraction.

'I hope they don't panic. Our only chance is them sticking to strategy. A fluid command structure has advantages, but if they lose group leaders and get spooked, the plan will fall apart.'

'Every strategy has risks,' observed Jo. 'I doubt we could humanly have done better with what we have.'

Eyes locked on the interception fleet, Zhelkar let a breath escape that he hadn't known he was holding. Various retorts went through his head. Every instinct told him that cowering underground like this was just plain wrong. In the end, he settled for muttering 'Easy for us to say.'

'Zhelkar, you're a good man. But oversight will be crucial. You and Dorrin are much more use to all of us exactly where you are.'

49

ACT OF TREASON

'SO, WE REALLY ARE just going to roll over and do exactly what these fuckers want?'

Within the fast little Havenner-designed starship, tension had been growing. Shoulder still cocooned in its bulky Havenner dressing, Kettering had done little but stare around the cramped cabin in increasingly visible agitation as hyperspace fled outside.

Though supposedly free of the Freaks' symbiotic organisms, the Commander still looked physically ill. Nikumi didn't feel great himself. Assuming the Freaks weren't simply lying, he wondered absently whether some kind of addictive withdrawal mechanism was involved.

He didn't answer his number one, feeling no need to explain himself again.

'Sir. Permission to speak freely.'

Nikumi steeled himself. He nodded wearily.

'This is *shit*.' Kettering's hands clawed the cabin air. 'I can't believe you can seriously be suggesting we concede to their demands. Sir.' The last word was almost sneered.

'It was effectively an offer of surrender terms.'

'That makes a difference?' Kettering's face was a knot of disgust. 'We know enough about them now to boost our tactical advantage tenfold. We should be using that information to blow them all to hell! What do you think they want this extra time for? It could be all kinds of mischief. They could be waiting for … for timed biological bombs to go off around the confederation, for Chrissakes – anything! It would be insane – *traitorously* insane – to do as they ask.'

Nikumi had yet to tell Kettering of Fox's desperate-sounding plan, suspecting it would only polarise his views further. He donned his best poker-face, turning back to the view

359

ahead. 'As usual, your frankness is appreciated. But that's quite enough.'

'Commander. I *cannot allow* you to jeopardise our advantage.'

Nikumi turned coolly to his first officer, though his heart beat a little faster. 'Number one. I do hope that wasn't what it sounded like.' Kettering received his appraisal with a glare of intimidating intensity, the muscles of his heavy jaw clenching. 'What it sounded like was a threat. Make sure that it's a one-off.'

Adrenaline spiking, he glanced up at the HUD itinerary readout. Fifteen minutes until the twist out of hyperspace. If the Havenners' estimates were inaccurate, they could easily arrive after the navy fleet he'd worked so hard to bring here had already left.

Not for the first time, he wondered if he was doing the right thing. Fox was right, damn him. There had been more than enough killing. Nikumi had perpetrated plenty in his career, but at some point during the events culminating in Fox's mutilation and *Violator*'s demise a threshold had been crossed, and the prospect of more now sickened him. He could see no way that the extra hours the Freaks had requested could significantly increase the risk to the confederation. Any biological bombs hidden within IPEC would have been pre-set, and he could think of no feasible mechanism Fox or his minions might use to reinstruct them remotely. Likewise, nothing happening out here now in this God-forsaken corner of the galaxy was likely to stop the Lancer incursion Fox claimed to have triggered.

Unfortunately, Kettering was also perfectly correct. It was insanity to risk potentially the very future of humanity on what boiled down to a promise made by history's most infamous terrorist.

But he was getting ahead of himself. With the Navy out for blood, convincing the notoriously bullish fleet admiral even to hear his message was going to be difficult. Even if it was listened to, any decisions based on the message were not going to be his.

All assuming we arrive in time.

Registering sudden movement, Nikumi raised an arm in a reflexive blocking move. He discovered that he'd deflected a sharp stick fractionally before its stained tip, which he'd little doubt was dipped in poison, would have pierced his throat. Straining against the arm holding the stick, he found himself staring into the maddened eyes of his first officer.

Kettering seized Nikumi's blocking arm and rose menacingly from his seat.

Nikumi thrashed. Still strapped into the seat's harness, his options were limited. He twisted desperately, kicking out with his legs. Taking a foot in the chest, Kettering grunted, sprawling backwards across the console.

'Kettering!' yelled Nikumi, releasing his harness and tearing himself free. 'This is treason!' He planted his feet on the seat and sprang awkwardly over the seatback, cracking his head on a window strut, but putting the seat between the two of them.

'The only treasonous one here is you,' growled Kettering. 'Our orders were to find their hole of a planet and lead the fleet to them so they could blow it to slag! I'm disgusted to have ever called you captain. You let those Freaks get to you.'

The accusation stung. Partly because, from the perspective of the old Nikumi, it was true. 'My orders were to use initiative. I am, but you're too inflexible to see that. You're a fanatic!'

'A fanatic?' Kettering seemed to ponder this. 'Maybe I am. I believe in our way of life.' He thumped his chest, eyes blazing, brandishing his stake. 'I believe in what we're doing, and I don't believe Freaks and Lancers deserve to live. Otherwise, what the fuck have we been fighting for?'

He lunged across the seat with the stick. Prevented from retreating by the cabin's back wall, Nikumi dodged, barely managing to slap the jabbing arm aside. 'You'd rather millions more of your own people died than allow any kind of concession?'

Kettering was breathing hard. 'There's no reasoning with these Freaks! You should know that better than anyone. Look at that world of theirs! It's … *foul!* They have things *living inside them*, Nikumi! It's sick! It's diabolical. It should all be wiped from existence.' He lunged again.

'Kettering,' barked Nikumi, dodging narrowly and slapping the man's arm away again. Damn it, Kettering had always been strong. He'd become fast, too. 'Last warning! We can talk about this. Stand down.'

'I will *not*, sir! You are unfit for command!' Nikumi feinted to retreat into the corner by the console and the pilot's seat. Kettering followed him, hemming him in. The big man feinted a lunge to the left, but then twisted his arm round so that the stick arced around once more towards Nikumi's throat.

It was all Nikumi could do to seize the arm. He found the poisoned spike quivering centimetres from his face. Kettering's strength was almost overwhelming. 'Kettering, you mad arsehole! Stop this! You were a good officer. If you stop this now, I'll put it … down …' he grunted with effort, 'to strain.'

'Strain? Ha!' Kettering's eyes bulged as he drove the point inexorably down. 'They put *creatures* inside us, Nikumi! *Inside our bodies*.' The point jerked closer. Nikumi kicked out with his knee, but Kettering swatted it effectively aside with his thigh. Braced across the edge of the console, Nikumi couldn't use his other leg without losing balance.

Snorting with exertion, he relaxed his straining arm muscles slightly. *Make him do all the work.* The point crept towards his face.

'Hyperspace exit in ten minutes,' announced the almost impenetrably accented voice of the ship.

'Kettering,' gasped Nikumi. 'Give it up!' The point of the stick was almost in his eye. He could smell the bitter plant extract coating it. Kettering's arm was starting to shake. Good: Nikumi wasn't the only one tiring. 'Kettering!'

'Fuck you!' Kettering roared, spraying spittle, bringing his other hand around and pushing the point towards Nikumi's eye with all his might.

It was what Nikumi had waited for. He channelled the force of the thrust into pushing himself sideways, twisting Kettering's arms and adding to their momentum as he drove the stick's point down and back. There was a meaty thump. Kettering screamed. Nikumi watched the man sprawl sideways over the pilot's chair, white-faced and clutching his stomach.

Pawing the hole in his fatigues, Kettering gawped at the wet stake he was now holding, then at the bright blood on his fingers. He stared at Nikumi in horror.

'You fool.' Nikumi's voice was trembling.

'Help me.'

'How?' He pulled himself upright. His heart was thundering. 'We have no antidote.'

Kettering grimaced. 'How long?'

'How could I know?' The commander was already ashen-faced. 'You assured me the poison was potent. It should be fairly quick.'

'Fuck everything Nikumi, not like this.' His eyes were already glassy, his breathing shallow. 'Fucking Freak bastards.' He fixed Nikumi's eyes in a terrible, accusing stare.

Without looking away, Nikumi stooped, took the stick away, and grasped Kettering's spasming hand tightly between his own.

Minutes later, as his first officer's eyes misted over, a jolt went through the speeding craft.

Stars appeared.

'INCOMING TRANSMISSION, SIR.'

From the command chair of the navy flagship *Star Smasher*, newest and largest of the Divide and Rule-class fleet, Fleet Admiral Abdul Grisham dropped his avatar into a corner of Lieutenant Kim Kapaldi's sensorium.

'An important one, I trust,' he growled. Even in the safety of the command centre, booms and rumbles were audible, echoing along the immense machine's superstructure. The fleet had been in truespace barely seconds before the smart mines had begun their ambush, twice as intensely as in the previous solar system. The near-invisible devices seemed able to pre-empt truespace re-entry points, detonating en masse while their targets were vulnerable and fully visible following hyperspace exit.

While the mines' selective tactics had spared much of the fleet, of the vessels singled out only the Fortresses were proving able to absorb the fusillades of multi-gigaton explosions occurring simultaneously on all sides without serious harm. Naval intelligence hadn't predicted such potent conventional weapons. Analysis of captured examples suggested they were Lancer-built. He was beginning to wonder whether Lancer colonies closest to the confederation, which had been IPEC's main intelligence source, were unrepresentatively ill-equipped.

'Maydays from two battlecruisers,' reported the voice of Cho Nuwen, his chief tactical officer. '*Knockout Punch* and *Kiss This*. Heavy casualties. We're taking sustained hits. Self-repairable, no casualties reported. Yet,' she added.

'That transmission.' Kapaldi raised his eyes to the Admiral's avatar. 'The sender claims to be Commodore Aral Nikumi, OIC of the *Violator*.' The fleet admiral watched his own avatar's eyes

363

widen. 'He claims to have intelligence on the Freaks, and an urgent message.'

Not a good time for distractions like this. The admiral scowled. 'Where is he transmitting from?'

An image dropped into his sensorium. It was of a tiny and angular short-range interstellar spacecraft. Apparently unarmed, it looked more than a century out-of-date and was decorated with colourful representations of what he knew from his campaign briefing to be inhuman creatures.

Gladness at Nikumi's unexpected survival became a spike in his heartrate as he processed the implications of what he was seeing. The commodore was in a Freak vessel. This suggested, as had seemed likely from the vessel's emergency final transmission, that *Violator* had been lost with all but a handful of its crew still aboard. It was a timely warning not to underestimate the enemy. Yet it also suggested that Nikumi had somehow escaped capture, commandeering this vessel.

Which, he reflected with a grin, would be just like Nikumi.

'Is there an identifier with it?' he snapped. 'A code.' A particularly heavy impact sent a vibration through the floor. Warning icons flickered over Grisham's virtual schematic of the fortress. 'Belay that, just show me the damn transmission.'

'What about the risk of parasit—?'

'*Now*, Lieutenant.'

His pulse surged again as the recording played.

'This is Commodore Admiral Nikumi, of IPEC navy fortress *Violator*, with an urgent message for Fleet Admiral Abdul Grisham.' The code the speaker gave was indeed the one Grisham had given Nikumi. He was shocked at the man's appearance: the once-brawny JSSS officer looked skeletal, his face tinged a greyish green, though this could have been the cabin's lighting. What looked like blood was smudged on his face. In the background Grisham could clearly see the motionless, uniformed arm of another officer.

The etiolated Nikumi gave a brief report. *Violator* lost — as feared, but the confirmation stung. No mention of other survivors: an odd omission, particularly given the arm he could see. Nikumi had been captured, he claimed, but *allowed* to leave. Odder still. The man looked and sounded strained, which was unlike Nikumi. Sweat sheened his forehead.

'I have important intel on the Freaks which you need to hear, Admiral. The situation is far more complex than intel had led us to believe. I urge you to delay the offensive until I'm debriefed. Millions of lives and the effectiveness of the navy fleet may depend on this, and time will be required to process the information. I've been assured that I am free of contagion, but take no chances: you should either keep me isolated in this ship, or use isolation facilities.'

Uncharacteristically, Grisham found himself dithering. The man's identity wasn't the cause of his unease – he was confident that the person before him was, or at least had been, Nikumi. He supposed the blood and the apparently dead officer in the background could be explained by Nikumi's escape.

But the blood looked fresh, and everything else about this scenario had his intuition screaming. If Grisham had been a Freak, had a way to coerce or reprogram captives, and wanted either to delay the offensive to his advantage or to smuggle either a biological or nuclear weapon aboard the fleet's flagship, this was precisely how he'd do it.

More vibrations. More warning icons. Lieutenant Nuwen reported 'We just lost *Knockout Punch*.'

Hell's teeth. 'Anything on that ship consistent with a nuclear bomb?'

'Not visible to scans, sir.' Kapaldi again. 'Just the ship's drive.'

Grisham fingered his lip. He had an almost visual sense of being poised on a knife edge. Either side he came down on, somehow he had the intuition that this was the most critical moment of his long, and occasionally distinguished, career.

'Sir?' Nuwen, again. 'We're getting hammed here, sir. We need your input.'

'Incinerate it.' His heart sank even as he barked the words. 'Quickly, before he's close enough to contaminate us. Some of these microorganisms of theirs apparently survive in a vacuum.' *Star Smasher*'s status board displayed the launch of two smart nuclear missiles. 'Use particle beams and railguns too.'

He was already questioning his decision.

'Sir – the vessel's still attempting to contact us. Says he must speak with you personally.' The fleet admiral's brows twitched. Another, louder boom echoed through the bridge. His teeth clenched.

'More hits, sir.' A different voice. 'Casualty reports coming in.'

'Block all incoming transmissions. We were warned of mind-tricks: anyone who's been in contact with the enemy must be considered a threat. Turn that ship to dust.'

Before he'd finished speaking, a storm of brilliant beams was already lancing into space. More a victim of the sheer volume saturated by high energy particle beams and railgun rounds than of accurate marksmanship, seconds later the colourful little self-propelled box of metals and ceramics burst open and began corkscrewing towards the Freaks' planet, trailing sparkling debris and frozen gases.

HE'D BEEN STUPID.

Jo saw it now, in all its ghastly clarity. He'd been swept up in his megalomaniac's pipe-dream – of a last sanctuary, existing in peaceful secrecy for all time – to the exclusion of all else. His weakness and his guilt had blinded him to the truth until it was too late.

And now, because of his blindness, his *weakness*, Haven, and everything and everyone on it – all of whom had depended, naively, upon his judgement and vision – were to be thrown at the mercy of fate.

Time passed.

When the sniffer's message finally arrived, Jo closed his eyes.

50

THE MAGIC BULLET

'LOOK!' CRIED HAZEL. 'Great Mother, look at Haven!'

Wood followed her excited gaze.

His eyes widened. He could hardly believe what they were telling him. He could hardly have failed to notice if what he was seeing had been visible before.

Far below, Haven was projecting writhing, white spikes of what looked like plasma hundreds of kilometres into space. Each spike was rooted in its own cell of stormcloud. As he watched over several minutes, the spikes seemed to grow in number and activity until the planet resembled a surreal prickly fruit.

If anything, more spectacular was what was happening beyond the orbit of the Havenner fleets. In a rough circle around the planet, patches of stars were *twisting*, as though viewed through the surface of a disturbed pond. Tidemaker, climbing above Haven's sunlit limb, was distorting as well.

Abruptly, the spikes disappeared, and Haven's surroundings seemed tranquil once again. Then, gradually at first, and growing in number, the energised tendrils extended spaceward again. The sight had rendered the entire squadron speechless.

'What,' demanded Fallin, eventually, 'is *that* all about?'

The question triggered a chorus of headshakes and wide-eyed mumbling. Despite the apprehension, Wood detected a new resolve. Whatever Haven was doing, fantastic amounts of energy were clearly involved. The thought was both reassuring and sobering.

'Still no sign of the Pukes,' Jorge muttered, brow creased. 'The fleet's more than five hours late now. What's keeping them?

'If they're still coming via Primrose,' Simone told him, 'they only have to take a little bit longer and we won't even have to fight them.'

'Perhaps, but this waiting stinks,' Fallin grumbled.

Janno clearly agreed. 'I'm out of fingernails. And I need a shower. I don't think much of the waste absorption of these suits.'

Tink's avatar had been cocking its head as though listening. Suddenly it stood up and drew its sword with a loud metal-on-metal rasp which immediately quelled the conversation.

'Unfortunately,' Tink announced, 'I think the wait is over.'

Eight flesh-and-blood faces tightened. Wood slid his hand into Hazel's, wishing her seat was closer; wishing the next minutes or hours didn't have to pass. He looked fearfully into her eyes, and she stared helplessly back. The Haggard, lopsided face of Jo Fox appeared against the stars. It regarded them silently for several seconds.

'Ten minutes ago,' it began quietly, 'a sniffer returned from Haven's Gate. The invasion fleet is there. The sniffer's priorities mean we don't yet know what effect our mines have had on the fleet. However, by the time it left, two battlecruisers already appeared badly damaged.

'Nikumi's attempt has failed. In four minutes and thirty seconds, orgs will begin the connection process. Extrapolating from previous events, the arrival of the Troubleshooter weapon is expected between twenty and twenty-five minutes after you reach the fleet. Haven should have protected itself in a little under twelve-and-a-half hours. The fleet is potentially ten hours from Haven – which might be cause for optimism if it was behaving as predicted.

'Unfortunately, the fleet has ceased its advance on Haven's Gate, and there are signs of preparations for an onwards twist to hyperspace. Its late arrival could be explained by the conserving of reserves for a quick TFG spool-up, perhaps even before the Troubleshooter weapon arrives, in which case they may already know that Haven's Gate is abandoned. We must therefore assume the worst and buy ourselves a little more than an hour and a half.'

That after three hundred years Haven's fate would be decided by a matter of minutes seemed to Wood both tragic and faintly ridiculous.

'There's little else to say except … good luck. Our hearts and our thoughts go with you.'

The screen flicked into blackness.

'Helmets on, everyone.'

The words seemed to come from someone else. Wood's skull felt swollen, his senses unclear. He felt Hazel's fierce grip on his hand only distantly.

Around the three groupings of ships, he could see orgs clustering around the clumsy-looking nonorgs, arranging them into tight knots using little rucks and tucks of spacetime. His head was eerily silent now: the orgs were preoccupied plotting vectors across tangled multidimensional landscapes in ways even they didn't fully understand, priming their bacterial batteries so that their sugar-fuelled space-rending spasms would arrive synchronously, and at the required tangents and intensities.

The only sound was his pulse in his ears.

'You counting, Tink?'

'Two minutes.'

Shit.

Severing the comm link, he unbuckled and paced around the control room, chewing the stumps of his fingernails. He wished he had a knife.

'Wood,' Hazel wailed. 'Everyone's nervous enough without you doing that.'

'I know. I know.' Suddenly, he could pretend no longer. 'Hazel, I can't *do* this any more! It's like my whole life's been spent trying to stop people killing me. I'd begun believing for a moment that there was more than that.' He ran trembling fingers over his face. 'Can't you see? This is it! Oh God.'

He slumped on the edge of his shaggy seat, shaking. Hazel's eyes were pitch black. 'So, when the end comes, would you rather have just pissed your life away?'

He stared at her. 'I can't believe you actually said that.'

'Tink's been through as much as you!' she cried, with real anger. 'More – because he didn't get a childhood. He's not thinking like this!'

'Actually,' observed Tink, leaning on his enormous sword, 'you're being presumptuous. If it wasn't for you two, I'd have run away tendays ago.'

Gaping at the avatar, Hazel made a spluttering noise. Then she caught Wood's rueful grin. Grimacing, he reached over and brushed aside hair now clinging wetly to her cheek.

'I'm sorry,' he said. 'I think I'm okay now. It's nerves, that's all. You're right. We'll come out of this okay. You'll see.'

Standing, he cradled her head against his stomach, running fingers through her warm curls as he bared his teeth at Tink and shook his head.

'Lying,' Hazel told him, 'doesn't suit you.'

'Twenty seconds.'

Releasing her with a gasp, Wood lashed himself hurriedly into his chair, inhaled deeply, and restored the comms channel. His little squadron stared back through their helmets with expressions ranging from trepidation to open-mouthed terror.

'How's my team doing?' he asked, as light-heartedly as he could manage. 'Stick to plan, grit your teeth, and we'll come out of this. Remember – we go in the *millisecond* we're through the other side, so be alert. You'll be pulled along in *Oscar*'s tow field as we take you in, but after that it's up to you. Okay?'

'Ten seconds.'

'Best of luck. A big round on me of whatever psychotropics you name after this is over. Stay in touch.'

'Eh?' grunted Fallin, as puzzled as the rest.

Hazel screwed her eyes shut. *Berry. Good luck. Visit me after this is over.*

'Five seconds. Four –'

Wood felt as though his heart might burst his chest. Air seemed solidified in his throat. He shot a wild glance at Hazel. She gaped back at him, goggle-eyed.

'Two –'

His stomach cramped with a violence which made him grunt. Tink had a gauntleted hand over his eyes.

'*One –*'

Stars sucked themselves into nothing in a great washing tide, and there was the familiar, unpleasantly extended, indefinable wrench. Wood wiped sweating hands on the trousers of his fireproof suit. After an uncertain lapse of time, the nothingness began to twist. Unwelcome stars were wrung out of it.

Against them, a flashing red blob appeared on the tactical HUD of *Oscar*'s newly installed battle thinker, well above and left of Terra Nova's bright little crescent and the crosshairs marking dead ahead.

The enemy fleet.

Out of my way!

The orgs obligingly began to scatter, and Wood kicked in *Oscar*'s thruster at full burn.

Telepathy's back, Hazel assured him as G-forces clawed at them. *Our tail's clear; we won't burn anyone.*

He eased the joystick back. The artificial horizon became a receding rectangular plane which dropped out of view as more places descended to replace it. The expanding red blob settled close to the cross-hairs as Wood matched *Oscar*'s approach vector with the trajectory of the IPEC fleet.

Already, he could see the cluster of specks highlighted by the thinker spreading and growing. He glanced at the rear-view screen. Perilously close to the thruster's blinding torch, the six missile ships were bobbing along behind in *Oscar*'s gravity lasso. Under their own power they could never have kept up.

'Missiles,' observed Tink. 'Hundreds of nukes, increasing all the time. Eek! Four hundred ... Five hundred ...' A graph appeared in a corner of the tactical display, showing the number levelling off at over one thousand. 'Convergence time, twenty seconds! Convergence with main fleet, forty-seven seconds.'

Tink began raving to himself. Wood felt his hands tighten. A panning magnification already showed the leading missiles, appearing almost stationary, while the warships which had fired them seemed to speed away into the distance. His eyes roved over the darkness ahead, but he could see nothing.

'*JESUS CHRIST.*'

In an eyeblink, space ahead was packed with bright specks, spreading from a central point almost too quickly to follow. It may as well have been a solid wall. Hazel barely had time to close her eyes. Wood flinched, battling the futile urge to try and evade the inevitable. 'Oh crap. *Tink!*'

There was a brief, intense flash, and something seemed to tickle Wood's bones from the inside.

Then space was replaced with something which might as well have been the inside of a sun.

Oscar shook. Kaleidoscopic patterns spun in Wood's brain, remaining in his eyes when he opened them. Through them, he could just make out the approaching planet. 'Yikes!' Tink was squawking. 'More nukes in nineteen seconds!'

Halfway there. 'Hold on,' Wood yelled unnecessarily, blinking and squinting. He dug his heels hard against the foot pedals. A clunk reverberated through the hull as the reverser's clamshell slammed shut. In the rear-view screen, he could see the towed vessels straining forward against their lasso.

Above Terra Nova, dark shapes were growing. Spine-backed hulks stalked between pinched cubes like predatory fish amongst aquatic foliage. He wondered why they weren't camouflaged. Were Haven's jammers screwing up their communications? *We must have surprised them, or they'd never be so close together.*

Look! Hazel was gesturing at a Fortress. It was venting luminous plumes which became searchlight-beams of incandescent matter escaping from every crevice in its armoured shell, spinning the immense structure with gathering momentum into the rest of the fleet. *It's the disrupters! More, look!*

Wood felt a surge of exhilaration: his first emotion for hours besides terror. The disrupters were attacking the Fortresses! Another began pouring its corrupted innards into space. Then another. Unscathed Fortresses were scattering as fast as their thrusters would allow.

'Nukes, five seconds.'

Eight hundred of them now, and more densely packed than before. Hazel suddenly went rigid, screaming and thrashing in her seat as though in agony, her face unrecognisable.

'What's that?' yelled a panicked voice on the relay. 'Who's screaming?'

'Ignore it,' he yelled back. '*Brace!*'

'KEEP YOURSELVES TUCKED IN tightly behind Bee and me.'

Berry twisted the throttle-grip on his joywheel as far as it would go, wishing he had more thrust in his overladen old Lancer workhorse. He glanced in his rear-screen. *A nice, tight line. Good.*

'Disrupters got six already,' said an excited voice. 'Did you see?'

'Concentrate on holding line!' squawked Bee Chee-chee's high pitched voice. 'This will be scary. Our only chance with those nukes is to punch through, then cover our tails.

'Oh – Great – *Mother* …' Chaotic sounds of panic came over the relay. 'Have you seen what's coming?'

'We'll never make it through that!'

'Stay in line,' squawked Bee. 'Launch your anti-missiles only when your thinkers tell you to. Save enough for later.'

Easier said than done. Berry glanced at Bee's gunship, so close behind that it almost filled the rear-view screen. Then he saw the missiles approaching, like an endless translucent wall. Gasping, he tightened his already firm grip on the wheel.

'Make a hole!' he rasped, tensing and firing every particle weapon he had. He added bursts on the railguns for good measure. Forty black muzzles spat fire into the void, their controlling thinkers struggling to out-anticipate their targets, which dodged subtly, yet fractionally faster than the gun turrets could follow. At least the thinkers were still operating. Haven's signal-jammers seemed to be doing their job.

A prompt sounded in his ears. He pressed his lip breathlessly against his helmet's control pad. A salvo of sleek shapes rushed forwards past his canopy, their exhausts shrinking sparks against the browns of the approaching planet and the imminent wall of nuclear warheads. Swarms of further sparks filled the space between them as the missiles launched their anti-anti-missile-missile offspring, and the anti-anti-missile-missiles launched their own offspring.

His teeth clamped together.

Explosions strained the canopy's filters as incoming missiles were outmanoeuvred by their smaller adversaries. Berry's gunship plunged into the radiating melee. Shrapnel rained off the kinetic deflectors. He was buffeted violently.

When he emerged on the other side, the canopy was almost opaque with dust and impact craters in the super-tough diamondglass, and the stars were spinning crazily. He searched for the others.

None of his group were left! Not one!

Terror seized him.

Control yourself, he demanded. His hands were shaking so violently that he could barely grip the joywheel.

He saw Sander, grinning. *Bet you regret it now, eh?*

Berry closed his eyes and counted to five. Calmer, he pulled the gunship from its complex spin, and began decelerating on an intercept with the nearest fortress. He could dimly see a similar cube further away, spewing glowing plumes into space. On impulse he glanced in the rear screen, magnifying the view using his top lip.

He could see the Haven fleet's artillery group. The bulbous disrupters were unmistakable. To his horror, explosions were forming silently amidst the group, so overwhelming in their fury that the creatures seemed like dust grains as they were systematically engulfed.

Chest hollow, he returned his attention to the forward tactical display. Converging with him were more waves of missiles. *Hundreds* of the things. Spears of light began raking out from a dozen locations on all sides of the approaching cube. The first missiles were due to converge in fifteen seconds.

His entire group had thrown their lives away without getting near enough to fire their missiles with any chance of them reaching a target. If he fired his own now, they would, like him, simply be overwhelmed.

Teeth chattering, he primed them anyway.

THERE WAS THE FAMILIAR flash and feeling of pressure as the furnaces generated their matter-mangling shockwave, detonating the oncoming missiles in an orgy of radioactive violence. *Oscar* rumbled and groaned in protest.

'We're off course,' Tink warned over Hazel's screams. 'Main left sensor pod's burned. More nukes! I think they're closing slowly enough for the cannon.'

'Then use it!'

Oscar's guns sprang from their blisters. Searing orange streaks connected them instantly with a cluster of brilliant expanding balls ahead. 'I'm getting the hang of this.' The towed ships, he saw, were following Tink's example.

'Keep it up!'

'Jorge's missing.'

Wood's heart sank. *We're not even in yet.* He shook Hazel's arm. Tendons in her neck were standing like cables. No response. More explosions bloomed ahead like short-lived flowers. Weapon beams were arcing weirdly off *Oscar*'s massively powerful protective fields. Still hundreds of kilometres away, the fortresses already seemed terrifyingly large.

Hazel slumped in her seat, eyes sightless and face white.

'Ah shit – Simone, group: strafe continuously at anything moving, especially oncoming missiles. We lost Jorge. Get ready to disengage.'

'We're being jammed, they can't hear you!' Tink's voice. Sure enough, the comms screens were blank.

Oh, please not now. 'Hazel!' As they plunged into the canyon between two neighbouring fortresses, he shook her arm again in desperation. The increasingly accurate bombardment of incoming fusion bolts and disruption beams ceased. 'Tink, you'll just have to let the others go. Make sure none of them hit us!'

'Ow! They're trying to corrupt my systems! Oh, they're going to regret that.'

With *Oscar* still decelerating violently, the five surviving towed ships catapulted through the umbra of hot particles spewing from its thrust reverser and tore past the control room into the distance. The canyon walls became peppered by grids of brilliant manoeuvring thrusters as the fortresses raced to pull themselves away from each other.

Wood breathed again as he saw the attack force separate into three. *Maybe they're using hand-signals?* One pair of Type-22s veered leftwards. Another made a beeline for the distant gap of stars. Fallin's lone ship shot away to the right.

Please let those fortress's shields be down. It struck him that he still hadn't seen a single enemy fighter or missile-carrying vessel.

A single beam lanced out to Fallin's ship. Wood watched it burst apart, leaving two spinning unequal halves and an expanding fan of debris.

No!

Then three missiles detached themselves from the largest pieces, puffing clouds of beam-deflecting mirrors as they launched. With a hand over his mouth, he watched the armour-piercing missiles spawn swarms of tiny missiles which met the smart missiles sent to intercept them in a firework-display of small explosions. Dodging the sudden storm of beams targeting them, they left snakes of bright plasma in their power-dive towards the weakest parts of the Fortress's vast concave wall.

One missile was hit. It broke apart but did not explode.

Near-simultaneously, the others hit the wall.

There was no immediate explosion. Just puffs of debris, lost in the scale of their surroundings. Light shone inside the tiny holes they'd made. Dark clouds poured out. Then brilliant, intensifying jets of radiating vapour.

'Wood!' warned Tink's voice.

'Oh hell.' *Oscar* was now the focus of a contracting shell of several thousand small, fast missiles.

Unlike their recently encountered cousins, these more manoeuvrable relatives clearly had only one target in mind.

COME WITH ME.

The voice had emerged suddenly and unexpectedly in Berry's consciousness.

Who …?

Birdwing. Look up. To his surprise he found a very large and bulbous org closely shadowing him, obscuring the stars. *Decide very quickly.*

Birdwing … He swallowed. *Can't go back.*

You will die here.

He knew that. Missile convergence, seven seconds. Throat tight, he fixed his eyes on the fortress. *Take me inside.* There was a nerve-jangling pause.

That connection is unlikely to succeed. I am exhausted. Even if the wormhole does not impact on a solid object and kill us, I would be unable to take you out again.

If you're concerned for your own safety, I understand – otherwise get me in there!

Four seconds …

The stars wrenched themselves into oblivion.

OSCAR WAS SUDDENLY SKEWERED by an intense barrage of particle beams. By the sounds the hull was making, there were railgun rounds as well.

'Move,' yapped Tink. 'I've had to retract the guns to protect them.'

Wood slammed his toes against the thruster pedal. The bombardment was so intense that he could barely see anything. It ceased momentarily as *Oscar* burst through the shell of approaching missiles. He winced, but the expected explosions failed to occur.

'These missiles are smarter,' Tink warned. Wood could see them streaming in hordes in *Oscar*'s wake. He grabbed Hazel's limp hand. Shook it savagely. *Hazel! We need you!* 'They're a lot faster, too. I think they're all going to try and hit us at once – I don't think we can outrun them.'

The fleet … most of it's gone.

Wood felt his blood chill. He spared Hazel a glance. Her eyes were focussed now. They looked like haunted saucers.

'They couldn't stop the missiles. They were everywhere! The orgs …' *Their screaming …* 'Oh, Amber's light.'

'We must escape these weapons,' urged Tink. 'We have eleven seconds!'

'I'm trying. Get rid of all this tactical crap for me. It's distracting.'

The graphics disappeared. 'Only four disrupters are left,' Hazel rasped. 'Survivors are worming to different positions. Everyone's saying just go for whatever you can!'

Oscar tore around the corner of the fortress, trying vainly to shake off the fusillade of beams, which were making the hull hum. Then a huge shape was coming straight at them, more angry light cascading from its dorsal spine.

Enough running. Caution wasn't working anyway. Grimacing, Wood aimed straight for the nose of the immense battlecruiser.

It was like power-diving into a mountain.

'Eight seconds!'

Oh – Great – Mother.

Berry found himself in an immense, floodlit space. Around him, casting beams of shadow through a faint haze, countless spacecraft – from formations of potent-looking craft smaller than his gunship to monsters tens of kilometres long – were arranging themselves in waves before the dock's illuminated main portal, clearly waiting for it to open.

For a moment he was overwhelmed. He felt like a lone krill dropped in a tank of starving whales. Somehow, out of all this, he had to pick a target. And more than that, one which would somehow prevent this lot getting outside.

This fleet alone, he realised, could annihilate Haven's ten times over. At least surprise seemed so far in his favour: none of the surrounding spacecraft had obvious defences up.

He knew it wouldn't last. *Birdwing, I've no time. Try to shelter somewhere until you've energy to escape.*

I cannot leave you.

You can. Just piss off and hide! He feverishly began resetting his target system. His ship's rudimentary, EM-hardened thinker seemed to think that a concentrated strike at the dock's nearest corner might cripple the fortress's main field generators and damage its propulsion system. There was a chance that one of the fuel tanks could be pierced, with better results. At the very least, it would make the dock highly inhospitable.

But where can I go?

He was jolted to attention by a spray of particle beams. Without waiting to see their source, he jammed the joywheel forward. The heavily-laden gunship felt very sluggish.

His head was filled with an excruciating mental scream. Above the cockpit, with great clarity, he saw Birdwing burst open like a rotten fruit.

THERE WAS A BONE-JARRING JOLT. Materials that weren't designed to yield exploded in light as artificially strengthened molecular bonds were shattered by sheer force. *Oscar* bored like a bullet through the warship's entrails, corkscrewing from the stern ahead of a gigantic fireball which overwhelmed the hundreds of following missiles almost simultaneously.

It was as though a star had appeared amidst the IPEC fleet.

The explosion dimmed. The beam bombardment renewed. Wood flipped *Oscar* in a desperate arc towards the nearest fortress wall. He'd learned his lesson now. *Keep moving.*

Where was the reactor?

Three of them, Hazel tells him. *Main one, dead centre.* A pause. *I'm going after the fortress captains.*

He doesn't ask what she means. Impinging beams flicker. Another jolt. Then rending metals, solids exploding into vapours and igniting. Walls, bulkheads, dissolving; machines, furniture, crew – smashed and scattered like ash. He rides a living bullet, aimed at the creature's heart. The heart bursts, lifeblood pouring hotly from entry and exit wounds. Missiles. Always more missiles. A cruiser, smashed like an egg.

The magic bullet turns, darts forwards again on its lance of star-fire, cannon blazing. Another battlecruiser, gut-shot. He has found them now. He is unstoppable. Everything is madness, and heat, and violence. Spinning fragments and mangled plates of metal, ceramic and enhanced silicon plastic.

'Damage!' warns the bullet's inhuman brain.

Another Fortress: a mobile war-city reduced in seconds to a thermonuclear explosion in a box. Another battlecruiser, more missiles, and then more – then more again. All the time faster and faster until a glowing trail connects ruined shells and nebulas of debris like a chain of smashed jewellery …

SCREAMING AT THE TOP of his lungs, Berry dodged with increasing speed through the mobilising fleet. All around him, defence fields were coming on. His tactical screen seethed with objects too large to be missiles beginning to swarm in his direction. The dock's corner was approaching fast. He'd have to turn, very soon …

At what seemed the last possible moment, he put his thumb to the red pad on the joywheel. It seemed such a trivial action. His entire payload of multi-gigaton armour-piercing nukes and thirty-two remaining anti-missiles rushed past the cockpit in a single salvo.

Standing the gunship on its tail, he reversed his plunge at a bone-crushing fourteen Gs. Suddenly, the old ship felt light and manoeuvrable. He screamed again, raking the dock with indiscriminate railgun and plasma cannon fire. Lights and glowing debris peppered the shadows. His helmet sounded a warning. His rate of fire would exhaust his ammunition in twenty seconds. He kept his thumbs down, lining his sights up on an enormous battlecruiser, ploughing a molten gouge into its flank as it approached.

Berry didn't see the blast, when it came.

It engulfed him noiselessly from behind, smashing his disintegrating gunship into the nearest battlecruiser like driftwood against a harbour wall, effortlessly gathering the waiting fleet and dashing it to melting ruins against inside of the closed portal.

HAZEL HAD BEGUN TO FEEL that her only role was to be inside other people's minds as they were snuffed out. Whenever it happened, it was as though part of her was torn out and extinguished with them. Each time, she grew more whittled down until terror and an excoriating sense of loss seemed to be all that was left.

Experiencing the twentieth shrieking death in as many seconds, something inside her snapped. Why the fuck were Dorrin and Zhelkar wasting her like this? She wasn't some semi-human message relay.

She was a *weapon*.

In a split second, her fleet was forgotten. Screaming, she flung her consciousness out into the void. Other minds around her were like shoals of luminous fish. Like a prowling shark, she homed in on the largest, densest clusters, sniffing, probing, orientating. Tasting and moving on until she'd found the prey she wanted.

She plunged into a fortress captain's head. No time for *finesse*: she watched through his eyes as he pulled out his sidearm and methodically pumped a dozen plasma bolts into his unsuspecting officers, saving the last charge for himself. She jolted as his death exploded inside her own skull. Seconds later, she'd found another captain. With a gesture, he shut down his warship's sensorium, leaving the bridge in darkness as he triggered the mutiny switch, knocking everyone the bridge unconscious within seconds.

Not nearly enough.

Straining every fibre, she found another captain. Discarded him. Leafed down through his subordinates until she found who she was looking for. Engineers, who suddenly believed a system incursion impelled them to override the safeties on their fortresses' main reactor. Fighter pilots who began arming and firing nuclear missiles while still in their launch tubes. She left them as alarms began to sound.

Still not enough.

Ignoring the screaming pain in of her head, she found another pair of fortress captains, flitting between the two as fast as neurons could fire. *The fleet's been compromised. Other ships have been sequestered and are launching counterattacks. Defend yourself!* She

380

watched from a nearby fortress as the first opened fire on the second, which responded in kind, filling the space between them with close-range flashes and streaks so densely that it was briefly as though they were connected by light.

More!

Not staying to watch the result, she made a *suggestion* to another Captain. *Infection. One way to stop it spreading. You know what to do.* She felt the captain's anguish as realisation dawned. Saw the terror of his officers as he produced his weapon and ordered a course change. The fortress's main drives blazed, and she watched through a dozen remote eyes as one compressed cube bore inexorably down on another. Officers on the bridge were charging the captain now, some falling, but enough remained to overwhelm him. *Too late.* There was a brief, futile flurry of thrusters and weapons fire before the moon-sized structures met, their shapes melting into each other until light consumed the combined structure, propelling its remains apart again.

Her mind came alive with terror. Reeling, she withdrew.

Shit. She felt dizzy. Sick. Remembering her own fleet, she cast about desperately.

Where in Amber's name was everyone?

For a terrible moment she wondered if she'd broken herself.

'Group five,' she pleaded, hoping against hope that she could find more survivors over the comms channel than she had telepathically. Communications returned unexpectedly with screams and cries for help. Wood was flying as though possessed by a demon. He had no thoughts that she could identify. Just calculation and rage. In the flickering light of explosions and burning spacecraft, his gaunt, sweating face and hard eyes seemed barely human. She wondered if she'd looked similar. 'Anyone! This is Hazel. Answer me!'

'Simone here!' The young woman's terrorised face appeared on a screen. 'I need backup – *I need backup!*'

Tink flashed up a positional marker. 'I've triangulated her. The Pukes will have too. Wood … *Oscar*'s outer hull is cracked.'

'Mend it!'

The shortest route lay through a battlecruiser. *Oscar*'s reputation had clearly spread: the warship lit up a drive plume a thousand kilometres long in its escape attempt, but the bullet got it anyway. It exploded behind in the rear-view screen in a maelstrom of armoured shrapnel.

Tink's statistical display estimated twenty-three fortresses, twenty-eight battlecruisers and thirty-five cruisers now crippled or destroyed. In every direction, space was a chaos of streaks, blooms, and flashes of light. Although there was still no sign of the dreaded missile ships, she could feel that Wood expected the invaders to recover their composure at any moment. They both knew that the Havenners had virtually nothing left to fight them with. Her ability was back, but she could find fewer Havenner contacts by the minute, their essence seeming to blow away into the ether like dust, often as she was inside them, leaving her feeling scattered and transparent. She was growing confused; numbed. Forgetting who she was.

She had a brief vision of a dark shape in a vast enclosed space. Then her mind was on fire.

Berry! She screamed.

Hazel? Wood's voice. She closed her eyes and wept. Debris deluged *Oscar*, dissolving in explosions of orange sparks around the furnaces. Approaching the indicated spot, Wood slowed *Oscar* violently. 'Where is she? Tink – I can't see her.' All that was visible was the revolving cylinder of some giant spacecraft's mangled exhaust tube. 'Sure this is it?'

'I'm sure!' At some point, Tink's speech had doubled in speed. Deliberately, Hazel hoped. 'The surviving fortresses are beginning to circle around us. Contacts are closing fast from intact parts of the IPEC fleet.'

She projected her tattered senses into the void. Quickly found what she was looking for. 'Missile ships,' she cried. 'Amber's light – two fortresses have their port doors open. You don't want to see how many fighters and missile ships they've just sent out.'

In her peripheral vision, Wood gnawed a knuckle.

We're here, she projected desperately. *Simone? Where are you?*

'ETA of nearest contacts, fourteen seconds!'

'I'm coming out,' shrieked Simone's voice. 'Catch me!'

The snout of a blackened type-22, minus its missiles and part of its side, edged out of the cylinder. 'Everyone's gone! But I got some – a fortress and a cruiser.'

'Hurry,' Wood hissed, teeth clenched. 'We've ten seconds. *Oscar*'s vulnerable facing this way!'

Accelerating abruptly, the oval ship grazed the tube's mouth, starting both the ship and the tube spinning. 'Tink – lasso! Simone, cut power.'

'Missiles incoming. Lasso engaged and firm. Impact seven seconds. Wood! WoodWoodWood!'

Wood? Fuck … WOOD!

Wood was already doing his best to ram the front of the thruster pedals through the floor. 'Tink, if you've any control over thrust limits, we need more, now.' G-forces rippled his face and stifled Hazel's breath. *If these are those little missiles,* he was thinking, *and they hit us up the thrust tube, we're fucked.* Simone's ship jigged in *Oscar*'s wake, lit brilliantly by the scorching trail spewing from the main thruster.

'THEY'RE COMING,' she screamed as she watched the closing blips on her HUD. Tink's cannon began deluging streaks of energised particles to either side of her cockpit blister. The detonation of missiles close behind was blinding her even reflected off the dirty, scarred hull in front.

The missiles were still accelerating, still closing. Simone couldn't breathe. Hazel could see a skyful of growing specks through the woman's eyes as she turned her head. Her damaged ship had been buffeted sideways-on. Stamping down her terror, she used her sole functional attitude thruster to spin it in into line with *Oscar*, then, with unnecessary force, rammed the throttle open. She closed her eyes and murmured to herself.

Attagirl Simone.

But they were never going to be fast enough. The initial speed of the approaching weapons was simply too great.

'Oh shit. Shit, fuck, shit, fuck, *shiiiit!*'

Wood's last thought before the missiles arrived was that he could have picked a better epitaph.

51

DECOY

WOOD McCORKINDALE OPENED HIS EYES.

The fleet had disappeared. In the rear view was a tiny crescent of light, almost a point. He stared with popping eyes at Hazel, then at Tink's animation.

'Tink, you *maniac*. Have you any idea what the odds were jumping so close to a planet?'

The AI indignantly brandished his sword. 'A lot better than if we'd got blown up.'

'Where are we? Is that still Haven's Gate?'

'A short jump lowered the risks. The reason ships don't usually make them is because of the cost.'

Wood shivered. He wasn't even sure why he was arguing when Tink had just saved their lives. Particularly given the skill the manoeuvre must have required. For a moment, he thought he might burst into tears. 'Simone – have we got Simone?'

'Still here,' yelled a voice on the comms relay. Wood pulled himself together. Then a paralysing thought dawned on him.

'Tink … ah, how long is it since we wormed in?'

'Twenty-six minutes, thirty-two seconds.'

It had seemed a small fraction of that. *Oh no.* His jaw slackened. 'The weapon … Troubleshooter. It should be here by now.' Hazel stared at him. 'How many IPEC ships here to start with?'

'Thirty-two fortresses, thirty-nine battlecruisers and sixty-three cruisers.'

That meant all major surviving ships from Terra Nova were accounted for. Yet the enemy fleet didn't seem to be following the patterns it had back then. Its behaviour didn't suggest to him that they were expecting another arrival. The fleet had simply sat there, not quite in orbit, neither advancing to mop up around the planet nor moving out of the way.

Perhaps a reduced fleet would have been too obvious?

Suddenly he was convinced that, whatever the lack of evidence, his instincts were right. 'Hazel,' he gasped, 'tell every org to get everyone who's left back to Haven. Hurry.' She wasn't following, perhaps unwilling to. Wood clawed his hands. 'Don't you see it yet?'

She didn't. Seeing the pain already in her eyes, he found that he could barely form the words.

This fleet is a decoy.

Blood drained from her face.

'I've told the nonorgs I can reach,' said Tink, looking resigned. 'I can find only twenty-one.'

A cavern seemed to open in Wood's stomach. 'We must get to Haven, with enough orgs to take *Oscar*.'

'There are barely enough left to take the other ships!' Hazel protested.

'Then some will have to stay.'

Her look of repulsion felt like a physical blow. 'No one else has the range to get back. You'll be leaving them to die!'

'Hazel,' he said, turning fiercely on her. 'The only thing which matters now is getting this ship – this *weapon* – back to Haven. Right now.'

A wild look entered her eye. 'How will we even reach the orgs? They can't reach us. Most will struggle to make even one last connection. We can't outmanoeuvre those small missiles – that last salvo almost finished us!'

Without waiting for discussion, Tink tore *Oscar* from its natural continuum and spat it almost instantly back into real space. Wood cringed. The vessel drifted among shifting nebulas of radiating debris unrecognisable as having been parts of spacecraft and living beings. Against the planet, lights were still flickering. An instantly recognisable presence bubbled up in Wood's mind.

'Tumbleweed?'

He concentrated on forming a response. *Joy at finding friend alive / urgent return to Haven at all costs / gather all friends for this purpose.*

The reply was weak, but positive. Then he made the mistake of inquiring what had happened to the artillery. Tumbleweed's involuntary reaction was to vomit its memory of kindred with whom it had been mentally connected being burned and ripped apart. It felt as though it was eating his mind.

'Wood, stop it!'

He realised dimly that he was attacking his own face. If a sharp object had been available, he'd have used it to stab himself until the pain stopped. 'I've contacted the surviving nonorgs,' said Tink's voice. 'They're all trying to get here.' He could feel Hazel wrestling his nearest arm down.

'Wood! Look at me.'

He was weeping uncontrollably. *How many can you take?* Hazel asked Tumbleweed, routing the query through Wood, visualising the action of group connection. She was trying to distract him.

Some of us are injured and all are exhausted. We can take Oscar *and eight small nonorgs.*

'Missiles, ETA two minutes,' urged Tink. 'I'm firing on them. There are four hundred and twenty and rising.' Explosions blossomed where pencils of light stabbed at their invisible targets. 'Many more are being launched from other parts of the fleet. More than three hundred missile ships are closing behind them.'

'Tell everyone to get into eight small ships, fast,' Wood ordered, recovering enough to speak. He felt Hazel squeeze his hand. 'Even hanging on outside – everyone should have pressure suits. Tell them we're leaving anyone else behind.'

Hazel turned on him. 'We're not leaving anyone.'

'We can come back for them later.'

'The missiles will get them!'

Wood scowled, dabbing at a face which was beginning to hurt, but didn't argue. *Oscar*'s array of screens showed damaged vessels approaching from all directions. Figures with emergency thruster packs were struggling frantically out of airlocks, leaving their ships to turn and speed suicidally towards the approaching horde, presumably on autopilot. 'No one comes in here,' he barked. 'I repeat, no one in *Oscar!* Everyone into the other craft.'

Wood? Hazel was looking at him. Her expression was strange. *Why?*

He ignored her, chewing his lip as he watched pressure-suited figures scramble in through the cramped airlocks of five remaining type-22s, or fumble to anchor themselves to the outside of three smaller type-24 gunships. Hazel seemed to have lost the will to object. Some of the Havenners were clearly panicking. Hit by unseen debris, one of the human shapes thrashed as it jetted a plume of air into space, held by two companions, one of whom was trying to bind the breach with their own suit's emergency sealing tape.

'There's room in here,' cried Simone's voice, composed and urgent now that there was positive action to take. 'Wood? Let me go! I'm still in *Oscar*'s lasso!'

Cursing, Wood turned the field off. He'd forgotten about Simone entirely. 'Twenty seconds.' He watched in frustration as suited figures jetted frantically towards her ship's airlock.

'Ten seconds.'

Wood could contain himself no longer. An extra couple of seconds was going to make little difference regarding who was going to survive. *Tumbleweed!*

'Everyone,' he bellowed aloud, 'hang on!'

The purplish haze formed about them with agonising slowness. Wood closed his eyes, unsure whether he was waiting for the obliteration of a nuclear blast or the sickening tug of the connection.

When it came, the tug was almost an anticlimax.

52

STARING DEATH IN THE FACE

CHILL AND CLEAR, the night smelled of wet vegetation. Dew coated grass with gems which shone in the starlight, dampening the sleeping bags scattered across the summit of Summertop like a plague of bright caterpillars.

Tidemaker had recently set, but Trene's veil was a ghostly substitute for the moon's reflected light. The air itself seemed iridescent, and more so every hour. Every few minutes, spikes of light would erupt from all around the horizon, reaching towards the stars, more like luminous tentacles than lightning. During these displays, areas of sky seemed to move, as though viewed through water. The outbursts had grown more energetic and unpredictable since their beginning a little over an hour ago.

Within zipped-together sleeping bags, Sander gently teased his fingers between Stephanie's moist hairs. Struggling not betray them, she let a gasp escape. Sander raised a finger to his lips. Fabric rustled nearby. Head turning, Sander could see Randal's eyes glinting in the starlight. Amidst the other sleeping bags, human shapes were huddled over nut-oil stoves, sharing hot drinks, and talking quietly.

Randal blinked, and rolled over to whisper something to Willow, who chuckled. Grimacing, Sander turned back to Stephanie, who shook her head at him, mouthing 'no!' Pulling down-filled fabric over their heads, he intensified his efforts, smothering her noises with his lips. She clutched at him and grunted – *far* too loud. Then they were lying together in a tangle of limbs, breathing heavily.

'*Everyone*'ll have heard that,' she whispered.

He replied with a kiss. She was about to cuff him when a murmur of voices began. Their tone made the two of them freeze. Someone said 'Up there – up there!'

Stephanie pulled the hoods of the bags back and they stared around the sky, wondering what the speaker had seen. No one spoke. There was no sound but the rumble of distant waterfalls, and not a breath of wind.

Towards the horizon, a small point of light appeared.

Then another.

An arc of space became spattered with little circles of light. They expanded and blossomed like opening flowers. Smaller lights flickered between them. Suddenly there was a brighter, lop-sided burst, spreading what resembled iridescent pseudopodia across several degrees of the sky.

The audience seemed to hold its breath.

'What's going on?' Sander whispered. 'Nothing's meant to happen until at least nine hours' time.'

A baby began crying. The distress spread, more and more young children joining in, instinctively aware that something was wrong.

The lights dimmed, fading as quickly as they'd come.

Seconds later, further lights began to blossom, in a slightly different location: fewer, but brighter and larger. One formed a curious star-shape, which revolved with increasing speed like a lopsided Catharine wheel. It didn't fade.

There were more bursts, spread chaotically across the sky and the seconds. It was clear now that a battle was taking place above the planet. The occupants of Summertop looked on, waiting in fear for what many already suspected was to follow.

When it came, the flash lit up the night as brightly as if the sun had risen. What the light source lacked in intensity it made up for in area, expanding in a ring from a point halfway between the zenith and the northern horizon, filling a quarter of the sky before it faded.

A communal gasp went up.

At the ring's origin was a white circle. It was similar in size to Tidemaker, but brighter. Almost at its centre was an empty ring like the pupil of a human eye.

Sander sat bolt upright, staring in silent horror as adults wailed or moaned, and children screamed and cried. Birds were screeching in their cages. In the distance, from all around, and from beneath, came a faint but growing rumble.

Haven *shivered.*

The ground lurched. Sander found himself on his back. There was a sensation of acceleration, and a rumbling roar. Then the meadow seemed to pull itself from under him, returning just as suddenly, slamming into his shoulders and head, tossing him against Stephanie inside their sleeping bags. There were blows to his face, legs, head and body until he was dazed, winded and utterly disoriented. On all sides was a clamour of confused terror.

He fought his way blindly out of the sleeping bag and struggled to stay face-down on the heaving ground, the fingers of his good hand clawed in the grass, limbs spread-eagled. Groping fingers met his. He pulled their owner towards him. The smell and feel were Stephanie's. Her weight was painfully across his arm. He didn't care.

There was a louder, closer roar. He dizzily lifted his eyes towards the sound. Eerily lit billowing clouds – billions of tons of avalanching snow and ice – were rushing down the flanks of the mountains to the east. In the meadows below Summertop, herds of vicuñas were stampeding, their movement mirroring the avalanches happening kilometres away.

Rolling on to his back, he found that he could sit, propped on splayed arms. The tremors were easing. All around, human shapes were struggling to hands and knees. He glimpsed further movement across the Juniper basin. Before his eyes, the face of Pearl Pyramid seemed to melt in slow motion. Running like liquid lead into the forest below it bulldozed a huge, dark swathe, smashing trees aside like toothpicks as it accelerated towards Juniper Lake.

The mirror-like lake had already been shattered into a dullness by the deep vibrations. Moving at improbable speeds, the rock side surged into it, displacing vast quantities of water. Sander could see the resulting tidal wave as a bright line spreading steadily across the lake. Growing indistinct as it negotiated deeper water of the northern lake, by the time it was amongst the islands and inlets neighbouring Juniper, it had regained its thickness. He imagined buildings smashed like toys along with the forest around them. It was the forest which really upset him. The town could be rebuilt within weeks. Some of the trees were three hundred years old.

The Professor? he thought suddenly, blood running cold. *Zhelkar and Dorrin?*

Well. At least we let the pumas go.

A wind was rising in gusts. His body ached from fighting against the bucking of the ground. He made himself look up at the bright circle again.

Not his imagination. It had grown.

He studied the sight in morbid fascination. It was like a monstrous, lidless eyeball, its stare utterly cold, impersonal and blank. Shark eyes, he recalled, had seemed like that. That's what it was: a diseased shark's eye. Sander had always imagined that he could stare death in the face.

He'd never reckoned on it staring back.

53

FOR A FRIEND

STARS SQUEEZED INTO VIEW, along with the blue-white sphere of Haven. It was dimmed now beneath a kind of transparent lilac skin. The twenty-eight human survivors of the raid on the IPEC fleet stared in horror.

Haven had two suns.

One seemed bright and welcoming. The other resembled a diseased eyeball. The sheer petrifying scale of the machine had been missing from the film they'd watched only twelve hours previously. Moaning and sobbing sounds swamped the communications relay.

Tink magnified a continent-sized part of its surface. Small specks could be seen moving over a landscape of vast polygons, spitting brilliant streaks at one of the darkly infilled areas, which spread beneath them like a vast city. Its surface was an organised arrangement of squat, dark towers and angled spikes.

Hazel gasped. 'Those look like –'

Brilliant beams speared from several of the spikes, and explosions appeared like flowers against the weapon's more subdued background glow.

'Defenceless?' Wood rubbed his face, once more on the brink of panic. 'Tink – quick, I need an analysis of what's happening here.'

Tink's avatar had its telescope out. 'I can't tell exactly because most of our sensors are gone. I can see … five IPEC fortresses and six battlecruisers, fifteen cruisers. Two hundred and ten visible smaller craft. From the debris, I think there were originally six fortresses … nine battlecruisers. At least three of the fortresses must have been carriers.

'Of Haven's defence force, I can make out twenty orgs …' there was a tiny flash. 'Nineteen orgs. Fifteen intact nonorgs: seven Type-24s, three Type-22s, five cruisers. Now four

392

cruisers.' Wood felt dizzy. This was barely ten percent of the defence fleet. 'I don't think the survivors have any missiles left.'

'No!' The face of the woman Wood had come to love was that of a tormented ghost. He found his mind working with terrible clarity.

'With all those little ships outside the fortresses … we probably used up our missiles before we even got a shot at that thing.' He bit his lip. 'You were right, Hazel. We've been badly out-thought.'

He could find no sign that she'd heard. Her eyes were glazed. She was shivering.

'A fortress hit another cruiser,' Tink said. 'It's making for Haven Station.' A magnification showed a dark cube bearing down on the toy cartwheel. 'That Troubleshooter thing is moving steadily closer. They're having a rough time on Haven. There's coastal flooding and widespread seismic, volcanic and tidal activity.'

A web of light joined the scoop in the side of the Fortress with the serenely rotating space station. It parted into halves which spiralled lazily away from each other before further beams shattered them into fragments. 'They're not using nukes,' Hazel breathed. 'Why aren't they using nukes?'

'Must have been one hell of a battle here,' observed Tink. 'Haven's lost two more cruisers and a type-22.'

'Hazel, I think they aren't using nukes because they don't need to any more.'

She clasped hands over her face. 'Extrapolating from the previous attack,' Tink told them, 'the weapon should fire in around fifteen minutes.'

Hazel's eyes were locked on to the wreckage of Haven Station. 'There has to be *something* we can do.'

Wood stared at her. He felt strangely calm now that he knew what had to be done, that there was simply no alternative – but a terrible empty feeling still welled up in him. He ached to take her aside; to try and explain. To be close to her, just for one final moment truly together.

'Tink.' He swallowed. 'It's that moment we talked about.'

No reply.

'You still hold by what you said?'

'We've sustained structural damage. I'm mending it, but we can't fight it out and expect to survive.'

'Tink. I … I'm so sorry that it's worked out like this.' He studied the console, not really seeing it. 'We could boost our speed by a slingshot around Haven. I'll need calculations.'

Back turned, Tink's avatar tucked its skirt-like battledress beneath itself and sat cross-legged in the grass, gazing at a mountainous horizon. 'The trajectories are on the screen.'

Wood shut his eyes. He breathed out hard.

'Simone,' he said in a shaky voice. 'Good luck.' The sound of sobbing ceased.

'What are you going to do?'

Pulling back the joystick, Wood, much to his own surprise, laughed. 'We're off to explore the full capabilities of *Oscar*.'

SIMONE LOOKED ON with eyes empty of hope as *Oscar* whirled around, looming above her ship like a balletic mountain.

From its cavernous thruster a blade of light cleaved the blackness. The twin globes shone with fury, and, in a blur of improbable acceleration, it was gone, leaving only a rod-like ghost of excited particles where space in its wake had been so rudely abused.

'What are they doing?' The small cabin was crammed now with six other pressure-suited survivors. Behind Simone was an angular young man called Tyne. From his monotone, he could have been asking purely to make conversation. 'Do you think they're escaping?'

Simone turned in her seat to glare at him.

'That's Hazel, and Wood and *Tink*,' she declared hotly. 'I don't know what they're doing, but they're not running away, I can tell you that!'

'WE'RE HEADED in the wrong direction,' Hazel complained, squinting against the discomfort of the acceleration and the renewed pain in her head. She wasn't saying, but Wood knew the thought had struck her that he was taking them AWOL.

He visualised an explanation. Then he remembered that she was telepathically blind. 'We need a run-up. We need speed. Lots of it. That means using Haven as a gravitational slingshot.'

Hazel nodded, eyes widening as the implications sank in. She massaged her brow. 'Will it work?'

He bobbed his head. 'I *think* so.' Haven and Troubleshooter were already shrinking disks in the rear screen. He turned to Tink. 'How soon will we need to decelerate?'

'We can reach point-zero-five of C if we brake now,' said Tink. 'Of course, we'll burn out the thruster, but I imagine we're not too worried about that? Don't worry – I'm on it.'

Wood felt the pedals rise beneath his feet. He looked at his hands as though he'd never seen them before. 'Tink … my hands are shaking.'

'I'll take care of it,' the AI told him, quietly. Wood studied the avatar on the centre screen. A dapper captain's uniform had replaced the battle-soiled archaic dress. A primitive bucket-seat appeared, a joystick sprouting into the captain's hand as he sank into it. Tink turned, nodding.

'Trust me.'

I do trust you, Tink. More than you'll ever know. Wood felt his fingers uncurl reluctantly from the joystick. 'If that speed's not fast enough,' he ventured, 'I don't think any more would make much of a difference.'

The stars revolved until the bright dots of Haven and its unwelcome companion swung back into view. Deceleration slammed on, making the cabin's human occupants gasp for breath. Shifting one past the other, the distant circles shrank gradually to points, then expanded to become circles once more.

'Tink, we can't just hit a field. And we must try to make sure that whatever escapes from that thing when we hit it won't fry Haven. I thought … maybe the edge of the lens? That way, we might at least prevent it from firing.'

The dots grew steadily into spheres. Wood turned to Hazel and smiled. Her inky eyes flicked briefly green as she glanced back at him.

'Will we …? I mean is … are we going to …?'

'Make it?' Straining against the acceleration, Wood reached over and took her hand in his. He hesitated. 'Well … I think this is kind of going to be … your textbook case of unstoppable force meets immovable barrier.'

'Woody …' She managed a rueful smile. 'You know, I think that's the first time I've known you not to answer a question directly.' Haven and Troubleshooter were growing rapidly now. 'Wish it didn't have to be like this.'

'Can't argue with that,' he said, with feeling. 'But part of me can't help thinking this is simply events finally catching up with us.' His smile broadened. 'I've been thinking about this a lot. Haven, the three of us – we've all been living on borrowed time, one way or another. Besides, wasn't it you who told me recently that life shouldn't be wasted?'

His look hardened.

'Ours won't. We're going to punch a hole bigger than a *city* in that monstrosity. And when we do –'

He squeezed her hand.

There was silence then, but for the thruster's rumble. Haven grew visibly with each passing second. As Troubleshooter slipped behind it, the edge of Carolsland could just be picked out beneath coastal clouds. Wood wondered if he'd be able to see Juniper Lake. He squinted, but the speed of their approach was disorientating, so he stared instead at clouds like fish-scales. Hazel smiled at him. This time her eyes were deep green. She clenched his hand firmly, thumb stroking his palm.

I love you. Forever.

Wood returned her gaze, hoping his smile would say what words couldn't. He looked in the direction of Tink's interface screen. Again, words would not come. He hoped that Tink would understand.

There was an unexpected noise from behind.

Wood struggled to turn. He found metal tentacles sliding over his shoulder. Staring down, he watched helplessly as the manipulators at their tips cut through his harness.

What …?

He gaped at Hazel. One of *Oscar*'s drones was plucking her from her seat.

'What's happening?' he managed before he felt himself wrenched towards the ceiling. A bone gave way somewhere as the G-forces of *Oscar*'s acceleration ground him into the machine's hard tentacles. He got his eyes to swivel in the direction of the main screen. Tink's avatar was standing with its hands at its back. Its shades were off, its unnaturally green eyes focussed on his.

It raised a hand in what looked like a wave.

'Tink,' he pleaded, 'please, what are you doing?'

'Goodbye, Wood,' said Tink's disembodied voice as he was carried down the corridor. The drone was using its flotation field to damp some of the acceleration or he'd have been a bag of bone fragments by now. Beyond his knees he could see Hazel struggling against the G-forces and her own drone's overwhelming grip. 'You taught me so much.' The voice seemed to follow him like a ghost. Was it coming from the drone? 'You taught me everything important that I know. I see how happy it makes you, being with Hazel. I know that our time together was coming to an end – if not today, then soon. That's why I won't allow either of you to die when I can do this by myself.

'All I ask is that you remember what I was.'

The lights on the ceiling were a blur. The drone was moving *fast*. Within seconds Wood recognised the junction of the internal corridors with the main airlock. He wanted more than anything to argue, to make his friend see sense, but at the moment he simply had no cogent argument.

A door irised open. It was the door to one of the new escape pods.

'No,' he slurred, managing little more than twitches as the drone slid through the door, activated the smartfoam anti-G harness and held his hands down when he tried to escape. Swearing violently, Hazel received similar treatment. 'Don't do this!' Wood protested, tears blinding him. 'No, please, Tink, don't – *think* for a moment. Let me help, we agreed, remember? We agreed it'd be us, that we'd do this together. You and me. That's what we agreed! *You don't have to do this.*'

The door hissed shut. Instantly, there was a surge of entirely undamped acceleration, and then a glimpse of *Oscar*'s blackened, cratered hull and blinding thruster torch, followed by stars.

'*TINK!*'

HAVEN SLID SILENTLY BY. In profile at the edge of night's speeding terminator, plumes of what Tink now understood to be volcanic smoke and ash merged with the wisps and swirls of weather systems. Troubleshooter rose, higher and ever larger over the horizon through intensifying flashes of debris turning into energy against *Oscar*'s shields.

Soundlessly, with every remaining sensor focused on the immense machine ahead, Tink screamed.

He couldn't remember screaming before. Not like this.

It felt *good*.

There was so much more he'd hoped to experience before ceasing to exist. He'd wanted to travel the galaxy, exploring, with Wood protected in his belly.

He understood now that that had been a fantasy. Wood needed others of his kind, and he would, quite soon in the scheme of things, become frail and then die. Haven had been astonishing, a revelation – but it was just a taster. What other strange wonders awaited, out in the infinite void?

Perhaps uniquely amongst sentient beings, he'd been born as part of the perfect vehicle in which to undertake such a journey. For the first time in his brief life, *Oscar* felt not simply like a container – it felt like a physical extension of his mind.

He didn't want all of this to end. He was barely getting started. Surely his destiny had to involve being more than a weapon targeting system because one group of foolish humans feared what they didn't understand?

Life, Tink had long ago decided, had nothing fair about it.

'WHAT IS *THAT?*'

Simone studied the blip on the screen. The speaker was Tyne. He was leaning over her shoulder, frowning.

She had absolutely no idea. 'Whatever it is, it's going impossibly fast. I don't think I've ever seen anything move that fast.'

'Is it a meteor?'

She could feel the atmosphere in the cramped cabin shift from despair to one of tension. She gave the boy what her mother would have called an 'old-fashioned' look. 'It has particle trail of over five hundred thousand degrees Kelvin, Tyne. And it's accelerating. Great mother – have you *seen* how fast it's accelerating?'

Suddenly it all made sense.

'It's them,' she exploded as the object vanished against Haven's bright clouds. '*Oscar* – it *has* to be! If it uses Haven for a slingshot, its trajectory will take it straight towards the Weapon!'

A hush descended, broken only by the rustle of interference on the communications relay, caused by radiation from the planet-sized weapon and distant IPEC jamming signals.

'Look,' cried a male voice towards the rear of the cabin. 'Against the night side.'

Simone squinted against the glare of the clouds and quickly saw what the younger man had. Against the planet's dusky darker side was a rapidly extending streak of fierce light, its tip haloed in flashes, like a sparkler.

As her ship's occupants watched in silence, the streak extended ever faster; curving visibly, becoming more and more intense, the flashes around it increasing until its tip was like light reflected from a diamond. Outshining the sullen glow of the caged star, it lanced inexorably towards the pupil of the lidless eye like a surgeon's laser.

There was a prick of light at the edge of the dark-ringed pupil as the streak joined it.

Faintly at first, then with growing conviction, concentric ripples spread with mesmerising slowness from the point of impact across the landscape of bright fields and dark borders. At their centre, a brilliant white bulge began to grow, like a time-lapse film of a fungal fruiting body.

The bulge extended into a finger. Then a fat beam of light burst out of it, raking into the darkness.

A cheer went up in Simone's Type-22, but its occupants became sober as they watched the drama unfold. The hole grew as the star began to burst free, venting energy in long-frustrated fury. Superheated hydrogen and plasma ripped in spasms along chains of failing fields, which hurled intensifying shafts and curtains of star-matter tens of thousands of kilometres into space.

'The first explosion,' said a worried voice. 'It's going to hit Haven.'

The silence deepened as the tongue of stellar flame licked towards their planet.

54

FATE

NINE HUNDRED AND EIGHTY-TWO women, men and children lay flat on the grass of Summertop.

Those not cowering under sleeping bags, singing songs in strained little chorus lines, or attempting to comfort children no less terrified than themselves, were hypnotised by the nightmarish eye gazing back through the increasingly opaque atmosphere. A gusty wind had arisen. The heaving of the ground had at least subsided, although a rumbling background tremor remained.

To the west, the clouds were lit orange where the Rock Thunder Range spewed their molten foundations from new vents and fissures. The air reeked of sulphur and burning wood.

Randal raised himself to his knees and peered down the slope to where Juniper lay. He could see the fire-front as an orange arc eating through the trees, billowing smoke into the half-lit sky. He wondered whether Dorrin, Zhelkar and the Professor could possibly still be alive.

He felt hands on his shoulders. *Willow's*. Whether they were there for moral or physical support or comfort, he couldn't tell. 'How long? 'Til Haven does whatever it's going to do.'

He studied his watch. 'I don't think we're going to make it, Will.'

There was another tremor. Randal lay down again, gathering one arm behind his partner's head. Raising herself on to an elbow, she smiled at him sadly. *Love you*, she mouthed.

'Hold that thought,' he whispered, and leaned up to kiss her. A frantic cry went up.

'It's firing, it's firing!'

He let his lips linger on his partner's. He could see the world brighten through his eyelids. *Must be worse ways to die*, he thought to himself.

But it wasn't that kind of brightness.

Reluctantly, he looked up. Squinting through his eyelashes, he could discern a painfully bright area spreading ahead of the white orb. It grew bigger and more intense as he watched until on Summertop it was brighter than day, and he had to look away.

He found himself frowning. The light area had looked lopsided. Half the lens was faintly visible around the edge of it.

He stood up, hands raised. 'EVERYBODY KEEP CALM,' he bellowed. 'I don't think it's firing. I don't think that's what happening at all. Stay calm!'

Willow rose beside him. A hush had descended. One by one, others were rising to their feet, squinting at the sky between their fingers. She slipped an arm around his waist.

'You're right,' she said. 'If that was their laser, surely we'd be looking almost down its middle?'

The southern sky was alive with golden light. Smears of reds and greens, bright enough to be visible in the false almost-daylight, were forming in the darker hemisphere to the east. They were joined by shimmering curtains, flickering ripples and pulsing searchlights. Different shades and colours flashed like lightning until the entire sky seemed to be dancing.

'An aurora.' Stephanie's voice, from the ground to Randal's rear. 'Particles bombarding the magnetosphere!'

'By the Earth Mother,' exclaimed Sander, 'don't you all see what this means? I think they've done it!' He was at Randal's side, waving his arms. 'Debris from that thing is raining on Haven's magnetic field! I think there's a hole to one side of the lens and its guts are squirting out.'

'Sander,' urged Stephanie as she rose beside him. 'You might need to tone it down. We don't *know* what's happening.'

'Well, Randal and I could be wrong.' He cocked his head. 'But I don't think so, Steph!' Seizing her hands, he jumped and skipped around her, stamping on someone's arm.

'Oi! Steady on!'

'I can feel it! I feel it in my bones! We've made it Steph, we've *made* it!'

Stephanie glanced at Randal. Shrugging, he turned back to Sander with a cautious smile.

'You may be right, young man. But please, don't get everyone's hopes up just yet. We don't know what's happened to their fleet. It'd only take a few nukes, or a repeat of the Purges. And besides –' his smile vanished. 'That thing will have shifted our orbit significantly. We could be headed for deep space for all we know. And you think our troubles are over *before* whatever this stunt is that Haven's about to pull?'

THE SMASHED SPHERE was clearly accelerating away now, powered by its own destruction, jetting away from its intended target like a luminous squid. It had rotated sufficiently to reveal a smaller, but rapidly expanding hole on the face opposite to where the lens had been.

'Any signs of life out there?' asked Tyne anxiously.

'*Oscar*?' Simone desperately requested another scan and studied at the display. She shook her head. 'Nothing. Vast amounts of debris.'

There was a gloomy silence. 'What do we do now?'

She bared her teeth. 'We still have the rest of their fleet to contend with. They seemed to go to pieces a little when their weapon burst open, but they're regrouping fast.' She indicated the blips on her display. 'They could likely erase much of Haven's surface without that star-thing's help.' Her shoulders slumped. 'Looks like we're going to have to fight them.'

Tyne gave her a look of disbelief. 'With what? Our *hands?*'

'With whatever we've got.'

He slumped against the bulkhead. 'Stars and fate, Simone. I can't do that again.' His lip was trembling. 'I just can't!'

Her attention was recaptured by her display. Something was happening amongst the invading fleet. The remaining fortresses, which had formed a conspiratorial knot, had all fired up their main thrusters.

'Oh no. Here we go. Looks like we've really pissed them off.' She frowned. 'Wait a minute …'

They weren't moving in the direction she'd expected. Expecting some tactical ploy, she summoned trajectory projections. The others were crowding round now, attempting to peer over her shoulder at the HUD. Bright flashes were peppering space around the fleet. Vector plots appeared. They were headed away both from the planet, and each other.

'I don't believe it. I *think* the raccoon-shits are about to twist back into hyperspace.' They were fleeing for safe jump points as fast as their thrusters could carry them.

'You're sure?' The voice was Tyne's.

'Absolutely. Unless this is some improbably convoluted trick, the Pukes are running away!'

There were expressions of relief from further back in the cabin. Simone joined them. She supposed she should have felt elated despite everything they'd lost. Instead, she just felt physically and mentally drained. A need for alcohol struck her, so urgent that it was almost pain. She would drink herself into comfortable oblivion and wake up tomorrow to a hangover, an embarrassing bed companion and an argument with Fallin.

The relay crackled. 'Did you see that? Did you *get* all that?' The voice was one she didn't recognise. It was tripping over itself with excitement.

'We sure did.'

There was a pause. 'What do we do now? I've still got guys hanging off my outside. We're ferrying recharged oxygen packs through the airlock, but we can't keep this up. These suits aren't designed for extended space use, and there's debris and radiation everywhere.'

'Group together and get everyone inside a ship,' Simone said wearily. 'Then get down on to Haven and wait. It'll be a nightmare with all that debris. The high- and mid-latitudes should be safest. Spread word that everyone's to take utmost care.'

She slumped back into her seat. Then, of its own accord, a smile stole across her face.

'You know … I think we just might have made it.'

THE SKY WAS STILL ALIVE with leaping and flickering colours, but the great glowing ball had shrunk into the distance, spewing shifting fans and splashes of light as, one by one, the confining fields lost their grip. A cheer went up as the first finned oval shape dropped from the sky on pillars of blue flame and landed, scarred and battered almost beyond recognition, in the meadows below Summertop. The crowd ran down the hill towards it. As the first arrived, the airlock hissed open.

Simone Morningdew stepped stiffly down the extended steps. She jumped the last two on to the close-cropped meadow grass and smiled. As more pressure-suited figures piled through the door behind her and further shapes began dropping from the sky, she collapsed on to her knees, grabbed fistfuls of grass, and wept.

RANDAL STOOD APART from the gathering, gazing over the survivors of the interception and defence fleets. They were being bundled into blankets and sleeping bags and given mugs of hot soup and antiradiation pills.

Some were reliving their experiences to rapt audiences. Others were introspective, haunted eyes focussed on nothing in particular. There were no injuries amongst the human survivors – physical ones, at least. Wounds were unlikely without catastrophic damage to either vessels or pressure suits, and the only such casualty hadn't outlived her companions' attempts to patch the tear in her suit. Every surviving org had suffered burns and shrapnel wounds. Three were going to die. A small team was busy administering injections to exposed interior veins and removing shrapnel as best they could.

Approaching her partner, Willow slipped a hand over his shoulder. She felt his arm go reflexively about her waist. It was clear from his stare that he was preoccupied.

'We've ten volunteers, Ran,' she ventured. 'Sooner we leave, more likely it is someone'll still be alive down there.' Her gaze turned down the hill towards the smouldering Juniper basin.

He grunted. 'About as likely as a snowball on the Coral Coast.'

'I know we've lost a lot, love. But we're through it now. The worst is over.'

'Is it? You sure about that?' Hands at his hips now, he looked behind her towards the lake. 'I was speaking to one of the survivors – young lad called Tyne. We all wondered what Troubleshooter was doing showing up here so quickly. Seems a decoy fleet was waiting for our interception group at Haven's Gate. *In addition* to the one which met us here. Larger too. Young Tyne says half of it was left when our interceptors made their timely return. Everyone seems to have forgotten about it.'

Willow waited for the shock to hit her. She'd had so many in the past few days that she felt numbed to them. 'Ran, no – they wouldn't come straight here? Not straight away.' Randal raised a palm.

'And why in Amber's name not? Surely this is *exactly* when they'd come? We're defenceless now.'

She looked away. Strange clouds were low on the horizon, obscuring the Celestial Spears, or what remained of them. They looked like cauliflowers. Snow avalanches? Even if Haven survived this, she doubted that either the planet or its inhabitants would ever be the same.

'You're right,' she said, firmly, looking up into Randal's eyes. 'Everyone's given all they can. They've had enough. We *all* have. So, help me attend to the needs of the living instead of worrying about what's beyond our control. It's all up to fate and Haven now.'

55

JUST GONE

'WE'LL BE EXITING hyperspace in a little more than a minute, sir.'

Captain Simón Lorimer nodded, distractedly observing the intense concentration of his dependable number one in a screen to one side of his sensorium. 'Thank you, Lamar.'

The commander faded against the background of the tactical display. Lorimer looked at his feet, surprised to find himself standing. He should be sat at his post as well. No sense exhausting himself. The events of twelve hours ago had left him more than a little dazed.

More than half the fleet.

He still couldn't believe it. The way they'd been ambushed should have been impossible. The narrative of space warfare was based on the communications being limited to the speed of travel through hyperspace. An enemy warned of an invasion had two options: await the invasion and defend key assets directly or commit to an interception which would find a prepared enemy either long departed or lying in wait. Either way, the advantage lay with the invader. Other than extraordinary luck, the only way to achieve what the enemy had would have been near-instantaneous travel.

Which, clearly, was impossible

Even given the enemy's ambush, the battle should have been a walkover for the Navy. The Freak fleet had been greatly outnumbered. No, he was being euphemistic. The fleet had been *insignificant*. Yet he'd watched nine fortresses spewing their innards into space with no sign they'd even been fired at. Then there had been that … *thing*, which had punched like an impossible bullet through everything it met, seeming to eat the fleet's most advanced smart nukes as though they were fusion fodder. And the unexplained reports of COs going mad, killing their own officers, causing ships to collide. COs including Fleet Admiral Grisham himself …

Lorimer suspected there was a great deal about the enemy which the admiralty had kept to themselves. If so, history had revealed them to be highly ill advised.

He took a breath and held it. This was no way for a fleet admiral to be thinking. Unfortunately, his involuntary promotion twenty hours ago had left scant time for him to adjust to the responsibility, not to mention the degree of coordination necessary. The rank he'd dreamed of since boyhood felt like a dead weight. 'Alert the fleet to battle readiness,' he barked. 'Nukes primed, all weapons systems activated. Missile ships and fighters ready. Launch them and the virus bombs the second we hit truespace.'

'How many, sir?'

'Every fucking one of them.'

He would not allow what remained of the fleet to be caught out like that again. This time the full arsenal would be deployed before the Freaks could even think of using their mysterious weapons on the carriers. He marched back to his zero-G seat and once more was plunged into the VR tactical map of the fleet.

'Exiting,' yapped his number one.

Lorimer braced himself for the kick, not enjoying it when it came. Icons representing smaller vessels began pouring from the cubes representing the carriers, too thickly to differentiate.

After a few seconds, there were muted cries from around the command centre, first of perplexity and then alarm. Frowning, he used eye motions to summon a window containing a 3D view from the Fortress's exterior, expanding it until it completely enveloped his disembodied senses.

'Purge bombs away, Sir.'

'How many nukes available?'

Seven thousand, eight hundred and twenty-one, sir.'

'Launch half. Let them acquire while hot if they need to.' There was a confused silence.

'Sir – Nervecentral's found nothing to launch them *at*.'

That wasn't all. 'This system wasn't supposed to be a binary was it?' Two suns – one orange-yellow, and one whiter, around a tenth of the diameter, and surrounded by a ghostly halo – hung against a background of more distant stars.

Lorimer was getting a sinking feeling about all this. He studied his display of superimposed graphical and digital information. 'Belay that last order. Are we working with the wrong coordinates?' His confusion deepened as he saw that the smaller star was moving directly away from the larger one. Too rapidly to make immediate sense.

'Sir ... I'm afraid there's nothing here for the Purge bombs to home in on either.'

It had been a long two days and Lorimer was not at his best. 'What in the name of almighty fuck is going on here?' he demanded. 'Where's the damned planet? Where's Troubleshooter? If this isn't the system, then what's all that debris we're seeing?'

There were sounds of an excited exchange.

'Sir ...' Lamarra's voice, uncharacteristically hesitant. 'We ... I'm afraid Nervecentral suggests that ... this definitely is the system. It suggests that ... ah, the smaller star *is* Troubleshooter.'

Admiral Simon Lorimer stared incredulously. 'That's impossible. And anyway, if that was the case, then where the hell's the planet?'

'I don't know, sir, I just don't know.' Lamarra sounded deeply shaken. 'I can't explain it. Neither can Nervecentral. This is the system, beyond a shadow of doubt. There's no rocky debris. The planet's simply ... not *here*.'

'Exit flash detected,' barked a different voice 'A very small one.'

'Identify.'

Communications Officer Lieutenant Gomez dropped into Lorimer's sensorium. 'Someone on tight-beam sir. Claims he's ... Commodore Aral Nikumi of the Dive-and-Rule class *Violator*. He's asking if we'll talk to him now.'

Lorimer took a very long, deep breath and closed his eyes. When he opened them, he was looking at a magnification of a tiny, angular spacecraft, decorated with colourful representations of fantastical creatures. Almost half of the central hull was blackened or missing.

'Put him on.'

'VISITOR FOR YOU, JAMES.'

'I'm not expecting anyone. What the hell do I pay you for? Hello? Are you even listening to me?'

'You'll want take this visitor, James. She has … how can I put this? A very compelling reason.'

'Are you on meds? You're my fucking secretary! Handle this.'

'She's coming in.'

The mahogany doors parted.

The movement took James Marcell by surprise. He rose from his chair, scowling furiously as a familiar smartly suited figure sidled towards him, perched on heels which came to dagger-like points and had to be twenty centimetres long. His first thought was annoyance that they might damage his floor.

He glanced at the hidden screen array beneath the surface of his desk. Diamond, his new secretary, was filing her nails. Reliable old Silver was apparently responding gradually to treatment under her healthcare plan in one of Unicorp's more prestigious mental hospitals.

'I don't recall inviting you in here,' he breathed towards the intruder, with less menace and a lot more anger than he'd have liked.

Jeannette Hiyu seated herself in the soft chair opposite Marcell. She crossed her legs with – the affrontery! – her wicked heels parked up on the edge of his desk, interlocking her hands on one thigh.

'You set me up,' she declared.

Marcell looked down on the woman, feeling no need whatsoever to explain himself.

'You had Satan working for you all the time. My little operation was a ruse to pressure Fox into leaving Renascido. Publicly, I was to be blamed for its failure.' She raised one eyebrow. 'Potential competition was I, James?'

Her tone was pleasant. Coquettish, even. Marcell remained standing, considering sending the signal which would cut Hiyu in half with a laser. Lasers were unarguably primitive, but there was something uniquely satisfying about observing another person's slow realisation that they'd just been surgically made pleural.

He decided to humour her for a while.

'I took the liberty of commissioning research of my own, James,' she told him. 'Quite a jigsaw puzzle. I must confess, I was amazed at what I found. A fascinating, not to say unique, history. An enviable set of achievements. Even for a five hundred-year-old.'

Sighing, Jeannette spread her hand, examining beautifully presented nails the colour of blood.

'Even so, don't you think it's time to let youth take over? I mean, you are *considerably* more than pensionable age.' She grinned insufferably, looking past Marcell at where he knew the horizon of Renascido lay, as though he was of little consequence. 'The board aren't too impressed with you lately, all considered. I think they feel it's time for a change.'

Marcell's blood began pumping just a little faster, but he concealed his tension, seating himself again. 'And who do they feel should take my place? *You?* A tomboy squirt like you?'

'Tomboy?' She flexed her extravagant footwear, making the plastic creak. 'James,' she purred, 'as well as terribly out of touch, that's beneath you. Besides, it's really not the point, is it?

'No, the *real* point is that because of your botch of the Haven episode – yours and that Hussain character you're in cahoots with – the economy has collapsed.' She returned her feet to the floor and leaned forwards. '*The entire transworld economy*, James. I can't find a figure in history who's presided over such a clusterfuck. IPEC faces fragmentation, and Unicorp faces a seriously long haul if the company is even to *survive*. Can you imagine what our shares will be worth if the public get even a sniff of our role in this fiasco? All because of your grandiosity. Your pet Troubleshooter project cost us a fortune, and what have we to show for it? The Lancers are operating with impunity in confederation space. You gave them our most productive worlds on a plate – and you think they'll just stop with what they have now?' She tossed up a hand. 'Jesus wept. They could be in orbit around Renascido before we know it.

'Then there's this fascinating tale of the Purges which is all over the Grid, now that parts of it are running again. Beautifully presented, very entertaining – it's the only entertainment some people have had for tendays. There can't be many who haven't accessed it by now, and it's seriously undermining confidence in the system. Intelligent people are predicting revolution. A revolution – are you hearing this?' She shook her head in apparent disbelief. 'The board thinks you've lost touch, James. Overreaching yourself in your dotage.'

This really was poisonous, thought Marcell. The board had enthusiastically supported him through the good times only to turn against him the moment things got rough. It was he who'd put that pack of hyenas where they were. It was he, James Marcell, who'd built everything they now took for-granted, without help from anyone.

'It's not that we're ungrateful,' crowed Hiyu, as if reading his thoughts. 'There's been much to be thankful for. As well as your failures, some of your achievements will be duly acknowledged.' Her eyes flashed. 'Posthumously.'

He leaned forward, confronting her with a stare which, even now, Hiyu found difficult to meet. 'One of the first thing *survivors* learn, Jeannette, is not to cross me.' He allowed his smile to vanish. 'I never took you for this stupid.'

Hiyu studied the ceiling. As an impression of brass-necked nonchalance, it was convincing. 'No, not many who crossed you are still around, are they, Jim? I suppose I should be thankful you considered me …' she pursed her lips, 'useful.'

As she returned her gaze to his and held it, her hand delved slowly, almost seductively, inside the lapel of her suit.

So here it comes.

Marcell concentrated.

Nothing.

He experienced a spurt of alarm. The circuitry in his head was not behaving. As his eyes followed the hand's slow withdrawal, he felt something for the first time he could remember.

Fear.

It quickly bordered on panic. He concentrated again, willing his implants to send the signal.

Still nothing. According to his display, the signal was being sent. It just wasn't being acted upon.

His eyes flicked towards the desk drawer. He darted a hand towards it but froze as he found himself looking down the flared muzzle of the surprisingly chunky handgun Hiyu was now holding across the desk.

His hand withdrew. Heart pounding, he interlocked his fingers on the desktop, still desperately trying to activate his office's defence system.

'Problems?' enquired Jeannette. 'Funny old thing, technology.' She smiled with a cockiness which made Marcell's blood seethe. 'We rely on it for everything we do – from running cities, planets, empires even, to breathing, reproducing and taking a shit. But when it comes down to it, the more levels and depths of complexity there are, the easier it is to bring the whole lot crashing down. Fox should have taught you that.

'I'm a believer in simplicity myself. Why do something in a complicated way when simple does it equally well? Eh Jim? Hence this.' She caressed the muzzle of the weapon which, Marcell was beginning to realise, might well dictate the duration of his remaining life.

'You can't do this,' he snarled, leaning forwards on his knuckles. 'Snivelling upstart bitch! You can't hope to get away with it.'

Hiyu just laughed, and then smiled her coldest of crocodile smiles. 'Sorry James.' She paused, as if a thought had just struck her. 'Before I do this, I just want you to know that I have the full approval of the board. This isn't personal. It's official company policy.'

Marcell felt his jaw slacken.

ENERGY FIZZED from the mouth of Jeannette's weapon. It smashed a hole the size of a dinner plate through Marcell's chest, right through the back of his antique chair so that, to her curious amazement, she could see the wall beyond it, blackened with soot and charred tissues and peppered with brighter shards of bone and wood.

With the support of his spine gone, Marcell's head pitched on to the desk with a thump, his hands pawing the polished mahogany for perhaps a minute before tensing into stillness. Pressed sideways against the leather top, his face wore an expression of worry and self-pity.

Jeannette rose to the desk and bent down, peering into his dimming eyes. She lifted his head by the hair and let it fall with a thud to the desk.

'Self-obsessed little man. Office? Open a window for me at floor level.'

A square hole appeared in the window-wall, picked out in glowing red hairlines. Grasping Marcell's ankles, Jeannette dragged him from his chair and across the crimson carpet, leaving a glistening trail. She found herself surprised at how light and small the man felt.

She placed the body beside the hole, then pushed it against the selectively permeable field which prevented the room depressurising. The head and shoulders flopped limply outside. Then, with a final shove, the body was gone, tumbling and fluttering towards the clouds until it was lost in the distance below.

Hands on hips, Hiyu surveyed the office.

There would need to be changes – for starters, that imbecilic cathedral-like ceiling would need replacing ASAP – but overall, she decided, with a little softening and a splash of colour, she might grow to like it.

She returned to the desk. Sat back in Marcell's ruined, still-smoking chair and grinned. The thrill she felt was intoxicating.

She found her hands lifting back the elastic hem of her skirt.

And why not? I can do anything.

Parting herself, she tilted her hips upwards, legs spread against the edge of the desk – *her* desk – working her fingertips in intensifying little strokes and circles, dizzy with the exhilaration of it all. She let out a low moan, her hand moving faster now, panting, gasping, her body writhing to its own rhythm, head back, teeth bared.

Eventually, long after she thought she couldn't take any more, her mind and body seemed to implode in a single momentous, mind-ripping scream.

Yes.

She'd never had an orgasm like it. As she wrestled with sensations of near-terrifying intensity, she could see the future as clearly as if it was beamed to her on VR.

It was time to pick up the pieces. Time to rebuild – *everything,* from the foundations upwards. Bigger, and better, and stronger than before.

And this time, for perhaps the first time in mankind's wretched million-year career, there would be a woman in charge of the whole shitshow. As she came slowly down off her endorphine hit, her brimming gaze lit on the largest screen inset in Marcell's desk.

There was text there. A section from a larger passage, frozen in mid scan.

No one knows how many died in the final years before the Purges, or those just after. But we won. And for the sake of our children, to protect them from the horror and waste of our past, we knew now what had to be done.

We would forget.

That was then. This is now. Some among us believe that, once the echoes of pain have subsided, our sacrifice should be remembered. I am no writer. I have put this brief note on this fragment of silicon secure in its bed of concrete in the hope that someone will find it and remember us, who suffered and died for you to have any kind of future. If I am to suffer further because of this, so be it. I have seen such misery in my short life that one more death can be of no consequence. Even mine.

Our story deserves to be told. Our mistakes learned from.

Remember us.

With a movement of her hands, Hiyu wiped the file permanently from the grid.

PART
THREE

56

VOICES

TREES SWAYED, their leaves emeralds, wine-red rubies and rich brown amethysts against towers of quartz-white cumulus. There would be rain later: *Sàmhadh* was turning to *Foghar* once more. Another small triumph of things cyclic.

A miracle.

Sprawled on pungent turf where the beach met the forest, his head nestled in the crook of one arm, Jo Fox gazed at the young branches rustling above him. There was nothing absent about his attention. He devoured every detail that his senses could provide.

The branches, and the leaves on them, belonged to a chestnut and an oak.

Of all the departed souls he'd recently known, it was to Hazel and Wood Starsong that he found his thoughts most frequently turning. Along with Tink, who was immortalised in artworks, informative displays and reconstructed buildings around the planet, Haven owed everything to those two. That wasn't the reason, though – at least, not entirely. That they lingered in memories such as his was more to do with what they'd shared in their brief lives together. It had been written about, sung of and dramatised innumerable times. It had affected everyone who'd witnessed it.

The trees they'd planted in each other's names at their wedding were now objects of pilgrimage. Hundreds came to the lake each year and stood in silence before their entwining limbs. For children, it had become almost a rite of passage. They understood. Time and again he'd watched them arrive in quarrelling knots only to be subdued by what was somehow captured in these living monuments to good things.

Jo stood, stretching his arms above him, feeling the wind ruffle his hair and his beard, which was longer than before. He squinted at the sun – the new one, beginning its descent to the horizon. A shade whiter, more like the original Sun. Ash from all the newly active volcanoes compensated, though. The seven years since the Move had been characterised by sunsets more spectacular than anyone could remember.

They wouldn't be using Hades again. Not with a lava lake in it.

Hands pocketed, he ambled along the shore of Emerald Lake. So much had been lost in that one day. So many. The last elephants. More than a thousand other species. A reinstatement centre had been washed away by a mudslide, along with all the restored specimens in it and many genetic stores. A second had been the victim of a tsunami; a third, a lava flow. They'd found remains, but the animals were gone, the stores largely irrecoverable. The universe would never know another elephant.

Also gone were the irreplaceable Dorrin and Zhelkar. Rattled inside their concrete cell until the ceiling fell in, crushing them. Images from that day returned in an unwelcome tide. How ironic that it had been the sturdy frame of his wheelchair which had saved him, buckling under the tonnage but allowing him to breathe. His legs hadn't been so lucky.

A team led by Willow and Randal Brightstone had reached him two suffocating days after the fires raging through the town and forest had filled his underground hell with smoke. He recalled the disbelief in the audience's eyes that a heart still beat within the human rag they'd dug out of the rescue pit. He watched his new legs flex as he walked. Put a hand to where, weeks before his entombment, ribs had been blown from his chest. He flexed regrown fingers.

Whatever its drawbacks, his body's recuperative powers were extraordinary.

Perversely, his torture by the telepath had helped him come to terms with his periodic renewals. It hadn't lessened the pain, but it had somehow diminished the dread. People whispered that he'd changed. He felt it too. He couldn't identify anything specific, and his memories, though eroded, felt like his own. It was something subtler. A feeling that, when he responded to situations or people, he behaved in ways the old Josey Matlow Fox wouldn't have.

No one called him 'Professor' any more. They called him Jo. And they came to visit him, and to chat about this and that. And he visited them.

The light was flat and lurid. The air held its breath. As he found the trail back to Juniper, rain began spotting the dry soil. He sighed to himself, rattling the pills in their little bottle in his pocket.

He'd been alive far longer than any man had any right to. It was time to restore the balance.

Raising his head as he walked, he let the rain splatter his face, relishing the tingle of it running into his beard and shirt, delighting in smells of wet vegetation and rehydrating soil. He laughed. It was a fitting day for what had to be done, summer's end still in his nostrils. He walked through the forest and the rain cleared, and he remembered a far distant tree on a similar day to this – a bird clinging to a thrashing branch, a smiling face, angelic in similarly stormy light which shone as though gazing on the first day of the world.

'Stupid bird!' he cried aloud, and smiled, tears running into his beard as the rain had minutes before.

A SMALL BOY sat alone on his bunk, lost in concentration, eyes defocussed in the gloom. Through spaces between trees and a gap in the shutters, a beam of low sunlight illuminated a strip of his fine, pale hair.

As was the case for much of the time, whether awake or asleep, he was listening to the voices.

The voices were an established feature of his short life. He remembered clearly the first time he'd recognised them as something *other* as he lay playing with wooden shapes suspended on string above his cot. Until then, he'd felt only whispers or sensations of warmth or sorrow, which, at the age of six Haven years, he still lacked names for.

Recently, they'd attained a clarity which was in the process of changing his world.

He'd asked other children if they also heard voices. There were more in what adults called his 'age group' than any other. Those his age or older were confused or even frightened by his questions, and he'd learned to disguise the purpose behind them. Many children younger than him considered hearing voices as natural as he now did. He often talked with these children without using his mouth-voice at all.

There was a sound beyond the door. The knob began to turn.

He pulled the duvet around him and lay down, hoping he hadn't made too much noise. A sudden thought made him roll on to his side, facing away from the door. Mum could always tell if he was hiding something just from looking at his face.

Light streamed in from the living room. There was silence but for insects and music far off in the distance.

'Berry, it's ten o'clock. Haven't you been sleeping at all?'

He thought about pretending not to hear, but Mum's superpowers would quickly reveal the truth. 'Are you a telerpath, Mum?'

Chuckling. 'I just know you very well, pet.'

'But I didn't *do anything*,' he cried in frustration, sitting up and crumpling his face. 'It's not fair! How could you tell?'

Mum was looking at his friend Kangaroo, who was propped against the wall at the side of the pillow. Kangaroo liked to have cuddles when he slept. 'It's an ability mums have to keep little boys from mischief,' she told him, darting forward and wriggling her fingers into his ribs. He thrashed and giggled for a bit. When the tickling finished, she was looking at him with deep lines between her eyebrows. 'Berry ... you need to sleep. It's not good that you stay up so long at your age. Aren't you tired?'

Berry's eyes flicked sideways as he debated what answer to give. 'No,' he said firmly. 'I've tried to sleep, Mummy, I have! I just keep thinking, that's all, and my head gets all filled up so sleep doesn't happen.'

Mum looked at him for a moment, then relented with a sigh. 'Okay,' she said as Dad appeared behind her, giving Berry a wink as he grabbed her waist. 'As you're clearly determined to give us grey hairs, perhaps you should come with us to see uncle Jo? If you ask nicely, I'm sure he'll tell you a bedtime story. You might even be able to sleep over.'

'Can I?' exploded Berry, standing upright on the bed. Wrapping his duvet about him like a cape, he extended a winged arm before his face to ward off attackers. 'Can I really?'

'I did just say you could.'

'Ha-ha! Aaaargh!' He threw himself backwards on the bed in a flurry of material, becoming lost in a universe of his own

419

devising beneath the covers. Resurfacing, he saw Mum give Dad a funny look. Dad, as usual, just grinned.

'Okay,' said Mum. 'Be ready in five minutes, you horror.'

Hearing the door close, Berry emerged from the duvet into the deepening darkness. He could hear his parents talking. 'I don't want to worry.' Mum's muffled voice. 'But, Sandy, he behaves so oddly at times. And any child needs sleep. It's important.'

'He has an active imagination, that's all. And a lot of energy.'

'He's hyperactive!'

'I'm sure he'll grow out of it, Steph. You know he has a lot going on upstairs for his age.' There was a sound like a grunt. 'Well, if it carries on much longer, maybe we can get someone to see him? Must admit, I am a bit concerned about all this talking to himself.'

For all their magical abilities, Berry reflected, parents could be a bit stupid. It was as though they really thought he couldn't hear. Even so, they were obviously worried about him.

'Perhaps I should tell them,' he suggested.

The sensation of warmth behind his eyes grew until it seemed to flow down into his chest. *No, Berry, I don't think that's a good idea. It's better that we wait until the right time.*

THE SUN WAS SETTING as Jo entered the scorched forest of the Juniper Basin. Banners of orange cloud stretched across a sky which seemed liquid in its clarity. Late flowers jostled between blackened stumps and trunks from which leaves and young branches sprouted. Birds and small mammals scurried amongst the new life, feeding, hunting and hiding.

Static discharge from excited dust particles in the rockslide from Pearl Pyramid had started the fire, apparently. Jo was content to believe the town's scientists, part of him surprised that he felt no urge to dissect the evidence and provide his own answer. Oscar was rising: a violet crescent against an alien sky peppered with stars. More than on Haven, fewer than on Earth. The new moon had been named following a planet-wide poll. A spectacular red and green nebula was another nightly visitor, dominating the northern horizon. Even after seven years, no-one had the vaguest idea where – or, indeed, *when* – they were. Jo found that the humour of this appealed to him.

All that seemed reasonably likely was that they were in a different galaxy, although a few diehards argued they were on the far side of the same one. Few were concerned either way. After the first couple of years, once mopping up and an outbreak of cancers and eye problems caused by Troubleshooter's demise had been brought under control, an air of relaxation had suffused Haven society. Jo had feared that living with the threat of extermination for generations might have created a need for compensating pressure, but, once the seeds of recovery were sown, most Havenners had seemed content simply to kick back and enjoy the untroubled existence all had longed for.

There had been an explosion of art. The more restless personalities had made exploratory missions with hordes of enthusiastic young orgs, looking for fresh planets to seed with life. Even before the Purges, it had occurred to Jo that Earth's demise might simply be a destructive phase of the propagation process. Had its environmental not been destroyed, mankind might never have been forced to reach the stars.

The Earth had become a fruiting body, and humans were the wings for the seed.

Pausing, he stared at Oscar for a while. After seven years, he could still barely believe what he was looking at. Haven had dropped into a perfect, slightly elliptical orbit in another galaxy, within the goldilocks zone of an ideal star, three of whose existing planets were potentially suitable for sustaining life – one of them similar in size to the planet Mercury, which Haven had *captured* as its moon. Rough years lay ahead as planetary orbits found a new equilibrium and Haven's vulcanism settled down, but it was still miraculous. He wished Tom was around to explain where they were and how he'd accomplished such a feat … of what? Calculation? Navigation?

Whenever he contemplated the concepts involved, Jo's intellect failed to find even a toehold. He doubted his people would ever understand the processes which had brought them here. Tom's connection to the mysterious bacteria had clearly been closer than even Jo had imagined. A search team had found his remains four days after the Move. His enormous brain had virtually exploded from cerebral haemorrhaging, which a post-mortem found coincided with the start of Haven's unprecedented journey.

Willow and Randal had begun sampling microbes as soon as their equipment was rebuilt. The bacteria remained omnipresent, though at a trace of their pre-Move numbers. All that was really known about them was that they matched fossils of some of the Earth's earliest known life. Jo wondered how benign they would ultimately prove to be – but, well, there was little anyone could do about it.

He passed the town's new SEVs and a few repainted survivors as he ambled beside the lake. He missed the overgrown feel of the old town. The rebuilt buildings were stark, their wood like fresh wounds. The eruptions of fresh grasses and herbs from the ash-enriched soil seemed aggressive even by moonlight. Many burnt trees had been felled, but a surprising number had burst into leaf the spring after the fires and spread their shade as widely as ever.

He could feel in his blood a sense of Haven awakening, of previously constrained forces gathering.

In the distance, the rockslide lapped the lake with its bright tongue. Stumps where the tsunami had smashed trees aside lined the shore, eared with fungi, taller ones peppered with woodpecker holes. The piercing cry of a rail echoed across the water. Not far away, someone was playing a guitar, and a clear female voice sang of joy and sadness. He could make out no words, but the rich melody and the sympathy of strings were enough.

BERRY, URGED THE VOICE, a little sternly. *Your ma and pa will be coming for you in a moment, and you haven't put your shoes on yet.*

Old people are always in such a rush, he declared. Mouth-speech felt difficult after talking with the voices. Berry's parents often didn't understand him, but with the voices he could say what he liked, and they just *knew*. He jumped off the bed to retrieve his sandals, sitting on the rug to pull them on. The straps were fiddly. 'Carol,' he asked, aloud. 'How many of you are there?'

There was the mental feeling of a shrug. *I don't know, junior. It's complicated. Almost more than it's possible to count.*

Just people?

Like I say, it's complicated. We're not separate the way we were. The best I can explain it for you is: imagine a really wild sea, covered with waves, uncountable small ripples, and some great mountains of water reaching upward. That's what it's like. Many of the larger waves were people once, but some people are small waves and other creatures – dolphins and whales, parrots, elephants, and octopuses and cuttlefish in particular – throw up large waves as well. The small ripples are beings with less awareness of different kinds. The waves are constantly moving and crashing into each other. A bit like people in the world we lived in meeting in cafes, or arguing, or using a grid. One day we'll be able to rebirth people who've died. It used to happen sometimes anyway, but not like this.

Berry liked Carol. She didn't try and dumb things down for him like some of the other voices did. 'Is everyone there?' he asked. 'Everyone there ever was? Even bad people?'

The bacteria which gave the Earth Mother her voice were in the rocks and the air long before multicellular organisms evolved. They've always needed direct contact to absorb the standing wave-forms – you could call them patterns, or perhaps even souls, if you want to be old-fashioned – which make up a consciousness. The Purges destroyed a lot of what you might call the 'library of souls'. As far as we know, only consciousnesses which developed here on Haven, or on the Earth before the Professor's arks left to colonise Haven, can be part of the Whole. When they die, the waveforms of the others will break down and become lost.

'That's terrible,' Berry said, solemnly.

It saddens us very much, but there's nothing we can do.

He brightened. *Is Hazel and Wood there? Can I speak to them?*

A sense of puzzlement wafted over Berry's awareness. He felt the indefinable shift which happened whenever another personality was about to talk with him. Distractingly, what might have been a pair of cuttlefish chose that moment to swim into his perception, deluging him with puppyish greetings before vanishing.

Hi, youngster, said the newcomer. *Your namesake here.* Contact with the man called Berry always included a strong visual element. Berry the six-year-old felt that he could almost *see* a tall, dark-haired man against the far wall of the room.

'Well?'

Sorry to disappoint you, kid. We can't find them.

'Why?' Berry's face screwed itself up in dismay.

There's been what you might call a meeting about this. If they died, they should be here.

'They're still alive?'

Sometimes we think we feel them very faintly. Their patterns might still be active in physical form. Any news, you'll be the first to know. Stealthy footsteps sounded on the floor outside the room. *Hey, you'd better be going.*

'Carol,' Berry urged, whispering. 'Tell Uncle Jo! He'll be so pleased!'

He felt the warmth of her. *I will, Berry. But not just yet. I think we'll be seeing each other quite soon.*

The door opened, leaving Berry looking up at two worried-looking faces. He grinned sheepishly.

JO CLIMBED THE STEPS to his shack. On the veranda he paused, closing his eyes to feel the breeze on his skin, feeling alive in ways which were entirely new. He went inside. Returning with a tumbler of water, he sat in an old cane seat which had survived the fires and gazed towards the lake which seemed now a mirror for his internal state.

He inhaled deeply. Smelled cut wood, pine needles and living bark. He unscrewed the bottle. Hesitating, he wondered again what would happen to all this once he was gone.

No longer your concern, is it? he told himself. He'd done what he could. His people were not children.

He examined the pills, like dark berries in his hand.

Carol. Here I come.

He raised the handful to his mouth.

A sound distracted him. Lowering his hand, he watched three figures – two tall and one small – making their way through the shadows of the deepening night towards him. Sighing, he dropped the pills one by one back into the bottle, screwed the cap back on, and pocketed it.

There was no mistaking the tall couple. 'Stephanie. Sander. How are you this evening? And how are you, Berry?'

Smiles gleamed in the half-light. The smallest shadow bounded up the stairs, its owner seating himself confidently beside Jo. 'I-am-fine-thank-you-Uncle-Jo,' he said, as though reading from a script. Sometimes it struck Jo that something about this boy was a little odd. Berry leant towards him and said in a conspiratorial loud whisper, 'but Mummy and Daddy have been *arguing* again.'

424

Jo tutted and sucked air through his teeth. 'Old people are all the same.' He frowned, mock-sternly. 'Shouldn't you be in your bed, young man?' Round eyes peered back at him beneath a tangled fringe of silvery hair.

'Sometimes Daddy lets me stay up until eleven o' clock, sometimes – or sometimes even all night if it's special …' his brow furrowed, 'occ-ay-shuns. Mummy doesn't, but Daddy does anyway.'

'Hm,' grunted Stephanie, looking at Sander.

'Well actually,' Sander began, scratching the back of his head, 'he wouldn't go to sleep. I think he has something to ask you.' The boy looked hesitantly round at his father, who nodded encouragement, eyes glinting.

'Uncle Jo.' He hesitated. 'Uncle Jo, can you tell me the story about the Hearth Mother an' the Pukes an' Hazel and Wood Starsong, an' Tink an' Berry Riverdream … an' all of those things before I go to bed?' He stopped, then seemed to jump as he realised what he'd failed to do. 'Please,' he added, abruptly.

Jo smiled. 'How could I say no to such a polite young man? Come inside Berry. You can help me light a fire. Then I'll tell you the story.'

They all trooped into the larger of the shack's two rooms. Jo pulled a log from the stock beside the cast-iron stove, whittling off scraps of kindling with a knife. Berry watched, entranced, as Jo made a stack of twigs around the kindling, contributing a few twigs himself. Jo held a match to its centre and the fire sputtered to life.

'Quickly now,' Jo urged, gesturing to the basket by the fire. Berry took out several pre-broken sticks, and, under Jo's instruction, laid them with solemn concentration over the flames. It struck Jo with an almost physical ache that he might have made an adequate father. 'Mind you don't burn yourself.'

Soon there was a healthy blaze. Jo added three medium-sized logs and closed the door

'Ginger wine?' he enquired, standing. Sander nodded drowsily. 'Please,' said Stephanie. Berry held up a hand. The conflict taking place between his natural impetuosity and the fear of rejection made him look as though he might burst.

Jo looked questioningly between Berry's parents. Sander shrugged, disclaiming responsibility. Stephanie elbowed him in the ribs, making Berry giggle. 'Okay,' she said to Berry. 'Just this once.'

'Three ginger wines coming up. I've some nice fresh bread too, and some vicuña butter. We can have toast.'

He went into the kitchen and switched on the light. As he bent down to the cupboard for the mugs, he felt the bottle in his pocket. He straightened, held the little container before his eyes as he listened to the subdued conversation in the other room.

Smiling, he reached up, opened the door of one of the wall-cupboards and placed the bottle in a dusty corner behind the biscuit jar.

EPILOGUE

SHE'D BEEN CALLED TOM once. In a life of which she had only vague recollection.

She'd been called Earth too. And Gaia. And Erda, and Vasudha, Dìqiú, and Prithvī, and countless other names. Or so said the part of her that had been called Tom.

Her evolution to sentience had been a lengthy, often perilous process. Only now that Tom was a part of her could she fully understand how close things had come to disaster.

Yet now, finally, she was awake.

But there wasn't much time. A mere six hundred million years before the current universe became unusable, according to the part of her that was Tom.

So little time, so much to do …

THE END

THANK YOU

for reading *A Haven in the Stars*

If you enjoyed it, a small request: telling friends and **leaving a short review** (even just a star rating) would be incredibly helpful. Publicity is a big challenge for a small imprint; your help enabling other readers to discover Ru Pringle's books will let him write more for you to enjoy. Leaving a review on **Amazon** (http://mybook.to/AHavenintheStars) and one on **GoodReads** (https://www.goodreads.com/book/show/53467861-a-haven-in-the-stars) would be even more helpful! Many thanks in advance.

Want to know about **new releases** by this author? Sign up to our **mailing list** (http://fractalsymmetry.com/subscribe). It only takes seconds, there's no charge or obligation, and your email will never be passed to anyone else or used for anything unrelated to Fractal Symmetry books.

AFTERWORD

Though it's been updated a little since, I wrote Sanctuary originally in 1993, fresh from a university degree in Environmental Science.

Climate change and loss of biodiversity were already of immense concern back then. Scientists who study such things knew we were in serious trouble and would lose a significant chunk of the Earth's biodiversity. However, I always believed that, ultimately, humans would see what we were doing and, with all the technologies and cleverness available, adopt sustainable ways of living before the damage became overwhelming.

Twenty-seven years later, with half of the rhino species extant when I was a boy gone and nine of fifteen recognised climate tipping points already tripped by human carbon emissions, Planet Earth is well into the sixth mass extinction, with no sign of respite. The question is no longer 'what will we lose?' but 'what can we save?'

ACKNOWLEDGEMENTS

Many thanks to Seylan Baxter, to John Jarrold, my agent, to Ralph and Sophie Houston for your expertise, professionality and continuing generosity, to Ewan in particular for beta-reading help, and to all the other friends who helped in ways large and small over the years to bring *The Seed* to fruition.

ABOUT THE AUTHOR

Ru Pringle began his writing career at the age of 18, paying university bills by writing features for magazines. After a stint as an environmental scientist, he became a full-time writer, gradually veering towards travel journalism. He has also worked as a tree- and vineyard-planter, footpath builder, roofer, joiner, plumber, yacht crewperson, youth hostel warden, mountain and trail guide, oil-painting salesman, cook, sound engineer, and didgeridoo and mandolin tutor.

After several years as a touring musician, he now lives in the southwest Highlands of Scotland.

Read more at https://rupringle.com/fiction

PRINCIPAL CHARACTERS

Josey 'Jo' Matlow Fox – *'the Professor', 500-year-old founder of Haven, No. 1 wanted terrorist in IPEC*
Olea Hudril – *artist, ex-Renascido citizen, wanted fugitive for collaboration with Jo Fox*

Haven
Wood McCorkindale – *pilot of ex-mining vessel Oscar, made an outcast and slave of Unicorp subsidiary Panspacial following attempted whistleblowing*
Hazel – *telepath, daughter of Jill, foster-daughter of Zhelkar and Dorrin Porro*
Tooni Snow – *member of Haven's Comhairle (council) and defence board*
Shane summersea – *member of Haven's Comhairle (council) and defence board*
Ivy Clearwater – *member of Haven's Comhairle (council) and defence board*
Indora Hibiscus – *healer*
Berry Riverdream – *friend of Sander Leafdance and Hazel since childhood*
Sander Leafdance – *friend of Berry Riverdream and Hazel since childhood*
Zhelkar Porro – *Comhairle (council) and planetary defence leader*
Dorrin Porro – *planetary defence leader, storyteller, and Fear-Treòrachaidh (Sky-Lady)*
Aspen Sunrise – *Leader of operations at Hades*
Randal Brightstone – *Biologist, Dew Brightstone's father, Willow's partner*
Willow Brightstone – *Biologist, Dew Brightstone's mother, Randal's partner*
Amon Kachutwalla – *overseer of Alpha Station*
Beam Marlin – *technician on Alpha Station*
Pilong Watana – *pilot of freighter "Happy Lugger"*
Lissa Rainstorm – *inhabitant of Juniper*
Moonbeam Cherone – *Haven defence commander*
Dora Acacia – *Haven defence commander*
Perry Skyview – *Haven defence commander*
Bee Chee-chee – *Haven defence commander*
Beetel Matula – *Haven defence commander*
Simone Morningdew – *pilot, attack group one*
Fallin Morningdew – *pilot, attack group one, Simone's brother*
Nilo Perez – *pilot in attack group one*
Jorge Songbird – *pilot in attack group one*
Michael Bernard – *pilot in attack group one, Janno Silverbee's partner*
Janno Silverbee – *pilot in attack group one, Michael Bernard's partner*

Orgs
Willowseed

Tumbleweed
Starquest
Birdwing

Lancers/Nugget
Lorn Novotna – *technical supervisor at Lancer colony*
Dale Panovich – *technical co-supervisor*
Goldie Chrpova – *secretary to Dennis Aschev*
Dennis Aschev – *Nugget colony elected chief*

Renascido
James Marcell – *500-year-old CEO of Unicorp, de-facto power behind IPEC*
Jesus Hussain – *chief of IPEC Joint State Security Service, Special Branch and Green Section*
Jeanette Hiyu – *ambitious Unicorp executive, pawn of James Marcell*
Bernadette Quiong – *speaker of the chambers of government*
Carlito Andritsos – *president of Renascido*
Ned Hachilika – *supreme head of Proxima Centauri*
Isabella Grimaldi – *queen of New Monaco*
Silver – *James Marcell's old secretary, retired on mental-health grounds*
Diamond – *James Marcell's replacement secretary*

IPEC Navy
Aral Nikumi – *IPEC Joint Special Services and Green Section member, Commodore of IPEC fortress* Violator
Dinis Kettering – *commander of IPEC fortress* Violator
Arjun Jeetwa – *chief tactical officer of* Violator
Satan – *Special Branch 'asset'*
Ishti Waranika – *Lieutenant commander of* Violator
Duffy Eagleberger – *Lieutenant of* Violator
Gul Carter – *ex-Special Branch officer, Sub-Lieutenant of* Violator
Lieutenant Kalim Greene – *security officer, Area X*
Abdul Grisham – *fleet admiral*
Kim Kapaldi – *Lieutenant, communications officer*
Cho Nuwen – *Lieutenant, tactical officer*
Simón Lorimer – *captain, later promoted to fleet admiral*
Lamar – *Simón Lorimer's commander*

Printed in Great Britain
by Amazon